THE SENECA SONG

A Novel

By: Peter Perkins

"Give me two healthy, highly intelligent, and attractive young adults, place them into seclusion with little to no supervision, and if they don't end up killing each other, I can pretty much guarantee they'll fall in love."

Anonymous

Acknowledgments

To my loving wife, Giao, who I adore and without whose support and guidance this novel couldn't have been possible.

To Robin Venturelli, my Beta editor, for her time and all the invaluable contributions she made as I completed my manuscript.

To the author, Jay Greenstein, the toughest and most demanding coach an aspiring writer could ever be fortunate enough to find and to work with.

Chapter 1

Traveling down the gravel road that led to his family's cottage always gave Dan the sensation he was barreling head-first into the lake at the base of the hillside. Visually, it really did look like it ran straight into the water. It started off with this nice, gentle slope until it got so steep, so quickly, it reminded him of that first hill on a rollercoaster. For reasons he never understood, he always got a rush driving down that narrow road. When he was little, it scared him because he thought his family would crash right into the water and they would all drown. That would have been tragic, he thought to himself. Now, having crested the ridge, Seneca Lake came into full view. He was almost there.

With the end of the school year rapidly approaching, he continued toward his destination down through the vineyard and orchard that bordered the road, ready to begin what could be his final summer at the lake. If you didn't have firsthand knowledge of the area, you'd think the road was nothing more than an access for farm implements. It was only when you reached the collar of hardwoods lining the lake that a stranger would discover they were entering a private community of about twenty small cottages nestled up against the cliffs that formed the lake's shoreline.

Following a blind curve onto a big loop near the bottom, he rounded the corner and standing right there in the middle of the road was a huge, white-tailed buck. Panicked and slamming on the brakes, he skidded to a stop as the deer stared at him with this look of superiority, snorted once, followed by him springing off into the woods and disappearing out of sight. "Oh, Christ," he muttered to himself. "First time I come up alone and I almost total the damn car. Lovely." His heart now racing, he paused for a moment to calm down before once again driving off.

He covered the remaining distance uneventfully, then parked on the crushed stone driveway adjacent to the tiny cottage. In checking the clock in the car, it was only 4:30, so there was still plenty of sunlight remaining. After exiting the vehicle, he paused briefly to take in the view of the lake, something he never tired of. "Yes!" he proclaimed with a small pump of his fist. With only about ninety days before his senior year began, he was more than ready for summer vacation to start.

Looking around the Wallace property, everything appeared to be totally normal. That was expected. Being here solo wasn't, and that felt really strange. He let himself in and went about stowing his gear along with getting organized for the weekend. Though the property wasn't far from Watkins Glen, it was very secluded. Maybe you had a phone. Assuming you had a TV, you got a maximum of two stations. His family had neither. There was a radio for music and information from the outside world, but that was it. If you wanted to stay abreast of the news, you drove to the gas station at the top of the hill and bought the local newspaper. Like it or not, you made your own entertainment. Most cottages had the same owners for years and everybody knew each other. Of course, that also meant his neighbors would be watching and wondering what he was doing there by himself. Quite frankly, Dan wasn't entirely sure why he was there by himself either.

Done with his tasks, it was now time to start enjoying the lake. After all, that was the whole point of coming. He headed out the door onto the large deck facing the lake, grabbing the boathouse keys off a hook as he passed by and walked to the wooden stairs built up against the cliff that led down to the docks. Unlocking the boathouse, he passed directly through and out the opposite end to the main dock and twin boatlifts. Other than a few small tree branches scattered along the dock that he kicked into the water, everything else appeared in good order. Stretching his arms and turning his face skyward to take in the warmth of the sun, it was time to relax. He set up a beach chair on the end of the dock, settled in and started enjoying the scenery. Decisions on what to do later could wait.

Almost immediately, the tranquility was broken by the deep bass rumble of an old speed boat. Though his view was obstructed by the neighboring docks, the sound was unmistakable. It was his neighbor, Hartmann, and his perfectly restored 1948 Century Resorter. As it cleared the docks and came into view, Dan couldn't help staring. He loved that boat; its varnished mahogany hull, polished brass fittings, and miniature American flag. The words 'Seneca Song' with little music notes as quotations were painted across the stern. As he sat there admiring the boat, he did a complete double-take to confirm what he thought his eyes were telling him. The woman in the boat that should have been the elderly Mrs. Hartmann wasn't Mrs. Hartmann at all, nor elderly. Instead, it was a girl, and a very attractive one at that. He sat there wondering, who the heck is that?

Hartmann idled out past the end of his dock and just when he started to throttle up, the engine coughed violently, followed by a massive explosion. The engine had backfired and it sounded like a shotgun blast, both startling Dan and scattering the birds in the trees along the shoreline. With a final belch of smoke out of the exhaust, the engine simply died. Hartmann turned the ignition key once, twice, three times, but the Gray Marine engine stubbornly refused to fire.

At the same time, the current was taking Hartmann and his passenger further and further from shore. Dan knew the boat was too large to row, and paddling in would take forever, assuming Hartmann had a paddle on board and that he was strong enough to even do that. And while Dan may have been wrong, it didn't look to him like Hartmann's new first mate possessed the required skill set either. Clearly, Hartmann had a problem and it was getting much worse by the second.

"Hey," he shouted at them. "You need a hand?"

"Do you mind?" Hartmann yelled back.

"On the way!" Dan immediately dropped their rowboat into the lake, hopped in and began rowing out to the stranded Hartmann. "That didn't sound too good," he called out while quickly glancing at the girl, trying not to get caught in the process.

"Yeah, it sure didn't. No idea what's wrong with her. Probably something electrical."

"Well, toss me a line and I'll tow you in."

Hartmann complied by throwing him a rope that Dan tied off on the transom of his rowboat. He then began towing him back to his lift and in no time at all, they'd arrived.

"Thanks, Dan. I really appreciate it," Hartmann called out while untying his boat.

"My pleasure, Mr. Hartmann. Glad to help." Before Dan started rowing back to his place, he snuck another quick peek at the girl and caught her staring right back at him. Damn! She's checking me out, he decided. He also noticed she had some of the most amazing blue eyes he'd probably ever seen, but something was wrong. They were brooding, sad even. She's really unhappy about something he realized.

After returning to his place, he retook his seat, went back to relaxing and then started thinking about all of this. The Wallace's and the Hartmann's had both owned their properties for about the same amount of time and never once in all those years had Dan seen this girl. He sat there wondering, who could she possibly be? Something's not right here, he decided. While sitting there considering the situation, a loud voice abruptly yelled down from the top of the steps.

"Hey, Wallace!"

4

Chapter 2

Twisting in his chair to look back at the top of the cliff, Dan saw his neighbor and classmate standing there. "Hey, man, what's going on, Gary? Grab a chair and come join me," he yelled back. His friend immediately headed down and brought a chair along with him from the boathouse as he made his way out to the end of the dock.

"Yeah, I saw your brother Henry's Chrysler pull in and thought it was him. Where's he at?" he asked, sitting down with a thud.

"Henry's gone, man. Enlisted in the Coast Guard. Right now, he's in Cape May, New Jersey, for basic. Left his car behind and told me I could drive it while he's gone."

"Really? He enlisted, huh?"

"Yep. Didn't want to take a chance on getting drafted and being shipped off to Vietnam."

"Oh, come on, man. He wasn't going to get drafted and sent to 'Nam."

"Easy for you to say. You never have to worry about getting drafted," Dan stated bluntly.

"What the hell is that supposed to mean?" Gary snapped at him.

"You know exactly what that means," Dan fired back, well aware that Gary had some kind of health problem providing him a 4F draft status.

"Well, we aren't talking about that," Gary responded, now thoroughly agitated.

"Okay, sorry, Gary. Calm down, alright?" Dan replied, gesturing with his hands.

"Fine. I'm calm," he responded, his voice now returning to normal, then pausing briefly before speaking again. "Anyway, that was nice of him to leave his wheels for you."

"Oh, I was totally shocked. I expected he'd sell it rather than let it sit or let somebody use it."

"Who's paying the insurance?"

Dan paused to consider that for a moment before answering. "You know, that's a darned fine question, Gary. He didn't bring it up, so I assume he is. Knowing him, though, that's probably not a good assumption to be making. It wouldn't be unlike him to just cancel it and not even mention it."

"Yep. For sure. That would be Henry. In fact, he may have already done that, so you better be extra careful."

"Thanks, and you make a good point. I'll have to check on that when I go back down to Elmira. So, when'd you come up?"

"Dad and I came up a couple days ago. He's run down to Watkins right now to pick up plumbing parts from the hardware store, but I expect him back shortly."

"Which means you skipped school again, huh? He doesn't care?"

"Guess not," he responded laughing. Not known for being one of the better students at his school, Dan knew Gary was on a career path to nowhere, but it didn't matter. He enjoyed Gary's company and he liked him as a part-time friend. Dan had known him since they were in kindergarten and they'd spent a lot of time together here at the lake.

"How long you planning to stay?"

"I don't really know. Never came up alone before, so I guess we'll see. If it's too boring, I'll head home. If not, I'll probably stay through Sunday, maybe even get up early Monday and drive straight to school.

Plus, I've got work. It doesn't really matter, though. For the first time in my life, I'm not relying on someone else for transportation. Heck, if I feel like it, I can just pack up and leave whenever I want."

"For sure. Hey, your parents coming up?"

"I doubt it, Gary. We were all just up last weekend for Memorial Day. They didn't mention any plans to, but you never know. I suppose they might show up."

"Cool. I saw you had a big crowd last weekend."

"You should have stopped by."

"I thought about it, but decided not to."

"Hey, by the way, any idea who that girl is I saw riding in Hartmann's boat earlier? Never seen her before."

"That's Hartmann's granddaughter. My dad stopped by to visit with Hartmann and he told him she's spending the summer."

"The whole summer? Really? That doesn't sound right. What's her name?"

"No idea. Haven't talked to her. Actually, I've only seen her a couple times outside their cottage, either on the porch or down on the dock. Pretty good-looking chick, huh?"

"Oh, yeah. Super pretty. She looks especially good riding in that boat."

"Couldn't agree more. Hey, I've got an idea," he said, lowering his voice and leaning forward in a conspiratorial fashion. "Let's walk down to the point! Maybe we can get a look at her when we're passing by the Hartmann place."

"Okay, sure. Let's go." Dan popped up from his beach chair and the two of them headed straight up to the road.

7

As they were walking to the point and getting closer to Gary's place, they saw that his dad had returned. "I'll be right back," Gary announced before running up to his cottage to let his father know what he was up to. He disappeared inside and was right back out in less than thirty seconds. "Okay. All set." That addressed, they continued their walk toward the steep access road that led down to the point.

The point, as it was called, was one of those rare areas along Seneca that was relatively flat. Cut from glaciers thousands of years ago, a large portion of the lake's shoreline was stone cliffs. This particular piece of delta-shaped land was really large compared to the other lots in their community and was cut in half by a creek, creating two separate properties. Dan never understood why, but neither piece of land had a cottage, even though he thought they were, without a doubt, the most desirable lots in their little neighborhood. The only thing ever built was a nice, long dock but no boat lift. According to what he'd heard, the land was owned by two local farming families that were related. The dads were brothers or something. He wasn't sure. Dan had only seen the owners maybe a couple of times in his entire life. The rest of the time, the land just sat there unused.

The creek was one of the favorite places for the boys in the community to explore. Though small, the little creek had cut a deep gorge through the shale bedrock over the millennia. The washed-out shale, coupled with the wave action from the lake, was what had formed the delta. The sides of the gorge were very steep and, at some points, more than thirty feet tall. There were also multiple waterfalls, both large and small, scattered along the entire length of the little gorge. When he was very young, it was common to see smelt swimming up the creek at night during the spring spawning season. Now, the numbers had declined significantly to the point where you only saw a few each season.

The boys would typically hike up through the creek and its waterfalls, checking out all the flora and fauna. At some point, they'd decide they'd gone far enough and simply backtrack to the lake. It was really serene and beautiful, but a little strange because it was so remote and incredibly still inside. You could hear nothing except those noises created inside the gorge itself. Apparently, all the sound waves from the outside world simply passed over the top of the steep-sided ravine.

As they walked by the Hartmann place, there was no sign of the girl. Once they arrived at the point, the two messed around, hanging out on the dock, checking out the creek, and just generally killing time until they got bored and decided to head back. As they passed the Hartmann place again, this time they saw the girl standing on the porch. She looked over briefly and Gary gave her a small wave of the hand, but she didn't wave back or even acknowledge them. Once they were well past and out of earshot, Gary turned to Dan, "Man, she is smoking hot, good looking!"

"Yep. No doubt about it. All these years and I've never seen her before. I wonder what her deal is?"

"No idea. First time I've seen her here, too, man." Like Dan, Gary had spent a great deal of time at the lake beginning when he was a toddler, and his place was basically right across the road from the Hartmann's. If he hadn't seen her, she hadn't been up before, and that added even more to the mystery of her presence.

Arriving back at the Wallace property, the two went about preparing a simple supper and afterwards they sat outside listening to the radio put out a steady stream of Jackson Browne, Steely Dan, Carol King, McCartney's new band Wings, and other popular rock groups. They gossiped about different people at school and things in general until darkness began to set in. Gary finally stood up and announced, "Well, I guess it's about time for me to head home. Hey, what do you think about maybe doing some fishing in the morning? I've got bait at the house."

"I'm in. Let's do it. We can take our boat." Dan knew that for whatever reason, Gary's father didn't allow him to take their boat out alone. Apparently, his dad didn't trust him, although Dan didn't really understand why. Maybe his dad thought he was lacking in the common-sense department because Gary's boating skills were actually quite good. Regardless, they had no choice but to take Dan's boat or fish off the end of the dock, which wouldn't be nearly as much fun or successful.

"You got it. Well, enjoy the rest of your night, and I'll see you in the morning."

"Okay, sounds good, Gary. See you tomorrow." After he left, Dan got up and made his way into the cottage. He cleaned up a little, got organized for the morning then decided to call it a night. Now, well past dark, he locked both doors and promptly headed to his bedroom.

Sleeping there alone that first night, something he had never done, proved to be a real challenge. Every little leaf rustle, creak, or noise he heard sounded like it was right outside his window. The noises would fire up his nerves and simply prevent him from calming down or falling asleep. It was actually very unsettling. When he finally started to relax and had just about gone under, he heard a new, bizarre sound right outside his window. His head popped up off the pillow and he lay there wondering, what the heck was that? It almost sounded like there was a person out there and his senses immediately went on full alert. Dan carefully pulled the curtain back trying to see outside, but it was simply too dark. A few seconds later, he heard it again: footsteps.

He definitely didn't want to, but somehow, he was going to have to find the courage to see who or what was outside. What with the old windows in the cottage that were already antiques when the property was built, along with the paper-thin wooden doors, the building wasn't much of a castle. If it was a person and they wanted in, there was really no way to keep them out. Right or wrong, having decided he had no choice but to investigate, he slipped silently out of bed and crept quietly into the kitchen.

He grabbed the large flashlight they kept on top of the refrigerator, hoping the battery was still good, along with a Billy club that hung on the wall near the front door. With his heart racing and as carefully as possible, he opened the cottage door, slipped outside, and around the corner in the direction he thought the noise came from. He took a step, paused, listened, took another step and paused again. Standing like a statue for what seemed an eternity, while also trying to slow his breathing, he finally heard them again: more footsteps in the leaf clutter.

They were directly in front of him, maybe twenty-five feet away. It was so dark he couldn't see anything at all, but there was definitely someone or something there. That was certain. He carefully raised the flashlight, pointing it in the direction of the sound, and with a good grip on the Billy club, he hit the switch illuminating the night. Standing right there on its hind legs facing him was the source of the footsteps. It was an adult male raccoon, and as soon as the light hit its eyes, it bared its teeth and started hissing at Dan scaring the crap out of him. Its initial reaction was to come at him. Never having confronted a raccoon before, should he battle it or just run back into the cottage: fight or flight? He had absolutely no idea, but he would have to decide quickly because the raccoon was still coming towards him.

At this point, his instincts simply took over. He was three or four times the size of the raccoon, so he responded to its advance by yelling, faking a charge at the beast, and raising the club over his head in a threatening fashion. The animal hesitated briefly, then started towards him again. Dan yelled even louder that time, faked another charge, and swung the club at the animal. Fortunately for him, that was enough of a threat for the raccoon. It wheeled around and disappeared into the night as fast as possible. Thank God for that, he thought to himself, his hands shaking slightly from the encounter. The last thing he needed was trying to fight off some wild animal all alone and in the pitch-black night.

Mystery finally solved, and the problem dealt with, Dan made his way back into the cottage and locked up again. He returned the flashlight and Billy club to their assigned locations and climbed back into bed, hoping that was the end of it. Eventually, his heart stopped pounding. There were no more strange noises outside and he finally found that elusive sleep he'd been searching for. He didn't stir again until the next morning. That's when he woke to the chirping birds in the trees outside the cottage windows and the familiar sound of waves crashing against the stone cliffs down below.

Chapter 3

Dan lurched upright in his bed, temporarily confused, head swiveling back and forth, as he tried to orient himself. Sitting there momentarily, he wondered where he was and what time it might be. Almost immediately, he remembered the raccoon and realized he was at the cottage. He pushed his blonde hair back off his forehead, slipped out of bed and checked the wall clock in the kitchen. Though it was already broad daylight, it was still early. But that was a good thing, especially if you're going fishing. Gary was also an early riser and could easily show up at a moment's notice. Knowing this, Dan immediately went about starting his day, eventually making his way down to the dock to load up the gear they'd need.

Done with all his chores and loading of the necessary fishing gear into the boat, Gary still hadn't shown up. This was odd, he thought. Fishing at Seneca was best done early. As there was still no sign of him, he decided not to wait but just walk down to his place to see what was holding him up. Approaching the cottage, he noticed their car was missing. That's strange, Dan thought, deciding maybe his dad's gone to Watkins again. He jogged up onto the porch and knocked on the front door. "Gary, you home?" No answer. He knocked again. "Gary!" Nothing. He waited a few more seconds with no response, turned, and walked off the porch, heading back down the driveway towards the road.

"They're gone."

Dan looked up in the direction the female voice came from and saw the girl standing in the shadows outside the Hartmann cottage. "Oh, hi. Yeah, they probably went down to Watkins."

Stepping from the shadows, she replied, "No, I mean I saw them loading up their car. They've left for the weekend. Gone home apparently, wherever that is."

"Really? Well, that stinks. We were supposed to go fishing." He hesitated for a second before speaking again. "Hey, my name's Dan."

"I know what your name is. You helped my grandfather yesterday." Then she paused for a moment. "My name's Yani."

"I'm sorry, Ronnie?"

"No, it's Yani," she enunciated carefully while she just kind of stared at him. "I know. It's a weird name."

"I don't know if it's weird, but it's certainly different."

"You're being too nice. It's weird. Just admit it."

Dan started laughing at that. He wasn't sure why, but he found her candor really funny. "Okay, you win. It's a weird name." He hesitated briefly before speaking again, first looking down at his feet before looking back up into her eyes. "You know, I've been coming here my whole life, and I've never once seen you here before. What brings you this year?"

"My parents decided to ship me here for the summer. Kind of like exile, you know, like Napoleon had to."

Dan couldn't help it and started laughing again. "I'm sorry. I don't mean to laugh, but 'exile like Napolean'? Seriously?"

"Yeah, something like that."

Dan stood there studying at her. "Well, unless you want to fill in as my fishing partner, I'm looking for something to do. You interested?"

"Right. Like, I've just met you, and now you want me to go fishing with you? I think I'll pass on that."

"Well, I'm not doing anything else. It's a really nice day. You want to go for a walk or something?" Dan asked, gesturing with his arms out at his sides, trying his best to appear nonthreatening.

"Or something?"

"Yeah, I thought maybe you might want to have a look around and see something other than your grandparents' cottage."

She stood there staring at him for what felt like an eternity when, in reality, it was only a couple of seconds. "Yeah, okay. Let me tell my grandmother. She'll want to know where I'm going. What should I tell her?"

"Just tell her you're going for a walk with one of the Wallace boys. She'll know who that is."

"Okay, I'll be right back."

The girl went inside and, in less than a minute, was right back out. "She said, 'Fine'. Let's go before she changes her mind," and she started walking. Dan walked along next to her, trying to figure out what to say next. Fortunately, Yani took care of that for him.

"Who's Henry?"

"Henry? That's my older brother. Why do you ask?"

"My grandpa asked if I was going for a walk with Henry. I told him no, and he said good. Why would he ask about Henry and why wouldn't he want me hanging out with him?"

"Well, Henry's got a bit of a reputation. He fancies himself as some kind of a rebel like a James Dean or someone. I love him dearly, and we're very close, but personally, I think incorrigible is a better way to describe him."

"Oh? Is that right?"

"Yeah. Like when it comes to anything that has an engine, he only knows one speed, full blast, which drives the neighbors nuts. Oh, and he's never met an argument he didn't want to start."

"I see. So, where's he at now?"

"He's gone off to the Coast Guard. Enlisted so he could avoid the draft."

"Avoid the draft, huh? Okay. So, where're you from?"

"A small city called Elmira. It's about an hour south of here."

"Never heard of it."

Dan laughed again. "Well, it's not much of a city, but it's where I was born and raised. Actually, I don't even really live in the city. I live out in the country, a couple miles outside of town. Where do you live?"

"I live in Youngstown…Ohio. Ever heard of it?"

"Believe it or not, I have. I don't know anything about it, but I have heard of it, probably in a book I read or history class or something. I think it's right next to the Pennsylvania border. Right?"

"Yes, that's exactly where it is. You like books and history?" she asked, an inquisitive look on her face.

"Yeah, very much."

"What kind of books do you like?"

"Well, mostly books about things like wars, Indians, famous battles, or maybe famous war heroes. Stuff like that," Dan explained, trying to sound serious in response to her question.

"If you had to go to Vietnam, do you think you'd be a hero like that Audie Murphy fellow?"

That caught him totally off guard and he thought about that for a second before answering. "The most decorated war hero ever? That

16

Audie Murphy? Well, I really don't think there's any chance of that, but I also know I definitely don't want to find out either." She didn't follow that up with any more questions about wars or heroes, and Dan was greatly relieved. He hated thinking about Vietnam and the possibility of having to go there.

They walked along in silence for a moment, leading in the direction of the point, and he found himself staring at her. He couldn't help it. It was shocking how beautiful she was up close. She was wearing cut-off jeans, a loose-fitting tie-dyed tee-shirt that was nicely filled out, and brown sandals. Her shoulder length hair was perfectly straight and auburn in color. She had the most amazing blue eyes. He'd never seen eyes that shade of blue, and they had this fascinating luminescent quality. It almost seemed like they sparkled. Her ears had perfect little detached lobes. They were pierced, but there were no earrings.

Her lips were full, and as far as he could tell, she wasn't wearing a speck of makeup. The face was perfect. She didn't seem to have a blemish or an imperfection anywhere. Yani was relatively tall, he guessed only a couple inches shorter than him, and she had an absolutely striking figure. Her legs were sculpted, hips perfectly proportioned to her upper body and she looked like she could have been a track athlete or a dancer. Coupled with those amazing eyes, in a word, she was stunning.

Out of nowhere, she turned and looked at him with her head cocked sideways. "What're you looking at?"

"Excuse me?"

"I said, what're you looking at?"

Again, Dan was caught completely off guard by the question and a little embarrassed that she caught him staring, so he just told her the truth. "Has anyone ever told you that you're incredibly beautiful?"

17

"Yeah, sometimes, but I would appreciate it if you don't stare at me," she responded sternly, and the look on her face meant it.

"Sorry."

"Has anyone ever told you that you're really handsome?"

"No, I don't remember that ever happening."

She said nothing more. They continued walking along, and after a moment, she turned to him, "Well, you are." Dan had never thought of himself as being good-looking, then it dawned on him. As he had watched her staring at him in the boat and on the road, she was almost certainly judging him, probably trying to decide if he was someone she wanted to talk to or not. Apparently, she had decided he was worth it, or maybe she was just desperate to talk to someone her own age.

"Thanks," was his less than witty response. Right or wrong, he concluded that this Yani girl didn't like playing games, so he didn't even attempt to be coy. He decided that, unless she responded otherwise, it was best to just be straight forward with her, and so he was.

"I'm seventeen and I'll be a senior in the fall. How about you, Yani?"

"Same. This is my senior year coming up, too."

"We still have classes for a couple more weeks. Actually, I have school on Monday. How come you aren't in class?"

"Yeah, well, my mom wanted to get rid of me as soon as possible, so she went to the guidance counselor at school and asked if there was any way for me to finish up early. That way, she could dump me as soon as Memorial Weekend. He told her I could take my finals early and I'd be done for the year. She made me take the tests, and now here I am in Paradise until Labor Day," she stated mockingly. "They come back to pick me up Labor Day weekend when I go back to Youngstown."

"Did you know she planned to send you here?"

"Nope. She and my dad set all of this up behind my back and just dropped it on me."

That this would happen seemed really strange to him. "So, you came up last weekend?"

"Yep. We drove up on Saturday."

At this point, Dan was beyond speechless. What Yani's mom had done to her sounded awfully harsh and he found it terribly confusing. Why would she do something like that? There had to be a reason, but this was hardly the topic Dan anticipated from a girl he had literally just met. At the same time, he thought to himself that if she'd been brought up here Memorial Weekend, maybe he was the first person her age she'd had a chance to talk to about this. Maybe she just needed to vent a little and get it off her chest.

"Where're we going?" she asked.

"I thought we'd walk down to the place we call the point," he suggested, correctly assuming that she hadn't been there yet, so this would be something new for her.

"Okay. Lead the way. Never been there."

The road was lined on both sides with large oak, hickory, and walnut trees, and it was entirely enveloped in shade. The only sounds were that of their sandals on the dirt road, the light breeze blowing through the tree tops, an occasional bird chirping, or a squirrel rustling through the leaf clutter on the forest floor, looking for fallen nuts. They walked along in silence until she finally spoke again. "You know, the last time I vacationed here, I was just a little girl, and I remember nothing at all.

19

I've seen pictures of me sitting in the Seneca Song, though, so I know I've been here. I've got to admit, it's really beautiful here at this lake."

"Why doesn't your family ever come up?"

"My mom and dad aren't interested. They say they hate coming here. It's too primitive and boring."

Dan knew that he was biased about Seneca and couldn't understand why people didn't love this place as much as he did, but some people just didn't. That's just the way it was. "Sorry to hear that."

"Don't be. If you never go someplace, you never know what you're missing."

While true, that sounded rather sad to him, and with all this depressing talk, he was starting to question whether he even wanted to hang around this girl. By this time, they'd reached the top of the steep roadway leading down to the point. "Be a little careful," he told her. "Sometimes, if you're only wearing sandals, it can get slippery. You might start sliding and you can lose your balance."

"Okay," and just as she reached over to grab his bicep for an assist, her feet went right out from underneath her, and down she went with a resounding thud right onto the dirt road.

"Oh, my gosh! Are you okay?" he asked, while reaching down to help her up.

Waving him off, she replied, "I'm fine. Actually, I think I bruised my ego more than anything else," she stated as she got up off the road and started dusting off her butt.

"Okay, grab hold," and she immediately did as he suggested. They made their way down, and when they got near the bottom where it was leveling out, she let go of his arm.

"You want to go sit on the dock?"

"Sure. I guess."

She walked along next to him out to the end of the long dock while staring off across the lake. They took a seat and she continued staring out across the water while saying nothing. Dan decided not to force the issue and sat there silently, as well. Eventually, she spoke. "So, now you know my story. What are you doing up here all by yourself? Why aren't you back at home hanging out with your buddies?"

"That's a fair question. As I told you, I live out in the country, but my friends all live in the city so hanging out with them isn't easy. They can simply walk or ride a bike to each other's homes whereas, up until very recently, I needed a ride. Most of the time, that simply wasn't available."

"But you've got a car now. Why don't you just drive and go see them?"

"Well, I could, but you'd have to know my friends. If I did that, I'd just end up being a free taxi cab for everyone. No thanks. Anyway, in years past, I've always come up with my brother Henry and spent most of the summer here. Either my parents or my grandparents would bring us. Things changed a couple years ago when Henry got his license and bought a car. He started providing the transportation and then we'd come up together."

"Things have changed again now with him being gone, but I've been coming here my whole life, so even though he's not around, I thought I'd still come up and see how things went. I mean, what are my alternatives? I've got a part-time job at a grocery store, but what am I supposed to do the rest of the time? Hang out at home and do nothing? So, I asked my dad if it was okay to come up by myself. He gave me this weird look like I was nuts or something but ultimately agreed, thus here I am," he answered, while gesturing with his arms out.

"Plus, it's not like there's no one to hang out with. There are actually several families on this road who have boys that I go to school with, like that Gary across the street from you. He and I don't hang out together at school, but I see him there every day. Bottom line is that I don't know what's going to happen. If it's too boring, I won't be spending much time here. If I'm enjoying myself, I'll be here all the time, just like every other summer."

"I see," was the totality of her response, though he thought he sensed a hint of disappointment in her voice. At that point, she went quiet again, staring out at the distant shoreline. The only sound was that of the waves gently passing beneath them as they sat on the end of the dock.

While they took in the view and the peaceful surroundings, a huge houseboat went by way out on the lake. The waves created by its wake were equally as large and they watched them slowly approach from the center of the lake like soldiers marching across a parade ground. They eventually crashed heavily against the shoreline, interrupting the serenity of the moment. It generated no verbal response or reaction from her whatsoever. Nothing. Several minutes later, the thunderous sound of an approaching speedboat began to fill the air. It rapidly came into view from the south, and the boat disappeared just as quickly heading north. "What the heck was that?" she asked.

"That, Yani, is what is called a Donzi. It is currently the fastest boat on this lake. It's got an eight-cylinder engine and it's a real rocket ship. I'm not sure about that particular one, but they come with different size engines, all of which have a ton of horsepower. There's no such thing as a slow Donzi and there's only a handful of people on the lake that own them. I'm told they're really expensive."

"It's impressive."

"It is, but I still like the Seneca Song better. It's got that classic look that I just love."

"Interesting," she said, then she simply went quiet again and, with the exception of waves continuously striking the shoreline, they sat there together in silence. Finally, she slapped both her hands on her knees, looked over at him and announced, "Okay, I think we should go," with a nod of her head reinforcing her declaration.

"No problem. Back to your place or somewhere else?"

"My place. I think it's getting closer to lunchtime and my grandmother told me to be back before noon so I can help her get the food ready."

"You've got it," and they began the walk back up the hill to her cottage. This time, she made sure to hang onto his arm. The whole time they were walking, Dan was thinking to himself, why did she want to leave so abruptly? Am I too boring? Did I say something to offend her?

Initially, they strolled along in silence and as they neared her grandparents' cottage, she stopped and turned to face him. "So, what are your plans for the afternoon?"

"Right now, I don't have any." He paused, not sure what to do next. "You want to hang out?"

"Actually, I would."

Thrilled that she wanted to see him again, he responded, "Okay, I'll come back after lunch. How's that sound?"

"That sounds pretty good. So, I'll see you after lunch then."

"Okay. See you then," and he left her standing there in front of her cottage.

Chapter 4

Dan returned to his place and began the process of undoing all of the preparations he had made for the now-aborted fishing trip. After that, he kept himself busy with other chores, followed by lunch. Once he was totally certain the Hartmann's had to be finished with their midday meal, he took a deep breath to muster up the courage necessary to go see this girl, all the while hoping she hadn't changed her mind, then headed down to her cottage with fingers crossed. Upon arriving, he knocked on the screen door and her grandmother instantly appeared. "Hey, Mrs. Hartmann. Can I talk to Yani?"

"Oh, hi, Dan. Yes, she's right here. Hold on a moment," and she turned and walked away. Waiting patiently, he could hear muffled voices coming from inside, but, in short order, she appeared and stepped out the door.

"Hi," was all she said.

He responded in kind, following up with, "You want to go for a walk?"

"Sure. Where're we going?"

"If it's okay, I thought I'd take you down to my cottage so you could see our place."

"Yeah. We can do that."

"Okay, let's go," and he began leading the way. They walked along without speaking and when they reached the Wallace property, Dan led her inside, held his hands out in a grand gesture and announced, "Well, this is it."

"It's cute," she told him. Dan had been inside the Hartmann property a number of times over the years. He knew theirs was way nicer than

24

his, so he appreciated her saying that. After he gave her the thirty-second tour of the tiny two-bedroom cottage, not knowing what to do next, he asked, "You want to go down to the dock?"

"Sure. Lead the way." They took the stairs down, passing through the boathouse and out onto the main dock.

"Hey, let's go for a boat ride," he suggested while glancing down towards the wooden motorboat parked in the lift.

She pointed down at the small boat sitting there. "In that thing?"

"Absolutely. Look, it may not be the Seneca Song or a Donzi, but it runs really well, it doesn't leak and I think it's fun."

She hesitated for a second, shrugged her shoulders and replied, "Okay, I guess."

"Hop in," he instructed her and she willingly complied with his request. Dan dropped the lift cradle until the boat floated freely, climbed in, pulled the engine cord and the Evinrude outboard started on the second attempt.

"All set?"

"Yeah, sure."

Dan backed the boat out, swung the bow around so it was facing north and off they went. Yani sat on a boat cushion on the front bench seat with her back to him and as they picked up speed, her auburn hair began trailing out behind her. He found the right throttle speed so that they would cruise smoothly and settled back in the boat.

His brother Henry would have done the exact opposite. Henry went out of his way to make any boat ride as uncomfortable as possible for all parties involved. For whatever reason, he thought it was hilarious watching passengers bounce all over the boat's interior as he slammed across the waves. As a result, a lot of people had gone for a ride just once with Henry, which he found terribly amusing in a rather malevolent way.

After they'd been cruising for a while, Dan started to throttle back and yelled out to her, "Hey." She swung around to face him. "I want to show you something." She simply nodded and turned back around, facing the front again. He continued to cut back on the throttle, getting closer and closer to the shoreline and a small rock outcropping sitting just off shore. Eventually the water became so shallow that he cut power completely and tipped the engine up into the boat so the prop wouldn't hit the stone lake bed. Grabbing a paddle from the bottom of the boat, he guided them up to the rock outcropping and paddled right up next to it. "According to what I've been told, this big chunk of rock here is the one and only island in the entire lake."

"It's not much of an island."

Somehow, Dan knew she wouldn't be impressed, and he laughed. "Yep. It's not much of an island, but it's the only one we've got."

"I see," was all she said.

After a few minutes of floating around the 'island', Dan asked, "Well, you ready to go back?" and was shocked by her response.

"Actually, no. Can you take me out into the middle of the lake?"

"Yeah, sure. We can do that." He stuck the paddle into the lake bed and pushed until they were in water deep enough to restart the engine. Dan fired up the Evinrude, and off they went skimming across the waves towards the middle of the lake with Yani's auburn hair streaming out behind her. It was a gorgeous day and she was a gorgeous girl. There were huge cumulus clouds overhead, a gentle breeze, and, in no time at all, they were out in six hundred feet of water. Yelling out to Yani over the sound of the engine, "Okay, now what?"

"Stop," was all she said, raising her hand. Dan killed the engine, and they began drifting along on the current. "I just want to float for a while," she said softly, her back still to him. He didn't know what to say, so he simply sat there silently thinking that whenever she was ready, maybe she'd start speaking. Other than the sound of the waves lapping against the side of the boat and the occasional call from a seagull passing overheard, it was total silence while they floated along. For what seemed like the longest time, she just sat there. Dan couldn't begin to imagine what she might be thinking about or staring at when she slowly spun around to face him. For a moment, he thought he detected a tiny teardrop, but maybe not.

"You know, my grandparents are really nice. They treat me great, but they're old, I don't know them very well and we really have nothing to talk about. Thanks for the boat ride. I needed a break."

"I think I understand. When I was little, my grandparents used to bring me up here all the time so I kind of know what it's like. The difference is they would always bring my brother, Henry, so at least I had someone fairly close to my age to hang around with. Do you have any brothers or sisters?"

"I have two younger sisters."

"What are their names?"

"Lisa and Robin."

"Wait a minute! Their names are Lisa and Robin, but they named you 'Yani'?"

"I'd rather not go into that right now."

"Okay. If you say so." Not wanting to anger his new found acquaintance, he decided to drop it for the time being. The question could always be revisited at a later date, assuming the opportunity presented itself.

27

"What about you? How many brothers and sisters do you have?"

"Six."

"What? No way. What are their names?"

"There's too many for you to remember, but not only do I have six brothers and sisters, I also have more than thirty cousins."

"Do you know their names?"

"Know their names?" he replied laughing. "Actually, I know every one of them personally. We all grew up within about an hour's drive of each other. I can hardly recall a moment in my life when I was ever alone except maybe when I was using the toilet. The good news is that I like most of my siblings and cousins and, for the most part, I enjoy hanging out with them. There are times, though, when I sure wish I could just be alone and not have to share my personal space with somebody else."

"What number child are you?"

"Four."

"So, you're the middle child. Lucky you," she stated sarcastically.

"Very funny. You know, this is actually the first time I've ever been up here at the lake by myself."

"Are you lonely?"

"Well, I was a little lonely last night, and I had a run in with a raccoon, but it wasn't too bad once things calmed down and I finally fell asleep."

"Stop. What do you mean you had a run-in with a raccoon?"

"Yeah, well, I kept hearing these stupid footsteps outside my bedroom window. It was freaking me out and I couldn't sleep. So, I decided I needed to check it out. Fortunately, when the raccoon saw me, he took off."

"Seriously? You heard noises outside, and rather than just stay indoors where it's nice and safe, you decided to go outside?"

"Okay," he replied, gesturing with his hands. "Maybe that wasn't the best idea, but our cottage isn't exactly a fortress. If it was a person and they wanted to get inside, there's no way to keep them out. I figured I kind of had no choice but to go confront whatever it was."

"Oh, God," she said, shaking her head and staring into her lap. Looking back up at him, she asked, "So, when are you leaving?"

"Well, I've got school on Monday, so I was either going go down tomorrow or maybe first thing Monday morning Haven't made up my mind yet."

"When're you coming back?"

"I have to work at my part-time job at a grocery store and I've got class every day, so right now, the plan is to come back next Friday afternoon."

"You should stay and go down Monday morning."

Dan turned and looked off towards the far shoreline for a moment to contemplate her request. Turning back to face her he replied, "Okay. I guess I can do that," nodding his head in agreement.

"Good. It's settled. You're staying until Monday," was all she said in response, and then she looked away again to stare out over the lake.

Now, he wasn't really sure what to think. She seemed awfully negative, and he didn't know how to feel about that. Did she want him to stay because he was a distraction from the boredom or because she liked him? At the end of the day, he decided that it really didn't matter. She was so incredibly beautiful that even if she simply wanted to use

29

him as cheap company, it was worth it to be so close to a girl this good-looking, at least for a little while. There certainly weren't any girls like this at his school, not even close.

She sat there for the longest time, not saying a word. Out of nowhere, she spun around again and announced, "Okay, I guess we better head back."

"You got it," and he fired up the Evinrude. Fifteen minutes later, they were pulling into the boatlift. He parked the boat, raised it out of the water, locked the lift wheel, gave her a hand getting out and they walked back up to the road. Yani gave him no indication that she wanted to walk back on her own, so he just kept strolling along beside her until they got to her cottage.

As they arrived at the little front porch of her grandparents' place, she turned to face him and asked, "Are you going to be around later?"

Staring into those hypnotic blue eyes of hers, the response was easy. "Sure. What time do you want me to come back?"

"How about right after supper?"

"Okay. I'll see you after supper."

"Perfect," and, with that, she walked straight into her cottage while Dan did an about-face and headed back to his place. He spent the rest of the afternoon mowing the lawn, raking a little, and doing chores around the property. When he got hungry, he went inside and grabbed a snack. When he got hot, he jumped into the lake and took a swim, and it wasn't long before it was supper time and another opportunity to talk to this fascinating Yani girl. He counted down the minutes until he was sure the Hartmann's had to be finished eating, took another deep breath to build up his courage, then headed towards their cottage.

Chapter 5

As Dan made the short walk down to the Hartmann's, he couldn't help thinking he must be living some kind of a dream and that somebody really needed to pinch him so he'd wake up. Just this morning, he'd met the most beautiful girl he'd ever seen, and already they'd spent most of the day together. Now, at her request, they were going to spend part of the evening together. When he walked up to the Hartmann place and knocked on the screen door, neither Mr. nor Mrs. Hartmann answered. Instead, Yani came to the door herself. "Hi. How are you?" she asked, as she stepped outside.

"I'm good. How was supper?" he answered back, trying his best not to sound too stupid.

"It was fine. Grandma's a good cook and she always makes something nice. This evening we had pork chops, corn on the cob and, fresh, home-grown tomatoes."

"Gosh, that does sound good."

"Play your cards right and maybe you'll get invited over for supper some evening," she stated with a little gleam in her eye and a smile on her lips. That was the first time he'd seen anything resembling a smile out of the girl.

"I'll do my best," he replied, returning the smile.

"So, what are we doing?"

"You know, I thought we'd walk down to the other end of the neighborhood. I'm guessing you haven't seen how the other half of our little community lives."

"And your guess would be correct."

"Okay, so let's go," and they proceeded with their walk, cruising along at a very leisurely pace. It was a lovely evening and there was still plenty of sunlight left, so there was no urgency. First, they walked past the fork in the road that led up the hill to the main highway, past Dan's place, and, finally, into the part of the community that Yani hadn't yet seen. While every cottage was unique in its exterior design and color, they were all located on lots of the exact same size and, with few exceptions, they were all about the same square footage, falling in the range of 500 to 750.

There were a couple that had been converted into year-round properties, but the vast majority had no insulation or heat, making it impossible to stay there during the winter months. If the owners were outside when they walked by, they would wave, and sometimes, the owners called out a greeting. Dan would always make a point of responding in kind.

Continuing to walk, she commented, "You know, this is a really cute community."

"Yeah, it's nothing fancy, but we like it. Heck, a fair percentage of these cottages don't even have hot water, let alone heat. It's kind of funny. When I was a little boy, we had heat, but no hot water. The old furnace eventually rusted out. You couldn't repair it because I was told you could no longer get parts, so it was ripped out and thrown away. In the meantime, the women in the family put their foot down and said that if we didn't install hot water, they weren't coming back. Lo and behold, all of a sudden, we had hot water, and later on, we even installed a small, hot water shower."

"Hold on a minute. If there was no hot water or shower, how did you bathe?"

"Ah, yes. Bathing. Fascinating concept," he replied laughing. Looking at her with a straight face, he told her the cold, hard truth…literally. "In reality, you either grabbed a bar of soap and went down to the lake or you didn't bathe. Have you gone swimming yet?"

"Nope. Not yet."

"We'll have to take care of that. Anyway, most of the year, the lake water is pretty chilly, which is probably the biggest reason the woman started protesting and demanding indoor hot water. Bathing in the lake most times of the year will definitely take your breath away and the women wanted no part of that."

"I see."

"Getting back to the issue of heat, my dad is a really big fan of wood-burning stoves. We had one of those here for a while to supply heat, but it took up too much floor space and generated too much ash and dust. My mom complained about all the filth. She's got enough cleaning to do at home, so we pulled it out. Now, once the cold weather arrives, we just close up the cottage, turn off the power and wait until the next season arrives when we open everything back up again."

"Interesting. So, how old are most of these places?"

"I don't know exactly. I believe my grandfather bought the lot around 1950 or shortly thereafter. My grandfather, my dad, and my uncle built the cottage not long after that, which would mean some time like 1952 or '53. You should probably ask your grandfather. I bet he'd know. Your family bought and built around the same timeframe. The only thing I can tell you for sure is that it's been here longer than I've been alive."

"So, these places have been here that long?"

"Oh, yeah. Before this community was created, the land was owned by the farmer at the top of the hill. It made for lousy farmland, and it wasn't great waterfront because of the cliffs, but it had some value as lakefront. Anyway, he had it legally broken up into individual lots and sold them off one lot at a time, acting as his own developer. He also put in these dirt roads, including the one we're walking on right now."

"Fascinating," was her total response and then she went quiet again. Dan figured she was probably digesting everything he told her when, out of nowhere, what sounded like a miniature horse came galloping up behind them. Dan looked back over his shoulder just in time to see a large, brown dog charging in their direction. As it went flying by, it bumped into his leg, almost knocking him down.

"Ruby, damn it! Watch where the hell you're going!" he yelled at the dog.

"Wait. You know that dog?" Yani asked, sounding somewhat astonished as Dan staggered a bit to regain his balance.

"Yeah, that's the Snyder's dog, Ruby. She's a really good dog, but sometimes she forgets how big and powerful she is."

Seemingly out of nowhere, a man shouted, "Ruby, you dumb ass! Get back here!"

"And that would be Mr. Snyder," Dan said to Yani with a big smile as the dog's owner ran past with a leash in his hand.

"Hi, Dan," he said almost breathlessly as he ran by them chasing after his dog.

"Hey, Mr. Snyder," Dan replied to Snyder's back as he continued running after his pet. Meanwhile, Ruby was still barreling down the road like a mad woman heading in the general direction of the forest located where the road came to a dead end. As they watched, she pulled up short and started bellowing. All of a sudden, out of the brush charged the raccoon. It stood at its full height on its hind legs, baring its teeth, clawed paws up by its head in a threatening posture while hissing at the dog. Ruby started snarling and circling the raccoon, looking for an opening to attack. All the while, the still-running Mr. Snyder was yelling at Ruby to stop.

"Oh, Christ. Hold on a minute," Dan muttered as he took off running towards Snyder and the two crazed animals. While he loved baseball, he wasn't particularly good at it, but he had a strong and fairly accurate arm. As he ran along the road, his eyes searched back and forth until he saw what he needed: two rocks the perfect shape for throwing. He stopped briefly to retrieve them and started running again towards the melee up ahead. Mr. Snyder was yelling, and the animals were snarling at each other, circling and getting ready to battle. As soon as Dan got within about thirty feet, he let loose with the first rock, firing a fastball towards the raccoon. He got lucky and it found its target.

The rock struck the raccoon right in the ribs and you could actually hear it hit the beast. The amazing thing was it didn't even flinch or yelp, but it had to have hurt. It just stared at Dan and continued hissing and snarling. When Dan reared back to launch the second missile, the raccoon must have reasoned he couldn't possibly win, so he decided the best course of action was retreat. That way, it could at least live to fight another day, and it slowly started backing away. When the rock went whistling past his head, the raccoon knew the fight was over. He turned and high-tailed it deep into the forest. Ruby came to a stop at the forest's edge and continued bellowing until Mr. Snyder finally caught up to her, got the leash on and began admonishing her.

"God dang it, Ruby! How many times have I got to tell you to stay clear of that 'coon?" he scolded the dog as they headed back towards Dan and Yani, who had now caught up to him. Approaching the two of them, Mr. Snyder called out, "Sorry, Dan. Didn't mean to be rude, but thanks for your help there. By the way, nice shot with that rock."

"Pure luck, Mr. Snyder, but thanks. Glad to lend a hand and I totally understand. I had a little problem with that same raccoon last night."

"Is that right," Mr. Snyder replied with a surprised look on his face as he and Ruby came to a halt directly in front of them.

"Yeah, I'd gone to bed and kept hearing these strange noises outside the bedroom window, so I slipped outside to see what it was and got rudely greeted by that stupid 'coon."

"Well, I'll be," he responded, mouth slightly agape, then he quickly turned to Yani and smiled at her. "Oh, hi. I'm Mr. Snyder," he said while extending his hand.

"Hi. Nice to meet you, Mr. Snyder. I'm Yani," she answered back taking his hand in return.

"Hi, Yaa…"

"It's Yani."

"Oh, that's an interesting name." It was obvious he wasn't going to attempt repeating it again, hoping he got it right on the second try.

At this point, Dan broke into the conversation in an attempt to stop any potential confusion. "Yani is the Hartmann's granddaughter. She's just up here paying them a visit."

"Well, isn't that nice. Are you enjoying yourself?"

"Yes. As a matter of fact, I am," she replied, while taking a quick sideways glance at Dan. Mr. Snyder noticed that and smiled at the two of them. As they stood there engaging in small talk, Ruby, being the dog that she was and having calmed down, decided she needed to start sniffing around Dan and Yani.

Mr. Snyder noticed that, as well, and told Yani, "Hey, feel free to pet her. She's super friendly, if maybe a little bit too nosey!" he yelled down at Ruby, who lowered her head in shame at being scolded yet again. Yani bent down and gently stroked the top of her head. "Hello,

Ruby," she said softly and got rewarded for her affection with a nice, good dog kiss.

"I just don't know what I'm going to do with her, Dan," Mr. Snyder said sadly, slowly shaking his head. "Whenever I see that nose go in the air and she jumps up, I know she's gotten a whiff of that damned 'coon and, immediately, it's off to the races for her. One of these times, I'm afraid that 'coon is going to decide to fight back and that'll be a disaster I really need to avoid. I don't want to keep her tied up, though. That's one of the nice things about coming up here. There're no leash laws, so she can just run around and be free."

"I don't know what to say, Mr. Snyder. Fortunately, raccoons are kind of nomadic. After a while, he'll get bored with this area or start looking for a girlfriend and he'll move along. Hopefully, it'll be sooner rather than later."

"Yeah, hopefully. Anyway, I'm going to take her back home now. You two enjoy the rest of your evening. Good to see you, Dan."

"Likewise. See you later, Mr. Snyder."

They were already at the far end of the community, so the two of them simply reversed course and started heading back. "Well, that was certainly exciting," she announced, "and nice job with that rock," she said, smiling and tapping him lightly on the arm with her fist. "I'll bet that left a mark."

"Well, I had to try and do something. Those stupid raccoons have teeth like a cat to go along with their claws. I don't think that it's big enough to actually kill Ruby, but it could cause some serious damage to the dog and we definitely don't need or want that. Ruby's kind of a part of the community."

"I see. Well, somehow, I have a feeling we may have seen the last of that raccoon. Between you hitting it with a rock and a big dog harassing it, I think it may start looking for a new place to live."

"You think? Well, I don't believe we'll have to wait long before we find out."

They had now just about reached the Hartmann cottage. Yani turned to him, "So, you still planning to spend tomorrow up here?"

"That is the plan."

"Good. So, I'll see you in the morning, okay?" she replied, smiling at him and lightly touching his arm.

"Yep. I'll see you in the morning," he answered back. Yani turned and disappeared into her cottage, leaving him standing there with the same thought he had when he walked up earlier. Someone, please pinch me and wake me from this dream.

Chapter 6

The following day, anxious and excited to spend more time with his new friend, he walked to their cottage, knocked, and Mr. Hartmann came to the door. "Oh, hi, Dan. How are you today?"

"Hey, Mr. Hartmann. I'm good. Can I talk to Yani?"

"Yep. Hold on a second." He simply turned around, yelled out "Yani!" and walked back to the chair he'd been occupying before getting up to answer the door.

Yani appeared immediately, stepped outside and started walking. Dan followed suit and asked, "Where're we headed?"

"You tell me. I barely even know where I'm at."

"Okay. I have an idea."

When they reached the road that led down to the common beach area, Dan pointed to the left and they headed down the hill right up to the water's edge. He stepped into the clear lake water and she followed suit. It was cool, comforting and felt really good. They waded along through the water until they got to the end of the little community beach, where they simply turned around and headed back to where they began. Yani hadn't spoken a word the entire time.

He finally broke the silence by saying, "You know how to skip a stone?"

"Nope. I've never even tried."

"Here. I'll show you." Dan bent over and began searching the beach for the perfect skipping stone. When he spotted one he liked, he picked it up and whipped it sidearm across the water. It probably skipped more than a dozen times before disappearing below the surface.

"There. Now you try."

Yani bent over, picked up a stone and threw it towards the water. It went straight into the lake, never skipping once.

"I guess I need some practice."

"Well, the first thing you need to do is get the right stone. That stone you chose wasn't a good one. You need a really flat one." The beach was made up of broken pieces of shale that had fallen from the cliff walls over the millennia. Some had split perfectly when they broke off the cliff walls and others hadn't. Some were too large to grip properly and some too small. Dan showed her which types worked best and picked one that he liked.

"Take this stone. This is a good one," and he handed it to her. "The next thing you need to do is lower your arm and throw it sidearm so it glides across the water on the flat surface of the rock. Here. Give it a try."

She took the stone, reached back, dropped her elbow and whipped it towards the water. It skipped two or three times before sinking. He actually saw a glimmer of a smile.

"Good job. Now you're getting the hang of it." Dan reached down, picked up another 'good' stone and handed it to her. "Here. Try again."

She repeated the throwing motion. This time, the piece of shale skipped five time and the smile got just a little bigger.

"Okay, that's enough teaching. Now you're on your own." Dan picked up a stone, whipped it out across the water and it skipped at least a dozen times. As they took turns skipping stones, Dan noticed movement behind him. Looking back over his shoulder towards the road, he tapped her on the shoulder. She turned around and found herself looking at a very large, brown dog sitting there at the top of the stone beach staring back at her.

"Is that Ruby?"

"Yep," he nodded.

"Hey, Ruby. Come here, girl," she called out softly, and the dog came towards her tail wagging like crazy. Ruby came right up to her and rubbed against her leg while Yani petted her. "She's really nice," Yani commented.

"I told you she is. Ruby's only problem is that, occasionally, she forgets how strong she is. Other than that, she's a sweetheart." Yani petted her for a few more minutes, and once Ruby had gotten enough attention, she simply turned around and trotted back off up the hill towards her home.

They skipped stones for the next thirty minutes or so. Every time Yani threw a good one, the smile got just a little bit bigger. After a while of stone skipping, she announced that her arm was getting tired.

"Okay, so you ready to leave?" and she nodded in agreement.

They started walking up the hill away from the beach when she asked, "So, where are we headed?"

"I thought we'd go down to my place, but we don't have to. We can go somewhere else if you'd like."

"You have a car. Can we go into town?"

"Oh, so you won't go out fishing with me, but you will go for a ride in my car?"

"Maybe something's changed," she responded, a serious look on her face.

He hesitated for just a moment before replying back and then nodded. "Okay, yeah, sure. We can do that."

"Wait a minute," she stated, staring at him. "You just hesitated. Is there a problem?" she asked, her head tilted to the side and a hint of suspicion in her voice.

"Easy, Yani!" he responded cautiously with palms up. "There's no problem. I just had to think about the insurance for a second cause it's not my car. It's my brother, Henry's. Anyway, I'm pretty sure everything'll be fine. Come on. Let's go." Now satisfied with his response, they headed for the Wallace cottage with her tagging right along and a little skip in her step.

Hopping into the car, she told him, "Okay, let's swing by my place first so I can tell my grandparents where I'm going. They'll want to know."

"You got it." Dan drove the short distance to her grandparents' place, and while she went inside to tell them where they were headed, he turned the car around and waited for her to return. After informing her grandparents, she climbed back in, and off they went to Watkins with the windows down and the radio on.

"So, where have your grandparents taken you so far?" he asked as they drove along the lake road heading down the hill towards town.

"The only places I've been to are the IGA grocery store, Tobey's donut shop and the laundromat. That's it."

"They haven't even taken you to the state park yet?" he asked somewhat incredulously.

"Nope. Didn't even know there was one."

"Yeah, it's really beautiful and very popular, too. It's a little late, though, to be going there. Plus, those sandals you're wearing won't work. You basically walk the length of the park through this gigantic really deep gorge and that takes at least a few hours. I'm guessing they probably haven't told you about it because it would be too difficult a walk for them, so they haven't even considered it as an option. Maybe we can do that another time."

"So, what are we going to do?"

42

Dan thought about it for a second. "Hey, I know,' he said excitedly. "There's a really famous racetrack here called Watkins Glen International. It's huge, and it could be interesting for you to see. It's super famous. Have you ever noticed the street signs in Watkins?"

"I have. There are these little race cars sitting on top of the street sign poles. I was wondering what that was all about."

"I've only been to that track once before, but they hold a lot of big international races there over the course of the year."

"When was it that you went?"

"Last fall. I overheard some of my buddies from school talking about going to a race and they asked me if I wanted to come along. We camped there at the track and watched the racing on the weekend. I'd never seen anything like it. The cars had these huge engines, no fenders, and the drivers' cockpits were wide open. It was actually really cool to see up close."

"Okay. I suppose that could be interesting. So, do you think we can actually get in?"

"I think it should be open," he answered cautiously. "I don't know if there's any racing going on right now, but if there isn't, I think we can get on the property. Let's take a chance. Okay?"

"Well, I don't really know anything about racing, but okay," she replied, shrugging her shoulders.

They drove on into town, past all the little souvenir shops, the street signs with their little race cars on top, antique stores, and family-owned restaurants on Franklin Street when Dan turned up the steep hill leading back out of town.

"There's not much flat around here, is there?" she asked, smiling at him.

"Nope. If you want flat, you're aren't going to find much of that around these parts," he responded laughing. They drove several more miles up the hill until they came upon a large sign announcing the presence of the racetrack with an arrow directing traffic to turn right. Dan made the turn onto the county road leading to the track entrance. Shortly after that, huge billboards started coming into view. There were massive signs for Ford Racing, Texaco, Chevrolet, Mopar, and Sunoco. There were signs for Winston cigarettes, Marlboro, Miller High Life, Budweiser beer, and many other major sponsors scattered around the racetrack property. Next, the control tower appeared, and shortly after that, the different grandstands started coming into view. Finally, they reached the main entrance to the property. Sure enough, it was open.

As he drove through the main gate, a large black man in a security uniform with a sidearm on his belt came out of the guard shack located there and held his hand up, indicating Dan needed to stop. "Uh, oh. This doesn't look too good," Dan stated nervously to her.

The security guard walked up to the car and leaned his face down into the side window, first looking at Dan, then turning and staring at Yani. "Can I help you two?" he asked pleasantly.

"Yes, sir. We just wanted to come in to see the track."

"Okay. Well, the track is open for visitors today, so that shouldn't be a problem, but there are rules. Now, you do realize that there are restricted areas you're not allowed to enter, right?"

"Yes, sir. I've been here once before and I do know that."

Wagging a big finger in Dan's face, he said sternly, "Do not go into any area marked 'restricted', okay? The last thing I want to hear is my radio blasting out a report about two kids being in a restricted area when they aren't supposed to be there."

"Yes, sir. Got it. Stay out of restricted areas."

The security guard slapped his hand twice on the window sill of the car door. "Enjoy your visit," was all he said as he turned and walked away. Dan immediately drove off before the guard could change his mind.

"Whew! For a second there, Dan, I thought he was going to make us leave."

"Yeah, I was almost certain of that myself," he responded as they pulled into the track grounds. "Anyway, here it is, Yani, Watkins Glen International."

"Whoa!" she exclaimed. "Look at this! It's huge!"

"Yep. It's almost three and a half miles long."

"I had no idea."

"Hey, I told you it's a big deal. They get famous drivers from all over the world racing here," Dan explained as they drove deeper into the track property. For the next hour, they drove around the grounds, taking the private roads through several tunnels that led into and out of the infield. They drove throughout the campgrounds, including the one where Dan had slept with his friends, and around the different grandstands. They even stopped at the souvenir shop for a look at the different driver's gear and other racing memorabilia available for purchase.

"You recognize any of these names: Richard Petty, Jackie Stewart, Mario Andretti, A.J. Foyt?"

"Never heard of them," she replied back and he just laughed.

"Of course, you haven't. What was I thinking? So, all of these guys are really famous and they've all raced here."

"Come on, Dan. Be serious. I've never even heard my dad mention auto racing, let alone seen him watching a race on TV."

"Hey, I was just checking," he said laughing again, while Yani gave him this dirty look and a half-hearted smack on his shoulder.

After the souvenir stand, they continued on their tour of the track property, making sure to avoid the restricted areas. There weren't a lot of people there, but there was a lot of activity around some of the garages. At various times, race cars of different types would go flying by in test runs, followed by the track safety vehicles trailing behind at a distance.

"Okay, Dan, so there's cars out there driving around. Can we drive on the track?"

"Well, yes and no. You can pay to take a drive around the track, but they won't let us do that," he responded with a big smile.

"Well, why not?"

"Couple of reasons. First of all, I don't have what's called a senior operator's license. I only have a junior operator's and they aren't going to let me on the track for that reason alone because of insurance requirements."

"Boy, car insurance sure seems to be a big deal around here."

"Yes, yes, it is, but on top of it, there's no way they'd let me take *this* car out there."

"Why not? *This* car seems fine to me," she replied, emphasizing 'this' as Dan had.

"It's all about safety. An old car like this one we're driving might leak oil, antifreeze, or brake fluid. If I take it out on the track and it leaks fluids, it could cause a car following later to lose traction and crash. That would be a very bad thing. There'd be a lot of really unhappy people. Plus, someone could get hurt."

"That sucks because I'd really like to drive on that track. That would be so awesome!"

"So would I, Yani. So would I," he responded, looking into those luminescent blue eyes. Frankly, I'd drive you just about anywhere, he thought to himself. "By the way," he offered. "Of course, you've heard of Woodstock."

"Of course. Who hasn't?"

"Exactly. Well, the farm where that took place is not all that far from here. Anyway, rumor has it that they are scheduling Woodstock II for next summer and it's supposed to be held right here at this track."

"Cool. Think you'll go?"

"It's way too soon to know about that. Maybe. Anyway, I don't think there's anything else I can show you here. We've seen pretty much everything there is to see. So, you ready to head back up to the lake?"

"Sure. I guess so," she answered while staring at the track facilities out of the window. "You know, at first, I thought this would be really boring, but it was actually pretty interesting. Good choice, Dan. I enjoyed this, but now you've got your work cut out for you because now you're going to need to come up with something that's even better."

"Oh great," he sighed.

"Don't worry, Dan," she laughed as she reached over and gently touched his arm. "You're doing just fine. You'll think of something."

Chapter 7

The next morning, he got up early and made the drive to school, thinking that Friday couldn't possibly arrive soon enough. It was now June 5th, and school ended in seventeen days. The anticipation of the school year ending had been building for some time now.

On the way to school that morning, he was suddenly struck with an idea. When the class day ended, rather than leaving and going straight home, he went to his guidance counselor's office. Even though the door was wide open and his counselor was sitting there all alone, out of respect, Dan knocked anyway. His counselor looked up with a smile, "Oh, hi, Dan. Come on in and take a seat." Once seated, his counselor leaned forward with arms folded on the desk and asked, "So, what can I do for you?"

"Mr. Kubinski, I have a question about graduation."

"Okay, what's on your mind?"

"I was curious," then he hesitated briefly, wondering how his counselor might react to his question. "How many credits do you actually need to graduate?"

At that time in New York, high school was similar to college in that you needed a certain number of credits to graduate, but it was one of those things no one ever brought up or discussed. It was just kind of taken for granted because almost no one ever failed. Kids did drop out occasionally, but if you hung in there, simply attended school, and stayed out of trouble, they'd find a way to ensure you graduated. Gary was a good example of that. He was a borderline student, but somehow, some way, the school would see to it that he passed and graduated.

"Well, that's an easy one," Kubinski responded. "Eighteen and a half."

"Can you tell me how many I have right now?"

"Sure, though I'm certain you already have more than enough." He turned and opened a filing cabinet drawer behind his desk, pulled out a folder and started flipping through the pages it held inside. "Let's see here. Assuming you pass all your finals, and I know you will, you'll have exactly twenty-one and a half going into your senior year."

"So, I already have more than enough credits to graduate?"

"Well, yes and no. You need eighteen and a half total credits, but they do need to be in certain classes. According to your transcript, let's see here, after this year ends, you'll still need…oh, yes. Here we go. You'll still need a semester of English, one in a foreign language or shop, and one for PE."

Dan had exactly the answer he was looking for. When he returned in the fall for his senior year, he'd only need one more semester, an easy one at that, and he could graduate. The timing would be almost perfect. At nearly the exact same date as the fall semester ended, Dan would also be turning eighteen.

"Okay, thanks, Mr. Kubinski. I appreciate it."

"Wait. That's it? That's all you wanted to talk about?"

"Yeah, somebody was talking about it in study hall today. No one knew the answer, so I thought I'd ask. Anyway, thanks again," and he stood to leave. That was a complete lie. No one in study hall had asked about that, but Kubinski was friends with his dad. If he was suspicious of Dan's motives, he might say something to his father that could result in Dan having to lie to his dad. He would lie if he had to, but he didn't like doing that. It was too easy to get caught. It was always better just to avoid getting in that position in the first place and simply eliminate a potential problem for himself.

"Okay, well, I'm not going to get a steady stream of students knocking on my door now to find out how many credits they have, am I?"

"I doubt it, Mr. Kubinski. You want me to say something to them?"

"Yes. If they get all worried and desperate, tell them that their next report card will state exactly how many credits they've accumulated. Now, it won't tell them what classes they still need, but it will give them their cumulative credits to date."

"Okay, thanks, Mr. Kubinski. I'll be sure to tell them if it comes up again."

"You're welcome, Dan. You have a good evening and please tell your dad I said hi."

"Will do. Thanks, again."

While leaving, Kubinski stared at his back as he walked away, wondering what that was all about. Why was Dan interested in how many credits he had? He was one of the best students in his class year and there was no question that he would graduate on time. He shook his head, closed up the folder, put it back in the filing cabinet and returned to what he had been working on before Dan showed up.

Dan walked away in possession of the information he needed. Now he could put a plan in place. Graduation was within easy reach. He had decided some time ago that it was time for a change. School was no longer challenging and had become downright boring. Now, it was time to do something new. Turning eighteen and graduating at the end of the fall semester made him legal to do just about anything and everything. "Yes!" he said quietly with a small fist pump as he walked away.

Chapter 8

When school ended the following Friday, Dan hopped in the Chrysler and immediately headed for the cottage, pulling in a little before 4:30. Anxious to see his new friend, he let himself in, changed out of his Levi's and short-sleeved button-down shirt into shorts and a tee-shirt. That done, he headed directly for the Hartmann's. When he walked up, the front door was wide open, and he could see Mrs. Hartmann inside. He knocked on the screen door and stepped back, hoping nothing had changed and that Yani was still there at the lake. Her grandmother came to the door, opened it and he politely asked, "Hey, Mrs. Hartmann. Can I talk to Yani?"

"Yes, Dan. Hold on, just a second. I think she's been waiting for you." She walked back to the interior of the cottage. He could hear voices but couldn't quite make out what was being said when Yani suddenly appeared in front of him.

As she opened the screen door, she looked at Dan smiling and said, "Hi." The clothes were different, but she was dressed exactly the same way as when he last saw her: shorts, a tee shirt, sandals, and no makeup. He paused briefly to take in her beautiful eyes. They were truly amazing and sparkling as much as ever.

"Hi," he replied back, amazed at how relieved he felt just to see her again.

Yani stepped off the small porch and they began walking. It was now Friday, June 9th. According to his estimates, there were about 89 days left before she would be leaving.

"Where're we going?"

"Let's go down to the point," he suggested.

"Okay. Let's go."

At first, they walked in silence until they were out of earshot of her grandparents' place when she asked, "How was school and work?"

He was a little surprised that she remembered he had a job. Obviously, she'd been paying attention when he told her about it the previous weekend.

"Everything was uneventful. I went to school every day. In the evening, I went to my job at the grocery store on the days I was scheduled and that was it. How was your week?"

"It was very quiet up here. It seemed like most of the cottages were deserted. The highlights were two trips to the grocery store in Watkins with my grandmother, boat rides in the Seneca Song, or watching the one TV station they get. The rest of the time, I just read books, helped my grandmother in the kitchen, or sat outside. That was it. I don't really feel comfortable walking around by myself."

"I totally understand. Well, let's see if we can't make your weekend a little more interesting."

"I was hoping you'd say that."

They walked down the steep hill together, with her holding onto his arm, making sure she didn't fall like she did the first time she made the trip. When they reached the flat area between the lake and the cliffs, she looked around and stated, "This is so nice. I still can't get over the fact there's no cottages here."

"Yeah, I don't know what the deal is. I've always wondered the same thing. I think I told you that the people who own the land live locally. I'm just guessing here, but maybe it's because their homes are so close there's no need for a cottage? They can just come here, use it when they please, and go home afterwards. I don't know what else it could be. The really weird thing, though, is that I never see anyone using it. On top of that, I've never once had anyone show up when I was here."

"Hmmm," was her only response to that information.

They walked out to the end of the dock and sat with their feet dangling in the cool, fresh water. After they'd been sitting for a while, Dan turned to her and announced, "You know, you gave me an idea last weekend."

"Oh? What was that?"

"Well, I was thinking about how you took your finals early. I didn't even know you could do something like that and it got me to wondering, what else don't I know? So, on Monday, I stopped by to see my guidance counselor. He told me that I already have enough credits to graduate and that I just need three more classes in the fall to meet all the state requirements. That's it."

"So, you're going to graduate early? Is that your plan?"

"I think so."

"Have you told your parents?"

"No."

"Are you going to?"

"I haven't made up my mind yet, but I'm thinking probably not. I don't actually have to put in for graduation until finals week next January. The fall semester ends pretty much exactly when I turn eighteen. Maybe I'll change my mind, but I doubt it. Besides, I don't want to deal with my folks pressuring me to stay in school. If I graduate, I'm done with school. There is no going back, so there's nothing they can do about it. I think they'll be pissed, but, oh, well."

Yani didn't pursue that line of questioning any further but moved on to another. "Well, if you graduate early, what are you going to do?"

"Once I've graduated and turned eighteen, legally, I can do pretty much anything."

"Which is?"

"Well, my parents won't kick me out of the house. That's not their style. So, I'd probably get a job and work full-time somewhere in Elmira until the draft comes up for my birth year. If I get drafted? Well, you know what happens if I do. If I don't? Well, maybe I register for classes at the local community college for the fall semester. My parents don't have money to pay for my college, so that's all I'd be able to afford. I already sat for the college boards, so with my test scores and my grades, I know I'll get in. The other alternative is that I could just enlist like my older brothers to avoid the draft. My guess is I'll probably get drafted and won't have to worry about making any decisions."

"I see," was all she said and they sat there silently. Dan could tell that Yani was thinking about what he had just told her. After a few minutes of no sound except the lapping of the waves against the pilings of the dock and the rocky shoreline, she turned to face him. Placing her hand on his arm and looking him in the eyes, she said, "I, for one, think you should just graduate. After all, who knows what the future holds," she told him with a tone of calmness as she nodded her head once for emphasis. Both of them knew exactly what that meant, and it didn't need to be spoken out loud. If he got drafted, there was a very good chance he could end up in Vietnam.

"Okay, then it's settled. I'm graduating early."

She smiled, removed her hand from his arm and stared off across the lake. They sat there quietly until it was near supper time, then casually strolled back to her grandparents. Once they arrived, he asked her if he could come back once she was done eating. Her response was exactly what he had hoped for. "If you don't, I'll be really disappointed."

Dan went back to his place, ate, cleaned up, and sat outside listening to the rock station on the radio until he was sure enough time had passed that the Hartmann's had finished eating. He walked down to their place and knocked. This time, Yani answered the knock, came straight outside and they walked away together towards Dan's place.

"What're we going to do?" she asked.

"I think we should take the boat out."

"Your little motorboat?"

"No. The rowboat." Dan had decided ahead of time that it would be much better to take the rowboat. That way, they wouldn't have to yell over the sound of the engine. It would be more peaceful and easier to have a conversation, assuming she was interested in doing that. When they got down to his lift, she climbed into the rowboat and sat in the back, facing the bow. He lowered the boat into the water until it was floating freely from the cradle and climbed in. Holding onto the side of the lift, he pushed against it, propelling the boat through the water until it cleared the end of the dock. He grabbed the oars, slipped them into the oarlocks and started rowing away from the dock.

"When I was a little boy, this was the only boat I was allowed to take out," he explained, as he made these smooth, easy strokes with the oars. "When I was very little, it used to have a small gas engine, and my grandfather used it for fishing. The engine was this little Johnson brand of outboard. It was really small, and eventually, it just stopped running. Like a lot of the other things we've had around here over the years, you couldn't get replacement parts, so I guess my grandpa finally threw it away. Anyway, ever since, we've only used this as a rowboat."

Even though it was more difficult, he started off rowing against the current. Having learned over the years that rowing was hard work, once you got tired, it was a heck of a lot easier to row back home with the current helping than it was against it. He headed out away from shore and rowed down to the cove just past the Hartmann cottage. Mr. Hartmann was down on the dock doing something with the Seneca Song and looked up as they were rowing past. Yani waved to him, he waved back and then returned to whatever it was he was involved with. The water was smoother in the cove because the point that jutted out from the shore acted as a block for the wind and waves. Once there, Dan stopped rowing, put the oars in, and they just sat there drifting with the boat rocking gently back and forth.

"Hey, before I forget, my grandma said that I have to be home by dark."

"Okay. Well, we don't want to make Grandma angry, so I'll make sure you're home in time."

"Thanks," she said with a nice smile. Yani didn't seem to smile too much and it made Dan happy whenever she did.

After they'd been drifting for a while, he looked up to face her, "Hey, I know you didn't want to talk about this the other day, but I'm still curious about your name. Feel like maybe telling me about that?"

Yani paused for a moment before finally speaking. "Yeah, well, my parents are seriously weird, and I don't mean that in a good way." Dan started laughing. He found the frankness with which she spoke sometimes to be really refreshing. He simply couldn't stifle the laugh, but he didn't say anything else because he wanted her to continue.

"Before I was born, somehow my parents got interested in East Indian mysticism, but it seems like they're always into the latest fad. After the Indian thing, they became beatniks, and now they're like hippies. I've never caught them, but I'm pretty sure they smoke pot. I'm shocked they didn't go to Woodstock. They're definitely the type. All I can figure is they must not have been able to find a babysitter for the four or five days it would have taken. They're huge Beatles, Stones, and Zeppelin fans, but for some strange reason, they were never into

Elvis. I found that interesting because they're into every other fad. Maybe he's just too commercially popular with normal people and not weird enough. Maybe they're racists. Who knows? I'm not sure."

"Anyway, for my mom, everything's always all about her. It's never about anyone other than her. As she tells it, when she got pregnant and started looking at names, she thought it would be really cool to give her kid some kind of odd Indian name, not even considering for a moment if that might cause any problems for the kid. If she thinks something's cool, well, that makes it cool, and don't you dare question that. I guess she had some boy names in mind in case she had a boy, but I don't know what they were."

"Actually, my name isn't even Yani. That's a nickname. My real name on my birth certificate is 'Sunayani' and that's not even the stupid part. I was curious if these names had any meaning, so after searching for a long time, I finally found a book in the library that actually had a listing of Indian names and what their meanings were. Sunayani means a girl with lovely eyes. How retarded is that, you know? It's totally redundant. I think it's pretty obvious when you look at me, wouldn't you say?"

"Yes. I would say it's pretty obvious," he replied, trying unsuccessfully to subdue a smile.

"Right. Now, as for the Yani part, that name means 'peace' or 'peaceful'. I don't know what your opinion of me is so far, but I'm thinking 'peaceful' is not exactly how I'd describe myself."

"Perhaps not, but I don't really know you that well yet," and he started laughing again, though secretly he was sure hoping he would get to know her that well.

"So, there you have it. Any other questions?"

"Can't think of any right now," and he smiled once more, but this time, he didn't try to hide it. She stole a sideways glance at him but didn't say anything. They started rowing again and watching the sun descend towards the crest of the hill on the opposite side of the lake. When the sun began to set, Dan suggested it was time to go back.

"Hey, you want to try your hand at rowing?" he asked.

"Sure. Why not? I've never done that."

"Okay, well, we'll need to switch seats so you can row."

"Why?"

"Trust me. You can't row from that seat."

Yani shrugged. "Okay." He grabbed the gunwale to balance himself and started to stand to switch seats. When she stood, she didn't realize she needed to hold onto something for balance. The boat immediately began rocking severely from their movement, for which she was totally unprepared. Losing her balance, she started falling, and it was obvious she was going backwards right out of the boat.

"Dan!" she shrieked, reaching out for him. Just before she reached the point of no return, he managed to snatch hold of the waistband of her shorts, praying to God they wouldn't rip. Fortunately, the fabric held and he pulled her back into the boat. She fell right on top of him as he collapsed back onto the seat, and all he could think was, God, she feels great. Yani's face and lips were so kissable and so close, he had to fight off the urge of trying to make out with her. Somehow, he restrained himself, though it took a tremendous effort. She looked at him, smiled sweetly and said, "Thank you."

In return, he softly replied, "Be careful," and he helped her get seated. "By the way, how are your swimming skills?" he asked with a laugh as he switched to the back seat.

"I can swim just fine," she answered with attitude.

Now that she was safely seated, Dan went on to explain how to make a proper stroke with the oars and the importance of placing her feet against the ribbing that ran across the bottom of the boat. That way, she could brace herself while she rowed, using her legs as much as her arms to propel the boat. At first, she had problems getting the blades in the water at the right angle, but after a couple of missteps, she figured it out.

"Good job, Yani," Dan said smiling, and she returned the smile along with this little look of accomplishment. Once they got close to the dock, they switched seats again. This time she held on, kept her body hunched low, and didn't even come close to falling. He parked the rowboat in the empty lift and took her back to her cottage just as dusk was fully settling in. Walking along, he turned to her laughing, "You know, I'm not sure which would have been worse: you falling out of the boat and having to walk home soaking wet or you having to walk home soaking wet with no shorts."

"That's not really that funny," she responded, smiling reluctantly while poking an elbow in his side.

Still laughing, he replied, "See you in the morning?"

She placed her hand on his arm, "The earlier, the better."

Dan smiled. She removed her hand and they parted ways for the evening. As that weekend passed by, they spent their time together going for walks, boat rides, and just getting to know each other. Dan wasn't sure how she felt, but for him, their conversations were becoming much easier, and now he was a lot more comfortable in her company. When Sunday night came, they said their goodbyes, and the following morning, Dan got up and drove to school. It was now June 12th, and the end of the school year was getting ever closer.

Chapter 9

Dan went to school each day and to his part-time job on the days he was scheduled. While he was at work on that Thursday evening, the store manager walked up to him as he was restocking the shelves in the canned goods aisle.

"Dan."

He turned around, "Yes, Mr. Givens?"

"Would you stop by the office before you leave today?"

"Yes, sir." At that point, Givens just left him standing there without saying anything more and simply walked away. Dan never gave it another thought and immediately returned to what he had been doing before Givens had stopped to speak with him.

Mr. Givens was both a man of few words and little personality. Most of the employees didn't like him, but it was a good place to work, and they paid well, so the employees just put up with his cold demeanor. The only people Givens was nice to were the customers and a couple of key employees. Of course, Dan knew Givens had to do that. Otherwise, it would be really bad for business, and that, in turn, could cost Givens his job.

When his shift ended, Dan went to the office as ordered and Mr. Givens was seated at his desk studying some paperwork. He didn't even bother to offer Dan a seat. He just looked up at him and stated, "Dan, I'm changing your work schedule for the summer. Beginning next week, you're going to start working weekends."

Dan stood there stunned, not sure what to say next, when the words just came tumbling out. "I'm sorry, Mr. Givens, but summer vacation starts next week. I've got plans for the summer and I don't think I can work weekends."

Givens just stared at him blankly and, after a moment, he stated, "Well, if you can't work weekends, then I guess I won't be needing you any longer."

Dan returned the stare and calmly informed him, "Well, then, Mr. Givens, I guess that means I'm quitting." What he was really thinking was, forget this job. Not even a team of horses could keep him from spending his time at the cottage with Yani.

Givens studied him a few seconds longer before looking over at the head clerk and telling her, "Helen, Dan's quitting. Can you give him his final pay?"

"Yes, of course, Mr. Givens," was her only response. Dan stood there while the head clerk checked his time card, made some calculations with a pencil on a piece of paper and counted out his pay. She placed it in a small envelope, turned around, and handed it to Dan without speaking or even acknowledging him. Dan took the envelope and thanked the lady in spite of her rude behavior. He silently walked out of the store without saying anything to his coworkers, several of whom were watching him, and then proceeded straight home.

When he walked in through the back door of his house, his mom was standing there in the kitchen preparing food, which seemed like the place where he almost always found her. Of course, when you have to cook for a small army, that was what you did. The rest of his siblings were either scattered throughout the house or playing outside when he came in. A couple of the youngest immediately went into the kitchen to see him.

"Hi, Dan. How was work?" she asked out of habit.

"I just quit," he said straight out.

"You just quit? Why, honey? Don't you need the job?"

"Givens told me that I have to start working weekends beginning next week and I told him I can't do that."

"Well, why not, son?" His dad had overheard the conversation and had walked into the kitchen to join the discussion. "Are you sure this is a good idea? Good jobs are hard to come by, you know," he said with that serious 'dad' look on his face.

Dan sat down at the kitchen table and faced them both while one of his little brothers stood beside him, leaning on his leg. Dan put his arm around him and gave him a quick hug. "Well, in case you've forgotten, I turn eighteen this winter. This could be my last summer to do what I want. I mean, come this time next year, I could be getting drafted and going off to war."

"Well, I understand that, son, but I don't think that's really going to happen. So, what are you going to do for money in the meantime?" his dad asked while maintaining that serious 'dad' tone to his voice.

"Dad, between mowing lawns, shoveling snow, my paper route, and this job here at the grocery store, it seems like I've been working pretty much since I was ten years old. I've got more than enough money saved to last the summer. When fall comes around, I'll figure it out."

"Well, okay, son, I guess." Fortunately for Dan, his dad left it at that and the discussion on quitting his job ended there.

"By the way, I'm headed up to the cottage tomorrow after school, and I doubt I'll be coming home until Monday."

"Okay, son. Thanks for letting us know," his dad responded. "So, I guess that means we'll see you up there because we're planning on coming up to the cottage this weekend, too, if that's okay with you. The weather report says it's going to be a beautiful weekend."

"Well, of course, it's okay with me, Dad. Why wouldn't it?"

"I don't know. Seems like you want to be by yourself these days."

"Come on, Dad. Be serious. This has nothing to do with me wanting to be by myself. I just want to spend as much time up at the cottage as I can this summer. You coming up tomorrow or Saturday?"

"We'll be up Saturday morning."

"Okay, great. So, I'll see you sometime Saturday morning at the lake," and that was the end of that conversation.

The next day, at 3:22 on the dot, Dan was walking out of school and heading to the cottage. The drive had now changed from routine and unremarkable to one of great anticipation and eagerness at the thought of seeing Yani. As soon as he arrived, he went straight to the bedroom and changed out of his school clothes into shorts and a tee shirt. When he started for the door and the walk to the Hartmann's, he froze as he recognized a now familiar figure standing on the other side. Without knocking or waiting, Yani opened the screen door and casually strolled inside.

"I saw the car coming down the hill and I've been waiting for you," she stated as she continued walking straight towards him. Once she reached him, she put her arms around his neck and kissed him like she really meant it, shocking Dan in the process.

"Certainly, wasn't expecting that," he said softly, "but I'm definitely not complaining."

"Well, I thought it was about time we kissed and I was getting tired of waiting for you to make the first move," she told him while caressing his cheek. "Besides, I really missed you."

Dan stroked her auburn hair in return while looking into those dazzling eyes. "Yeah, I agree on the kissing part, but I bet you didn't miss me as much as I missed you."

"Oh, is that right?" she responded, as she released him from her grip and took a seat at the kitchen table. "So, how was your week?"

"Well, I quit my job."

She didn't even bother to conceal her glee when she heard that hopping right out of the chair, bouncing up and down and clapping her hands. "Why?" she asked excitedly.

"Well, the manager wanted me to start working weekends and I told him no."

"So, when's your last day?"

"Yesterday," he stated smiling.

She gave him another big hug, after which he very carefully pushed her away. "Okay, now don't get too excited, Yani. My folks are coming up tomorrow to spend the night, but they'll be going home on Sunday around lunchtime or shortly thereafter."

"Okay. That's fine. My grandparents are taking me to meet a great aunt and uncle of mine who live somewhere not too far from here. I'll probably be gone most of the day. You'll be done with school soon, right?"

"Well, let's see. Based on my precise calculations, today is the 16th, and school ends the 21st, so that means I have five more days and then I'm done until fall."

"Cool. So…does that mean you'll be able to start spending more time up here?"

"That's the plan."

"Excellent!" she said just a little too enthusiastically. Dan couldn't help but smile back at her. She was so happy. It was obvious to him why.

"Come on. Let's go outside," he suggested, as he led her onto the large deck facing the lake where they sat at the picnic table. "So, I told you how my week was. How was yours?"

"Well, it was exactly the same as every other week so far. We went to Watkins a couple times to do some shopping at the IGA store. My grandpa took us out for a few boat rides, I did a bunch of reading, watched a little TV, helped my grandma in the kitchen, and that was pretty much it."

Dan hesitated for a moment before speaking again. "Yani, I'm kind of curious about something."

"Yeah, what's that?"

"Have you talked to your parents since you got here?"

"Nope, though I do know that my grandpa has spoken to them at least once. He called them from the pay phone at the top of the hill. I'm not sure what they talked about because I wasn't there, but he told me he spoke to them."

That seemed really strange to him. She'd been here now for about three weeks. He didn't talk to his parents a whole lot, but he had never gone three whole weeks in his life without speaking to them. "You okay with that? I mean, why didn't your grandfather take you along so you could talk to them, too?"

"I don't understand. What do you mean?"

"I don't know. It's not like I sit around with my folks having deep discussions all the time, though with six brothers and sisters, someone's always talking. There's never a quiet moment with the exception of when everyone's in bed, but the idea of not speaking to my folks at all for three weeks just seems kind of odd. Don't they wonder how you're doing?"

"Maybe, but you'd probably have to know my mom better to fully understand."

"Okay, I guess, but what about your dad? Don't you two get along either?"

"Oh, no. We get along just fine. I've got no problems with my dad whatsoever. At the same time, he does pretty much whatever my mom orders him to do."

That remark only left Dan with more questions when a chipmunk suddenly stuck its head around the corner of the deck staring up at them and ending the conversation about Yani's parents. When Dan spotted the chipmunk, he pointed and whispered to her, "Hey, look."

She swiveled around to see this little creature staring up at her. "Oh, how cute," she said very softly.

"Yeah, they sure are. As long as I've been coming up here, there's always been a couple living in that stone wall there" he said pointing at the wall along the top of the cliff. "With all the walnut, hickory, and oak trees we've got, I'm sure they never go hungry. It's probably a pretty good place to call home if you're a chipmunk."

Yani got up very slowly and carefully started making her way towards the chipmunk. As soon as she began moving in its direction, it disappeared in a flash.

"What'd you think you were going to do, pet it?" he asked laughing.

"I don't know. I guess I just wanted to see how close it would let me get," she responded while laughing along with him. After a moment, she spoke again. "You know, Dan, the more time I spend here, the more I think I understand why you like it so much. I mean, it's very quiet and serene, but you're so close to nature. It's actually kind of comforting in a way."

"Yeah, it really is. It's a pretty good place to get away from all the stress and forget about life for a while. Hey, enough of that, though. Let's listen to some music."

"Okay, definitely."

Dan went inside, turned on the radio, and they just sat there together quietly holding hands and looking out over the lake while Creedence Clearwater's 'Fortunate Son' played in the background.

As they were sitting there taking in the view, Gary suddenly appeared from around the corner of the cottage. "Hey, Dan, what's going... Oh, shoot! Sorry, man! I didn't realize you were with someone."

Dan and Yani discreetly released their hands. "It's okay, Gary. Have a seat," Dan instructed him.

"You sure?"

"Of course. Come on, man."

"Okay, thanks."

"Gary, this is Yani. Yani, meet Gary."

"Hi...Yani? Am I hearing that right?"

She looked at him and smiled. "Yeah, you're hearing that right. How are you, Gary?"

"Yeah, I'm good, I'm good," he said awkwardly while staring at her.

"When'd you get here, Gary?" Dan asked, trying to pull his attention away from Yani, who he continued staring at.

"Huh? Oh, me and my parents just pulled in."

"Cool. You guys up for the weekend?"

"Yeah, how about you?"

"Same. My folks are coming up tomorrow. Dad said the forecast is for a beautiful weekend, so they want to come up and enjoy the lake. He said they're planning to spend the night."

"Cool," and he could see that Gary had, once again, started staring at Yani.

Well, I can't blame him, Dan thought to himself. She truly is amazing to look at.

Knowing Yani didn't like to be stared at, Dan brought Gary back to earth again. "Okay, you two. It's Friday, and it's only about 5 o'clock. We should do something. How about a boat ride? Yani?"

"Sure."

"Let's go."

The three of them got up and headed down to the dock. Dan left the cottage doors wide open and the music on. No one was going to mess with anything while they were gone. Gary was very experienced around boats and Dan didn't even need to tell him what to do. When the boat was loaded, Dan and Yani hopped in. Gary stayed on the dock and lowered the boat until the prop was fully submerged. Dan yanked on the starter cord and the Evinrude fired on the first pull. Gary dropped the cradle until the boat was floating freely then climbed in with them. Dan put it in reverse, backed out of the lift and around until the bow was facing out into the lake. He slid the shifter into forward, hit the throttle and off they went bounding across the water.

There were lots of folks sitting out on their docks or swimming, and as they cruised by, people would wave to them and they'd wave back. It was simply ideal weather and everyone up at the lake was having a good time. Once he'd gone a mile or so, Dan swung the boat away from the shoreline towards the other side of the lake. He made a big, sweeping arc way out into the center of the lake and beyond, continuing to head in the opposite direction of the cottage.

They zipped along across the waves with the wind blowing their hair back and the pleasant smell of the lake filling their nostrils. There were lots of other boats out on the water, and some of them were pulling skiers. Dan's boat wasn't powerful enough to do that, but sometimes, they would tie a skim board or a disk off the back with a ski rope and pull those. They went way down past Peach Orchard Point when he swung the boat around again and headed back towards the cottage. As they went by the Hartmann place, Mr. and Mrs. Hartmann were sitting in lounge chairs on the dock next to the lift where the Seneca Song sat in all her glory. They all waved to the Hartmann's and Yani's grandparents smiled and waved back.

Dan drove the boat way out away from the shoreline, U-turned back towards his dock, lined it up with the lift and throttled back. As they reached the lift's opening, he shifted into reverse, throttled up a little to stop the boat's forward momentum, killed the engine and slid gracefully into the lift, never touching a thing. Gary grabbed hold of the dock, stopped the boat completely, hopped out, and, without being told, started rolling it up. Dan and Yani followed suit and they all headed back up to the cottage.

"Well, that was fun," Dan stated.

"Yeah. That was cool," Gary replied. Yani was all smiles.

When they got back up to the deck, the song 'Ohio' by CSNY was just finishing as the disk jockey switched to the top-of-the-hour news. First up, of course, was the latest casualty count out of Vietnam. Fortunately, that news report didn't last long, and after a couple of minutes, they were right back to playing music. The three of them sat around the table and just relaxed while they listened to the radio.

It was fast approaching six when Yani turned to Dan. "I need to go. Grandma's going to be serving supper."

"You want me to walk you?"

"No, I'm fine. You stay here with Gary."

"Okay. See you later?" he put it in the form of a question.

"You better," was her smiling response.

As soon as she was out of earshot, Gary leaned into Dan and punched him on the arm. "You snake in the grass. Damn, that chick is super cute."

"Easy, Gary," Dan replied with a smirk on his face.

Gary sat back and slapped his leg. "God dang, she's good looking!"

Dan said nothing and just sat there smiling. What else could he do? What Gary said was true and as long as he didn't screw it up, she'd be his until at least Labor Day.

After they sat there for a while listening to music, Gary stood and announced, "Well, I got to go, too. My dad said I've got to mow the lawn before dark."

"Okay, man. Guess I'll see you tomorrow."

"Yep. Later, Dan," was his response.

"Later, Gary."

After he'd left, Dan went inside, made himself a simple meal and went back outside sitting at the picnic table to eat while the song 'War' by Edwin Starr played in the background. Once he'd finished, he carried his dishes back inside, cleaned up, and headed straight to the Hartmann's. Along the way, he saw a couple other neighbors outside and waved to them as he strolled along. When he was approaching the Hartmann's, Yani came walking out.

"I heard you coming."

"I can tell." She smiled and walked along next to him as they headed to the point. This time, she didn't ask where they were going. Now she knew that when they headed in that direction, that was their destination.

On the way, they saw Gary up in his yard pushing his old lawn mower, a thin cloud of blue smoke spitting out behind the engine. He looked up, gave a quick wave, and went right back to cutting grass. When they reached the point, they walked out into the water, enjoying the cool feeling on their legs. After a while, they went up on the dock and sat with their legs dangling in the water, holding hands.

Eventually, Yani turned to him. "What time are your folks coming up tomorrow?"

"Not sure. If they're coming up to stay, which they are, they usually come up pretty early so they can enjoy as much of the day as possible. If I had to guess, I'd say they'll probably be here no later than ten. What time are you leaving to go see your relatives?"

"Well, Grandma says we're going to have lunch there. I know they'll want some time to visit, and they tell me it's about an hour's drive. I'm guessing we'll probably leave around 9:30 or so and be back around 2 or 3."

They sat there again in silence for a while when Dan abruptly turned to her. "Hey, you want to meet my folks?"

She stared at him for a moment. "Do you want me to?" she asked, a surprised, but pleased look on her face.

"Yes," was all he needed to say. She gave his hand a squeeze and went right back to looking out over the lake with a contented smile on her face while leaning her head against his shoulder.

After several minutes of silence, Yani turned to him, "So, what have you got in mind?"

"Well, the normal routine is that after supper and we've finished cleaning up, I typically build a bonfire and we all kind of gather around to enjoy the evening; maybe toast some marshmallows, and that's about it until bedtime when the fire gets put out and we go inside. I'm thinking that the best time to bring you by is once I've got the fire going and everybody's sitting outside."

"That should work really well. By that time, supper will be over, and my grandparents will be settling in for the evening themselves. I'm guessing you're going to come down and get me, right?"

"Yes. That's exactly what I'm thinking."

"Okay. That's perfect. Consider it settled."

"Settled it is," he replied, smiling at her as she gave his hand another good squeeze to make sure he knew she was pleased with his plan. They continued sitting there together just talking until the sun began to set below the hillside on the opposite side of the lake. Once the sun had almost completely disappeared, the two of them made the short walk back to her place. He dropped her off for the evening thinking to himself the entire time that tomorrow couldn't possibly come soon enough.

Chapter 10

As ten o'clock arrived the next morning, Dan was sitting out on the deck patiently waiting for his folks. A half-hour earlier, he'd noticed the Hartmann's car heading up the hill, so he knew Yani was gone. While sitting there, he soon heard the sound of a familiar car coming down the hill. Assuming it was his parents, he got up and walked out to meet them. Sure enough, they pulled up to the cottage, and his mom, dad, and three younger siblings all piled out. His oldest sister, who still lived at home, hadn't come. Apparently, she either wasn't invited, had a better offer to do something else, or didn't feel like making the trip. That wasn't unusual.

Functionally, Dan's family was split in two. There were the three oldest, the three youngest and Dan, who didn't fit with either group. He was too young for some activities and too old for others, but he could care less. For as long as he could remember, that was just the way it always was. He was quite used to looking after himself. The other obstacle was simply space. Trying to squeeze two adults and four children into a sedan was a real challenge, especially when one of them was a young woman like his older sister. Of course, you could do it, but it wasn't comfortable. Therefore, Dan was typically left out if only part of the family went some place. If the whole family went, they would have no choice but to take two cars. Today was a good example. If his sister had come, she would have almost certainly driven separately with one or more of his siblings to keep her company.

Dan immediately walked over to them, "Hi. Can I give you a hand?"

"That would be great," his dad responded. "I brought some more gas. Can you carry that down to the boathouse?"

"No problem. Hi, Mom," he said warmly, greeting his mother and giving her a hug.

"Hi, Dan. How is everything?" was her response, smiling back at him.

"Just another wonderful day at the lake."

"Yes. I see that," she replied, while continuing to smile.

Dan grabbed the gas can out of the trunk. It weighed a ton, but the only way to get fuel for the boat was to haul it up from town. There was a marina down the lake towards Watkins that sold gas, but you only went there if you were desperate. They charged a huge premium, mostly because they could. He lugged the gas down to the boathouse and returned to the cottage to find his parents unpacking everything they'd brought along with them.

"You need more help?"

"No, we've got it, but thanks.

"Okay. Well, as you don't need me, I'm going to go fill the gas tank,."

"Sounds good," was the response from his dad. He headed back down to the dock where he went about the business of refilling the gas tank for the boat, which was no easy chore. First, he'd have to disconnect the heavy steel tank from the engine and set that on the dock. After which, he'd refill the tank, get back in the boat, lift the full tank off the dock, set it in the bottom of the boat, and reconnect the hoses to the engine. Because of the weight of everything, coupled with the boat's rounded bottom and the lift's swaying, it was always a major challenge to keep your balance while moving all that weight.

Normally, he'd end up with at least one bruise on his body somewhere after banging against either the gunwale or the lift. Plus, he was supposed to do all of this without spilling a drop of gas in the lake so he didn't pollute. Start to finish, it took him about fifteen minutes, but now they had plenty of gas, at least for the time being. He had no noticeable bruises and hadn't spilled any gas. It was a success.

Work complete, Dan grabbed a large tube, threw it off the end of the dock, dove in and swam to it. He pulled himself up from inside, settled in, and just floated in the waves out in front of the dock. Before long, all of his siblings were in the water floating in their own tubes. Play in the Wallace family was more like open warfare. They didn't just peacefully float around. Oh, no. They attacked each other unmercifully, splashing each other in the face along with the goal of knocking the other person out of their tube and, with any luck, maybe even drowning them.

Eventually, they got bored with tormenting each other and came back to shore. At some point, Dan's mom had gone up to the cottage to start getting lunch ready. A brass bell hung outside the door leading to the deck. If she tried to yell down to the dock that it was time to eat, no one would hear her because of all the noise and mayhem. If she rang the bell, though, everyone would hear that and know it was time to come up to eat. Today was no different. They weren't back on the dock more than a couple of minutes before the bell started ringing.

After lunch, his dad decided to take the boat out for a little cruising. There was really only room to comfortably seat four, so Dan and his mom stayed back. She kept busy doing dishes and picking up the clothes that had gotten strewn everywhere when people changed into their bathing suits. Once finished, she picked up a magazine she'd brought along with her and went out to the deck to read and simply enjoy the peace and quiet. There wasn't a lot of that for her at home.

Dan decided he was going to walk down to one of the neighbors to see if they were up for the weekend. Their son was one of his classmates and they were pretty good friends. He announced to his mom where he was headed. She said, "That's fine," and he walked to the neighbor's place. Sure enough, they were there, so he stopped in and visited for a while. He left and came home when he heard his dad returning from the boat ride.

They spent the rest of the day down on the dock swimming and hanging around until it was time for supper. His parents had gone up a little earlier to start preparations. His dad was in charge of the grill and his mom took care of everything else. When supper was ready, the bell rang, and they all clambered up the steps to the cottage. After supper, they picked up after themselves and then went back outside, leaving their mom with clean-up duties. That was the normal order of things.

As the unofficial bonfire builder, once sunset approached, Dan began building the fire. As soon as they had a rip-roaring blaze going, he turned around, started heading towards the road and called out, "Hey, Dad?"

"Yeah, Dan?"

"I'm going down to the Hartmann's for a second. I'll be right back."

"Okay," was the reply he got, but his dad was sitting there thinking to himself, why would he be going down to the Hartmann's?

Dan made the short walk there, knocked on the screen door and Mrs. Hartmann answered.

"Hi, Mrs. Hartmann."

"Oh, hi, Dan. Hold on a second. I'll get Yani."

As she was turning around, Yani was already walking towards the door.

"I'll be back later," Yani announced as she walked past her grandmother and out the door.

"Okay, honey. Have a nice time," was her response.

That was the question to be answered. Would it be a nice time? Dan and Yani would definitely know soon enough. Tonight, Yani wasn't wearing a tee shirt and shorts. She still had on the shorts, but they were a little nicer. She was wearing a pretty top that flattered her figure, but not too revealing and in excellent taste. The cotton top was a button-down with a pattern of blue flowers on a white background and it had a little white collar. The shorts also appeared to be cotton and were a matching blue. She was wearing gold earrings, something he'd never seen her do before. As usual, she was stunning in an understated way. It seemed that this girl was quietly confident in her own skin; just one more thing that he really liked about her.

They started slowly walking towards his cottage. She put her hand on his arm and looked up at him. "Hi. I missed you. By the way, are you still okay with this? You know, we don't have to do this."

"I missed you, too, and yes. I mean, what's the worst that could happen? They don't like you and you have to go home?"

"I suppose it's possible."

"Yani, somehow I don't think that's going to happen." He took her hand and squeezed it for a moment before releasing it. His folks were old-fashioned and not keen on public displays of affection. They'd keep their hands to themselves in his parents' presence. When they got to Dan's place, his folks were sitting on the deck right where he'd left them. They walked up together and Dan announced to them, "Mom, Dad, this is my friend Yani."

His mom looked up, shocked at what she saw standing there in front of her, and all she could say was, "Oh, my!" with her mouth hanging slightly open. His mom was a small woman, only about five feet tall. She had gray hair, was of English descent, college-educated, and tough as nails. His dad had wavy hair and a rugged build. He was of Scottish descent, also college-educated, and very religious, but unlike his mom, he was mild-mannered.

Yani walked straight up to his mom, extended her hand, and said, "Hi. My name is Yani."

His mom took her hand and shaking it gently replied, "Well, it's nice to meet you...Yani," her mouth still hanging slightly agape as she stared at the young lady standing there in front of her.

Yani next turned to his dad and repeated the greeting. She stuck out her hand and introduced herself. His dad took her hand and responded with, "Well, welcome, Yani. It's nice to meet you."

His mom was the next one to speak. "So, who are you?" she asked, still staring. That was so typical of Dan's mom. No need to beat around the bush. Let's get right to the point.

Yani turned to her smiling, "The Hartmann's are my grandparents. I'm visiting for the summer." Dan stood there laughing to himself. That smile could disarm almost anyone, maybe even his mom.

"Oh," was his mom's only response while still staring.

His dad stammered slightly then politely asked, "Well, you want to sit down and visit a bit?" while his mom just continued staring.

Yani turned and looked at Dan, waiting for a cue. He shrugged his shoulders, so she turned back to them and said, "Sure," and the two sat in a couple of chairs on the deck that were facing his folks.

His mom was still studying Yani when his dad asked, "So, do your folks live around here?"

"No. We live in Youngstown."

"Youngstown, huh. I don't ever remember seeing you up here before. Is this your first time at the lake?"

"No, I was here a couple of times when I was a little girl, but that's about it."

"Oh," he responded. "Well, what do you think? Do you like it here?"

"Yes. I mean, it's very quiet, but it's really beautiful."

"How old are you, Yani?" his mom asked from out of nowhere.

Here we go, Dan thought to himself. Let the interrogation begin.

"I'm seventeen."

"Really? You look a lot older than that. Why aren't you in school?"

"I finished early so I could come up here for the summer. I go back around Labor Day for my senior year."

"Do you have any brothers or sisters?"

"Yes. I have two younger sisters."

"Well, why aren't they here?"

"I think sending all three of us here would have been too much of a burden on my grandparents. They are getting older."

"Yes, I see," was Mrs. Wallace's droll response.

Next question: "How often do people comment on your looks?"

Yani didn't even flinch. "It happens sometimes. Not a lot."

"Oh, come on. I don't believe that for one second. I mean, look at you," his mom stated somewhat combatively.

"Well, maybe it does happen more often than I realize, but if it does, I guess I don't really notice." Based on Dan's limited experiences with her, he was pretty sure she was being totally truthful. While lots of people probably did comment on her appearance, Dan was fairly certain that she paid little attention to it.

79

His mom said nothing more for the moment. Apparently, she'd run out of questions for the time being. After a brief awkward silence, Yani turned to Dan, "Hey, why don't we go sit by the fire?"

"Great idea. Mom, Dad, we're going down to the firepit," he stated.

"Okay," his dad said. His mom just sat there watching them carefully.

The two of them walked the short distance down to the firepit and grabbed a seat on the bench that lined it.

"Good job, Yani," Dan said quietly. She looked at him and gave him a reassuring smile. In her heart, she was really glad that was over. She was surprised at how nerve-wracking it had been. Was she actually concerned about the first impression she would make with his parents, and if she was, what exactly did that mean?

Dan introduced her to his brothers and sister and they sat together watching the fire. It was a lovely evening. The smoke from the burning hardwood had a really pleasant scent to it. Little sparks would pop out every so often like those from a child's sparkler, and occasionally, his siblings would toss something on or poke it with a stick and stand there watching it burn. Later in the evening, they got out the marshmallows, and even Dan and Yani toasted a couple.

Eventually, the fire started to burn down and it was getting late. Dan turned to Yani, leaned in, and softly said, "It's time to go." She nodded accordingly, and they got up and walked back up on the deck.

"Well, Mr. and Mrs. Wallace, I have to go. It was really nice meeting you."

"It was nice to meet you, too," was his mom's reply, though she didn't bother to get up.

His dad had stood up and walked over to them. "Come back any time, Yani."

"Thanks. Anyway, I hope I see you again. Have a nice evening."

"I'll put the fire out when I get back, Dad."

"Okay, Dan."

They turned away and the two of them stepped down off the deck heading towards the Hartmann's. Once they were far enough away that they couldn't be seen or heard, they stopped. She turned towards him and put her arms around his neck. He returned the embrace and they kissed. God, her kisses are just so wonderful. I could kiss this girl for the rest of my life, Dan thought to himself.

When they finished kissing, she asked, "Well? How'd I do?"

"With this kiss or with my parents?"

"With your parents, stupid," she responded, staring into his eyes. "I know how I did with the kiss."

Dan smiled back at her. "Oh, you did just fine. My dad's easy. He welcomes anyone. That's just his nature. Mom is another story, but I'm pretty sure you passed the test. For some unknown reason, she's always suspicious of girls she thinks are just a little too pretty, and you certainly fall into that category. No idea why."

"Your mom asked a couple questions that were sort of awkward, but other than that, everyone was really nice to me. I like your family."

"Thanks," and they started walking again, this time at a slower pace while holding hands.

She looked over at him with that angelic face of hers, "So, what's the plan for tomorrow?"

"I figure they'll head out after lunch. My dad has to work on Monday and my brothers and sister all have school, so they'll want to get home before supper. I need to spend the morning with them, but after they leave, hopefully, I can spend the rest of the day with you. I've

81

already decided I'm going to sleep here tomorrow night and drive down to school Monday morning."

"Wait. What do you mean, hopefully?" she asked, staring at him with her head slightly tilted.

"Yani, honey, my dad taught me to never assume anything."

"Fair enough." She squeezed his hand and before they reached the door, they stopped for one more kiss, then said their goodnights.

When Dan got back, his siblings were already inside, but his folks still sat on the deck. As promised, he extinguished the fire and, assuming they might have questions, he sat down but without saying anything. Let them break the ice, he decided, and it didn't take long.

"How'd you meet her?" his mom asked.

"I was at Gary's. When I walked back down his driveway to the road, she was standing outside her cottage and she spoke to me."

"She spoke to you first?"

"Yeah."

"Seems awfully bold for a girl to do that."

"Well, I'd seen her before and I thought she was just trying to be helpful. She was just letting me know Gary and his dad had left."

"What kind of name is Yani? Never heard a name like that before."

"I'm not sure," he lied. "I asked and she said that her mom and dad thought it was a cool name, so that's what they named her."

"She's awfully pretty, but it seems kind of strange to me that she's up here without her parents or her sisters. Is something else going on? Is she in trouble or something, Dan?" his mom inquired, staring at him suspiciously.

"No, Mom," he replied laughing. "As far as I know, she's not in trouble. I'm not entirely sure why she's up here by herself, but what difference does it make?" There was no way he was going to tell her why Yani was there. As far as he was concerned, it was none of his mom's business.

"Yeah, I bet you do think a girl that looks like that is nice. Well, I'm going to bed." With that announcement, she simply stood up and went inside.

It suddenly dawned on Dan why she was being so combative. She's afraid of Yani. Not of Yani, per se, but of the threat she represents. With the exception of her two children in the Coast Guard, all of her other children live at home, and as soon as those two finish their military commitments, they'll be back, too. Yani represents the catalyst that could result in a child leaving the nest permanently. If he fell in love with her and they got married, his mom would lose one of her children. It was now clear to him. His mom was scared of her.

"Yep, I'm going in myself. You coming, Dan?" his dad asked, bringing him back from his thoughts.

"You know, Dad, the cottage is pretty full. I think I'll sleep in the boathouse. See you in the morning," and his father responded in kind.

He always found sleeping in the boathouse to be incredibly peaceful. You'd fall asleep with this reassuring sound of the waves lapping against the cliff. The only time it wasn't pleasant was if there was a storm. When that happened, the thunderous noise of the waves crashing and the rain beating down on the metal roof made it almost impossible to sleep. Tonight, the waves were gentle and he fell asleep almost immediately dreaming about the girl with the auburn hair.

Chapter 11

He woke the next morning to the sound of heavier waves crashing against the cliff. He could tell by the sound that they weren't storm waves. It must just be a little windy outside. He rolled out of bed, slipped on the clothes he was wearing the night before, and headed up to the cottage. His mom was already on the deck drinking coffee and there was no sign of his dad. He would be inside preparing breakfast.

"Morning, Mom."

"Good morning, Dan," she said smiling. She must have gotten over the Yani thing, he thought to himself.

"Where's Dad?" he asked out of habit, knowing in advance where he actually was.

"Inside," she answered, while motioning in that direction with her head.

Dan walked into the cottage and the smell of frying bacon hit him immediately. His dad didn't cook much, but he did a nice job with the grill and with breakfast. It wasn't unusual for him to take over the kitchen on weekend mornings. He'd never once heard his mom ask him to cook. He just did it.

"Morning, Dad."

"Morning, Dan. Sleep well?"

"Oh, yeah." He could hear his siblings beginning to stir in the bedrooms. It was probably the smell of the frying bacon that was responsible.

Before long, everyone was out of bed and breakfast was being served. Just like supper the night before, they used paper plates and ate outside at one of the two picnic tables on the deck. After everyone had

84

been fed, clean-up commenced and the cottage was put back in order. That done, they transitioned down to the dock to begin the day's activities of more swimming and boating. At one point, Mr. and Mrs. Hartmann took the Seneca Song out for a cruise. Yani was sitting in the back alone, and as they went by the Wallace property, she smiled and waved at Dan. He waved back and stood there enjoying that auburn hair flowing out behind her. Looking at Yani never got old. There were very few things that Dan thought were more beautiful than the Seneca Song. She was definitely one of them.

It was a lazy Sunday morning at the cottage. In years gone by, his mom would have gotten them up and marched them off to Mass at St. Mary's of the Lake in Watkins. Over the years, she'd relaxed those rules, and now, if they were at the cottage on a Sunday, they were given dispensation and weren't required to attend. They got the tubes out and floated around in the lake. His dad took the boat out multiple times to give people rides. On one of the trips, he let his younger siblings take control and drive slowly back and forth in front of their property. They came back to the dock after everyone had gotten a turn. His dad parked the boat in the lift and everyone got out with these big smiles because they got to drive. For a couple of them, it was their very first time, so they were absolutely thrilled.

When late morning arrived, his mom drifted quietly up to the cottage to start getting lunch ready. The ringing of the bell sometime later was their signal it was time to eat, and they all made their way up. The food was served. Clean-up took place. Dan and his siblings went back down to the dock for one final swim, while his folks started packing things up for the trip home. The time to leave came, and his dad walked down to the dock, announced they had to go, and his siblings headed up to the cottage to change out of the wet suits for the drive home.

"What are your plans?" his dad paused to ask before heading up.

"I'm going to stay here tonight and drive to school in the morning."

"You've got finals this week, don't you?"

"Yep. Three days left. That's it."

"Don't you need to study?"

"Dad, I've got A's in every class except one. I'll do some review before my exams, but there's plenty of time for that." Dan was the kind of kid all of his classmates loved to hate. He could literally sit for most tests while barely even studying and get an ace. He wasn't sure why, but school came really easy for him. Even if he didn't get A's on his finals, his class averages were so high there was no way he could even lose a letter grade. With the exception of the formality of actually taking the finals, he was done with his junior year. Plus, he wasn't telling his father anything he didn't already know. His dad knew Dan was one of the most intelligent of all his children.

"Are you sure? Finals are really important, you know," he stated with that 'dad' voice again.

"I'm sure, Dad. Don't worry. Everything's going to be fine."

"Okay, so we'll see you at home Monday after school?"

"Yes. I'm coming straight home from school. I promise."

"Okay." He turned and started back up to the cottage with Dan following close behind so he could say goodbye to his mom. He lingered near the car while they loaded everything up. As the rear doors closed and his mom was ready to get in the car, he said, "Bye, Mom. I'll see you tomorrow after school."

"You're not coming home?"

"No, I'm staying here."

She stared at him for a moment and replied, "Well, okay, I guess." He knew from her body language exactly what she was thinking. *I know why he's staying. He's going to be hanging out with that Yani girl.* She turned around, got in the car and closed the door. He stood there watching and waved goodbye as they drove off. They made the turn up the hill, and as soon as they were out of sight, he headed for the Hartmann's. When he walked up, the front door was open, so he knocked on the screen. Nobody came, so after waiting a moment, he knocked again. This time, Yani came to the door and motioned him in.

"Hi," she said, smiling. "Are your folks gone?"

"Yeah, they just left."

"We're sitting on the porch. Come join us."

"Okay," and he followed her out to where her grandparents were sitting at the table.

"Hi, Mr. and Mrs. Hartmann."

They both looked up and responded almost simultaneously, "Oh, hi, Dan." Yani pointed to a chair and Dan sat. Mr. Hartmann spoke next. "I see your folks were up this weekend. Have they gone back?"

"Yeah, my dad has to work tomorrow and my brothers and sister have school, so they headed down."

Yani turned to Dan. "My grandpa is going to take the boat out." She turned back to her grandfather, "Grandpa, can Dan come with us?" she asked somewhat excitedly.

Mr. Hartmann turned to his wife. She gave him a small nod of approval and he turned back to them. "Sure, why not."

Dan could not believe his good fortune. Riding in the Seneca Song would be an absolute dream come true. With that decided, Mr. Hartmann got up from the table. "Well, let's go." They all headed down to the dock and Mr. Hartmann turned to Dan, "You want to handle the lift?"

"Sure. Happy to."

The other three climbed into the boat, and Mr. Hartmann immediately flipped a switch on the dash, turning on the engine blower. Dan lowered the boat until the prop was in the water and stopped there. Mr. Hartmann waited a few more seconds to ensure all the gas fumes were cleared from the engine cowling. Satisfied the fumes were gone, he turned the ignition key, and the engine sprung to life. It has such a beautiful sound, Dan thought to himself. He lowered the boat the rest of the way until it was floating free of the cradle then climbed in with the others. Once everyone was seated, Mr. Hartmann reached down with his left hand and moved the floor shifter to the reverse position. It clicked smoothly into gear and he stepped lightly on the gas pedal. The boat immediately started backing out of the lift. They were off.

After they'd cleared the lift, he continued in reverse, swinging the stern around until the bow was facing out into the lake. Reaching down with his left hand again, he moved the shifter to the forward position. Then stepping on the gas pedal, they started out into the lake. Mrs. Hartmann sat up front leaning against the left side gunwale while Yani and Dan sat on the bench seat in the back. Mr. Hartmann was really gentle with the boat while bringing it up to speed, though it still didn't take long for the Seneca Song to fully plane out. Dan was sitting there thinking to himself, if Henry was behind the wheel, this boat would already be floored, and we'd be slamming across the waves with everyone bouncing all over the interior, trying desperately to find something to hold onto. That was definitely not Mr. Hartmann's style.

Yes, he eventually took the boat up to its top speed, but he navigated so that the ride was really smooth as they cruised along in comfort and style. Dan took a peek at the dash for a look at the speedometer. Just as he thought, the boat was traveling along at just under forty knots. He looked around the interior. The upholstery was in perfect condition and the wood finish looked brand new. The Seneca Song was everything Dan thought it was, both powerful and beautiful. He turned to Yani, smiling. She returned the smile, snuck her hand into his and held it while they skimmed across the waves, her hair blowing out behind her. Mr. Hartmann drove the boat several miles up the lake towards Geneva, made a big sweeping turn out into the lake's center and motored back in the direction they came from.

He continued on by his property, going way down past Peach Orchard Point all the way to Painted Rock just north of Watkins. At that point, he swung around again and headed back towards his cottage. The entire time, they were traveling at full throttle, though you wouldn't know it based on how smooth the ride was. When they got in front of his place, he turned the boat ninety degrees toward the shore and lined it up with the lift. Only at that point did he let off the gas. He throttled back completely as they got close, and right before they entered the lift, he reached down, put the shifter in reverse, punched the gas pedal a little to stop the forward momentum, then switched off the engine.

Without having to be told, Dan immediately hopped out of the boat. He and Hartmann lined it up so that it was centered in the lift cradle, then Dan began spinning the lift wheel until the boat was settled on the cradle and the prop came out of the water. The other three climbed out and Dan turned to Mr. Hartmann, "You want me to take it up some more?"

Mr. Hartmann looked down at the boat sitting in the cradle and replied, "Nope. I think that looks pretty good right there. Thanks, Dan."

"No. Thank you, Mr. Hartmann. That was great. I've always wanted to ride in your boat." He was so happy he could barely control his emotions.

"Glad you enjoyed it, Dan."

The four of them walked back up to the cottage, sat at the table together and made small talk. They asked him about his grandparents and how they were doing. They asked about Henry, wondering why they hadn't seen him around, and Dan explained that he'd enlisted in the Coast Guard. The sun was beating down on them and Mrs. Hartmann excused herself to go inside to get some iced tea. She came out a few minutes later with a pitcher and four glasses on a tray. She passed around the glasses, filled them with the iced tea and sat back down. After taking a long drink, Mr. Hartmann turned to Dan. "You're done with school this week, right?"

"Yes. We've got three more days. School ends Wednesday afternoon."

"So, what are your plans for the summer?"

"Well, this is my last summer before I turn eighteen. Next year, I could end up drafted and in the Army, so I decided I was going to spend as much time up here as possible. Who knows when I might have another chance."

"You're not planning to work?"

"No, sir. I've been saving my money and I don't need to work right now. Maybe I'll find work again in the fall."

"Well, I'm not getting any younger and some of these chores around here are getting a little hard for an old man like me. If you're up and I need some help, maybe you could earn a little extra money helping me out."

"You know, Mr. Hartmann, I'd be happy to do that."

90

"Good. Thank you, Dan." He paused for a moment before announcing, "Well, you three, I think it's time for me to take a little rest, so I'm going inside. I'll see you all later."

"See you, Mr. Hartmann," Dan said. Hartmann got up from the table and disappeared into the cottage without saying another word.

Dan turned to Yani, "You feel like going for a walk?"

"Yes," was her immediate reply. She stood up and looked at her grandmother, "We'll be back."

"Okay, honey," was all she said in response.

They walked back towards Dan's place, where they could be alone, and held hands as they strolled along. Dan turned to Yani, "That was really nice of you to ask your grandpa if I could ride in his boat."

"I know how much you love that boat, Dan, and I was pretty sure he'd take you for a ride. I told you before. They're really nice to me, and they love me. I guess they're just trying to make me happy knowing full well I'm stuck here until Labor Day."

"Well, I really do appreciate that. That was so cool! That boat is even nicer than I thought it was," he told her while squeezing her hand and smiling at her. Yani squeezed right back and returned the look. When they got to his cottage, they walked inside so they could be alone. She put her arms around him and gave him a really lovely, passionate kiss. "That was special," he said, smiling at her while looking into those iridescent eyes. "Hey, you want to sit outside?"

"Yes, but first, I want to do this," and she gave him another really passionate kiss. "Wow!" was all he could say. After the kiss, they stepped outside holding hands and took a seat on the deck facing the lake sitting there in complete silence, immersed in their thoughts. Yani was the one to break the silence.

"So, did your mom say anything else about me after I left?"

"Yes," and he stopped there waiting to see how she'd react.

She waited patiently and getting no more information, she asked again. "Well, what did she say, goofball?"

Dan paused before speaking. Yani didn't rush him. She just sat there calmly staring at him. "Well, I don't think that what she said is the important part. It's what she seems to be thinking that's important." He hesitated briefly, "And I think she's scared of you."

"What? That's crazy. Scared of me? Why?"

"You represent a threat to her."

"I have no idea what you mean by that. How can I possibly be a threat to your mom?"

"If you knew my mother, you'd understand." He paused again before continuing. "You see, it's like this. Except for her religion, her children are the most important thing in her life. She's not into material things. Her children are her most prized possession. Right now, all her children still live at home. Sounds crazy, but I'm convinced that she's afraid we might fall in love and get married. If that were to happen, she'll lose me to you."

"Well, that's not right. You have two brothers that don't live at home."

"Except she doesn't view them as having left home."

"How could that be? I mean, they're gone."

"In her mind, they're just on a kind of temporary assignment with the military. Once that ends, they'll be coming home. Look it. She wasn't much older than we are right now at the beginning of the Second World War. All the boys left to go off to war, and when it ended, they all came back home. It's the same thing in her mind now. My brothers aren't really gone. As far as she's concerned, they'll be back home before too long living with her again." He paused briefly before continuing with the discussion.

"Now you? You're different."

"Well, wait a minute. Haven't you had other girlfriends?"

"Yes, but they weren't steady girlfriends. We were just going out."

"Well, wasn't she worried they were going to steal you away from her?"

"Nope."

"Why not?"

"Because they were what I'll call 'regular' girls. She knew full well we were just dating and I wouldn't be marrying any of them."

"I still don't understand."

"Yani, honey, I've been raising myself since I was little. I rely on my folks for food, clothing, and shelter because I have to. I'm a minor. I've got no choice. But I've been making a lot of my own decisions and earning my own money since I was probably about ten. Heck, most of the time growing up, my parents didn't even know where I was, nor did they seem to worry about it, and they never asked. Look at what I'm doing this summer. Don't get me wrong. My folks love me and I know that. I don't want this to sound arrogant, but I'm as mature and probably more responsible than my older siblings. She knows I don't rely on her like my other siblings. They rely on my parents way more than I do. Heck, I'd never do it because it would be stupid, but I could probably move out on my own and somehow manage to survive. Sure, I'd make plenty of mistakes, but eventually I'd figure things out. And I'm pretty sure she knows that."

"Well, what does that have to do with me being a threat to her?"

"You're special. She sees that, and I don't mean special just because of your looks. You're not a 'regular' girl. She's a woman, and she's got a woman's intuition. She knows just meeting you that you're the kind of girl a guy could easily end up falling in love with and marrying. If that happened, I'd be lost to her forever and that's why she's scared. You see, whether you realize it or not, you're really mature, too."

"Damn," was all she said and she just sat there in thought, staring out at the lake. Dan didn't disturb her. He just sat there waiting. He knew she was trying to process what he had just told her and she'd start speaking again once she was ready. Several minutes passed before she turned to him, "Well, what do you think, Dan? Am I the kind of girl you could fall in love with and marry?"

"Yes."

"Okay. Well, why?"

He knew she'd ask the follow-up, so he was already formulating the answer in his mind. "Because you truly are that special person, at least for me. There's something about your soul and your spirit that makes you different from all the other girls. You're tough as nails emotionally because of how your mom treats you, but you don't have a cold heart. You're still full of love. Besides being really mature, you're smart, strong and beautiful. You're a little bruised right now because of your mom, but it's nothing that won't heal with time. What guy in his right mind wouldn't want to marry a girl like you? At the same time, we're both seventeen. You know as well as I do that getting married won't happen, at least no time soon. You have to return to Ohio. We both have to finish school and who knows if we'll ever even see each other again."

Yani went silent again and he wasn't at all surprised. This was a lot for her to consider. Quite frankly, it was a lot for Dan to think about. Neither one of them planned any of this. What if her mom hadn't decided to send Yani to exile at her grandparents' cottage? What if Dan had decided that coming to the cottage without Henry just wouldn't be any fun, so he hadn't come up? They would have never met, and none of this would have ever happened, but it did. He suddenly had a startling revelation. This was simply meant to be. What other explanation could there be? There was a greater force out there that had decided the two of them should spend the summer together at the lake. That at this point in their short lives, they simply needed each other. He suddenly realized, that's the only possible answer.

"Yani."

She turned and looked at him, but didn't speak.

"I don't know why," he started out very cautiously. "Maybe I'm wrong about this and maybe it sounds crazy, but I'm starting to think," and he paused for a second. "Maybe it was our destiny to meet. I mean, how else can you explain this? You're not even from around here. It's like you're a ghost or something that appeared out of nowhere."

Yani turned and faced him directly. "You might not believe this, but I've been thinking almost the exact same thing the last day or so." She stopped talking for a moment, just sitting there before speaking again. "So, if it really is true, Dan, what are we going to do about it?"

"I'm not sure," he said, looking down. "I need to think about this."

"I've already done that."

"Wait. You have?" he asked, with a puzzled look. That Yani had already been thinking about this caught him completely off guard.

"Yes," and her face had transformed from almost no expression at all to a very reassuring smile. "If it's really true it was our destiny to meet, well, there's only two possible paths for us to take. We either do everything we can to spend as much time together as possible until I have to leave, or we don't spend time together at all. I say we try to spend as much time together as possible. What about you?"

Dan sat there silently. His mind was spinning a thousand miles an hour. This was an awful lot to deal with. After what seemed like several minutes had passed, but in reality, it was probably only a few moments, he looked at her, took a deep breath, and replied, "Okay. Well, I guess that's what we're just going to have to do then."

Yani sat back in her chair smiling and said to him, "Okay, it's settled."

"Okay," he responded while simultaneously wondering what he was getting himself into.

"All right, so what are your plans?"

"Well, I'm going to spend the night here. Of course, I have to go to school tomorrow morning and finals start tomorrow afternoon. They end around lunchtime on Wednesday, so as soon as the last one's finished, I'm done until fall."

"When are you coming back?"

"Unless something happens between now and Wednesday, I'm coming back that afternoon once finals are over."

"Good. Then it's settled. We'll spend the rest of the day together and I'll see you right back here on Wednesday afternoon."

And that's exactly what they did. When the next morning arrived, he went back to Elmira. Once done with his last final, he got in the Chrysler, drove back to the cottage and found Yani already waiting for him sitting right there on the front deck.

Chapter 12

After parking the car, Dan got out and looked over at the very beautiful and charming Yani sitting there. It was now June 21st and there were approximately 76 days left before she would be leaving. "Well, I see you've made yourself right at home," he stated as he tossed his gear up on the porch by the front door.

"That's right," she said laughing.

"How long you been here?"

"Not too long. I missed you and I figured you'd probably be getting here about now. You told me your finals ended at lunch time. I was going to let myself in, but I thought that might be a little too bold."

"Breaking and entering? Yeah, that might be a little bold," he replied, staring at her as he hopped up on the deck and settled into a chair directly across from her.

"How were your finals?" she asked with that now familiar smile.

"Piece of cake. I know I did well. My folks will have nothing to complain about when they see my report card."

"Good for you. Now you can relax for the summer."

"Yep, but speaking of finals," he looked down at the deck for a moment, not sure how to proceed before facing her again. "That raises a question I've been kind of thinking about."

"And what would that be?" she asked, a serious look now forming on her face.

"Well, when you told me about your finals and your mom making you take them early, I felt like maybe you were leaving something out." He paused again before continuing. "Anything else about that you might want to share with me?"

She didn't speak at first. She just sat there staring back at him, studying his face. When she finally spoke again, it was in a quiet and subdued voice. "Maybe."

"Maybe…what?"

"Yeah, I told you everything except…" her voice trailed off.

"Except?"

"Except she left out one little detail when she told me I had to take my finals early."

"Which was?" he continued probing.

"If I failed, I'd have to repeat my junior year," she explained, now staring down into her lap.

"Seriously?" he exclaimed. "Oh, dear God! That is just awful!" he said, shaking his head back and forth as he leaned back in the chair.

"Yep. It was a win-win for my mom but not so much for me. Regardless of whether I passed or failed, I'd be done for the year and she'd be rid of me until fall. So, when I found out what would happen if I failed, you know what I did?" You could see from her body language she was starting to get really agitated discussing this.

"I can only imagine."

"I decided there was no way I was going to fail. If I did, my mom would have an extra year of controlling my life and I was not going to let that happen. For three weeks straight, if I wasn't eating or sleeping, I was studying. And you know what she did?"

"Anything she could to try and keep you from studying," he stated, staring straight into those luminescent blue eyes.

"Yes! Exactly! She would constantly come to my room with, hey, Yani, we're going to the mall. Why don't you take a break and come with us? Or, hey, Yani, we're going to the movies. Why don't you come with us? Or, hey, Yani, we're all going out for dinner. Why don't you come along? Anything to try and keep me from studying."

"Let me guess. So, every time she did that, you told her no."

"Exactly. I'd simply tell her no thanks and go right back to studying."

"That sounds really painful...and really stressful. Are you okay?"

"I wasn't for a while, but I am now that I know I passed and it's all behind me. Of course, meeting you certainly didn't hurt."

"Gosh, Yani, I'm at a total loss for what to say."

"It's okay, Dan. I beat her at her own game, and that's all that mattered. I've got one more year of school. After that, I'm done with her and can start working on the future."

"She was really mad when she found out you passed, wasn't she?"

"Oh, she was silently furious. There were no congratulations, no nice dinner out because of my accomplishment. Nothing."

"Sad," was his only response, and they both sat there in silence for several minutes.

Yani finally spoke first. "It's over, Dan. I've moved on." He could tell that wasn't true and that she was still wounded by the experience, but there was nothing to be gained by pursuing it further, though he did have one final question he absolutely had to ask.

"Yani, honey, why do you suppose she treats you this way?" he asked her as earnestly as possible. "There has to be a reason."

She paused for a long moment before speaking again. "Honestly, I believe in my heart that she truly resents me and has for a very long time."

"Yes, but why?"

"She hates me because I'm everything she wishes she was but never will be. She's shallow, petty, mean-spirited, cruel, and vindictive. Pick a personality trait you think is despicable and that describes her," she replied, looking down into her lap again.

Uh, oh, he instantly thought. Another shoe's about to drop.

"The worst part of it is, I'm convinced she didn't want me in the first place. I believe she wanted to abort me, but there was no way to do it."

"Wait. What could possibly make you think that?" he asked, a pained expression on his face.

"Because she talks about abortion all the time and how awful it is that it isn't legal. That it's a woman's right. That it's women's health care. I think when she got pregnant with me, she wasn't quite ready to start a family. She was forced into having me and was really pissed that she couldn't terminate her pregnancy. Apparently, I ruined her life plan. Now, every time she looks at me, I think it reminds her of that and I think she resents me for it."

"Ouch! Boy, that really hurts. My God, Yani. I am so sorry."

"It's okay, Dan," she said, now almost sobbing. "I think you already figured this out anyway, but can we change subjects now? Please? You're killing me." she asked, imploringly.

"Of course, but before we do that, there's one more thing I want you to know."

"And that is?" she replied, her voice slightly quivering.

"I'm sure glad she couldn't get that abortion."

"Thank you, Dan," she whispered, her voice still shaking ever so slightly.

He reached out and took her hand. "Come on, let's go inside."

"Okay."

They went into the cottage and Yani took a seat while he went about organizing his gear. Once finished, he sat down across from her. Fortunately, she seemed to have calmed down and he felt better about the whole situation.

"Yani, so there's something else we need to talk about," he said quietly.

"Oh, God! Now what?" she responded, getting highly agitated again with those huge blue eyes searching his face for a hint of what was to come next.

"Easy, honey," he responded with palms up, doing his best to keep things emotionally under control. "Okay, so we're going to try and spend as much time together as possible, but I can't just pretend my parents don't exist. My mom is not your mom, and my mom won't put up with that. Anyway, to keep things cool with my folks, I'll need to go home for a couple nights each week just to keep them happy, you know?"

"I understand. I figured that might have to happen. Thanks for being straight with me."

"Of course. Besides, I'll need clean clothes and other stuff anyway."

"Okay," she said and immediately followed that up with, "Hey, can you do me a favor?" she asked, looking down into her lap yet again.

"Of course. What do you need?"

Looking back up, she asked, "Can you kiss me? You've probably been here a half hour already and haven't even kissed me once yet."

"Wait. Kiss you? I don't know about that," he replied, making a face and laughing.

"Come here, you," and she leaned over to him while putting her arms around his neck. They paused for a moment to look into each other's eyes and then they kissed for a really long time. This girl is so awesome, and I am so lucky, Dan couldn't help thinking.

Once they finished, he said to her, "Hey, I don't mean to destroy the moment, but I came straight from school and haven't eaten. I'm starved. You hungry?"

"No, I already had lunch. You go right ahead."

"Okay, thanks." Yani sat there keeping him company as he got food out of the refrigerator. Once done, he sat back down at the table and started eating.

"So, have you got any ideas on what we're going to do the rest of the summer?"

"Actually, I do," he replied in between bites. "First of all, there are several really cool state parks in the area, and I'm not talking about your normal everyday city-type park. These parks are kind of like you. They're really unique and beautiful and like something you've never seen before."

"How's that?"

"Well, if I told you that, I'd spoil the surprise now, wouldn't I? You need to see them for yourself."

"Okay. What else?"

"Oh, there's lots of other things I've been thinking about, but I'm going to spring them on you one at a time. It'll be more fun that way. Besides that, there are the things I haven't even thought of yet."

"Okay," she said smiling, and she seemed satisfied with his answer.

Dan finished eating, did a quick cleanup, and sat right back down. "Ah, I feel so much better now."

"Good. Hey, let's go outside. Why don't you turn the radio on?"

"Great idea." They both got up, Dan turned on the radio and 'School's Out' by Alice Cooper was playing. How appropriate, he thought as they sat down looking out over the lake.

They relaxed for a while, listening to music, when Yani turned to him, "Hey, you feel like doing anything?"

He considered that for a moment. "You know, it's been kind of crazy this last week or so. I understand you're cooped up here most of the time, but why don't we just take it easy right now? I'll make it up to you. Maybe we can go for a swim later. It's probably going to get pretty hot."

"Okay," and she reached over to take a hold of his hand. She leaned back in her chair, holding his hand with her eyes closed and looking very peaceful. She's content right now, he thought to himself. Good. She needs that. As the afternoon rolled on, they simply sat there in idle conversation, listening to music as the heat continued to build. Eventually, it reached a point where Dan finally decided it was plenty warm enough and turned to her.

"Okay. I think it's time. Let's go for a swim."

"Sounds great. I need to put on a suit, so I'm going to run down to my grandparents' place real quick."

"Do you want me to come with you?"

"No. No need. I'll be right back." She got up, walked down off the deck and headed directly to her cottage. Dan stared at that beautiful image until she was completely out of sight, got up from the table, went inside, and put on his own swim trunks. In no time at all, she was back.

"Okay, ready," she announced.

"Let's go," he responded and they headed down to the dock. Once inside the boathouse, Yani stood there in front of him, peeled off her tee shirt, and dropped her shorts.

Facing him in a yellow bikini, she asked, "Well, what do you think?" She stood there with this beaming smile, waiting for his response. Somehow, he knew she wasn't asking about her suit.

"Dear, Lord," was all he could utter. She was an absolute sight to behold. He knew from the very first time he saw her that she was unusually magnificent for a girl her age, or maybe any age for that matter, but this was almost startling. Her shoulders, full, firm breasts, hips, legs, skin; nothing could have been improved on as far as he was concerned. Stunning didn't properly describe her. She looked like a movie starlet, except better. "You're perfect," he told her, as his heart started pounding.

"Thank you," she said, thoroughly pleased by the response as she moved to him, put her arms around his neck, and kissed him really hard. He wrapped his arms around her waist, pulled her close, and kissed her right back, thoroughly enjoying her passion.

When they finished, he looked into those iridescent eyes. "You ready?"

"Oh, yes. By the way, you know I've never actually gone swimming in the lake before," she responded giddily.

"Yeah, I remember you saying that. Well, this should be an experience," he replied in an understated fashion so she wouldn't notice the significance of his remark. The lake was so deep that it rarely got to a temperature one would call 'warm'. People always used terms like 'refreshing' when describing a swim in Seneca. As he had been swimming there his entire life, he was totally used to it, but most people had their breath taken away the first time they jumped in.

"Okay, let's go." Dan grabbed a couple of tractor-trailer tubes and rolled them out to the end of the dock and stood there for a second. "Alright, this is how it works. I toss the tubes into the lake. We dive in and swim to them. After that, you crawl inside and make yourself comfortable. The water is really deep, so don't be surprised that you can't touch bottom." He didn't mention the seaweed. That would be a little surprise for her. "Ready?"

"Yes, ready," she replied, laughing.

Dan tossed in the tubes. "Here we go," he shouted and immediately dove in. He popped up out of the water, swimming on his back while facing Yani who was still standing on the dock. She hesitated for just a second, then jumped right off into the lake.

When she broke the surface, she was screaming. "Ah! What is that on my legs?"

"Oh, that? That's seaweed. Just ignore it," he replied laughing as she swam towards him, slightly panicked. She reached him quickly, grabbed onto him, and immediately started to calm down. "Okay, into the tubes," he ordered. She let go and swam to her tube now well out past the seaweed. As the tubes were for tractor-trailer tires, they were really large, so she struggled to get in at first, but quickly figured it out. Now safely in her tube, Dan went back under, came up through the center hole of his tube, settled in and paddled straight to her. "Okay?"

"Yes, but what was that stuff grabbing onto my legs?" she asked, her voice shaking from the shock of the cold water.

"I told you. That was seaweed. It can't hurt you."

"I know, but it feels so creepy on my legs and the water is really cold!" she exclaimed.

"The water's not cold. It's refreshing," he replied laughing.

"Oh, God," was her exasperated response.

105

The sun was shining brightly; it felt really good, and they floated around for a while out front. Once you'd been in the water a few minutes, you no longer noticed the temperature and her blue lips had already returned to their normal pretty pink. After a while, Dan suggested they float down to her cottage and they paddled that way. The waves were barely a ripple so they were floating out front of the Hartmann's in no time at all.

Her grandfather was in the boat doing something and her grandmother was sitting up top on the porch. Yani called out loudly while waving at the same time, "Hey, Grandma, Grandpa!"

They both turned, waved back and you could hear her grandmother call out from the porch, "Hi, honey." They continued floating around for a while, occasionally splashing each other in the face just to be annoying. Yani thoroughly enjoyed getting Dan when he was least expecting it. In retaliation, he threatened to dump her from her tube, but never acted on the threat.

When they'd finally had enough, they made their way into shore, hauled the tubes up onto the dock, headed into the boathouse, and grabbed some towels. While they were drying off, Dan simply couldn't help himself any longer. She was just too irresistible. He reached out, pulled her to him and kissed her. She didn't even put up the slightest resistance, her lips welcoming him. He gently pushed her back onto the boathouse bed, lay down next to her, and they made out for a really long time. She smells and tastes so good, he thought. Is there anything about this girl that isn't amazing? When they finally finished and came up for air, she looked at him with those luminescent blue eyes and softly said, "Thank you." He couldn't believe it. There she goes thanking me for kissing her when I should be the one thanking her.

Chapter 13

Bright and early the next morning, Dan walked down to the Hartmann's and knocked. Yani walked over, opened the door and stood there with this expressionless face she often displayed.

"Hi."

"Good morning," he answered back.

"My grandpa wants to talk to you for a second," and she stood back from the door allowing him to enter. She nodded toward the kitchen and Dan proceeded in that direction. What was going on? Is this about all the time Dan's been spending with Yani or is there something else happening? Mr. Hartmann was seated at the kitchen table reading the newspaper, his morning coffee sitting next to him on the table. When Dan entered the room, he looked up and set his newspaper down.

"Good morning, Dan."

"Good morning, Mr. Hartmann. Yani said you wanted to talk to me."

"Yes. Remember when I asked if you might be able to help me out around here a little?"

"Yes, sir. I sure do."

"Well, the lawn needs mowing. Any chance you could do that for me sometime today?"

"Absolutely, Mr. Hartmann. No problem, though I thought I might take Yani for a walk right now. How about right after that?"

"Oh, there's no hurry on that. Whenever you get a chance would be fine."

"Great. I'll get it done sometime today for certain."

"Okay, that's perfect. You two have a nice time," he stated and then returned to reading his newspaper.

Dan turned around to leave and Yani was standing there watching him. Relieved there was nothing more serious happening, he approached her, she grabbed his arm and they started to head out the door when he paused to look at her feet. She was wearing her sandals. "You're going to need your sneakers."

"Oh? Okay, hold on a second." She disappeared into her bedroom and came right back out wearing the new footwear. "Ready." They walked out of the cottage together and turned right heading towards the point. "If we're going to the point, why do I need my sneakers?" she asked.

"Well, we're walking down to the point, but my plan is to take a little hike up the creek. Once we start up the gorge itself, you'll understand why immediately."

"Oh, sounds mysterious," she laughed in response as they continued on down to the point. When they reached the flat, he walked towards the little creek that cut through the gorge and started to climb down the short but steep bank near where the creek emptied into the lake.

"Careful," he said. "There's a lot of loose stone. It's really easy to slide and lose your balance, and we don't want you falling on your butt again before we even get started," he said laughing as he held out his hand for her. Smiling, she took his hand, one step forward on to the loose rocks, and immediately slipped, falling right on her backside. "I tried to warn you," he said, laughing again, while helping her up and giving her a hand the rest of the way down to the creek bed. As it was summer time and the dry season, there wasn't much more than a trickle of water.

"It's not much of a creek," she stated while looking around. Based on her past behavior and reaction to things, it was pretty much what Dan expected out of her.

"Somehow, I thought you'd say that. Well, this little creek here cut this gorge all by itself over a period of probably tens of thousands of years or more. You'll see," was all he said in response. "Before we start walking, you know that salmon swim up rivers to spawn, right?"

"Yes, I think that's kind of common knowledge."

"I would agree. Well, this creek here actually supports a kind of fish that spawn just like salmon do. They're called smelt and they are absolutely one of the best baits there is for trout fishing. They're also pretty popular as human food, too. Anyway, at night time during the spring, smelt actually swim up this little creek here and spawn. Amazing, huh?"

"No way."

"Yep, and they're really delicious, although they're pretty small, so it takes a lot of them to make a meal."

"If they're so small, how do you fish for them?"

"They use nets and scoop them out of the water as the smelt try to swim past. There's lots of creeks in the area much larger than this one where they spawn. You stand in the water wearing a kind of one-piece water proof suit called 'waders' that covers you from your feet to the middle of your chest so you don't get wet and freeze to death. The smelt spawn at night in the spring when the water is colder than hell and the creeks are full. The fishermen attach these metal nets to long poles. They reach out into the stream, scoop out the smelt, and dump them into a bucket on the bank of the creek. I've actually gone a couple of times and seen it done."

"Smelt, you say?"

"Yes."

"Never heard of them."

"What can I say," he said, holding out his hands and laughing. "They're a big deal around here. Anyway, let's go," and off they started. "Now, there's a lot of flat areas of shale and the goal is to find the flat spots as we walk up the gorge," he informed her as they started up the creek. "Sometimes it's not possible, but I'll do my best to lead you on a good path." Sure enough, they hadn't gone far at all when they came upon the first shale flat. It was only a few inches tall, and there was water pooled on it, but the water wasn't even an inch deep. They stepped up onto it and continued up the gorge, climbing the successive flats of shale, one after another. Sometimes, they were only a couple of inches tall, but sometimes they were a foot or two. Sometimes, they were very narrow and sometimes very broad. Sometimes there were no flat areas at all, and you had to step on loose, unstable rock to navigate your way.

"How is it that so much of the rock is flat like this?" she asked.

"Well, the bedrock in this part of the country where we're at right now is all shale. You know what kind of rock shale is, right?"

"I think it's called sedimentary or something like that."

"Yep. So, sedimentary rock is made from sediment, dirt that is, and it's deposited in layers in the oceans and hardens over millions of years. When it gets exposed to the elements of freezing and thawing, it fractures. That happens at the weakest point, and that's between the layers. The top layer fractures, gets washed away, and you're left with nice, flat stone like the stuff you see here in the gorge. Eventually, this will also break up and wash away, but we're talking a really long time before that will happen. Some of these flat areas haven't changed at all since the very first time I walked up this gorge as a kid. Some have changed dramatically."

110

"So, the creek is partially responsible for the rock breaking up and washing away."

"Absolutely. That, along with the freezing and thawing of the water over the course of the year. Like I said, this tiny little creek here cut this gorge. The lake itself was created a different way. That was done by glaciers that came down from Canada. Have you ever noticed that the rocks we use for the firepit don't look anything like the rest of the stone around here?"

"Actually, I have. They're like boulders and they have these little tiny speckles in the stone. I think those are what they call granite, right?"

"Yep. Those rocks are granite. So, what are granite boulders doing in a place where all the rock is shale?"

"The glaciers brought them."

"See how smart you are? That's exactly what happened. They were carried down from Canada, where the bedrock is granite. We actually hauled those boulders up from the lake bed to make the firepit because shale won't work. The heat would quickly fracture the stones and turn them into dust. Not so the granite because that was created from molten lava to begin with. It's used to heat."

"That's actually pretty amazing."

"Yeah, I think it's kind of interesting," he responded, shrugging his shoulders. The next waterfall they came to was closer to three feet tall. Dan climbed up first and helped her climb up behind him. Standing next to the pool of water collected on it, he pointed and said to her, "Okay, now look closely."

"What? Oh, my God! There's fish!" There was a school of about twenty minnows swimming around together in the pool. "How'd they get here?"

"That I don't know. I'm not sure if they swim up here during the spring when there's a lot more water flowing, get trapped when the creek dries up, or live here year-round and this is just their natural habitat. All I know is that every time I come in here, there's these little tiny fish swimming around in this creek."

"Dang."

"Here. Look over here. Right down next to the pool's edge."

"Holy cow! Crawfish! I've never seen one before in real life. I've only seen pictures."

Dan reached down and snatched one out of the water, grabbing it right behind its front claws. It was waving them back and forth frantically trying to find something to pinch, and he held it up for her so she could get a good look.

"They look just like a miniature lobster."

"Yeah, they kind of do, don't they? I've read somewhere that down in Louisiana, people actually eat these. You think it takes a lot of smelt to make a meal? It must take buckets full of crawfish!" he said and they both laughed. When she had finished inspecting the crawfish, he tossed it back in the water and it scurried away.

They were deep into the gorge now and the walls were thirty feet high in some places.

"Stop, Dan. Listen. It's so quiet," she whispered. "The only thing you can hear is the sound of the water running down the creek."

"Yeah, amazingly quiet. The walls are so steep and tall that somehow, they're able to block any sound from getting down in here. No one can see us and no one can hear us. I guess the sound waves from the outside world pass right over top." With that, he pulled her close and they kissed.

"I've been waiting for that," she said, staring into his eyes.

"Why didn't you tell me?"

"I was getting ready to," she replied laughing.

He put his hand around her waist and they continued together up the gorge. They'd stop occasionally to look at a flowering plant, salamanders, crawfish, or anything else she thought was interesting. As they climbed, the trek became increasingly difficult.

"This is getting kind of hard, Dan. How far are we going?"

"We're almost there. Just a little bit farther." They continued walking and climbing, and as they rounded a small bend in the gorge, suddenly it came into view. In front of them stood a waterfall that was more than twenty feet tall.

"My goodness!" she exclaimed.

"Yeah, pretty impressive, isn't it?"

"It's really impressive!"

"Believe it or not, one time me, my brother and a couple of other guys actually climbed this waterfall. One of the stupidest things I've ever done. We climbed it once, and we never climbed it again. It's just way too dangerous. We made it all the way to the top and back down again, but I was shocked none of us fell and killed ourselves. It was really stupid, but we made it."

"God, it's just so beautiful."

"Yeah, it's like our own little hidden treasure. It's so remote I bet few people have ever actually seen this. Look how hard we had to work just to get this far." They stood there for a while gazing at it and the water trickling down off the top. Dan had his hand around her waist, holding her close, and she was leaning her head against his shoulder.

When it was time to leave, he took her chin, gently turned her face towards his, kissed her and whispered, "Okay, let's head back."

They returned the same way they came, scaling down one waterfall after another, occasionally stopping to look at something she wanted to see up close, and by the time they got back to the lake, it was approaching lunch time. They climbed out of the creek, walked back to her cottage and as he was dropping her off, Mrs. Hartmann called out to him, "Dan, why don't you join us for lunch?"

He turned to Yani. She nodded her approval and Dan responded, "Gosh, thanks, Mrs. Hartmann. That'd be really nice," and he walked together with Yani inside to the kitchen. The four of them had lunch together and when they were finished, Dan turned to Mr. Hartmann, "How about if I mow that lawn now?"

"Mower's in the shed. If it needs gas, I think there's a can in there that should have plenty in it."

"Okay, perfect."

After he'd finished the lawn and put the mower away, Mrs. Hartmann called out to him, "Dan, it's awfully warm. Why don't you come up to the porch and have a cold drink?"

"Thanks, Mrs. Hartmann. I'd appreciate that," he called back. Yani and her grandfather were already on the porch. She'd been there the whole time watching him mow. He sat down next to her and Mrs. Hartmann brought out some lemonade. When no one was paying attention, Mr. Hartmann slipped Dan some cash and he discreetly stuffed it in his pocket. They continued sitting there for a while sipping on the lemonade when after a few minutes passed, Dan turned to Yani, "Hey, you feel like a swim?"

"Yes! I'll go change." She was back in no time at all. "Ready!" she announced. Dan thanked Mr. and Mrs. Hartmann and they headed back to his place. Dan went inside, changed into his suit, and was right back out. They headed down to the boathouse and when they got inside, Yani spun him around, clamped her arms around his waist and started kissing him. Once she was satisfied that she'd kissed him enough, she stepped back, stripped off her tee shirt and shorts, and stood there in front of him so he could enjoy the view.

"God, Yani, you are one seriously beautiful woman," was all he could come up with. Words couldn't adequately describe the girl.

She kind of skipped back over to him and started kissing him again while Dan held her close. After a minute, she said, "Okay, let's go swimming."

"Your wish is my command, my dear. Swimming, it is." He grabbed a couple of tubes, rolled them off the end of the dock, and dove in after them, appearing out of the water again on his back facing her. This time, she didn't hesitate and dove right off the dock towards him, popping up out of the water with this big smile on her face.

"Refreshing," she stated laughing. They climbed into their tubes and started floating out in the lake. It was mid-afternoon, the sun was shining brightly, and it was a really pleasant day. They went way out in the lake and just kind of hung out, not doing much of anything.

After they'd been out there a while, he looked at her and asked, "So, what're your sisters doing this summer?"

"I don't actually know."

"Does your family ever take vacations together?"

"Rarely. They've taken us to Disney World once and to the theme parks near Cincinnati a few times, but that's about it, though my parents are constantly going someplace for fun on their own. What about your family?"

"Other than coming up here, which we've done a lot over the years, our big vacation is going to Florida every Spring Break for like the last decade, but I didn't go this year. It would've been too crowded in the car, so I passed and stayed home. I've got another question, though. Didn't you talk to your sisters before you left?"

"Barely."

"Why's that?"

"Well, the tension in our house was really bad. Seems like everybody was walking around on pins and needles as I was studying for finals and getting ready to leave, so we didn't talk much."

"Do you normally get along with them?"

"Oh, yeah. When my mom's not around, we get along just fine."

"What happens when your mom's around?"

"They keep their distance. I think the expression is 'guilt by association.' They're afraid that if they're caught being nice to me, our mom is going to start treating them the same way she treats me, and nobody wants that."

"Nope. Nobody wants that," he answered back, shaking his head. That's really sad, he thought to himself, but he decided to drop the subject for the time being.

After some time had passed in silence, Yani turned to him and said, "I've got a question for you."

"Okay. What's that?"

"If you're so concerned about going to Vietnam, why don't you just enlist like your brothers did?"

116

Dan floated there for a minute, collecting his thoughts before he finally responded. "Well, there's something about that that just doesn't feel right."

"What do you mean?"

"You know, during the Second World War, my dad and all my uncles enlisted in the military, but they didn't do it to *avoid* serving their country. They did it so they *could* serve their country. They did whatever was asked of them and thank God, they all returned home. Far as I know, I only have one uncle that actually got shot, and he made a full recovery."

"And?"

"I don't know much about why we're actually fighting this war, but it seems to me that an awful lot of our boys are joining the military so they don't have to fight. They do things like join the Navy or the Coast Guard hoping they can avoid combat. Now, that may be the right decision for them, but I'm not sure it's right for me. I mean, let's be serious here for a moment. Only a fool actually wants to get shot at. Honestly, I just don't know what's right."

"So, what're you going to do?"

"I haven't figured that out yet. I'm still thinking about it. What do you think I should do?"

She floated there quietly for a few seconds considering his question. "I don't know."

"See? That's the problem."

They returned to silently floating there together. As it was a weekday, there were almost no boats out on the lake, and the solitude felt really good. At one point, Yani reached over and took his hand. Locked together, they floated there rocking gently back and forth in the waves.

After a fair amount of time had passed, he finally decided they'd been out long enough. "Okay, Yani. I'm getting water logged. Let's go in."

"No. I want to stay a little longer."

"Really? Okay, no problem. Just let me know when you're ready to go in."

Several minutes later, he looked over at her. "Hey, Yani?"

"Yes?"

"I don't know if the time is right for this, but," and he faltered for a second.

"But what?"

He squeezed her hand and said, "I've started liking you in a really serious way."

That big, beaming smile immediately appeared on her face. "Actually, I was hoping you had the guts to tell me that."

He was so relieved to hear that, knowing he hadn't totally humiliated himself.

"And I feel the same way about you, so there. Hey, I'm ready to go in now. Let's race."

With that, she let go of his hand, put her foot on his tube, and pushed just as hard as she could, sending him further out into the lake and launching herself towards shoreline while she paddled as fast as possible.

"Oh, so, that's how we're playing this, huh!" he yelled, spinning himself around and paddling towards shore. He kept wide of her as he went past so she couldn't grab hold of him and slow him down, laughing as he went by. When she floated up, he proclaimed, "Beat ya!"

"Yeah, barely," she laughed. He grabbed their tubes, tossed them up on the dock, and he followed her up the steep, almost vertical swim steps, which turned out to be a really bad idea. He simply couldn't help himself and took a long, hard look at her gorgeous figure as she ascended. As soon as they got inside the boathouse, he put his hand around her waist. In one continuous motion, he gently pulled her onto his lap as he sat down on the bed, rolling her over on her back and ending up on top with their faces mere inches apart.

"Smooth, Dan. Real smooth. You do that with all the girls?"

"Shush!"

Looking him straight in the eyes, she took his hand and placed it right on her breast. He needed no instructions on what to do next, slipping his hand right under her bikini top. Yani grabbed his face with both hands and kissed him passionately as his fingers found their way around her body. He swore he felt her quiver slightly while he explored her chest, moving from side to side to give her breasts equal attention. They lay there making out for a really long time before finally declaring a temporary cease-fire, at least for a little while.

Chapter 14

Now finished with swimming and making out, they made their way back up to the cottage. The radio was still on with Neil Young's 'Heart of Gold' playing as they sat down facing the lake. "Well, that was certainly pleasant," she said, a flirty look on her face.

"Yes, it definitely was, my dear. So, let's see, now you've rowed a boat for the first time, skipped a stone, went to the racetrack, hiked the gorge, and you've gone swimming in Seneca. Any other firsts so far?"

"Riding in the Seneca Song?"

"Nope. You said there are pictures of you doing that as a little girl, so technically, that doesn't count."

"Hmmm. I'll have to think about this some more."

"Don't worry. I've got lots of firsts planned for you." She smiled broadly. Keeping Yani mentally and physically stimulated while she was here would certainly help her cope emotionally. For that matter, it would help him, too. They sat there relaxing while watching the chipmunks play along the stone wall along with the robins, blue jays, chickadees, and woodpeckers that stopped by occasionally. When a downy woodpecker landed in the walnut tree in front of them, Dan pointed it out.

"You see that little guy right there?"

"Yes."

"That's called a downy woodpecker. My grandpa hates woodpeckers and he used to shoot them all the time because they make holes in the cottage. It's actually a federal offense to kill woodpeckers. My dad had to have a long talk with him to make him stop because he was worried my grandfather was eventually going to get arrested for it."

"But it's so cute. I can't believe he'd want to kill that."

"Well, if you knew my grandfather, you'd understand. You see the siding on the cottage?"

"Yes."

"It's called board and batten, and the wood is pine, which is really soft. The siding on your cottage is called shiplap, and it's made from hardwood. Anyway, not to bore you about siding, but when my grandfather built the cottage, he was a carpenter. Most of the wood came from job sites he was working at. The wood was scrap, so rather than let it go to waste, my grandfather hauled it up here and used it to build this place. Because it's pine, it's really easy for the woodpeckers to peck holes and then they can build nests inside the walls. So, in a sense, it's my grandfather's own fault that the woodpeckers like to peck on his cottage. If he'd used hardwood, they wouldn't do it."

"That's actually kind of funny."

"I think so, too. My grandfather would get so mad when he found a new hole. He'd be running around yelling, cursing and looking for his shotgun so he could shoot the poor bird that committed the mortal sin. He and my grandmother would start yelling at each other. I'll never forget the conversation my dad finally had with him." Dan raised his voice and waved his arms. "Well, the sons a bitches won't stop pecking holes in the cottage! It was hilarious, but I had to pretend it was serious." They both laughed really hard.

"Where are your grandparents now?"

"Right now, they're in Elmira, but in the winter, they go down to their second home in Florida."

"Will we see them up here this summer?"

"It's possible, but I doubt it. They're getting old and coming up here is really hard for them. I mean, look at our property. The land is really uneven. There are steps everywhere, so it's hard for an old person to walk around. My grandmother has arthritic knees. I've never actually heard her say anything or complain, but I think walking around here is fairly painful for her."

Looking around, she responded, "Yeah, I see what you mean. It would be tough, especially if it hurt to walk."

"Absolutely."

Other than the top-of-the-hour news broadcast on the previous day's Vietnam casualties, it was a beautiful and peaceful afternoon. When supper time finally arrived, they went down to the boathouse and Yani dressed. They got in one more really sweet, really long-lasting kiss and slowly made the walk down to her place.

While Yani was having supper, he prepared his own food and ate as 'Rocket Man' by Elton John played in the background. Once convinced Yani would be finished with her meal, he walked down, knocked, and she came out immediately. "Hi," was all she said, smiling at him. Dan looked down at her feet and she was wearing her sandals.

"Any chance you can change into sneakers again?"

"Yes, though I should know better by now. Never wear the sandals," she responded nodding. Slipping inside to change, she was back promptly and out the door. "Where we going?"

"I thought me might walk up the hill to the grapevines. You're going to be adding another first to your list."

"Okay," she replied reaching down for his hand. They walked up the hill about a quarter mile, and as they walked along, she looked over at him, "I can see why you asked me to put on sneakers. This is hard work," she stated through labored breathing.

"Yep. Folks don't realize how steep the hill is and how hard it is to walk it because they're always riding in a car."

As they trudged along up the road, she noticed these small trees all evenly spaced in the fields on the opposite side of the road from the grapevines. "What are those?" she asked pointing at them.

"Those are peach trees."

"Those little things are peach trees?"

"Yep and they're quite old. Those trees have been there for as long as I can remember. They may be small, but they produce a ton of fruit. Later this summer when the peaches ripen, the farmer will pick them and sell them at the little roadside stand he has up there along the highway."

"Really. Just like that, huh?" All of a sudden, a loud boom went off in the field and Yani jumped in response. "What the heck was that?"

Dan laughed at her reaction. "That was one of these little explosive devices the farmer uses to scare away the birds so they don't steal or damage his fruit. They're kind of like a firecracker except when a bird lights in the tree, that sets them off."

"What happens to the birds?"

"I'm told nothing happens to the birds, but I don't know if that is actually true or not. Supposedly, it just scares the heck out of them and it doesn't damage the fruit either. If that's really true, then leave it to a good farmer to figure out how to make a big bang, scare off the birds, yet not damage his crop."

"Amazing!"

"Yep. Come on," he said, turning left towards the field of grapevines. They stepped across a ditch into the vines and started walking down one of the long rows.

"Are we supposed to be in here?"

"Nope. Not at all. Just like the point, this is private property."

"Won't we get in trouble?"

"Yeah, well, I suppose we could, but I doubt we will. We're not going to do any harm, and once we're in the vines, it's more than likely no one will see us anyway. It's pretty hard to spot a person walking around in here unless you're looking really carefully."

"Well, okay. If you say so."

"Trust me on this. We'll be fine."

Together, they walked along the perfectly aligned field of vines. Dan pointed out the little bunches of grapes that had already started growing and the way the farmer pruned and hung the vines so that they grew in a very specific way. He also explained that, if properly cared for, these vines would continue to produce for a very long time, decades, in fact.

"How long before they harvest?"

"That's one of the interesting things about Seneca Lake and why these vines are here in the first place. I'm told grapes take a long time before they reach a point where you can harvest. The lake is so large and so deep that it creates its own ecosystem and keeps the air warm well into the fall, which prevents frost. That, in turn, gives the grapes the time necessary to produce the sugar content they need to be any good. Oh, and these aren't eating grapes. These grapes are for wine."

"Wait. How do you know all this stuff?"

"Well, I did grow up here. Plus, according to my teachers, I have this insatiable desire to try and know everything I can about the world around me. So, I guess maybe I should know about this, too. Don't you think?"

"Yeah, I suppose," was her sole response while she just kind of stared at him probably wondering what kind of a nerd she was hanging out with. He could tell her mind was working overtime. She was thinking about something and as soon as she was ready, she'd let him know. That was one of the things Dan had really grown to love about the girl. She only spoke when she had something she thought was worthwhile saying.

After walking through the long rows in the vineyard examining the young grapes and their vine structures, the sun started going down and it was now time for them to call it a day. They made a U-turn in the row and simply backtracked the way they came in. Once they had almost reached the road, another huge bang went off in the orchard and Yani jumped again while grabbing ahold of Dan. He couldn't help but laugh at her reaction. "Don't worry, babe. After a while, you get used to it. Some days, I swear, it seems like they go off every fifteen minutes or so."

"Easy for you to say."

He just shrugged in response. What more could he add? They crossed over the ditch onto the road, then walked down to his place where they spent a little quality time alone together. When the evening came to an end, he took his girl home then returned to his place thinking the entire time just how lucky he was to have met this really special girl from Youngstown.

Chapter 15

During that night, a good-sized storm passed through the area. Dan listened to the wind whipping through the trees and the booming thunder as he lay there in bed. When he got up Sunday morning and looked out at the lake, he could see it was really rough and that there were lots of white caps on the water. It wasn't cold, but it was very blustery out on the water with the wind coming from the south. Today would not be a good day for the lake, so he'd have to come up with something else to do. Once he'd finished starting his day and was certain the Hartmann's would be done as well, he walked down to their place, knocked on the screen door and Yani came out immediately. It was approaching mid-morning by the time he got there.

"Good morning," she said with that staid countenance she displayed often, though not nearly as frequently now as when they'd first met.

"Good morning to you. Sleep well?"

"Yes. Very well," she replied, as she reached out to gently touch his arm and they started walking in the direction of his place. "Quite the storm last night, wasn't it?"

"Yes, absolutely."

"So, what are we doing today?"

"I haven't exactly figured that part out yet, but I've got some ideas. The lake is way too rough to do any boating or swimming, at least it is right now. Maybe it'll calm down later, but it doesn't look good."

They strolled along in silence down the dirt road towards his place. Dan had now accepted that she simply didn't speak so she could hear the sound of her own voice. She also wasn't one of those girls who was constantly tittering because they were nervous. He hated that. Dan recognized this, so he didn't try to force it. Silence was okay. He was good with that. He'd determined that it didn't mean she was in a bad mood or unhappy at all. This was just part of her personality. Or maybe it was a learned behavior she used to protect herself. If you didn't say anything, you couldn't be attacked for your words. He wasn't sure. If it was the latter, he thought that was rather troubling, but he kept that thought to himself.

"Well, you said you had some ideas. What're you thinking?"

"Right. So, as we can't really do anything interesting here, I thought maybe we could go for a drive along the lake. How's that sound?"

"Yes. Let's do that. I could use another break from this place."

"Do we need to tell your grandparents?"

"How far are we going?"

"Not too far. I'm thinking Geneva and back."

"How far is that?"

"Probably forty-five minutes each way."

"Maybe we'd better tell them just so they know."

"Okay. Let me grab the keys and we'll swing by your place to tell your grandparents.

After informing the grandparents and heading out, as soon as Dan reached the top of the hill, he turned left onto the lake highway and started north towards Geneva. While it wasn't a good day for activities on the lake, all in all, it was still fairly nice outside. You didn't get a lot of that in the Finger Lakes region, so when you did, you needed to take advantage of it. As they headed north, Dan pointed out the various vineyards, landmarks, or other things he thought might be of interest, and her body language seemed to indicate she was enjoying herself. Off to their left, you could see Seneca Lake and get a real sense of just how massive it was at over thirty miles long and about three miles across at its widest point. The lake seemed to stretch on forever.

Large segments of Seneca had a collar of trees sitting along the tops of the cliffs that formed the shore line. Just like the trees on the road by their cottages, these were mostly comprised of oak, walnut, and hickory, with only an occasional coniferous. In between the highway and the trees were large, sloping farm fields, many of which were vineyards that ran parallel to the lake, but not always. Sometimes, the fields had cabbage, corn, both field and sweet, or alfalfa for livestock. Sometimes, they had orchards of peach trees or other stone fruits like cherries.

The inland side of the highway had some agriculture, but was much more forested. The opposite or west side of the lake didn't have nearly as much agriculture and was less developed. This time of year, the fields and forest were a shade of dark green. Come fall, the colors of the fields would change to mustard yellow, flaxen or ochre, and the trees to different shades of red, scarlet, russet, and brown. The coniferous trees would be the only green remaining.

As they drove along, they had the car windows down and music playing on the radio. The wind was blowing her hair back away from her face and Dan simply couldn't get over how astonishingly attractive this girl was. Looking over at her, he said, "You know, I'm pretty sure this is the road your parents drove when they brought you to your grandparents' place."

"Maybe so, but it doesn't look at all familiar. I suppose it's possible. I was in such a black mood at the time, though, I didn't even bother to pay attention. As far as I was concerned, I was on my way to prison camp, so it was kind of hard to find any pleasure in it."

"I understand."

At one point, she noticed a really large property alongside the highway that was entirely enclosed with a chain link fence.

"What's in there?"

"That, Yani, is what is called the Seneca Army Depot."

"What's it used for?"

"Well, we used to think it was simply an army storage facility for bombs, artillery shells and military stuff like that, but now we aren't so certain."

"What do you mean you aren't certain?"

"So, we used to tell ourselves that if there was ever a nuclear war, one of the safest places to shelter would be right here at our cottage because it's so remote, plus you'd never run out of water, which is kind of important. Now, rumor has it that the Seneca Depot is actually used to store nuclear weapons. If that is, in fact, the case, well, this area would be one of the first places to be hit by nuclear missiles and we'd all be dead," he laughed. "Anyway, the Army won't confirm or deny, so we don't really know, but there's nothing we could do about it anyway, even if it's true that they do store nukes here."

"That is really crazy."

"Yeah, but it's not the only thing that's interesting about the Depot. Watch carefully as we drive along. You'll probably see a surprise. Pay close attention."

Yani stared at the property as they drove. All of a sudden, she pointed out the window. "Look! This is incredible! White deer!"

"Yep. A few decades back, when they enclosed the property with the fence, a few white deer got trapped inside. They aren't albino. They're simply white-furred deer, and I'm told there's now a couple hundred of them. They allow hunting inside for the soldiers, but you're

129

only allowed to shoot the normally colored deer. The pure white ones are protected. Kind of cool, isn't it?"

"Yeah, they're really beautiful."

"Yep, and very tasty, too. Ever had venison?"

"Nope."

"My family hunts every year. It's my dad's favorite winter time activity."

"Do you actually shoot the deer?"

"Yes, and depending on the size of the deer, you could get anywhere from 50 to 100 lbs. of meat, so afterwards we take the deer to a butcher who cuts it up, and we freeze it to eat later."

"Interesting, and you like eating it?"

"Oh, yeah. Not everyone likes the taste of venison, but I do."

"I see."

They continued driving all the way to the north end of Seneca Lake and to the little city of Geneva. When they pulled into town, Dan swung by Hobart and William Smith Colleges to show her the beautiful old campus. He explained that they were technically two separate colleges, one for men and one for women, but were now run with a single administration and that the institution was well over 150 years old. After the tour of the college campus, he drove her through the park at the north end of the lake, followed by a visit to a local sub shop where they stopped for lunch. Once they'd finished eating, it was back in the car heading south towards Watkins and the cottages. Right before they reached Ovid, he turned to her. "Hey, we're going to take a quick detour. I want to show you something really unusual."

"Oh? Is this like another top-secret thing or something?"

"Nope. It's even creepier than that," he answered back, while making a strange facial expression.

"Well, okay, I guess," she replied with a certain level of skepticism and uneasiness.

He swung off the highway onto a two-lane road, rounded a corner, and there in front of them was this huge, imposing group of multi-story red brick buildings. "What the heck is this?"

"This, Yani, is the Willard Asylum for the Chronic Insane, and it's been here well over 100 years. It's always been used to warehouse the craziest of the crazies. It's an insane asylum."

"Oh, my God! Do they still use it?"

"As far as I know, there are still patients in there, though nowhere near as many as there were at its peak. I'm told that they've stopped accepting new patients, but continue to care for those that remain and will continue to until they die. From what I've heard, if you end up in Willard, you almost never leave alive, so you better behave yourself while you're up here at the lake. You never know. Maybe they'd make an exception and find a spot for you," he said laughing loudly.

"That is creepy. Let's get out of here, Dan. This place makes my skin crawl."

"You mean you don't want to go for the guided tour?" he asked with a smart aleck grin.

"No, I think I'll pass on that. Seriously, let's go, Dan. This place is freaking me out."

"Okay, easy girl," he responded and took the next left, leading them back to the main highway. Once on the road again, he turned to her, "Hey, how about if we stop for an ice cream cone? Maybe it will calm your nerves after the trauma of seeing Willard."

131

"Great idea. Let's do that."

There was an ice cream stand just off the highway in the town of Ovid that he knew well. When they reached it, he pulled in and parked in the crowded lot. It was a Sunday afternoon in the summer, so it was really busy. There were families and kids scattered everywhere on the property. The outdoor tables were all full, there was no indoor seating, and there were people standing in line waiting to place their orders. When they got out of the car and started walking towards the order window, Dan noticed that just about everyone had stopped what they were doing and turned to look at them. He could also see several people bent over in these hushed conversations, and he instantly figured out what was happening. They were all talking about Yani and probably him, too. She paid absolutely no attention to this at all. He understood now that she was used to this, guessing that this was her normal.

Wherever she went, people probably stopped and stared at her because they'd rarely seen a girl this beautiful. And it wasn't just her appearance. It was also the way she moved. Yani didn't walk across the parking lot. It was more like she was gliding across with her auburn hair bouncing in perfect rhythm to each step. Plus, with those luminescent blue eyes, she couldn't help but attract attention. Yani strode confidently up to the line with Dan in tow, turned to him and said, "I always have chocolate because they say it makes you happy. What're you getting?"

"Well, I want to be happy, too, so make mine chocolate, as well. A large one, please."

When it was their turn, Yani placed their order. Dan paid for it, and they started looking for a seat. A couple was just leaving, so they sat at the picnic table they vacated, which was adjacent to a family still occupying the other half. Dan could see the mom and dad taking these sideways glances, checking out Yani, but she acted like she didn't even notice as she went to work on her ice cream cone. At one point, the mom caught the dad taking one too many peeks at Yani. She smacked him on the arm and gave him that look of, 'Okay, mister, that's quite enough.' Laughing to himself because the dad had gotten busted, Dan was sitting there watching Yani and decided, you know what? She probably doesn't notice, and even if she does, she obviously doesn't even care.

There was no urgency or fixed time to be back, so they relaxed and ate slowly. When they finished and were walking back to the car, Yani reached down and took his hand, which instantly made his heart palpitate like crazy. On top of that, he could also feel all eyes now upon them. He was pretty sure that all the women must be sitting there thinking it's just not fair that she looks that good. While the men, well, the men were almost certainly sitting there thinking something else entirely. After they had hopped back into the car and were heading out, Yani turned to Dan, "Oh, by the way, my grandma said I can stay out a little later tonight if I want to."

"Yes!" was his less than muted response.

As they were pulling out of the ice cream stand and on to the street, Yani looked over at a large green space adjacent to the road and pointed. "Hey, what's up with that bird over there in the grass?"

Dan looked in the direction she was pointing, "Oh, that bird? That's a red-tailed hawk."

"Yeah, but what's he doing? It looks like he's trying to grab hold of something."

"I don't know," and just as Dan finished speaking, the bird took off flying right towards the windshield of their car, almost striking it. Dan slammed on the brakes, throwing them into their seatbelts as the hawk swung away and the car behind them blasted their horn.

"No!" Yani screamed. "He's got a squirrel in his claws and it's alive!"

Dan started driving again and looked over at her, "Unfortunately for the squirrel, he's probably taking it back to his nest to feed his chicks."

"I understand that, but the squirrel is alive. Why didn't he just kill it?" she asked with obvious anguish in her voice. "That just seems so cruel."

"If I had to guess, I think he's taking it back alive because the chicks will grow up to be predators and they have to learn how to kill. This is probably one of the ways the hawk teaches them that skill."

"Oh, God. I just wish I didn't have to see that."

"I understand, honey. Sometimes nature can be cruel, but they do what they have to do."

She just sighed and shook her head as they continued on back to the cottages. When they arrived, he dropped her by her front door, and as she got out, she turned to him and stated, "See you later." It wasn't a suggestion, so much as it was an announcement.

"Yep. I'll see you later." She shut the door and walked directly into her cottage.

Later that evening as he was approaching her place, Yani came walking out the door before he could even knock.

"I heard you coming."

"Yeah, you're getting pretty good at that."

She smiled at him, placing her hand on his arm, and the two of them started heading towards his place. When they got to his cottage, they went straight down to the dock, grabbed a couple of folding chairs, and sat on the end, watching the sun set. The wind had died down during the afternoon and the lake had finally calmed. It was going to be a pleasant and peaceful evening. They got up, took their chairs into the boathouse and headed up to the cottage. As they got to the top of the stairs, he announced, "Okay. Time for a bonfire. Have a seat."

"Wait. What if the raccoon comes around?"

"Oh, him? Ah, it's way too early for the raccoon. He won't be coming around until much later tonight, if he comes at all. Besides, he knows better than to mess with me," he said with this air of fake courage. She gave him a disparaging look and sat down on the bench next to the firepit while he went about the business of starting the fire. Once he had the kindling and logs stacked to his satisfaction, he lit it, went into the cottage and turned on the radio.

When he came back out, he sat down next to Yani on the bench with their bodies touching while the fire slowly began to take hold, and soon enough, the firepit was consumed with roaring flames. They sat and watched the fire and listened to the radio station's steady stream of the Rolling Stones, the Beatles, Elton John, Bowie, and all the other popular artists of the time. They didn't speak. There was no need. Just being in the presence of each other now was more than sufficient and really comforting. Before long, total darkness descended on the lake. Soon, the only light was that of the fire. Dan reached over and took Yani's hand. She looked at him, smiled and gave his hand a reassuring squeeze.

After some time had passed, Yani turned, looked at him and softly said, "Dan?"

"Yes?"

"Kiss me." Just like before when she was getting out of the car, this wasn't a request. This was a command and he knew instinctively that she didn't just want a little kiss. She wanted to make out and he didn't need to be told twice. He took her in his arms and when their lips met, she wrapped her arms around him and kissed him like she really meant

135

it. Her mouth was so warm and wet. Her kiss was so passionate. It was like heaven. When they finished, she put her hand on his cheek and quietly said, "Thank you."

This thing with Yani thanking him when he kissed her was something he wasn't sure he'd ever get used to. Not knowing how to respond, he simply replied in a hushed tone, "The pleasure was all mine," and it was. They sat together for as long as they thought they could, making out many more times before Dan reluctantly got up, grabbed the garden hose and put the fire out. He walked her home and as they got close, she stopped, turned and kissed him once more for good measure.

"I guess I'll see you tomorrow, right?" she asked with quiet confidence.

"Yep. That is the plan, honey. Sweet dreams. See you tomorrow."

She smiled, turned and walked into her cottage closing the door quietly behind her.

Dan should have felt like he was walking on air the whole way back to his place. Instead, he felt apprehensive and very unsettled. Sure, he was happy, but he should have been ecstatic. The most beautiful girl in the world was crazy about him, but come Labor Day weekend, she'd be gone. What was the point of all of this? He went to bed that night, trying not to think about that, but focusing on the happiness he felt when he was with her. As he was falling asleep, he decided that, come what may, he was going to try and make the best of it, spending as much time with the auburn-haired girl as he possibly could for as long as it could possibly last.

Chapter 16

"Dan?" The announcement of his name was accompanied by droplets of water flicked in his direction, which pulled him back from his contemplation of the clouds decorating the blue sky up above. With a few strokes of his hand, he swung his tube around to face Yani. The thought came that admiring her was way more fun than staring at clouds, but the frown she wore contrasted with her beauty.

"Yes, Yani?" he asked, then pausing momentarily before continuing. "Is there something wrong?"

"No…I just have a question."

"Okay. What's your question?"

"Do you believe in God?"

He couldn't help but smile. "Well, there's a question that comes out of nowhere. Here we are sitting in our tubes, floating out in the middle of the lake. It's a beautiful day. The sun is shining. There are really nice cirrus clouds drifting overhead, and out of nowhere, you want to talk about God; the subject of which has never even been mentioned before, not even in passing."

Continuing to frown, she asked again, "Well, do you?

Her tone said that his answer mattered, so he thought about the best way to respond. But to do that, he also needed to know why she asked and if she wanted more than a yes or no. He shrugged in resignation and decided that he would just tackle the subject head-on. What did he have to lose?

"Yes, I believe in God, but what brought on the question?" He waved a hand to indicate the lake around them, adding, "It's not exactly the kind of thing you expect on a day or location like this," but almost immediately thought to himself, actually, maybe the natural beauty of this place is exactly why she's contemplating God.

Her frown was replaced with a pretty smile as she said, "No, I suppose not." The smile faded though as she followed that up with, "But since you do, will you tell me why?"

"Sure. I believe in God because God has helped me in the past when I really needed it, which confirmed for me the existence of God. That's why."

"Like how?"

Let the interrogation begin. He thought about that for a moment before providing his response. "Okay, here's an example. So, when I was about eleven years old, I got a paper route. You've never been there to see it, but I told you before that I live out in the country, and that's where the paper route was. I don't know exactly, but I'm guessing it was about a four or five-mile round trip every day, seven days a week. When I got the paper route, I didn't have a bike, and at eleven years old, of course, I was pretty small. It took forever to walk the route, and I really needed a bike, but my parents couldn't afford to buy me one. If you're eleven years old and you're carrying twenty pounds of newspapers, walking all that way isn't easy. Enter God."

"Elmira has a minor-league baseball team. One evening, my dad announced he was taking some of us to the baseball game. We'd never gone to a baseball game before. We get there. I see there's a giveaway that night and the prize is a brand-new bike. I filled out my little entry card and dropped it in the box with the other cards, took my seat with my dad and spent the next six innings praying non-stop to God to let me win that bike."

"And you won the bicycle."

"Yes. Instant serendipity. In between the sixth and seventh innings, they had the drawing, announced the winner and it was me. God had answered my prayers, but now I had a new problem."

"Which was?"

"How was I going to get the bike home?"

"Right. Bikes aren't small. So, what did you do? Ride it home from the baseball game?"

"Not hardly. That would have been way too far and way too dangerous. Fortunately, and out of necessity, back at that time my family had a station wagon. Whoever it was that was in charge at the stadium told my dad to back the car up to the main entrance. Some men brought the bike out, loaded it into the station wagon, and with the rear window down and a wheel hanging out the back it just fit and we could drive it home."

"And you had the bike that you really needed."

"Yes, and you know what else?"

"No, what?"

"We never ever went to another baseball game."

"That's a fascinating story."

"Yes, it is, and it's totally true. Think about that for a second. I go to one baseball game once in my life. I don't know it in advance, but they're giving away a bicycle at that one game when I badly needed one and I win that bike. That's one reason why I believe in God, but it's not the only reason."

"So, why else?"

Dan took a minute to collect his thoughts before continuing. "Well, since the moment I was born, I've been surrounded by religion and the

Catholic church. I don't go to church now as much as I used to, but I grew up going to church at least once a week and oftentimes a lot more than that. My parents made me take religious instructions and I was even an altar boy for a few years. God and religion have been a part of my life since before I knew how to speak or walk."

"Yeah, but what does that have to do with actually believing in God?"

"Be patient. I'm getting to that. So, for Catholics, we have this thing called faith. That is, part of being a Catholic is that you simply believe in God. You accept that fact. There's a lot of other things we believe in, but let's keep it no more complicated than that for now. So, to answer your question more fully, in addition to having reasons to believe in God, I also have no reasons not to believe in God. I have faith that God exists."

"Interesting."

"Yes, religion is kind of interesting." He waited before speaking again. "So, Yani?"

"Yes."

"What made you want to ask about God?"

She looked at him with a puzzled expression, "I'm not sure. For some reason, it just popped into my head."

"Do you believe in God?"

She hesitated. "I don't actually know. My parents don't practice any religion and God is never even mentioned in my home. At the same time, I don't not believe in God. Maybe I just don't know enough about it."

"Have you ever been inside a church?"

"Nope."

"So, never been inside a church, synagogue, mosque, pagoda, nothing?"

"Nope. None of those places."

"That's kind of surprising. I mean, I go to school with lots of kids whose folks aren't church goers, but if you ask them if they've ever been inside a church or a synagogue, they'd all say 'yes'."

"I'm not sure what to say. Maybe my parents think there's something evil or dangerous about churches. Like I said, I don't remember church, religion, or God ever even having been mentioned. I've had zero exposure to the concept of God or a God."

"That's really amazing." Dan sat there rocking in the waves when he suddenly had an idea. "Hey, would you like to see the inside of a church? There's a really nice one in Watkins that I've been to many times. Maybe you can think of it as another one of your firsts."

She sat there in her tube, studying him for a moment. "Am I allowed to actually do that?"

"Of course. There are very few rules on who can or can't enter a church for services. It would be bad for business if they made it hard to go to church."

Considering that for a moment with this really serious look on her face, she responded, "You know what? I think I'd like to do that."

"Great. The church is called St. Mary's of the Lake, and it's right in town. When I was younger and we were here at the cottage, come Sunday morning, my mom would load us in the car and make us go to church. Heaven forbid we miss a week. It wasn't until fairly recently that she stopped doing that. I guess it just became too much of a hassle. That, or she figured more church for her children at this point wouldn't accomplish a darn thing."

"So, she would make you go to the church while you were here on vacation?"

"Yep and we used to just whine like crazy when she made us do that," he replied laughing.

"Oh, I bet."

"Hey, Yani?"

"Yes?"

"You know what else I believe in?"

"What's that?"

"I believe in angels and, more specifically, guardian angels."

"Okay, what the heck is a guardian angel?"

"Well, you've heard of angels, right?"

"Sure. Who hasn't. But what's a guardian angel?"

"I mentioned the whole concept of faith. Well, there's lots of crazy things that are part of religion and guardian angels are one of them. Something you hear a lot when you're a Christian kind of goes like this." Pausing momentarily, Dan continued on with his explanation, pretending to use an actor's deep voice. "Why would God take the time to help you and answer your prayers? What makes you so special? Isn't God busy dealing with other larger problems like war or famine?"

"I was thinking almost the exact same thing when you were telling me the story about winning the bike. Why would God take the time to listen to your prayers?"

"He probably wouldn't," Dan answered back, staring at her straight faced.

"Wait a minute. Now I'm totally confused. I thought you said that God answered your prayers," Yani responded, challenging him.

"I did, but I didn't say that God personally answered my prayers. He's a busy guy."

"And?"

"Right. So, that's one of the things that guardian angels do. When God is busy dealing with a nice war or a good famine, sometimes he assigns duties to his angels to carry out on his behalf. It was my guardian angel that probably ensured I won the contest."

"Seriously?"

"Yes, seriously. And you know what else?"

"You mean there's more?"

"Oh, there's a lot more, but I'm referring to something much more specific and it relates to you."

"Okay. I'm ready. Shock me."

"I believe you have a guardian angel," he stated, staring at her again with that same expressionless face.

She just lay there in her tube, almost speechless returning the stare "Okay, Dan. Now, this is getting really weird. So, I have a guardian angel. Me. Yani, who doesn't even know if I believe in a God or the existence of a God."

"Yes."

"And how is it you know that I have a guardian angel? I mean, you can't actually see angels, or can you?"

Laughing, he responded, "No. I assure you that I cannot, nor have I ever seen an actual angel. Maybe this is a bad example, but I've also never seen a whale, yet I know they exist."

"That is a bad example, but I think I get your point. Getting back to my guardian angel, how do you know that I have one?"

"Remember when we were talking, and I told you I thought that maybe it was our destiny to meet here at the lake, our kismet, if you will?"

"Yes. I clearly remember."

"Yeah, I kind of left something out at the time. I didn't feel comfortable enough at that moment to drop this on you because I didn't want to freak you out, but I think that our meeting was the result of actions taken by your guardian angel. There's no other explanation for you and me being here at the same time."

"Okay, let me see if I've got this straight. So, what you're saying is that even though I don't pray or believe in God, nevertheless, God assigned a guardian angel to look after me. The guardian angel knew that I needed someone in my life, so he arranged for you to be here for me when I needed you the most. Right?"

"Exactly."

"Bullshit! That is simply not possible," and she splashed him right in the face.

He couldn't remember having heard her curse before and he couldn't help but start laughing when she said that.

"How am I possibly supposed to believe that nonsense?"

Wiping the water from his eyes, he went on while continuing to laugh, "Well, as they say, God acts in mysterious ways. One of our core beliefs as Catholics is that sometimes God knows what we need before we do. Remember, God is all-knowing. I think God saw you, saw what a beautiful heart you have, knew that you were in pain, and decided to provide you with a means by which to ease that pain. I guess that kind of makes me your pain reliever," he said, laughing even harder now.

"Right. So, what am I supposed to do now, start calling you Tylenol or something?"

He knew he might be getting himself in trouble with this conversation, but he didn't care. It was just too much fun discussing religion with someone who knew absolutely nothing about it. "Let's just stick with Dan for the time being," and she splashed him again. She couldn't escape, though, and he got her right back, splashing her in the eyes.

"Ah! Stop!" and he did. He'd gotten even.

"Okay, when are you going to take me to the church?"

"The best time to go is either late Saturday afternoon or Sunday morning. As this will be the first time you've ever gone to church, I'm going to suggest the late morning Mass on Sunday. That one will be the fanciest, so you'll get the full pageantry of a nice, good Catholic Mass."

"How am I supposed to dress?"

"It's summer time and there are no religious holidays coming up, so you can wear pretty much anything you'd like. The only exceptions are no swimming suits, bikinis, or bare feet. The priests are just happy to see people attending."

"Okay. That sounds easy enough."

"Yeah, it's really easy. Hey, I've got another idea. After church, why don't we go out for lunch before heading back to the cottage? How's that sound?"

"Sounds perfect except for one thing."

"What's that?"

"You haven't said when we're going."

"Good point. Let's check with your grandparents first to make sure they don't have something planned for you that you aren't aware of. Once we know that, then we'll pick a Sunday to go."

"Okay, so that's settled."

"Settled it is. By the way, we haven't even touched on the whole Jesus thing yet."

"Jesus? What about him?"

"Tell you what, Yani. Maybe we better leave that for another time," and she nodded her agreement to that statement.

After confirming with her grandparents that they had no immediate plans to take her anywhere else in the near future, they decided to go on the coming Sunday. Dan would pick her up at 10:30 and the Mass was at 11:00. That would leave them plenty of time to drive down to Watkins, find a good place to park and a seat in the church long before the Mass started. After the Mass concluded, they'd pick a restaurant in Watkins, have lunch there and then head back to the cottage.

Chapter 17

When Dan got up Sunday morning, it was July 16[th,] and there were now about forty-nine days left before she was scheduled to leave. Rather than go with his normal lake uniform of shorts and a tee shirt, he decided that he'd wear his school clothes and put on a button downed short-sleeved shirt along with jeans. As he arrived at the Hartmann's, Yani came bounding out to the car wearing a yellow, pin-striped, collared blouse along with a knee-length white skirt. She was wearing gold earrings, and she had lipstick on. He'd never seen the lipstick before. Plus, her hair had now grown enough that she could put it up in a ponytail. Dan really adored that new look.

"Good morning, Dan."

"Good morning, Yani. You look extra pretty this morning."

"Thank you! I'm feeling pretty." She leaned over, kissed him on the lips, then carefully wiped the lipstick off his mouth with her fingertip.

"Well, that was really nice. Thank you, sweetheart!"

"Oh, you're welcome," she replied, smiling.

"Excellent. All set, honey?"

"Yes! Let's go to the church!" she replied, excitement in her voice.

When they got up to the top of the hill and started heading towards Watkins, Dan turned to her, "Okay, there's a few things you need to know before we get there."

"Like?"

"Catholics are really big on rituals and all these little things we do. For instance, we do this thing called the Sign of the Cross," and he demonstrated it to her. "There are little tiny bowls called fonts that hold water that's been blessed by the priest and is simply called holy water.

When I enter the church, I'll stick a finger in one of these fonts and do the sign of the cross to bless myself. Before we enter the pew to sit down and when we're leaving, we drop to one knee or what's called genuflecting. This is different from the Mass itself where there's times that we kneel on both knees."

"Should I be doing all these things along with you?"

"Well, you certainly can, but you don't have to."

"But if I don't, won't people know that I'm not a Catholic?"

"Yes, but as beautiful as you are, I'm pretty sure you can get away with it." She gave him a grateful smile for the compliment. "Which brings me to another question I just have to ask."

She slowly turned to face him with a look of suspicion. "Am I going to be unhappy with this question?"

"I certainly hope not. Anyway, here goes. What's it like to wake up every morning knowing that you're really beautiful?"

Her delayed response was totally expected and, when she was ready, she sighed, and sadly, the smile disappeared. "Well, I'm pretty sure you know you're not the first person to ask that question."

"Yeah, I kind of figured."

"Okay, here's what I think about your question. I realized at a fairly young age there was something unusual about my appearance. People, men and women, young and old, would stare at me all the time. When I first realized this was happening, it made me really uncomfortable. I thought I was some kind of a freak. I mean, when it's your face you see in the mirror every morning, you kind of take it for granted. I was confused. Was there something wrong with my appearance that I wasn't aware of?"

"So, as the years passed, I started to realize they were staring because, apparently, I'm more attractive than your average girl. I thought that people would eventually stop staring, but it never happened. It makes no difference where I go. People stare at me. I know that lots of the time, they're talking about me, and I'm not stupid. I know it's not just my face and eyes they're talking about. It's also my body. Women are probably thinking it's just not fair that I look this good, and men, well, men are probably thinking something else entirely."

They certainly are, he thought to himself. "We haven't been out together that much in public, but I sense the people staring and whispering all the time. You're definitely not imagining it. I'm convinced they are talking about you."

"Right. So, I decided a while ago that being beautiful certainly beats the alternative of being stared at because you're really ugly. Anyway, it's become my normal. Now, I don't even really pay much attention, with one exception."

"And that would be?"

"I'm no longer a girl. I'm a woman now. There are certain kinds of boys that, when they see me, they get really aggressive and it scares me."

Dan immediately reflected on the day they first met when she asked him not to stare at her. It made perfect sense. She wasn't sure whether Dan was one of those boys she needed to be afraid of or not.

"I mean, it's not even logical. For some bizarre reason, they think that just because I'm hot, I'm going to want to sleep with them, which, come to think of it, might explain why my mom has been telling me since I was fifteen that I'm nothing but a slut," she said, her voice trailing off.

"What?" Dan shouted in response. "Your mom told you to your face that she thinks you're a slut?"

Yani stared at her lap for a second before looking over at him. "I'm sorry, Dan. I shouldn't have told you that."

"Oh, my God, Yani! That is just awful!"

"I know. I know. Forget I said that, okay?"

"How am I supposed to do that? I mean, that's really disturbing that someone's mom would talk to them like that. There has to be a reason. Why would she call you that?"

"I have my theory," she responded with her expressionless face.

"And that would be?"

"Honestly? I think that by the time my mom was my age, she might have already slept with multiple boys."

"Well, that definitely doesn't sound too good, but what does that have to do with you being called a horrible name like that?"

"I think she believes that because she did it, therefore, I must be doing it, too."

"She's projecting."

"Exactly. In her crazed mind, she's one of these people who automatically assumes that any unsavory behavior they're guilty of, everyone else is almost certainly guilty of doing the same thing even though there's never any evidence of it."

"Actually, I've noticed the same thing in other people I know, and I never understood that, but, at the same time, I can't pretend like I didn't just hear those words.

"Well, you're going to have to, Dan, because there's nothing you can do about it. This is my problem, and I'll deal with it! Okay?" she yelled back at him.

"Yeah, right! Okay, Yani. Well, I don't know how someone deals with something like that, but okay," and they drove on in silence while the radio played 'Love Her Madly' by The Doors.

As they were approaching St. Mary's, he turned to her. "I'm sorry, Yani, but there are two more things I need to tell you. We do this thing called Communion. The priest hands out these little, round pieces of flat bread we call a Eucharist, and we eat them. They symbolize the body of Christ. I'll hold out my hands for the priest to place the little wafer in, but you can't have one because you're not Catholic. Those are the rules. So, what you're going to do instead is cross your arms on your chest. That signals to the priest that you won't be taking a wafer. Secondly, you're not supposed to talk out loud during Mass. It's kind of like being at the library. So, if you have questions, just whisper in my ear, and I'll do likewise if I want to tell you something. Okay?"

"Yes."

They were now parked in front of the church. "Alright, let's go," he announced. He walked around to her side of the car, met her there and they climbed up the marble staircase together into the church. Dan immediately spotted the holy water font, stuck a finger in, and performed the sign of the cross as she studied what he was doing. Looking around, he spotted seats that were in the center of the church that would give her a nice bird's eye view of the ceremony. He put his hand on her elbow, directing her to the open pew.

When they got there, Dan directed her in, genuflected, and took his seat next to her. He leaned over to her and whispered, "Okay, I'm going to say a few prayers. You just sit there and relax." He reached for the kneeler, put it down, knelt, did the sign of the cross again and began to

151

pray silently. Once he completed the litany of prayers he liked to go through, he did the sign of the cross one more time and sat back next to Yani, turning and smiling at her. She was so sweet. She returned the smile and immediately took his hand. He leaned to her ear, "Okay, I'm guessing here, but I'm thinking the priest is going to be wearing green today."

They didn't wait long before the organ started playing, the small summer choir started singing the opening hymn, and everyone stood. Many in the congregation sang along, as well. Dan normally would, but he decided he'd just stand there with Yani so that she wouldn't feel awkward. As the first verse was underway, out came the priest along with his two altar boys. Sure enough, he was wearing green vestments. Yani looked at Dan with a little smile and discreetly pointed at the priest, acknowledging his prediction. He smiled back and kind of shrugged his shoulders. "I used to be an altar boy," he whispered. "I'm supposed to know."

The priest called one of the altar boys over with the censer and began spooning incense on top of hot charcoal. It produced a huge smoke cloud that he waved repeatedly at the congregation to help disburse the smoke throughout the church. The Mass then progressed through the opening prayers, the readings, the priest's homily, various hymns, and, finally, preparation for Communion. When it reached Communion time, Dan exited the pew bringing Yani with him, and quietly reminded her to cross her arms. She walked up to the priest with her arms crossed, not really knowing what to expect, and he delivered a full-blown sign of the cross blessing while declaring out loud for the entire congregation to hear, "In nomine Patris et Filii et Spiritus Sancti. Amen." Yani was baffled and had absolutely no idea what to do next. The priest gently took her by the elbow, redirected her back towards her seat and gave Dan his Eucharist.

When Mass ended, they exited the pew. Dan genuflected, of course, and they headed out the way they came in. Typical of many religious services, the priest, reverend, or what have you was standing right outside the main doorway greeting the parishioners as they departed. As Dan and Yani were passing by, the priest spoke directly to them. "Good morning. Good morning. How are you two this glorious Sunday?"

Yani, rarely bashful, responded without hesitation, "We're doing well, Your Honor. How are you?"

"Very well indeed, though please, feel free to call me Father Sullivan."

"Okay, Father Sullivan. Thank you."

"I don't believe I've seen either of you here before. What brings you today?"

"Well, Father Sullivan, I've never been to a church before, and Dan here offered to bring me so I could see what it's like."

"Is that right? Well, we're very glad to have you," he replied, and you could tell by his countenance and the tone of his voice that he really meant it.

At this point, Dan figured he'd better intervene, or this conversation could get off track really quickly.

"Yes, Father, she's never been to a church before, but I've been here many times. Our families have property north of here on Seneca and during summer, this is where we attend Mass."

"Very good, my son. Well, young lady, what did you think of your first-time attending church?"

"It was not at all what I expected. It was really very nice. Quite beautiful, actually. I most definitely enjoyed the experience."

"And I'm certainly pleased to hear that. Thank you so much for coming today. It was a real pleasure having you here and I hope to see you again sometime. Until then, please enjoy the rest of your day."

"Thank you, Father. You, as well," Dan responded while directing Yani away before the conversation could proceed any further.

Safely back in the car and on the way to the restaurant, she turned to him, "Did I screw up or something?"

"Oh, heck no, Yani. Not at all. You did great. I never expected we would end up talking to the priest, but I should have told you ahead of time that you address a Catholic priest as Father and not Your Honor. That's my fault," he told her, laughing a little.

"Sorry."

"No, really. Everything's fine. Priests tend to be really nice people. It's part of the job description. I doubt he was offended, although it may be the first time in his life he was addressed as Your Honor." Dan couldn't help but laugh out loud at the thought of that.

"Hey, don't laugh at me."

"Oh, honey, I'm not laughing at you. I'm laughing at the situation. Let me tell you something. Priests are people, too. They're flesh and blood, just like us. I know darned well he almost certainly stopped us because you're really pretty, and he wanted to meet you. If I was there by myself, he wouldn't have given me the time of day."

"Are you sure?"

"Oh, yeah, but hey, what'd you think of a Catholic Mass? Did you like it, hate it, what?"

"There was really a lot going on. I was surprised: the singing, the smoke stuff, organ blasting, and what was it he said to me up there?"

"Ah, that, sweetheart, was Latin, 'In the name of the Father and the Son and the Holy Spirit, Amen'. You can't imagine how special that was. He actually blessed you while speaking Latin. That's extra special. You'll be filled to the brim with grace for the rest of the day."

"Grace? Okay, what the heck is grace?"

"Grace is what is given to us by God so that we might attain eternal life; it is impossible for us to attain eternal life apart from God's grace, and it is solely due to God's grace that we can be saved and enter into Heaven. It's one of our fundamental beliefs."

"You're going to have to explain that to me in much simpler terms because I have no idea what you just said."

"Don't worry, Yani. We'll save that for another time. Think of it kind of like this. The priest just gave you a whole bunch of God's love that will easily last you for the rest of the day. That's a really nice gift."

"This Catholic religion stuff can be very confusing and complicated."

"Yes, it can. Put it aside for now, though, and let's have lunch."

After eating and while on their way back to the cottage, Dan asked if she had any other questions about the Mass.

"I was surprised how beautiful it was inside with the stained-glass windows, the big stage, and everything."

"Yes. The stage is actually called an altar. It's pretty old, too. I think the original church was built sometime around 1865."

"You mean like back around the time of the civil war?"

"That's my understanding."

"Crazy. And what was that stuff they were burning? It had a really interesting smell that was actually fairly pleasant."

155

"That was incense. They burn it to help carry the prayers of the congregation up to heaven."

"What were you praying about?"

"My prayers? Well, some are standard things like asking God to forgive me for any sins I've committed recently. But there are other things I pray about, too."

"Like what?"

"Let's see. Oh! I said a prayer for you today."

"Tell me what you prayed. Please?" she asked excitedly.

"I asked God to bless you and protect you from harm, both physical and emotional."

"Why would you do that?"

"I told you before. I really, seriously like you. A lot. You now occupy a very special place in my heart, Yani."

"Thank you, Dan. I don't know what to say. I think that's probably the first time anyone has ever said a prayer for me." She actually cried a little bit before gently kissing him.

"If you ask me, Yani, I think it was long overdue."

Chapter 18

Dan was sitting on the front porch staring out at the lake when he heard footsteps on the driveway. Twisting to look over his shoulder, he saw Yani round the corner. "Well, good morning, sugar," he called out cheerfully.

"So, it's sugar now, huh?"

"Yep, and I was just getting ready to come see you."

"Sure you were. Well, I got tired of waiting, so I thought I'd come find you and make certain you haven't been tangling with any dangerous wildlife again."

"Nope. No interactions with dangerous wildlife lately, but haven't you ever heard the expression about good things coming to those who wait?"

"Yes, but I also seem to recall an expression about grabbing the bull by the horns or something."

"Touché," he responded laughing as she stepped up onto the deck, leaned over and carefully kissed him on the lips. "Thank you," he said softly. "That was super nice."

"You're welcome," she replied, gently caressing his head as she sat down next to him.

"So, how's everything down at the Hartmann cottage this morning? Peaceful?"

"Yep. Everything's peaceful. Grandpa's down on the dock doing something with the boat and grandma's busy in the kitchen. I'm guessing she's probably working on lunch already."

"Good deal. So, what are we doing today?"

"What are you asking me for? That's your job."

"Oh, I see. I didn't realize I had new job responsibilities again after quitting my last job at the grocery store," and he paused for a moment to think about it. "Well, I threatened to take you to that state park in Watkins. You interested in checking it out?"

"Sure. That sounds good. You were bragging about how awesome it is. Let's go see."

"You got it," he said while simultaneously glancing down at her feet. "Oh, good. You've already got your sneakers on."

"Well, I was hoping you'd be taking us some place where I might need them, so I came prepared."

"And you are one hundred percent correct in your assumption. It's very likely we'll have to walk through standing water at different points on the park trails. There'll also be a ton of climbing up and down multiple sets of stone stairs. As I told you the other day when we were talking about this, sandals definitely won't do. Anyway, you ready to leave now?"

"Yep."

Standing to leave, he announced, "Okay. Then, let's do this," and off they went.

As they drove along the lake road with the windows down and the radio on, Yani looked over at him, "So, tell me a little about this park we're going to."

"Okay. Well, it's super old, originally opening, I think, sometime in the 1860's, though I believe at first it was a privately owned park. What year New York State bought it, I don't even remember. Doesn't matter. Anyway, I know it's not very creative, but it's simply called Watkins Glen State Park"

"Yeah, they could have come up with something a little catchier. Maybe a good Indian name or something? Those seem to be really popular around here."

"That's a good suggestion. Yes, that would be a lot more interesting, and Indian names are popular around here. Now, you know our little private creek and gorge down at the point?"

"Yes."

"It's exactly the same thing except a million times larger with actual trails you follow and there are three different ones to choose from. We'll take the one that's kind of the medium level of difficulty. The gorge itself is like four hundred feet deep and has about twenty waterfalls and a bunch of cascades. It's not as beautiful as you, but for most people, the first time they visit, they are absolutely spellbound. It's not for the old or weak either, which is probably why your grandparents haven't taken you there. It's hard work ascending and descending through the park and typically way too difficult for seniors."

"Let's see. Oh, there's both a lower and an upper entrance. People sometimes park a vehicle and get dropped off at one end, so they only have to walk one way. We don't have anyone to drive the car for us, so we'll go up and walk back down. You don't want to start at the upper entrance, walk down, and have to walk back up to your car. By the time you did that, you'd be completely exhausted."

"Sounds fascinating. More or less, how long does it take to walk up and back?"

Thinking about that for a second, he responded, "Well, we're young and strong, so probably somewhere between two or three hours, depending on how many other people are on the trail. If it's crowded, which it frequently is, it takes a lot longer. In certain quarters, they say this is one of the top ten most beautiful state parks in America, so don't be surprised if you see a whole bunch of foreign visitors. This place is a really famous tourist attraction, and it's not unusual to see buses pulling up and dropping off loads of tourists."

"Okay, I'll be sure to keep an eye out for those pesky tourists," she responded, laughing. "Is there anything special I need to watch out for when we encounter them?"

"No, I don't think so," Dan replied back while laughing along with her. "Now, we both need to use the restroom before we start because once you get inside the gorge, there ain't no place," he informed her as they drove through the park entrance and up to the kiosk, where he paid the entrance fee.

After hitting the restroom, they headed for the trail, and he turned to her as they walked along. "You know, I just love government bureaucrats. Look at this sign in front of us here. It says there are 832 steps in the park, and they make it sound like it's no big deal. 832 steps? Heck, that's nothing, right? But if you start thinking of it in terms of a staircase, how many steps do you suppose there are per story in a typical building?"

"I don't know, maybe twenty?"

"Yep. That's a pretty good average. So, if you have 832 steps in the park, that's like walking up and then walking back down a forty-story building, and that ain't easy."

"Yikes! That's a real workout."

"For sure, and we'll definitely see people sitting and taking a break as we walk through the park. It can be extremely exhausting. The trick is, slow and easy, baby."

"Slow and easy it is."

"Oh, and one more thing. Watch out for wet spots on the steps. They can be very slippery, and if you go down on the stone, it'll definitely leave a mark."

"Got it!"

"Anyway, as your tour guide today, I've selected the Gorge Trail, which is about two miles long. There's one a mile longer and more difficult, but I don't think it's worth the extra effort. The Gorge Trail puts you as close to the water as possible, so that's the one we're taking. Personally, I also think it's the most beautiful."

"Sounds good to me. So, you're going to feed us afterwards when we're done?"

"For sure. We'll both be ready to eat by the time we finish this little hike," he said nodding. "Okay. Let's get moving," and they started off crossing the Sentry Bridge, followed by the initial challenge of the 120 steps making up the Couch's Staircase, where they came upon their first casualties of the day. It was an old couple, obviously in their seventies, sitting on the low stone wall separating the trail from the sheer cliff of the gorge.

"You okay?" Dan asked the couple as they walked up. The old man was in obvious distress, with bright red cheeks and little beads of sweat on his forehead.

"Yes," responded the woman, a worried look on her face, as the two of them stared up at Dan and Yani. "I think he just needed a minute to catch his breath."

The old man looked at Dan, "My chest feels kind of tight, though, and my left arm hurts," he said weakly.

"Oh, Christ," Dan stated, now serious concern on his face. "You stay right here and do not move!" He turned to Yani with a look of urgency, "Keep an eye on them. I'll be right back."

"Where you going?"

"To find help. I think he's having a heart attack," he called out over his shoulder as he high-tailed it back down the staircase and got the attention of a ranger standing at the base. The ranger immediately got on his radio requesting assistance and the two of them ran back up to the old man.

"Okay, I've got it from here, son," and just as the last syllable left the ranger's mouth, the old man's eyelids fluttered, his head pitched forward, and his chin hit his chest. "You two get out of here. Now!" the ranger barked as he went to work on the old man. Now on the staircase, you could see the emergency personnel hustling towards them at a full gallop.

Turning to Yani, Dan said softly, "We need to go," and they started out again on the trail. Once out of earshot, he turned to her, "You can't fix stupid. An old man like that needs to know his limitations. No way should they be in here trying to walk this park."

"Do you think he's going to be okay?" she asked, a concerned look on her face.

"Hopefully, but it doesn't look real good right now," he said, shrugging his shoulders. They carried on silently up the trail a short distance before turning to look back at the scene they left behind. The old man was now laid out on the stone trail surrounded by medical personnel while the wife stood off to one side, a hand up near her mouth, fingers trembling and eyes glistening. When Yani saw this, it was obvious to Dan that she was becoming upset. He took Yani gently by her arms, turned her to face him and quietly spoke to her. "Look it, Yani. I know this is a real downer, but it's not our fault. We did everything we could to help. He's in good hands now. Okay?"

"Okay," she replied, shaking her head up and down in agreement, a troubled look on her face.

"Good. Smile for me?" She did her best to smile back at him and they began walking again, soon approaching the first major waterfall known as Cavern Cascade.

"Okay, we're going to literally walk behind this waterfall, so get ready to get a little wet."

Hesitating momentarily, "Okay, wait," she said, before she continued walking behind the waterfall. "Ah! It's so cold!" she yelled, shivering slightly as the spray landed against her ankles. "What is it with the water around here that it's always so darned cold?"

"It's coming straight off the top of the mountain," Dan explained laughing. "It's a lot colder up there."

"Okay, stop," she instructed him. "This is actually kind of awesome looking through the backside of a waterfall."

"Yeah, isn't it?"

As they stood there admiring the Cavern Cascade, a group of tourists came out of nowhere and the leading one bumped right into Dan. "Woo!" he exclaimed, staggering to catch his balance.

"Ah, sumimasen! Sumimasen!" the man responded in a shocked voice while nodding repeatedly. As the group passed by between them and the waterfall, Yani reached over, grabbed Dan's hand tightly, and turned to look at him, almost laughing. The men all had Nikon or Canon cameras hanging around their necks that they held against their chests so they wouldn't bounce around, and they all bowed slightly as they walked past. Once the group was gone, the two of them burst out laughing.

"Hey, I told you not to be surprised about the tourists," Dan said, laughing loudly.

"What was that he said to us?"

"I'm not sure, maybe 'excuse me' or something?"

"Well, I'm glad we didn't accidentally collide with them," Yani giggled. "We certainly wouldn't want that to happen."

"No. No, we sure wouldn't want that," he said, shaking his head and grinning. "Come on. Let's go. We've got a lot more ground to cover before we get to the top."

They carried on with their excursion walking through the hand-cut spiral tunnel, under the suspension bridge, and down below Lover's Lane Lookout while moving higher and higher into the gorge. They walked past the Glen Cathedral, the sixty-foot Central Cascade waterfall, followed by Rainbow Falls and Frowning Cliff when Dan came to a halt.

"Let's pause here for a moment. I find this really interesting," he announced.

"Okay," she replied.

Pointing up at the cliffs, Dan stated, "What's so interesting about this to me is that this part of the gorge gets so little sunlight during the course of the year that there's ice on the cliff walls until really late into the spring time and almost nothing grows. I just think that's kind of fascinating."

"And it's really chilly here," she responded, shivering slightly because of the cool air.

"Oh, without a doubt. I'll bet it's probably a good ten degrees cooler here than at the entrance, and it rarely gets warm in here, kind of like Seneca Lake. Anyway, let's keep going."

After walking across the Mile Point stone masonry bridge, they approached the base of Jacob's Ladder. "Okay, Yani. Here's the final big test. 180 steps straight to the top. Ready?"

"Yep. Ready," she said beaming, and up they started on the final stretch. Reaching the top, they paused momentarily to catch their breath. "Man, this place is quite the workout," she offered while bent over with her hands on her knees.

"Yeah, I told you this park is not for the old or weak. Now you know firsthand."

"Okay, so what now?" she asked, straightening up. "We just turn around and head back down?"

"Nope. First, we're going to do this," he said as he pulled her close, giving her a really passionate kiss as they started making out.

When they finally paused, she gazed into his eyes, "Well, that could be a first."

"What could?"

"You initiating the kissing. Normally, I'm the one that has to get things moving."

"Well, we're going to have to do something about that," he replied as he pulled her back to him, and they began making out again. When they had finally satisfied themselves, they turned to gaze back down through the gorge while standing there holding hands.

"I've got to admit it, Dan. This place is really beautiful."

"I'm glad you like it," he replied, squeezing her hand. They stood there for several more minutes admiring the view when he turned to her, "Okay, Yani, now we're going to take what's called the North Rim Trail back to the main entrance. This will give you a different perspective, and it's not as physically challenging or crowded. Actually, it's usually fairly deserted."

"Okay. Sounds good."

As they walked along, out of the corner of his eye, Dan noticed Yani bending down to pick some of the wild flowers growing next to the trail.

"Woo! Yani! Don't touch those, honey!"

She snatched her hand back, stopped, and turned to Dan, a confused look on that stunning face. "What's the problem? Why can't I touch them?"

"Yeah, they're really strict here about picking the flowers or any plants for that matter."

"I don't get it. What's the big deal?"

"Well, think of it this way. You've got thousands of people walking through this park constantly. If they didn't have a rule prohibiting it, after about a week, all of the wild flowers and interesting plants would all be gone."

"I see. Never thought about it like that. Okay, no touching or picking the plants," she responded happily and they started walking along again.

As they continued the trek, Dan glanced up at the sky and the dark clouds that appeared to be forming overhead.

"Hey, Yani?"

"Yeah?"

"I think we may have a problem."

"What do you mean?"

Dan pointed up at the sky, and she looked in the direction he was pointing.

"Are those what I think they are?"

"Yep. I think we're about to get wet."

"Oh, great."

"Come on," he shouted as he started jogging and she immediately picked up the pace, following in his footsteps. "There's a shelter up ahead at Lover's Lane Lookout. With any luck, we can reach it before it starts raining." At about the same time they could clearly make out the shelter ahead in the distance, they felt the first rain drops. That was followed immediately by an incredibly strong wind gust from the leading edge of the thunderstorm, causing Yani to stumble and knocking her to the ground. As he helped her to her feet, he hollered, "Run!" and they both sprinted as fast as they could along the narrow trail towards the shelter up ahead.

With a half dozen steps to go, the skies began to open up. Bursting into the shelter now dripping wet, down came the rain pounding onto the shelter's rooftop while a huge bolt of lightning struck just a short distance away. The crack and deafening boom of the thunder causing the two to flinch and cower in response.

"Damn! That was close," she said as they straightened back up with their bodies now touching.

"Yeah, way too close if you ask me," he responded while pulling her to him as they started making out again. Totally isolated from the rest of the tourists, they made out for a really long time until they finally stopped and he looked at his beautiful girlfriend. "God, you are wonderful."

"You're not too bad yourself, Daniel," she replied back with this very satisfied look on her face as she stroked his wet, blonde hair.

"Thank you, sweetheart." They stood there together, holding hands for several more minutes before Dan finally announced, "Fortunately, this feels like the kind of storm that won't last."

"Well, I can think of worse places to be stuck besides Lover's Lane," she said softly as she leaned up and kissed him one more time.

"That was so sweet," he replied, smiling while staring at that gorgeous face. As he had predicted, the storm didn't last long at all and when the raindrops finally stopped, they started walking again towards the main entrance and their car.

"Dan! Look it!" she exclaimed, while pointing out across the valley.

"Holy cow! A rainbow and it's a beauty!"

"Yeah, you can see all the colors perfectly. Awesome!"

"Yep. It's almost perfect. Just not quite as perfect as you, my dear," he replied as they strolled along and she responded to his remark with that big, beaming smile of hers.

"So, Yani, what do you think of your visit to Watkins Glen State Park?" he asked as they continued strolling along together.

She paused for a second before answering and, looking deep into his eyes, she said, "It's absolutely spellbinding." And so are you, Yani. And so are you, he thought to himself staring right back at her.

Chapter 19

One of the things the Finger Lakes Region is not known for is great weather. He had no idea if it was actually true or not, but Dan heard a story once that Rod Serling of The Twilight Zone fame had seriously considered making the Ithaca area on Cayuga Lake a kind of Hollywood East. However, after they calculated the annual average number of sunny days that they'd have available for filming, that was the end of that idea. So, when a day like this particular day came along, hot, bright sunshine, but with very low humidity, you simply couldn't waste the opportunity to be outdoors. In a word, the weather was spectacular and the two of them were taking full advantage, relaxing in the rowboat anchored well out past the end of the dock with the radio tuned to their favorite station playing off in the distance.

Laying directly across from him in the boat was the equally spectacular Yani just staring at him with those hypnotic blue eyes, not even blinking, just staring. After some time had passed, she finally began speaking quietly. "You know, you've got me doing things I could never even imagine. You're constantly taking me places and showing me things that are really interesting and mentally stimulating. You teach me all kinds of new stuff. Seems like every day is different, and I have no idea what kind of surprise I'm in for next. You're always so kind to me and you never make me cry."

"Oh, come on, Yani! Please stop. Don't do this."

"Don't interrupt me, Dan," she countered, her face devoid of all expression. "You never have a harsh word or raise your voice to me. About the only thing you haven't done is promise me babies." After that statement came a long, pregnant pause. "Dan?"

Oh, no, he immediately thought. I know that tone of voice. She's getting ready to drop another shoe. "Yes," he responded carefully to her prompt.

"Dan," she paused again. "I want to thank you from the bottom of my heart."

There she goes again, thanking me. Why does she always have to do that, he thought with great exasperation, shaking his head from side to side. "Thank me for what, Yani? I'm really confused, honey."

She stared back at him with that expressionless face he'd seen so many times before. "For being here for me. I don't know what I would have done this summer if it hadn't been for you. I think I would have probably gone crazy from loneliness. Who knows? Maybe you saved my life."

"Okay, wait a minute. You make me sound like I'm some kind of an angel or something, and I can absolutely assure you, I'm definitely not one of those."

"Hey, you're the one that brought the whole guardian angel thing into this. Before I met you, I'd never even heard of them."

"Yani, honey, that's really sweet of you to say that and it certainly means a lot to me, but I am not your guardian angel. Yes, I said I think our guardian angels intervened on our behalf, but it's not like I didn't get anything out of this deal. Quite frankly, I consider myself the lucky one in this arrangement. I should probably be thanking you and I really mean that. Tell you what. Let's just call it even. Okay? Let's just call a truce on who's benefiting the most."

"Stop. That's total nonsense. You could just as easily be hanging out with your friends back in Elmira. For me? You're it. There is no one else. If it wasn't for you and you sharing your life with me, I'd be living here like a hermit and probably losing my mind in the depths of depression."

"Okay, fine. Have it your way. You are most welcome, but the pleasure really is all mine," he replied reassuringly as he reached over to touch her. She gave him a big, warm smile in return and he could see the love in her eyes.

As she reached out her hand to meet his, he saw her eyes dart sideways from some kind of a distraction off in the distance when she violently lurched up on the bench seat of the boat. The color drained from her face, her blue eyes went wide, and he could see her mouth form the words, 'Oh, my God'.

Leaning forward towards him, she shouted, "Dan, we've got to go! Now! Now!"

"Wait. Why? What's wrong?" he responded while spinning around to look behind him at whatever she was staring at, trying to see what the emergency was.

Pointing up the hill, she responded with shock in her voice, "My parents are pulling in. I just saw their car coming down the hill. Quick! You've got to take me in. If my mom sees me with you, she's liable to think I'm actually happy here, and then she'll force me to go home with them."

Dan jumped up from his seat and immediately started hauling in the anchor not even bothering to coil the rope.

"Okay. Go! Go! Take me in!" He started rowing as fast as he could towards shore when all of a sudden, he just stopped for no apparent reason. "What are you doing? Come on, man! Move it before I get caught!"

"Hold on a second, Yani. I've got an idea." Pointing up at his place and speaking with a measured calm, "If your mom sees you walking

171

down that road from my cottage, she's going to start asking questions, and you're going to have to lie or tell her the truth. If she catches you lying, you're dead meat. If you tell her the truth, it's just as bad. Right?" She shook her head in agreement. "So, here's what we're going to do instead. I'm going to row you down to your grandparents," he explained, pointing in that direction, "and you're going to climb up the swim ladder right up onto the dock. That way, maybe you can at least fool your mom into thinking you've been there the whole time. Okay?"

"Okay, brilliant. Now move it before I get caught!" and off he headed towards the Hartmann's dock. Yani buried her face in her hands. "It simply can't end this way," she sobbed, the anguish in her voice pronounced. "It simply can't end like this."

As he rowed along, he spoke softly but sternly to her. "Yani, honey, I know this is going to be hard for you, but you've got to suck it up. No fighting. No arguing. Don't give her any reason at all to force you to go home. Just be humble and cooperative. Hell, if it's necessary, just bite your damned tongue and pretend you're happy to see her. Please?"

"Okay, I promise you. I'll do my best."

Gliding up to the dock, Dan navigated the boat right up next to the ladder. Yani reached over, grabbed onto the ladder railing, stepped directly onto a rung and scrambled right up onto the dock.

"Atta girl," he remarked, and she turned around and gave him a thumbs up. "Good luck, sweetheart," Dan said quietly, so as not to be overheard. She responded by blowing him a kiss, then spun around to face the cottage.

Just as the rowboat drifted out of view of Hartmann's property, Dan heard her mom calling out.

"Yani!"

"Oh, hi, Mom! Gosh! What a nice surprise! Hold on. I'll be right up."

He took his time going back to his place. Once he arrived, he carefully coiled up the anchor rope and stowed it along with the oars. While he worked, he considered the situation. Estimating that the drive from Youngstown had to be the better part of five hours, there was almost certainly no way her parents were going to turn right back around and drive home today. That meant they were here for at least one night and possibly two.

Analyzing the situation, he thought to himself, well, if that's the case, the soonest they'll go back would be tomorrow afternoon or early evening. If they stay two nights, they'd probably leave to go back right after breakfast or lunch the following day, but Yani said they hated coming here, so it's more than likely they'll go home early tomorrow evening. Okay, now he knew what he was going to do.

Concluding that they couldn't be together, there was no point hanging around the cottage alone so he'd head back to Elmira and come back up tomorrow around supper time. If the parents were gone, and assuming she was still here, great. Things would be back to normal for the two of them. If not, they would be leaving the next day at the latest anyway, so he wouldn't have to wait long to find out what his fate was. Either way, they'd be gone, and she would still be here, or she wouldn't, and he'd have to cross that bridge when he came to it. If there was a bright side to all of this, he wouldn't suffer long before learning his fate.

As planned, he drove back up to the cottage the next day so that he arrived around supper time. He figured that it was probably too risky to just walk down to the Hartmann's to see what was happening, so he decided a little old-fashioned reconnaissance was in order. He got the boat out and motored down past the Hartmann place, making sure to stay well off-shore. There they were: five people out on the deck, and it looked like they were having a cookout. As there were only five, that meant Yani's sisters were back in Youngstown. They were old enough to be left alone for a little while, but her parents couldn't leave them alone for too long. For sure, they'd be heading home tomorrow sometime.

Right now, things looked pretty peaceful and he certainly hoped it continued to stay that way. As he swung the boat around in a big, wide loop and headed back to his place, he saw Yani turn and stare directly at him. She didn't wave, but he never expected her to. She knew it was him and that he was driving by to check on her. She was just making sure that he knew she saw him. Right now, everything looked calm, and that's the best he could hope for under the circumstances. Now, the waiting began in earnest.

The next day, right after they'd finished lunch, Yani's parents loaded up the car, goodbyes were said all around, and off they went on the long drive back to Youngstown, just the two of them. About five minutes after they were gone, Yani came popping out of her grandparent's cottage and started heading towards Dan's place, an obvious bounce in her step.

"Hey!"

She spun around to face the direction the voice came from, and out from the shadows of the trees stepped Dan.

"How long have you been waiting there?" she asked, as she slowly made her way towards him a smile gradually forming on her face. He just shrugged his shoulders not saying anything as she continued her advance. "And why exactly are you lurking about in the shadows outside our cottage?"

"I think we both know your mom probably wouldn't have allowed you to come down to say goodbye if she was taking you home."

174

"Probably so," she responded, while nodding her head in agreement with that statement.

"Yeah, well, I figured if that were the case, the best I could hope for was to at least get one final glimpse of you from a distance and, hopefully, burn the imagine of your beautiful face permanently into my brain," he hesitated, "And that, my dear, is why I'm standing here."

"Is that right? Well, as you can plainly see, they're gone, but I'm still here."

"And you can only imagine how happy I am to see that."

As she finished walking up to him, she put her arms around his neck and simply stood there studying his face for a moment. "Here. Let me show you just how happy I am," and, with that, she kissed him with all the passion she possessed. Once finished, she stared back at him again. "There. Now that that's been taken care of, interested in going for a walk?"

"Yes. Let's go down to the point."

"Yes, let's, and I'll tell you all about their creepy little surprise visit."

"Perfect."

Chapter 20

They started the short trip to the point, walking beneath the hardwood tree canopy lining the cottage road and through the shadows it created. Reaching out with his hand, she responded by spontaneously taking hold. "Man, I was freaking out, Yani. I thought for sure she was going to make you go home and I'd never see you again."

"You think you were freaking out? I thought I was going to have a heart attack when I saw that car coming down the hill. By the way, dropping me off at my grandparents' dock was pure genius and I mean that sincerely. My mom never even suspected for one second that I might have been out in the boat with you or any place else, for that matter. She was totally fooled and never questioned anything."

"Yeah, but what about your grandparents? Weren't you afraid they might blow your cover?"

"You know, I've come to the conclusion that I don't think they're even aware of where I'm at half the time. I come, and I go, and they don't even ask me where I've been or where I'm going. I don't know what to think, but no, they didn't blow my cover. In fact, they didn't even mention your name the entire time my folks were here," she stated, nodding her head for emphasis as they continued down to the point.

"That is truly fascinating. I thought at some point my name would definitely come up during a conversation."

"Not even once."

"I think they're protecting you."

"Wait. You think what?"

"I think the reason your grandparents didn't bring up my name is because they know if they do, your mom will start asking questions, and that can only lead to a bad outcome for you. Knowing your grandparents, I'm pretty sure that's the last thing they want to have happen."

"That never occurred to me, but you know what? I think you might be right. That's incredible to think that they would do that for me."

"Well, you've told me multiple times that they love you. So, what about the visit itself? Do you know if they told your grandparents they were coming?"

"Well, I haven't asked, but based on the reaction of my grandparents, I think the answer to that is a resounding 'no.' I think they just decided to come up here to check on me. Kind of a spur-of-the-moment thing, or maybe not knowing Mom. With her, it could have easily been premeditated."

"Yeah, agreed, but to check on you for what?" he asked with a puzzled expression.

"Your guess would be as good as mine. With my mom, it's impossible to say. It could be something as mean-spirited as her wanting to see me suffering firsthand to enjoy the pain and anguish I'm going through, or maybe she just wanted to see if I would be totally subservient and beg her to take me home. Either one is a distinct possibility, and neither one is out of the realm of possibilities."

"Crazy. Absolutely crazy," he replied as they reached the bottom of the hill. "On the bright side, though, it looks like you're going to be able to spend the rest of the summer here."

"I'd say you are most definitely correct about that, Daniel. I can't think of another circumstance under which they'd come back again except maybe if I was deathly ill, one of my grandparents had to go to the hospital, or something as catastrophic as that. I think she saw what she wanted to see, and that's that. I'm guessing that the next time I'll see them is when they come back to pick me up to take me home."

"So, what did you guys talk about for the better part of two whole days?"

"Nothing really significant. It was mostly just idle chit chat and nothing even close to being important."

"Did you ask about your sisters?"

"I did! My folks said that they're fine and just kind of hanging out this summer, not really doing much of anything."

"Did they even ask you what you've been doing to stay busy here at the cottage?"

"A little, though I wasn't really expecting them to. They never really show much interest in my life outside of my schoolwork. I don't actually know why. That's just kind of the way it's always been. They just sort of seem to take everything for granted."

"Okay. Well, the whole episode is still really strange, but fair enough. Hey, sit on the dock?" he asked, motioning towards it.

"Sure," and they walked out to the end and took their seats in silence with their feet dangling in the water as they stared out across the lake.

After more than a few minutes had passed, Dan looked at her, "Yani, you hear anything?" as he turned to face up the hill behind them.

"No. Why? You hear something?"

"Yeah, but I'm not sure what. It kind of sounds like a car engine, but there's something different about it, and it's definitely not a truck or motorcycle," he responded as he kept staring up the hill, trying to figure out what it was. Concentrating carefully, he turned to her, "I'm not sure exactly what it is, but it sounds like it might be coming this way."

"You know, I hear something now, too, but it does sound kind of strange."

"Tell you what, let's walk back onto shore just in case," he stated as he stood and helped her up.

"You think they're coming this way?"

"Maybe, and this is private property. We aren't actually supposed to be here, so if it is the owners, who knows how they'll react."

"Well, what do you think we should do? You want to walk back up?"

"If they're coming down here, we can't walk back up. There's no way to do that in time without being seen. The only way up is the road, and we'd be marching straight into them. Let's go over by the creek. We can wait there and see," he replied, leading her in that direction. As soon as they reached the creek bank, he turned to her and, in a hushed voice said, "Whatever it is, it's definitely coming this way. Hop down in the creek with me. We'll hide behind the bank. If necessary, we can walk further in and hide inside the gorge."

He led and she followed with Dan assisting so she didn't lose her balance as she climbed down through the loose shale. Now huddled and waiting behind the creek bank, the strange engine noise continued to get louder and more pronounced. Finally, as they peeked over the bank of the creek, an alien-looking vehicle began to appear from around the bend in the road and through the tree line as it made its way down the hill toward the lake shore.

"What the heck is that?" she whispered.

"I have absolutely no idea," Dan whispered back in response. "It looks like some kind of a car, but what kind? I have no clue," and they continued to watch in silence. Once in full view, they could see it was some kind of an unfamiliar car model that was a powder blue colored convertible. The top was down, and a middle-aged couple were its occupants. It had a front end that looked like no other automotive front end they had ever seen and a back end that was equally unique and different.

The front end reminded Dan of a duck bill platypus, the bottom of which sloped down and back towards the front wheels. The vehicle appeared to be about the same overall size as the British sports cars he'd seen driving around Elmira, but it sat much higher off the ground. There was no grill at all, just smooth, painted metal, and it had two really small doors for the passengers. The back end of the car had fins like models from the 50's, and it had this tall light stanchion mounted on top of one of the rear fenders. The front bumper didn't appear to be a bumper at all. It was just a simple round chrome bar that extended from one side to the other, and the rear bumpers were two vertical chrome loops.

The couple were talking and laughing, the radio was playing music, and it seemed like they had no idea they were even being watched. It also appeared they were on some kind of a mission of their own. Amazingly, they continued driving straight towards the shore line, and while they weren't going fast, they gave no indication of stopping. Dan looked at Yani and she just shrugged her shoulders. As the strange car had now made its way past their location, the two of them raised their heads up over the bank to get a better look.

"Oh, my God. I think I might know what that is," Dan said with excitement in his whispered voice. "I think that's what they call an AquaCar. No, wait. That's not quite right. It's something else," he mumbled with his eyes squinting in serious concentration. "I know! I think it's what they call an Amphicar!"

"What the heck is an Amphicar?" she asked with a puzzled look.

"I don't actually know. I've only heard about them. If I'm right, we'll both know in a second, though. Come on," and he climbed up the bank and out of the creek to watch, helping Yani to follow. Sure enough, the vehicle continued straight to the water's edge. As it reached the lake, the driver slowed down even more, and Dan could hear him shifting gears. Underneath the rear of the car, you could now see twin propellers on the rear of the car that had begun to rotate. The driver eased the vehicle forward into the water and, amazingly, off it went right out into the lake.

Once it was fully out on the water, the lady sitting in the passenger's seat threw her head back, both arms in the air, and you could hear her yell, "Whee!" The two of them just stood there staring with their mouths hanging open as the car continued further and further out onto the lake. After a few minutes, it eventually just disappeared over the horizon, heading in the general direction of Geneva.

"That is totally nuts, Yani."

"Unbelievable!" was all that came out of her.

"That is a damned car, and they are out there in six hundred feet deep water driving it like they don't have a care in the world. I didn't even see any lifejackets on them."

"That is so cool! I can't believe it!" she replied, staring out where the Amphicar had been just moments earlier.

"I'm not even sure I'd have the guts to ride in that thing."

"Oh, come on, Dan. That is so awesome. You'd do it in a second."

"Well, maybe, but I don't know."

"Do you know those people? Are they the owners?"

"Never seen them in my life, and they definitely aren't the owners. The owners are farmers, and those people certainly aren't farmers. The strange thing is that this is a private road. How would they know that they could drive down here and there'd be a shore line that would allow them to launch their boat car? Somehow, they must know the owners because they had to have prior knowledge about this road. That's the only way they could know. Almost no one knows the road leading down from the highway dead ends here. Someone had to have told them in advance."

They stood there staring for the longest time, and finally, she turned to him, "Hey, I want to wait to see if it comes back. I want to see how they get out of the lake. You okay if we wait?"

"Of course. Why not? Let's go wait out on the dock until it comes back," and they did. They waited and waited, but there was no sign of the Amphicar. Eventually, Dan turned to her, "Well, I'm starting to think they aren't coming back this way. I don't know where they would have gotten out, but I guess they found some place else to drive their boat car out of the lake. That sucks because I wanted to see it, too, though I think I may know why."

"And that would be?"

"I don't know much about these AmphiCars, but I've heard they have really small engines."

"Why would they do that?"

"Engines are extremely heavy. I'm guessing they probably had to use a small engine so the stupid thing would float. Sinking would definitely be bad for sales. Anyway, the road leading down here is super steep, and the only vehicles I've ever seen drive up are full-size pickup trucks, usually four-wheelers. I'm figuring that they knew that and already had plans to drive out somewhere else cause their engine isn't powerful enough to pull them up the hill."

"Okay, that makes sense. That small engine would also explain why the car sounds so weird."

"Good point, Yani. I'm sure you're right about that. So, what do you think? Head back up?"

"Yeah, I suppose we can leave. Besides, we can watch for it up top, and if they show up, we should be able to hustle back to the point in time to see them drive out."

"I agree. Okay, let's go," and they stood to leave.

"Man, I have some of the most amazing and bizarre experiences with you, Dan."

"Yeah, I kind of noticed that myself," he replied as they began the walk back up to the cottages. "By the way, you up for a bonfire tonight?"

"Sure. Sounds wonderful."

"Awesome. Okay, it's settled."

Chapter 21

The bonfire was just kicking into gear when Yani walked up, appearing out of the darkness like some kind of a beautiful apparition. "Hey, baby," he called to her as she approached. She didn't speak. She just glided up to him, took his face in her hands, and kissed him passionately.

"Good evening, Dan," she said softly while staring into his eyes. "I missed you."

"I can tell," he replied as he hugged her tightly against his body while returning the smile. "Care to sit?" She just nodded her response, so he took her by the hand and led her to the firepit.

"When I was walking up, I was looking at your fire. Am I imagining things, or is this the most beautiful fire you've built this summer? The sparks, the little explosions, the smell of the wood smoke; it really is quite lovely."

"I think the evening has a lot to do with that. I'm sure you noticed there's no moon tonight, and it's getting pitch black out. Add to that the fact that we're out in the country, and it makes it exceptionally dark, which, in turn, makes the fire appear exceptionally bright. That's probably what you're noticing. I mean, look at the sky tonight. It's nothing but stars."

"It really is amazing how many there are that you never actually see living in the city. It's impossible to count them all," she said while pointing up at the sky. "Oh, look! A meteor!"

"We should see lots of those this evening. It is a starry, starry night."

"By the way, what's up with your folks these days, Dan? They haven't been coming up much and you never mention them," she asked, a curious look on her face.

184

"I guess everything's okay. You know I spend most of my time up here, so it's not like I talk to them much these days. They seem to be fine; just busy looking after the house along with my siblings, I guess. I know my mom wishes I was around more. As for my dad, we get along just fine other than one thing he does that really irritates me."

"And what is it you find so irritating?"

"Well, we'll be sitting around the house, and out of the clear, blue sky, he'll ask me what I'm thinking about at that very moment. To me, it seems rather strange to ask somebody that, and it's probably why I find it so darned irritating."

"That does seem a little awkward and he just does it like from out of nowhere?"

"Yep. We'll just be sitting there. He'll turn to me and, for no apparent reason, ask me that weird question."

"So, how do you respond when he does that?"

"I just blow it off and don't answer. But you know what I really want to do when he asks me that?" he replied grinning.

"Tell me."

"Well, as I've explained before, my dad is a really conservative and religious man. I'm certain my mom is the only woman he's ever slept with. So, what I really want to tell him is that I'm thinking about some girl he knows from school wondering how I can get in her pants."

"Well, why don't you?" she asked, laughing out loud at the thought of that.

"My dad's a good guy. I know he doesn't mean any harm. Plus, I don't want to offend him. But I guarantee that if I answered him that way, he'd never ask that question again."

"And I'll bet you'd be right about that." After making that statement, she unexpectedly fell silent. Several minutes passed before she looked at him again. "Dan?"

Uh oh, he thought to himself. There's that tone again. She's going to ask me something that's really uncomfortable. "What's that, sugar?" he answered as he put his arm around her and pulled her close.

"Do you ever think about making love with me?" she asked, staring deep into his eyes.

He just about choked when he heard those words but gathered himself and responded, "Yani, I'd be lying if I said it had never crossed my mind."

"Well…I want you to make love to me, Dan."

"Wo! Hold on here a second!" he responded, shocked by her bluntness while at the same time leaning away from her, unconsciously trying to create distance between them. "You can only imagine how happy and excited that makes me feel to hear you say you want to be my lover, but it actually sounds like a really scary idea."

"Well, thanks for nothing!" she responded indignantly. "You just got done telling me that you've thought about making love with me. Now, I'm offering you the opportunity to do just that and you respond by telling me it's a scary idea? What am I supposed to think about that? Besides, I want to be your lover. It's not like I need any convincing!" she scolded him as she threw his hand aside. Now she was really angry.

"Hey, easy. Please. Calm down, honey. I'm sorry, but what about the really obvious, like maybe you getting pregnant."

"Yeah, well, about that," she said while staring down into her lap, the volume of her voice having dropped dramatically. "I haven't exactly told you everything."

"Oh, God. Go on," he replied shaking his head in frustration. With Yani, there always seemed to be more to the story.

"Right," she sighed before continuing. "So, ever since I turned fourteen and started looking like this," she said while gesturing at her body with her hands, "My mom was convinced that I was sleeping with every member of the football and basketball teams, so she put me on birth control pills."

"I see," was all he said quietly in response.

"Anyway, after she left from her recent surprise visit, I found a fresh supply of pills in my dresser drawer. She must have slipped them in there when no one was looking. Apparently, she thinks so little of me that she figured I was probably sleeping with every farm boy in the county and that I'd be needing them. So, getting pregnant is not going to happen."

"And I appreciate you sharing that with me, but what about the other part? What about falling in love, Yani? We've already grown extremely close. You know darned well that if we become lovers, that's exactly what's going to happen. And after that? You'll be leaving come the end of summer. What do we do after that? Pretend like it never even happened? I'm in love with you. You're in love with me and we're ripped apart. How are we supposed to deal with that?"

"I've already thought about this a lot, Dan, and I don't care. I've never slept with a boy and I want you to be the first. As for the falling in love part, it's too late, Dan. I'm already in love with you. You're probably the best thing that's ever happened to me. Please don't do this to me, Dan. Do not reject me. I need you to make love to me," she said with as stern a voice as he'd heard out of her since she scolded him for staring at her the day they first met. She closed her eyes, leaned in, and kissed him really passionately. "There. It's settled," she whispered. "You're coming with me."

187

She stood while taking his hand and began to lead him away from the bonfire. He didn't resist and instinctively headed in the direction of the cottage, but she immediately stopped him. "No. Under the stars down on the dock," she whispered, while touching his cheek. He reversed direction and they made their way to the stairs leading down to the dock assembly. Looking up and down the shore line for the presence of outdoor lights and seeing none, he knew that everyone in the community was inside for the evening. They would be alone.

When they got down to the dock, Dan grabbed two sleeping bags from the boathouse, spreading them out on top of each other for their makeshift bed. Yani stepped onto the sleeping bags and peeled off her top, her bra, and her shorts, but left her panties on. Removing those would be Dan's responsibility. She laid down on their makeshift bed and motioned for him to join her. He slowly stripped his clothes off, laid down next to her, and they immediately embraced.

With the waves lapping gently against the cliff, providing a rhythmic backdrop, they began the process of exploring each other's bodies. They took their time. There was no urgency, no risk of being caught. No one spoke. They were alone, falling desperately in love and enjoying every minute of it. As the bonfire began to burn down and the light up above diminished, they found their own rhythm. God, she feels, tastes, and smells just perfect. She is just so sensuous, was all he could think to himself. They worked their way towards climax under that night sky with meteors streaking back and forth and the waves on the lake lapping against the cliff. She wrapped her arms around him and clenched him as tight as she possibly could until the feeling subsided. They were spent, but completely satisfied. It was an incredibly beautiful experience for both of them.

As they lay there waiting for their heart rates to return to normal and clinging to each other, she pulled his head closer and whispered in his ear, "That was absolutely wonderful, but I knew it would be. Thank you, Dan."

His immediate response was, "No, thank you, sweetheart. That was really special," though, in his mind, he was thinking, why, the hell, does this girl always have to thank me when, I swear, I'm getting the better end of this deal? They continued to lay there, alternating between looking into each other's eyes and staring at the canvas of stars and little meteors flashing overhead. After some time, Dan whispered, "Wait here. I'll be right back." He retrieved a beach towel from the boathouse and came back out. "Come on," he said quietly, extending a hand to help her up. "Let's hop in the lake and rinse off," and she did as he suggested. The water felt absolutely wonderful, and once dressed, they made their way back up to the bonfire, where Dan tossed on one final log for the evening.

They sat there for the longest time holding hands, making out and watching the fire burn down when, out of nowhere, Yani turned to him. She leaned into his ear, and whispered, "Again, please."

He stood up, pulling her to him, and whispered in reply, "Your wish is my command."

After they had finished making love a second time and returned to the firepit, Yani turned to him and asked, "You didn't get to see all those meteors flashing overhead, did you?"

"No, I was kind of busy at the moment," he said, laughing quietly. "I knew something had happened because I did see the night sky light up a couple of times, but I didn't actually get to see it."

"It was truly magnificent, Dan. I felt like I was living a dream; you making love to me, meteors flashing overhead. It was a very special evening. It's almost like it was some kind of a sign or something."

"I think it was a sign from God."

"Maybe so, Dan. Maybe so."

"Yani, sweetheart?"

"Yes, Dan?"

"I love you."

"I know you do. I've sensed that for a really long time. I love you, too, Dan. Very much so. You make me really happy," then she paused, wrapping her arms around him and kissing him with tremendous affection. "Now, as much as I hate to say it because I really don't want the evening to end, but I guess you better walk me home."

"Okay. I really don't want to either but, you ready?"

"Unfortunately, yes." They stood up together and began the slow walk back to her place. There was no urgency. They could take their time. They were in love and enjoying every second of it as they walked along beneath the starry sky.

Chapter 22

The following evening, as they sat outside while Dan jabbed at the bonfire with his official fire-poking stick he kept next to the wood pile, he announced quietly, "Yani, I've got something I want to run past you."

"Is it something that's going to upset me or make me cry?"

"No, angel. It's not going to do that."

"Okay, well, go ahead. What's on your mind?"

"So, what happens after this is all over and summer has ended? What if I want to try and come see you? How am I going to do that?"

"I'm not sure. Of course, I've thought about it, too. Youngstown is so far from Elmira, Dan. It seems like visiting each other, the cost of long-distance phone calls, and maintaining that kind of long-distance relationship is almost out of the question."

"Agreed, but the key word you just used there is 'almost.' Difficult? Yes. Impossible? No. No, it's not impossible, not if we really want to."

"Well, for starters, of course, I'll give you my address and home phone number, so at least you'll have that."

"And I'm going to want those for sure before you leave."

She sat there looking at him for a long moment before asking, "You've got something else in mind, don't you, Dan?"

"Actually, I do."

"Okay, Daniel. Talk to me. What's going on?"

He turned to face her and told her exactly what he was thinking. "Yani, honey, I want to make a run to Youngstown to see your home, to see where you grew up."

"What! Are you dumb or stupid? That's a four-and-a-half-hour drive each way! How are we possibly going to do that?"

"Oh, I'm well aware of the drive time, but I've been thinking about this a lot. Having your address is one thing, but sometimes, tracking down an address isn't as easy as it sounds. I want to actually go to your house. I want to see with my own eyes exactly where you live so in the future, there won't be any issues in terms of finding it, which I hope I'll have a real need to do."

"I see," was her only response as she reached over and took his hand.

He turned to her, smiled, and said, "I love the way your hand fits perfectly into mine." She smiled back at him and squeezed firmly. Both of them just sat there staring at the fire for several minutes before Yani finally broke the silence.

"Okay, Dan. Actually, I really would like to see my sisters, so I'm willing to give it a try. What's your plan?" she asked with complete frankness. "Assuming we do it, how do we pull this off?"

"Right. Here's the way I see it. For starters, we have to be back here not much later than eight o'clock because that's when it gets dark. You know I'm not allowed to drive after dark, so we have to work backwards from there. As you've pointed out, it takes about four and a half hours each way, so that's nine hours of total driving time. If we leave at eight o'clock in the morning, that gives us three hours of what I'll call open time. We'll need some of that for things like stopping to use the bathroom, eating, refueling the car, things like that, but that still leaves us plenty of time to go to your house."

"What about my parents? What do we tell them? We just magically show up unannounced?"

"We don't tell them anything. They both work, right?"

"Yes."

"Do they come home for lunch, or do they eat at work?"

"They eat at work. I've never once seen them come home for lunch."

"Okay, so we go on a weekday when we won't even see them. That way, it's extremely unlikely that we'll accidentally bump into them. As you'll recall, they didn't give you any advance notice when they showed up here unannounced with questionable intentions. I don't think you owe them anything. Now, what about your sisters?"

"They'll be home alone. They're plenty old enough now that they don't need a babysitter during the day. They take care of themselves."

"Can they be trusted to keep their mouth shut?"

"What do you mean?"

"Can you trust them not to tell your parents you came home, because if your mom finds out we came and left without seeing her, she's going to be furious."

Yani was silent for a moment while she thought about this and finally replied, "Yes. I believe I can trust them to keep their mouth shut and not tell my folks, but what about my grandparents? I can't be gone for twelve hours and not provide them with some kind of explanation in advance as to where I'm going."

"And I think I may have a potential solution for that."

"Go on."

"We'll tell them I'm taking you to New York City."

"Oh, my God! There you go again, being dumb and stupid!"

"No, seriously. New York City is about four and a half hours east of here. It's the same amount of driving time. We can ask your grandparents for permission to take you to New York for the day just so you can see it; a once-in-a-lifetime opportunity, if you will. We tell them we plan to go on a week day so there's less traffic and fewer tourists making it easier to do. Less hassle, you know? If we're careful how we approach them, I think there's a pretty good chance they'll say yes."

"So, we tell them we're going to New York when in reality we're going to Youngstown. We do this on a weekday when my parents won't be home so we don't get caught in the act, and we leave first thing in the morning so we can be home by dark. Huh!" she stated while looking at him. "It sounds totally insane, Dan, but you know what? I think it might actually work."

"That's what I'm thinking, though there's still a lot of details to be worked out," he replied, nodding his head. They both went silent again and simply stared into the flames while their brains started problem-solving and planning for their clandestine road trip. For the next several days, if they weren't cruising out on the lake or involved in other types of lake activities, they were working out their plans for the trip.

First of all, they'd need road maps. Dan had one for New York in the glovebox of the car, but that meant they still needed maps for Pennsylvania and Ohio. Those were easy to come by, though. Any decent gas station would have maps, and they were inexpensive. They had to decide what they were going to do for food. Sure, they could have breakfast before they left, but they couldn't go all day without eating. What about lunch and supper? Do they make a picnic basket and take lunch with them, stop at a diner, or a combination of both? Do they wait until they're back at the cottage and have supper in the evening, or eat on the road? What about beverages? They're bound to get thirsty.

Dan estimated that they would need to stop for gas at least once for sure, but they should assume they would need to stop twice. That meant he needed to make certain he had sufficient cash for the drive because he didn't have a credit card. Fortunately, that problem was easily solved. He'd simply stop at his bank in town and make a withdrawal from his savings account. He had plenty in the account and he didn't need his parent's permission to access it. It was his account his mother helped him set up a couple years earlier when he first started earning a paycheck. They wouldn't even know he had accessed it.

And what about the car? While the Chrysler ran well, it was getting old. At minimum, he needed to check all the fluids to make sure everything was topped off and he also needed to check the tire pressure. If the oil was dirty, he'd change it. These were all things his dad had taught him and that he'd done multiple times, so he had the experience. Besides, he'd already told Henry he'd take care of the maintenance. That was their agreement. Even if they didn't make the trip, the labor wouldn't be wasted as he would have to do it at some point anyway.

All the work could be done the next time he made his semi-compulsory weekly guest appearance home. Plus, his dad kept a supply of the necessary fluids in their garage, so he should be all set in that regard. Last but not least, he'd check the spare, make sure it was properly inflated, and that the jack was in the trunk. While he was at it, he'd wash the car and vacuum the interior so they'd have a clean ride for the journey. Beyond that, he'd just have to keep his fingers crossed that the Chrysler could handle a drive of that distance.

The great unknown at this point was the grandparents. Would they even agree to let them make a trip of that length? When they approach them with the request, how should they position it? Is it a once-in-a-lifetime opportunity for Yani to see New York, a learning opportunity, or just for fun? Is there no way to position it that they could possibly agree to? There was only one way to find out, and that was to ask. Timing would also be important. Yani knew them best, so she should make the decision as to when and how they approach them. She came to the decision that the best time would be mid-morning after her grandmother had finished cleaning up from breakfast, but before starting lunch. Normally, this would be a time when her grandparents were just sitting around relaxing and enjoying the day.

When the two of them walked into the kitchen together, Yani spoke first. "Grandma, Grandpa?"

"Yes, honey?" her grandmother responded as her granddad looked up from the morning newspaper.

"Dan and I want to ask you something."

"What's up, sweetheart?"

Yani looked at Dan, "You want to tell them?"

"Sure. So, Mr. and Mrs. Hartmann, I wanted to ask you if you would allow me to take Yani on a day trip to New York City," he lied.

"Oh, my," her grandfather responded. "That's a pretty long drive."

"Well, it is, but it isn't complicated. I just take Route 14 down to Elmira Heights and pick up 17. That runs all the way to New York City, so I don't even have to worry about directions."

"I see," at which point he paused. "Well, when do you plan on going?" he followed up.

"Well, we don't have a date yet. We figured we better make sure it was okay with you first and not get ahead of ourselves."

"And assuming we agree to allow you to go, when are you thinking?"

"My thoughts are we go on a weekday, like a Tuesday, Wednesday, or Thursday sometime in the next couple weeks. Traffic will be lighter, and there won't be as many tourists. We were thinking we could leave first thing in the morning, say around eight. By doing that, we'd be home long before it gets dark."

"Do you know anything about New York, Dan?"

"I've been twice on chaperoned school field trips. Both times, we spent the night. I know all the famous landmarks and I figured we wouldn't do any walking. That way, we won't have to worry about finding parking, paying for it, and then having to try finding the car afterwards. We'd probably just drive around the city for a couple of hours so she can see it. Afterwards, we drive straight back here."

At this point, Yani felt the need to jump back into the discussion. "You know, this could be an opportunity of a lifetime, Granddad. I may never have another chance to see New York. It's not like my folks come to New York very often."

Her grandfather looked over at her grandmother and shrugged his shoulders. "I don't know, Ma. What do you think?"

"Let me think on this a bit, but I promise I'll let you know soon. I just don't want to be rushed into a decision."

"That's fine, Grandma. You take all the time you need. Like Dan said, we haven't even picked a date when to do this," Yani replied back.

"Okay, honey. I'll let you know," and with that, Dan and Yani exited to leave her grandparents alone so they could chew on the idea. True to her word, later that afternoon, her grandmother provided her decision. They had permission to go. Along with that decision, though, there was also a strong admonition to be careful and to not take any chances whatsoever.

That settled, now there was one final thing to consider. Dan had heard his dad say it many times, "You don't know what you don't know." In other words, it's almost impossible to think of everything you need to prepare for. Something unexpected almost always seemed to pop up. Would this happen to Dan and Yani? With their youth and inexperience, it was basically guaranteed. They were only seventeen years old. Of course, they'd overlook something or make a mistake along the way. All they could hope for was that something wouldn't turn out to be significant and that it would be a problem they could handle on the fly. They had no support network. It would be totally up to them and their problem-solving abilities to deal with whatever came along.

Later that week, when he was home working on the car, his dad came wandering into the garage. "Hey, Dan. What's going on?"

"Nothing. Just checking fluids, tire pressures, crap like that."

"You planning on going somewhere?"

"Not at all," he lied. "My deal with Henry is I'm responsible for maintenance, so I'm just holding up my end of the bargain."

"You want some help?"

"Definitely. I'd enjoy the company."

"Okay." With that, his dad stared at the engine compartment for a moment, headed to the toolbox, and came back with a big flat blade screw driver. Sticking his head under the hood, he leaned over and slipped the blade under the hold-down clamp for the master cylinder.

"Wo! Wo! Wo! Hold on, Dad. What're you doing?"

"You said you're checking the fluids. I figured I'd check the brake fluid."

"No, please, don't do that, Dad. God forbid we get air in there. I'll be down here for the next six hours bleeding out the brake lines and creating a huge mess."

"Oh, come on. That's not going to happen," he replied dismissively, doing his best to sound reassuring, and leaned in again to pry open the master cylinder.

"Dad, stop! Seriously! Please do not do that! The brakes are fine. You want to check something, check the transmission fluid, and, no, we aren't dropping the pan to check for metal particles," he stated, half laughing and half serious. He had to. His dad had a really bad habit of taking a simple task and turning it into a monumental project that always seemed to literally end up taking ten times longer than it should. That was the last thing Dan wanted or needed right now.

"Well, okay, but I don't think it would hurt anything just to check."

"I know, Dad. I know, but we aren't doing that. If you really wanted to check the brakes, you'd pull a wheel and inspect the pads."

"You want to?"

"No, Dad. I don't want to start taking the wheels off the car," he answered back trying to suppress his exasperation with his father.

"Well, okay," his dad replied, sounding almost disappointed. He walked back over to the toolbox, redeposited the screwdriver, and came back to the car to check the transmission fluid while Dan was busy with his tasks.

"Okay, transmission fluid is full. Anything else?"

"As a matter of fact, can you check the trunk to see if there's a spare and a jack in there? I haven't even looked, and it would be awfully embarrassing if I got a flat only to discover Henry didn't have a spare in the vehicle."

"No problem," and his dad headed to the trunk. "Yep. There's a spare and the jack. Want me to check the tire pressure?" he called out.

"Would you, please?"

His dad checked the pressure, gave it his seal of approval, and walked back to the front of the vehicle just as Dan was lowering the hood. "Okay, Dad. Everything looks good. The oil's full and clean, tire pressures are good. You said the transmission fluid is full, and I've filled the reservoir for the windshield washer. I'd say our work here is done," and together they headed towards the house.

As they walked along, his dad informed him, "Hey, we're planning on coming to the cottage for a few days beginning this weekend. We haven't been up much and we want to spend some time there."

"Okay, great. It should be fun. You coming up Friday evening or Saturday morning?"

"We haven't decided yet. Does it matter to you?"

"To me?" he asked. "Not at all. I can assure you that I'll definitely be there whenever you show up."

"Okay, good. Then we'll see you at the lake sometime this weekend."

"Perfect. It'll be nice to have someone cooking for me for a change," he grinned and laughed, knowing that upon their arrival, his mother would immediately take over the kitchen.

When he got back up to the lake later that week, Dan informed Yani of his parents' plans to come to the cottage on either Friday evening or Saturday morning and that they would be staying for 'a few days', whatever that meant.

"So, does that mean we're going to cancel the trip to Youngstown?" she asked.

"We'll see what happens. We haven't given your grandparents a specific date, so I don't see that it's a big deal if we put it off for a week or so. We told them we didn't have a date."

"Well, we just hold off until we know for sure, right?"

"Yeah. Let's play it by ear and see what they do."

"Okay, then that's what we'll do," and she left it at that.

Sure enough, when Dan's family got up to the cottage and settled in, his dad told him that they were probably going to stay until Wednesday or Thursday. It was somewhat flexible and depended on the weather as much as anything. As the days went by, Yani stopped by several times to visit. Each time, Dan caught his mom staring at her suspiciously, and he found the whole idea of Yani being a threat to her to be terribly amusing.

As they got into the week, it was apparent they would not be leaving early and, unless some really bad weather event occurred, they would be staying through Wednesday and going home sometime on Thursday. Dan knew they wouldn't be coming back the next week. They would never do that, so he and Yani informed her grandparents they would be going to New York City the following Wednesday.

When Tuesday evening of the next week rolled around, Yani's grandparents called the two of them into the kitchen for another discussion on their trip. They went over the schedule again and asked a couple more questions when Mr. Hartmann announced to the two of them, "You know, we've been thinking about this a lot."

Oh, no, Dan thought to himself. They're going to tell us they changed their mind and that we can't go, but he didn't.

Instead, Mr. Hartmann looked at Dan, "I know you went to a lot of trouble to make sure your car is in good condition for the trip. Her grandma and I have decided, though, that we would be much more comfortable if you would take our car. It's a lot newer and we would just feel better with you driving that."

"Holy cow, Mr. Hartmann. That is so nice of you, but really, I think my car will be just fine. It drives great."

"I understand, Dan, but we would just feel better if you would drive our car. We don't have any plans and we won't be needing it."

"Are you totally sure, Mr. and Mrs. Hartmann?" he asked, looking at both of them.

Mr. Hartmann looked at his wife and she nodded in agreement. He looked back at Dan and Yani, "Yes. Absolutely. We want you to drive our car. In fact, we're kind of adamant that you do take our car."

"Okay, well, then that's what we'll do, but I'm going to leave you the keys to my car just in case there's an emergency and you need a vehicle. The gas tank is full, the vehicle is spotless, and it's ready to go," he informed them as he set the keys on the table and pushed them towards Mr. Hartmann.

"That's fine. Thank you, Dan."

"No. Thank you."

"You're more than welcome."

Now the whole issue of having reliable transportation had been miraculously solved and they had one less thing to worry about.

Chapter 23

First thing the next morning, Dan walked down to the Hartmann cottage carrying a picnic basket the two had prepared the night before. He set it down by the front door and knocked. Yani immediately showed up to let him in.

"Good morning, everyone."

"Good morning, Dan," they replied in unison.

He turned to Yani, "Well, you ready?"

"Yep."

Turning to her grandfather, "Any final instructions, Mr. Hartmann?"

"Just be careful and come back in one piece. That's it."

"We will. I promise," and with that, they all walked out to the car. Dan loaded the picnic basket into the back seat. Yani climbed in front, and off they went, waving to her grandparents as they drove away. Rather than go north to jump onto the New York State Thruway, they had already decided they'd take the southern route that would take them through Jamestown. It was a more difficult drive, but it was actually faster, and they would be passing through a series of towns and small cities. That way, if they needed anything, they wouldn't have to wait for an exit on the interstate and hope the services they wanted would be available at that exit.

They drove down into Watkins and took the road up over the hill past the racetrack to the little town called Savona, where they picked up Route 17. That would take them all the way to Interstate 90, which, in turn, would take them into Ohio north of Youngstown. This was the biggest chunk of the trip, and that would take about three hours. Once they reached Jamestown, it was about eleven o'clock. They pulled over to fill the gas tank for the final stretch, use the bathroom, and have something to eat. Shortly after leaving Jamestown, they crossed Chautauqua Lake and continued on the remaining distance until Route 17 ran into Interstate 90. From there, they continued west until they reached Route 11 near Ashtabula and took that south. This would take them all the way to Youngstown. Once they reached the suburbs, Dan turned to her, "Okay, honey. You're in charge now. Tell me where I need to go."

"Okay, I've got this. Stay to the left here and go under Interstate 80," and Dan did what he was told. "Stay on this road until you see Gypsy Lane and make a left there," and again, he did as she instructed. "Now, hold on, I'm looking for…there, make a right," and he made the turn. "Next, we're going to be making another left. There!" she pointed. "Turn left there. Now, see that light blue house on the right?"

"Yep."

"Pull into that driveway and park," and he did as she ordered. "We did it!" she exclaimed while leaning over to hug him. "This is my house," she announced with a huge smile as she climbed out of her grandparents' car and headed towards the front door with Dan following close behind. In a corner by the door was a potted plant. She reached down behind it and produced a door key, holding it up in front of his face and smiling. Unlocking the door, she stuck her head inside and called out, "Lisa? Robin?" then walked directly in. Immediately, two young ladies came bounding into view, one from the kitchen and one from a bedroom, screaming and jumping up and down in their excitement. What they failed to notice at the time was a lady across the street peering out through the curtains of her front window.

"Yani! Yani! What are you doing here? We didn't know you were coming home!" they continued screaming as they ran to hug her.

"No one knows that I've come home, and no one can know. Okay? Don't tell mom and dad."

"If we can't tell them, why are you home?" Lisa asked, a confused look on her face.

"First of all, I haven't seen you in forever, and I was dying to see you. Secondly, my boyfriend wanted to see where I live."

"What? You have a boyfriend?" she gasped, while looking at Dan.

"Yes. His name is Dan. Isn't he gorgeous?"

Robin slowly walked up to Dan, staring up at him the whole time. "He sure is," she said, and the three of them broke into raucous laughter. "Yani! I can't believe you have a boyfriend."

"Okay, you guys. Stop it," Dan responded as he started to laugh, too. "You're embarrassing me."

Robin grabbed him by the hand. "Come on in, Dan," she said, smiling up at him.

"Okay, where to?"

"Let's go sit in the kitchen."

"Lead the way," and the four of them walked to the kitchen, where they sat around the table and visited for well over an hour. Yani told them all about their grandparents, the cottage, and what it's been like. She told them the story of how she met Dan and what they do together, and she answered all of their questions as best she could. She even told them that she had gone to church with Dan.

"Wait. You went to a church?" Lisa asked.

"Yeah, Dan took me to a Catholic church near the cottage that he's been going to since he was a little boy."

"Well, why'd you do that?"

"I don't know. After listening to him describe it, he asked me if I wanted to go see it for myself and I said yes," she explained as she looked over at Dan. "It was actually very beautiful."

"I want to go to a church," Robin blurted out laughing.

"Well, Robin, we're just going to have to see if we can't make that happen for you sometime," Dan replied, and Robin responded to that with a big, radiant smile of her own.

Yani went onto explain to them that she couldn't stay long. They would have to leave soon and that they couldn't tell their parents she and Dan had been there because of the problems it would cause with their mom. They seemed to understand the importance of that and promised they wouldn't say a thing. All the while, the two of them would sneak these little sideways glances at Dan, checking him out.

As their visit began to approach the two-hour mark, Dan turned to Yani and broke the bad news. "We need to leave soon."

"I understand," was her response. "Before we go, though, I need to ask Lisa something. Lisa?" she announced, as she stood from the table and walked in the direction of the bedroom Lisa had come out of when they'd arrived. Once inside, Yani closed the door and stared at her. "When we walked in the house, I saw you come out of this bedroom, my bedroom. By any chance, have you moved into my bedroom?"

"Mom had me move in here," she answered quietly while staring at the floor. "Mom said you wouldn't be needing it, so there was no point sharing a bedroom with Robin. Are you mad?" she asked, looking back up at her for some sign of forgiveness.

"I don't know how I feel. Am I going to get it back when I come home after the summer ends?"

"Of course. Why wouldn't you?"

"Remember you said that, Lisa," Yani said sternly.

"I will. I promise."

"Okay. Let's go," and she walked back out of the bedroom to the kitchen. "All right, Dan, I don't want to, but I know we have to. Okay, you guys. Hugs, please!" and her sisters took turns hugging her and telling her they loved her and followed that up by hugging Dan. Finished saying their goodbyes, her sisters walked them outside to the car and continued to wave as she and Dan drove off.

Dan turned to her, "That was really nice. I love your sisters. They're super cute, but what was that between you and Lisa?"

"That's my bedroom. She's using my bedroom and I wanted to know why?"

"And?"

"It's exactly what I expected. My mom moved her in there because, quote unquote, I wouldn't be needing it."

"Ouch! Sorry, sugar."

"Thanks, Dan, but I'm not surprised. I kind of anticipated this. Trust me on that."

"Understood. We can talk more about that later if you want to. In the meantime, you need to direct me back to Route 11."

"You got it," and she did exactly that. Once they got on Route 11, he knew what to do from there. They continued north on 11 until it ran into Interstate 90, where he took the entrance ramp onto I-90 east.

As they were cruising along the short stretch of Interstate 90 between Ohio and the exit they would take to reach the New York line, Yani was leaning over the dashboard working the radio to try and find a good station when, out of nowhere, a silver-colored muscle car went blistering past looking like it was going well over a hundred. The turbulence created by the speed of the vehicle violently shook their car as it went by. Before Dan could even react or look around, a state trooper went flying past in hot pursuit, siren blaring and lights flashing. Dan looked out at the road and traffic up ahead of them. His eyes got really big and he yelled out, "Oh, my God, Yani! I don't think he's going to make it!"

As the words left his mouth, he saw the silver car trying to weave through the traffic, but the driver miscalculated, clipping the back of a United Van Lines tractor-trailer traveling in the right-hand lane. The rear of the car lifted right up off the roadway and the vehicle began tumbling down the interstate. As they watched in horror, the driver was ejected right through the windshield. For a very brief moment, he almost looked like a gymnast performing a vault routine. The big difference was that the driver's arms and legs were splayed out in all different directions as he spun through the air with his long, brown hair trailing out behind his dazed looking face. It reminded Dan of a picture of a cat he saw once in a National Geographic magazine. The cat was jumping through the air. Its legs were pointing in every direction, and it was staring at the camera lens with that weird expressionless face a cat has.

The other big difference between the driver, a gymnast, and a cat was the landing. A gymnast and a cat would typically stick their landing. When the unfortunate driver landed, he did more of a complete face-plant onto the shoulder of the highway. Was the young driver already dead when he came back to earth? No one would ever know. He bounced once and settled face down on the asphalt. Vault routine complete. His body never even twitched.

At this point, Dan and the rest of the vehicles on the Interstate had slowed to a crawl. It was total carnage. There was broken glass, plastic, and metal strewn everywhere. The hulk of what was left of the vehicle was laying in the median with a trail of steam drifting towards the heavens from the now silent engine. As they drove past the body, Yani asked quietly, her voice quivering badly, "Oh…oh my God, Dan. Is he dead?"

Shaking his head slowly in the affirmative, he answered her. "I'm afraid so, honey. No way anybody could survive that." The state trooper had already pulled over and was busy trying to deal with the situation, putting out flares while the moving van driver had pulled to the side and was now out of his cab. More troopers were pulling up to the accident scene to help assist with the mess they were faced with. They all knew they were going to be there a very long time. The coroner would have to be called in and the body removed, accident debris cleaned up, and their incident reports would have to be written before they could even think about leaving. In the meantime, several of them took over traffic control as they'd have to partially shutdown the interstate until they were done. At this point, there was nothing that could be done for the driver, so safety came first. Once that was under control, they could cover the dead driver with a sheet.

After having cleared the accident scene, it wasn't long before they were back up to speed on the interstate. Dan looked over at Yani as they drove. She was kind of leaning forward in her seat, and tears were starting to slowly roll down her cheeks. Gradually, the crying became more pronounced and she soon began sobbing. Dan saw signs for a rest area up ahead and pulled in. After parking, he reached into the picnic basket in the back seat, grabbed some napkins they had packed for the journey, and handed them to her.

"Yani, sweetheart," he said to her softly. "Can I get you anything? Can I do anything for you?"

"Yes," she answered weeping. "Please take me back to the cottage. I want to go to the cottage."

"Right away," he answered gently and he began driving again. As the miles accumulated while he drove back to the lake, he glanced over at her periodically. Though young and no psychologist, he thought he had a pretty good idea of what was going on here. She's got a terribly abusive mother, a gutless father who won't protect her, and she gets shipped off to some God-forsaken remote corner of New York to spend the summer with elderly grandparents she barely knows. Now, she witnesses a guy getting killed when she's already under a ton of emotional stress. A person can only take so much, and maybe witnessing that boy die was Yani's emotional breaking point. He didn't know for sure, but he was really worried about her.

They drove along in silence until they got to the village of Bath. Dan pulled into a diner along the road so they could have supper and fill the gas tank. Yani just stared at her plate, picking at her food the whole time. When they got back to her cottage, they walked in, and she sat in a kitchen chair staring into her lap.

"Yani, honey. What's wrong?" her grandmother asked with a look of serious concern and angst on her face. Her grandmother looked over at Dan, "Dan, what's happened?" Her granddad had come walking in from the porch and just stood there looking at the three of them.

"She had a real bad experience on the way home today," Dan answered back as he set the car keys down on the table. "She saw somebody die in an accident."

"You mean you passed a fatality along the road?" her grandfather asked.

"No. She actually witnessed first-hand a young man die in a car crash."

"Oh, dear God, honey," her grandmother said as she put her arm around Yani to console her.

Yani turned and looked at her grandmother, "Grandma, I'd like to go down to Dan's cottage. Do you mind?"

"No, sweetheart. You two go right ahead. We'll be here if you need us."

"Thanks, Grandma."

Yani stood and walked slowly to the door, with Dan taking his cue and following right behind. When they arrived at the Wallace cottage, she took a seat on the deck. Dan went inside to turn on some music, came back outside and sat down next to her. Together, they looked out at the lake in complete silence. At one point, she reached over to take his hand and staring into his eyes, she said to him, "Once it gets dark, I want you to take me into your arms, make love to me, and tell me that everything is going to be okay." He thought he understood exactly why she might need that, so later that evening, he made it all happen. Afterwards, she thanked him…again.

Chapter 24

The next morning, Dan walked down to the Hartmann place and knocked on the screen door. He was caught completely off guard when Mr. Hartmann came to the door and stepped outside the cottage onto the front stoop without first speaking.

"Good morning, Dan," he said rather quietly, making it seem like he didn't want to be overheard.

"Morning, Mr. Hartmann. Yani, okay?"

"I'm not sure. She's sitting out on the porch right now," he replied, leaning his head in that direction, then he paused before continuing. "Can we talk a minute?"

"Of course, Mr. Hartmann. How can I help?"

He stood there for a moment, looking at Dan before speaking again. "Yani's not right. She's barely spoken since you two got back yesterday. Her grandmother and I are awfully concerned about her. Something's wrong."

"I'm sorry to hear that, Mr. Hartmann. She was really upset on the ride home."

Hartmann continued to study him carefully before asking, "Dan, did something else happen yesterday that you two haven't told us about yet?"

Dan looked down at his feet and right back up to meet Hartmann's stare. "Yes, Mr. Hartmann. Something happened."

"You want to tell me about it?"

Dan paused again before answering. "We didn't go to New York, Mr. Hartmann."

"I see," he replied and hesitated once more before he followed that up with, "Well if you didn't go to New York, where exactly did you go?"

"Youngstown. We drove to Yani's house."

"And...why'd you do that when you told me you were going to New York?" he asked, gesturing with his hands.

"Yeah, well, she wanted to see her sisters, and I wanted to see where she lived in case, you know, cause maybe in the future..." and Dan kind of shrugged his shoulders. "We figured you and Mrs. Hartmann would never agree to allow us to go to Youngstown, but you might agree to New York so Yani could see the city. They're the same distance from here, just opposite directions, so we'd be gone the exact same amount of time and you'd never be the wiser."

"Well, I guess I understand. Okay. Go on."

"Right. So, everything is going just fine until we get to her house. The girls are all super excited to see each other. Everybody's screaming and hugging and I think the visit is going just great, but I don't realize what's actually happened when we first arrived. Right before we leave, Yani has this private discussion with Lisa in one of the bedrooms and she closes the door so they can't be overheard."

"When we got back in the car and started driving, I asked her what's going on. She tells me that the bedroom they went into was hers, but that her mom has given it to Lisa because, quote-unquote, Yani won't be needing it." Mr. Hartmann just sighed, looked down, and shook his head from side to side.

"Later, when we were on Interstate 90 heading towards the New York State line, we witness this terrible accident. Some young guy was speeding and driving like a total lunatic. The state troopers are chasing him. He loses control because he's going so fast and crashes right in front of us. But that wasn't the worst part. During the crash, the car starts tumbling, and he gets ejected from the vehicle. So, we're sitting there in your car, watching this kid fly through the air. You could actually see his eyes for a second. The poor guy slams face first on the road and it's obvious he's dead."

"Oh, dear Lord," he responded, looking away from Dan.

"Anyway, Yani goes quiet but starts crying not long after that and she hasn't been the same since. I'm really worried, too, Mr. Hartmann," and the two of them just stood there for a moment, staring at each other in silence.

"Mr. Hartmann?"

"Yes, Dan."

"I want you to know that I'm sorry about lying to you and Mrs. Hartmann."

At that, Hartmann took a deep sigh. "Dan, I appreciate you saying that. Let me also say this, though. I don't know what we would have done this summer with Yani if you hadn't been here to keep her company. You've truly been a godsend. Tell you what. Let's just put this behind us and move on. Fair enough?"

"Yes. Thanks, and Mr. Hartmann?"

"Yes."

"I know all about Yani's problems with her mom and her home life. She told me."

"Yeah, it's a real bad situation," and he hesitated again before saying more. "Dan, I'm going to tell you something, and I'm going to ask you never to repeat it. Okay?"

"Yes, sir. I promise."

214

"We love our son, Michael, dearly, but we are incredibly frustrated with him when it comes to Yani. We're not oblivious. He lets her mom push him around constantly and does nothing about her abusive behavior towards their own daughter. It drives us nuts, but there's nothing we can do about it."

"And I think maybe that's why she's so upset."

"What do you mean?"

"I think a couple of things happened yesterday. First of all, I think that going home to see her sisters only to find out that her mom has given away her bedroom is just a reminder of what she's facing when summer ends and she has to go home. She's already under a whole lot of emotional stress because of her home life. Now, she witnesses this kid get killed right in front of her. I'd be willing to bet she's never been up close to death like that before. I saw my grandmother and a great aunt die, so it's not the first time for me. The kid was probably not much older than we are and I think that may have pushed her close to her breaking point."

Mr. Hartmann stood there silently and looked around for a moment before looking back at Dan. "Okay, we'll talk more about this later. In the meantime, I promised her grandma I'd take her to Watkins so she could do the shopping. Assuming she's willing, why don't you take her for a boat ride?"

"Sure. I've got plenty of gas in our boat. I can take her for a ride if you'd like."

"No, just go ahead and take my boat."

"What? You want me to take the Seneca Song? Mr. Hartmann, you can't be serious!" Dan said quietly.

"Oh, I'm quite serious, Dan. I've been watching you all summer. You've got a good head on your shoulders and a real steady hand when it comes to a boat. On top of that, you seem to always show real respect for other people's property. There's no way I'd ever let that brother of yours anywhere near that steering wheel, but you? Well, I trust you not to do anything foolish. Besides, her grandma and I can see what's happening. Yani is extremely fond of you, but she also trusts you, too. I think she needs you right now. Go on out front. She's sitting there, and the keys are in the ignition. We'll see you later after we get back from Watkins. Oh, and don't forget to run the blower first before you start the engine."

"Okay, Mr. Hartmann. Thanks. I won't." Hartmann put his hand on Dan's shoulder and redirected him to the screen door as he pulled it open to let him inside. Dan walked through the cottage and found Mrs. Hartmann in the kitchen.

"Good morning, Dan."

"Morning, Mrs. Hartmann."

"She's sitting out there," she said, indicating where Yani sat with a motion of her head.

"Thank you, ma'am," and out the door he walked. "Morning, Yani," he said softly as he walked up.

Yani looked up at him from the table with a half-hearted smile. "Hey," she replied quietly. "Sit down?" she asked, pointing to the chair across from her.

He didn't answer. He just pulled out a chair next to her and sat down beside her. She glanced at him briefly as he sat and then turned away.

"Everything okay?" he asked.

"Oh, yeah. Everything's just ducky," she responded cynically while staring off across the lake. As they sat there silently looking out at the water, he began feeling extremely awkward and confused because he had no idea what to do next. Normally, Yani usually seemed to break the silence. This time, she simply didn't, and it seemed like she wouldn't. Assuming that it was going to be up to him, he summoned his courage as best he could to try and start up a conversation.

"In the mood to maybe go for a ride and talk?"

She looked at him and then sighed. "What'd you have in mind, Dan?"

Thank, God. At least she's speaking, he thought to himself. "I figured we could go for a boat ride."

"You mean walk down to your place and take your boat?"

"No, I was thinking we'd take that boat," he said, looking down at the Seneca Song.

"Yeah, right. Like my grandfather is going to let us take his boat out."

"He told me I could. In fact, he told me I should."

"Really?" she responded sarcastically. "My grandfather just told you that you could take the Seneca Song without him even being here, let alone being in the boat with us?"

"Yes."

"Seriously. You're not making this up."

"No, Yani. I'm not making this up. He told me that he was taking your grandma down to the Watkins to do the shopping and that I should take you for a ride in his boat."

"Damn!" was her reply as she continued to sit there staring at him when, right out of nowhere, she just lit into him. "Who the hell are you, Dan Wallace?" she yelled while leaning forward in her chair and yelling right in his face. "My grandfather just offers to allow you to take his most prized possession in the whole wide world without him

217

even being in the boat? He offers to give you his car to drive to New York without you even asking? I've never seen anyone die, yet in a little more than a month, at least one and maybe two people have died right before my very eyes while in your presence. You've got me doing things and going places I never thought I would. You're constantly showing and teaching me things I could never even imagine existed. You're doing weird things like fighting off raccoons in the middle of the night; helping people having heart attacks. What the hell is next, Dan? We going to help some lady deliver a baby later today? Huh?" she continued with more really aggressive sarcasm in her voice.

Yani was rapidly escalating into one of her moods and she became extremely agitated. For Dan, it was always rather frightening whenever she got this way. She leaned back in her chair and turned away from him for a moment before turning back, pointing right in his face. "You've got me talking about religion and God and angels, going to church. It seems like everything you do is to try and make me happy. Make my life better," she yelled while slamming both fists on the table, shocking the hell out of him and rattling the dishes sitting there. "Worst of all, you made it impossible for me not to fall in love with you!" Then she began weeping.

"If everybody around here didn't already know you, I'd swear to God you must be one of those damned angel things you told me about!" she sobbed. Dan was simply speechless after this eruption and didn't have a clue what to do next. Not knowing at all how to respond at this point, he just sat there silently, returning her gaze.

Yani continued crying softly for the next couple of minutes before abruptly stopping and switching to a normal voice, which seemed to him to be very contrived at that moment. "Well, Dan, I guess that means we're going for a ride in grandpa's prized antique speed boat," she announced, shaking her head and raising her hands in a sign of surrender. With that, she stood and headed towards the stairs leading

218

down to the dock. Dan immediately got up from the table and trailed right behind her.

As they reached the boatlift, she turned to face him. "Okay. Now what?"

"I am going to need your help, if that's not too much trouble."

"Oh, not at all," she replied with even more sarcasm. "What exactly do you need?"

"Can you hop down in the boat and turn on the engine blower, please, while I start lowering the boat?"

She didn't reply. She just climbed down into the boat and, while pointing at the dashboard, asked, "Which switch?"

"That one right there to the left of where you're pointing."

"This one?" she asked.

"Yep. That's the one." She flipped the switch, and immediately, you could hear the blower doing its job. Dan lowered the boat until the prop was fully submerged and hopped into the Seneca Song with Yani. He turned the ignition key, and the Gray Marine started immediately. Hartmann had a secondary lift rope that allowed you to finish lowering the lift cradle from inside the boat itself. He finished dropping the boat into the water, slid in behind the steering wheel, and turned to Yani. "Have a seat," he said, looking down at the bench seat next to him, and she did as he requested. He reached down, put the shifter in reverse, turned around to look over his shoulder behind him, and backed the boat slowly out of the lift.

Once clear of the lift and dock, he swung the stern around so the bow was facing out into the lake. Before stepping on the gas pedal, he took a quick glance at the gas gauge to make sure they had plenty of fuel. Confirming they did, he throttled up, and they headed out onto the lake, rapidly picking up speed. Within mere seconds, her auburn hair was trailing out behind her head. God, her hair's getting so long, he thought to himself. She looks more beautiful every day.

He headed out north towards Geneva, first passing the 'island' then stopping briefly out in front of a very large, stately property right next to the shore. "Just as this is my favorite boat here on Seneca, that property right there is my favorite place on Seneca. It's called the San Felice. It was built in the early 1900's, and its original purpose was what they called a 'villa' hotel, which I guess is just a fancy way of calling it a small hotel for steam boat travelers on the lake. I just love the architecture, the stained-glass windows, wrap-around porch, everything about it. It's a private residence now." Yani said nothing in response.

After floating out front briefly with zero interest being shown by Yani, Dan took off again, continuing north. They passed the Lodi Point State Park and continued onward until they reached Sampson State Park, originally part of the Seneca Army Depot. Tapping her on the shoulder to get her attention, she turned to him. "If you go straight up the hill from here, that's where the Army depot and the white deer are." She nodded, indicating her understanding, but didn't speak or even change expressions.

They were now at the widest point of Seneca, approximately three miles across. He swung the boat out into deeper water and headed across to the far shore line and to the town of Dresden. From there, he headed back south towards Watkins. Yani still wasn't speaking, nor was she even making eye contact with him. Continuing south, a large, white building and dock assembly soon came into view, and Dan started slowing while navigating in closer to shore. Touching Yani on the arm again to get her attention and pointing, he said to her, "That white building up ahead there is a restaurant. You want to stop and get a drink? I'm getting kind of thirsty."

"Okay," was the entirety of her response, so he headed for an open slip, pulling into the first available he came to. He climbed out, tied off the boat, helped her up onto the dock, and they began walking in the direction of the main two-story structure known as the Showboat Motel. It had a full-length restaurant and bar on the first story, motel rooms on the second story, and an open-air patio on the front facing the lake. Next to it was a larger two-story white building that was exclusively motel rooms, their exterior doors facing the lake. Each had matching blue roofs.

Stepping up onto the patio, it was only late morning, so the restaurant wasn't busy with the lunch crowd yet. He sat them at one of the outdoor tables facing the water. When the waitress walked up, Dan turned to Yani, "You want something to eat or just a drink?"

"Just a drink," and she turned to the waitress. "Do you have lemonade?"

"Yes, miss, and you, sir?"

"I'll have a Coke, please."

"Lemonade and a Coke it is. I'll be right back," and in short order, she was. As they sat there nursing their drinks and looking out over Seneca, it was obvious to Dan that she wasn't going to start speaking. He was going to have to take the lead on any conversation they had, and so he did.

"You scared?"

"Of what?"

"Going back home when summer ends."

"Should I be?"

"Well, I know if I was in your shoes, I certainly would be. Plus, you're only seventeen, so there's not a damned thing you can do about it."

"Yeah, well, what is it you Catholics say when you have a problem? Something about carrying crosses or something?"

"It's my cross to bear."

"There you go. Well, my home life is my cross to bear."

"And while I wouldn't wish that on anyone, it's especially painful to watch when it happens to someone you love."

"So now you love me?"

Reaching over to take her hand, he answered, "Yes, Yani. I love you, and I especially love how your hand fits perfectly into mine." She gently squeezed his hand and gave him a reluctant smile in return. After finishing their drinks and paying the bill, Dan indicated to her that it was time to go. As they stepped off the porch and started the walk back to the boat, Dan saw a couple of young men standing down on the dock next to the Seneca Song. They seemed to be checking it out a little too closely as far as he was concerned. "I wonder what they're up to?" he asked rhetorically to no one.

As they walked up, Dan called out to them, "What's up, fellas? Can I help you?"

The taller of the two turned to face them, "This your boat?"

"Actually, it's her grandfather's boat," he replied as he gestured towards Yani.

"Man, this is really sharp. What is it?"

"It's a 1948 Century Resorter."

"Excellent! So cool! What kind of engine does it have?"

222

"A Gray Marine flat head six with a V-drive. She'll do just short of forty."

"Awesome! Hey, any chance we can go for a ride?" he asked, gesturing to his buddy next to him, who was standing there now staring at Yani with his mouth hanging open.

"Sorry. We're in kind of a hurry. We need to get back. They're expecting us to be returning any time now."

"Oh, come on, man. What's the big deal? We won't be gone that long. They'll never even know."

"Hey, I'd really like to help you out, but we've got to get going. Maybe next time."

"Seriously, man," he replied with a new, more aggressive attitude and the smile disappearing from his face. "You can't take a couple of minutes out of your busy schedule to give us a ride?"

"Okay, okay," Dan replied, now starting to get frustrated. "Let me put it to you another way. There're you two guys, and there's me and her, but you want us to take two complete strangers for a ride out there in a boat that we don't even own," he stated, pointing out into the middle of the lake. "You must have been smoking something, man, because that definitely ain't happening."

"I don't see what the problem is, man. Why can't you be a nice guy and just give us a quick ride in this stupid boat."

Apparently, at this point, Yani had reached the limit of her patience because she walked straight up to the guy and stuck a finger right in his face. "Look it, pal," she barked. "I'm having a really bad day and you aren't helping things. My boyfriend here says you're not getting a ride, so you're not getting a ride. Is that perfectly clear? Now, get lost, and while you're at it," she continued yelling while turning to point at his buddy, "Tell your friend there to stop staring at me!"

223

"Oh, yeah? Is that right? And who exactly put you in charge?" he yelled back, his jaw muscles now tightening.

With the tension rapidly escalating, Dan knew he needed to do something and he better do it quickly. Raising his arm as he stepped in between them, "That's it. Conversation's over. Yani, grab the stern line, get in the boat, and turn the blower on, please," he stated as he stared at the boy. She immediately did what he asked. Dan made his way to the bow while keeping his eyes on the boys as they stared back at him with aggression on their faces. Releasing the bow line, Dan walked the boat out of the slip, stepped onto the gunwale while simultaneously pushing off from the dock and drifted away into open water. The two boys stood there glaring at them, but the lead one simply couldn't help himself. He just had to get in the last word.

"Yani, huh? What the hell kind of name is Yani?" he yelled out.

"The kind you'll never sleep with, loser," she fired back.

Ouch! That had to hurt, Dan said to himself, stifling a laugh.

On the way back, Yani reached over, placing her hand on his. "Dan, hey, I'm really sorry I yelled at you this morning," pausing briefly before continuing. "And, yes, I am scared," she said, looking into his eyes.

"I appreciate you saying that Yani, honey, and it's okay. I understand how tough things are right now, but you know what?"

"What?"

"If anyone is strong enough to handle this, that would be you," he replied, trying his best to sound both reassuring and confident in his tone.

She smiled back at him after hearing that. "I sure hope you're right."

Once they got back out front of the Hartmann's, Dan lined the boat up while adjusting for the wind and current. He slid it into the lift perfectly without touching a thing while grabbing hold of the lift to stop the boat's momentum. He then hopped out, and started rolling it up until the prop was well out of the water. Yani climbed out after him and the two of them clambered up the steps to find Mr. Hartmann standing there at the top watching the two of them.

"Have a nice time? Everything okay?" he asked, a concerned look on his face.

"Yes, much better now. Thank you, Grandpa," Yani responded while smiling at her grandfather. He smiled back at her, turned, and discreetly nodded at Dan. From that day forward through the end of the summer, Dan had a free hand to take out the Seneca Song whenever he and Yani wanted to.

Chapter 25

Not having yet seen Dan that morning, Yani decided to walk down to his place to search for him. When she didn't find him in the cottage, she headed down to the dock assembly. Out at the end of the main dock, she saw Dan sitting there facing out at the lake. She walked out to the end and quietly sat down along side of him. He turned to her smiling and took her hand. "What are you doing, Dan?" she asked softly.

"I'm sitting here thinking about you."

"Tell me what you're thinking about."

"I'm thinking that summer is coming to an end and that I am going to miss you like you can't even imagine, and that makes me really sad."

She looked down into her lap and turned back to search his eyes. "Do you really love me, Dan?"

"Yes, sugar. I really do. You're the first girl I've ever loved. That's how I know for sure that I love you."

"Thank you," she said sweetly. "You can't possibly know how much that means to me because you're the first boy I've ever loved."

There she goes again thanking me, he thought to himself. He squeezed her hand to reassure her and announced, "We need to talk. Let's go for a ride." He stood and helped her up to her feet.

"What do you want to talk about?"

"Us."

"Where we going?"

"Montour Falls. You haven't seen that yet and it's worth seeing."

"Where's it at?"

"It's the next little village just south of Watkins. Do we need to tell your grandparents where we're going?"

"No. As long as I'm with you, they know I'm safe and they don't worry."

"Okay, let's go," he replied as they reached the car. Driving down the lake road, they had the windows down, the radio was playing, and Yani's hair was blowing back in the wind. Her hair had grown so much that summer that sometimes, like today, she now wore it in a high ponytail. It was a look that Dan absolutely loved. When they first met that Saturday morning in June, Dan thought it simply wasn't possible that she could look any more beautiful, but putting her hair up like that actually did make her even more perfect.

As they drove towards Watkins, they didn't speak. They just listened to the music on the radio. The Beatles, The Eagles, Carole King and Harry Nilsson all played while they drove towards Watkins. At one point, Yani reached over, turned the radio off and they continued the drive immersed in small talk as they headed down the lake highway into town.

While they were passing through Watkins, Dan turned to her, "Change in plans."

"Oh? Where we going?"

"I'm going to drive you down to my home. I want you to see where I live."

"Okay," she replied, nodding her approval, and they continued driving for the next thirty minutes through the various little villages and towns until they reached Elmira. They drove all the way across the small city and out the southern limits, leading towards Pennsylvania. They continued south out of town on the two-lane highway they were traveling on until Dan abruptly slowed down. Pointing up to the left, he announced, "Right there. See that house right there on the mountainside? That's where I grew up, and that's where I live."

It was a fairly large, old Federal style two-story house. It would have to be large, what with the size of the Wallace family. The house was brown in color with white trim and had a peaked roof with a round window in the center of the peak. The front of the house had nine identical windows with faux shutters symmetrically arranged around a single front door that opened onto a small stoop with stairs leading down to a steeply sloped front yard. Attached on the right side was a single-story addition, and the entire perimeter of the home was surrounded with juniper hedges. Sitting on the side of a small mountain, she could see that there was nothing behind it except a forest that reached all the way up to the sky.

"There isn't much flat around here, is there?"

"No, honey. Not much of that."

"When you said you lived out in the country, boy, you sure weren't kidding."

"Yep. That forest you're looking at that runs up the mountain behind our home? That was my playground growing up. I spent a lot of time exploring those woods." Yani just stared in amazement. Having been born and raised in a city, albeit a small one like Youngstown, he doubted she could mentally connect with what it must have been like growing up in an environment like this.

"Are there wild animals?"

"Of course."

"You mean like bears and things like that?"

"As a matter of fact, I have seen bears, but only a couple of times."

"Were you scared?"

"Of bears? No. They pretty much avoid humans and keep their distance. Besides, they aren't really apex predators. They're lazy. Think of Yogi Bear in the cartoons on TV looking to steal picnic baskets. They want to expend as little time and energy as possible to find food. They aren't going to involve themselves with larger animals like humans. Too much trouble, unless they're stupid enough to leave food out."

"Well, were you ever scared of any animals you saw?"

"As a matter of fact, I was. I accidentally walked up on a bobcat one time. It was so large that it almost certainly had to be a male. Anyway, you know that kind of evil look cats have where it almost seems like they're staring at you, trying to figure out how to kill and eat you?"

"I never actually had that thought, but now that you mention it, I know exactly what you're talking about."

"Right. So, I'm looking at this bobcat, and he's staring back at me and it just gave me shivers. It actually felt like he was trying to figure out if he could take me down and eat me. I slowly backed away, and once I figured there was enough distance between us, I turned and ran."

"Yikes. That does sound scary," she replied with a nervous laugh. "Anyway, are we going to stop at your house?"

"No. Maybe some other time. I don't want to stop by with you unannounced. If my mom's home, she definitely wouldn't appreciate that," was all he said in response. He eventually turned around and started heading back towards Elmira. "You've noticed these houses we've occasionally passed, right?"

"Yes, of course."

"Those were my paper route customers. Now you know why a young boy really needed a bicycle."

"Damn. You walked all this way every day?"

"Yes, I did." She just shook her head in astonishment.

"Even in the winter?"

"The season and the weather didn't matter. The papers had to be delivered."

"Man, that sucks."

"Yes, but the money was pretty good for a boy that age."

He continued heading back north, past his house, back through Elmira, and onto the lake road that led to Watkins and Seneca Lake. Yani had turned the radio back on, and they listened to music while driving along. As they reached the outskirts of a small village, he looked over at her, "Okay, we're coming into a place called Montour Falls, which was our original destination when we left the cottage. Now, don't ask me to explain why they named it that because it makes absolutely no sense, but the older I get, the more I'm finding there's a whole lot of things in life that make zero sense.

"Anyway, the Montour part comes from someone who was apparently a really powerful Iroquois Indian queen by the name of Catharine Montour, who lived and died here back in the late 1700's. Now, they also have a Catharine Creek named after her that starts not too far from here and ends at Seneca Lake, but the falls located in downtown Montour are actually called Shequaga Falls. However, no one seems to know that's the fall's real name because everybody simply calls them Montour Falls, even some of the people that live here. Confused yet?"

"Totally, but go one."

"As waterfalls go, this is a really nice one, and you can get really close to it. There's a small park in front of the shallow plunge pool at the base that's formed over a million years, but it's not like Watkins Glen Gorge or the little gorge by our cottages. Climbing up the falls is

230

not allowed. It's way too steep and dangerous, so we'll just take a short walk, find a seat, and enjoy the sound and beauty."

"Okay. That's perfect," she replied, and with that, he made a left turn down a side street and maneuvered his way through the little village until they came out right in front of the falls, where he parked on the street.

"Before we walk over to the falls, I want to show you this really special house. I'm pretty sure you've figured out by now how much I enjoy old stuff. Well, this is simply another example," he said as they walked down the sidewalk and stopped out in front of a large, white home with four huge columns on the front porch.

"This is actually someone's house and according to what I've heard, it was built around 1845. The architecture is what they call Greek Revival. Isn't it cool? I mean, how great would it be to have a house like this one where the view from the back porch is a huge waterfall?"

"It's absolutely gorgeous. Stunning, really. It would be so awesome to get into the backyard to see the falls from that viewpoint."

"Yeah, it sure would. Again, I know nothing about the owners, but it's obvious they've got some money. Okay, let's go." Dan reached down, took her hand, and led her towards the park. They walked all the way up to the barrier fence in front of the plunge pool and just stared at the falls and the water coming over. "I told you this is a pretty nice waterfall. It's amazing how many there are in this part of the United States. Seems like they're almost everywhere. Most of the locals just take them for granted and never bother to visit. I love to go and just stare at them. You know, Niagara Falls isn't even three hours from here. I've never been, but the first chance I get, I'm going."

"Oh, gosh, Dan! Let's do that! Let's go to Niagara Falls!"

"Seriously?"

"Absolutely. Heck, we drove to Youngstown. I'm pretty sure we could find our way to Niagara Falls and back."

"You know, there's some merit to that idea. Let me think about that," he responded as they continued to stare at the falls. After a few more minutes, he suggested they sit down, and they walked over to sit on a park bench that faced the falls. As they were getting ready to sit, he reached into his pocket, took out a folded-up piece of paper, and handed it to her.

"What's this?" she asked as she sat down on the park bench.

"Open it."

She carefully opened up the piece of paper, and on it were written out his name, his parent's phone number, and two addresses. "I don't understand. Why do you have two addresses?"

"Well, where I live, there are no street or house numbers. It's a highway, so the post office uses a different system for delivering mail. They actually number your mailbox, not the house. The other address is the physical address of my parents' house. If you wanted to write me a letter, you'd use the mailing address and, if for some reason, you wanted to come to see me, you'd need the other address to actually find my house. The post office that delivers our mail is located in a different town than where my parent's house sits. So, if you went there to look for my home, you wouldn't find it."

"This is wonderful! Thank you, Dan. Thank you so much," and she carefully refolded the piece of paper and put it in her pocket.

"You're welcome, and don't forget that I need yours before you leave."

"Oh, I won't forget. Trust me on that."

"I'm holding you to that, sugar," and she responded to his remark with a beautiful smile.

"So, what is it you want to talk about, Dan?"

"In case you haven't seen a calendar lately, it's now the beginning of August, and sadly, that means you'll be leaving soon."

"Hey, I'm still going to be here for another month. No need to rush things."

"Ah, but you're assuming your mother won't pull a fast one, show up early, and demand that you go home right then and there. Unfortunately, I don't think we can make that assumption." Yani didn't say anything in response to that. She just looked down into her lap without saying anything, and Dan left her to her thoughts. They sat there together in silence for several minutes. Even though it was a beautiful day, the park was totally deserted. It was just the two of them, their thoughts, and the sound of the water cascading down Shequaga Falls.

Finally, Yani turned to Dan, "Well…what are we going to do?" she asked while looking deep into his eyes.

This was one of the very special things Dan loved about Yani. To most people, it probably meant little or nothing. He supposed that lots of people might not even notice, but the fact that Yani always referred to the two of them using words like 'we,' 'us,' and 'ours' meant a great deal to him. It proved to him that she really did consider them a couple.

"Well, with the time we have left, I think we need to savor each remaining moment and this gift we've been given. Plus, there're still some things I want to do with you."

"Like what?"

"For starters, I want you to go to church with me one more time."

"Why do you want us to do that?"

"I want to ask God for a favor, and I want you there with me when I do that."

"Do you only pray to God when you need a favor?" she asked with this really sincere look on her face.

"Yeah, I usually only pray to God when I ain't got a prayer of succeeding," he replied, laughing. "No, seriously. It does seem kind of like that, but there really aren't any hard and fast rules on when you are or aren't allowed to pray. For me? I just pray when I feel the need. So, what do you think? You want to go?"

Yani nodded her approval at the suggestion. "Yes. Yes, let's go to the church again. I think I'd like that."

"Next Sunday?"

"That's a deal. It's settled. What else?"

"It'll require some planning along with the permission of your grandparents, but I kind of like your idea of going to Niagara Falls. That could be super awesome. Plus, I want to spend time doing the little things that make coming to the lake so special. We should go fishing. I also want to take you to the movies. Neither one of us has been this summer, and it's such a traditional kind of date night activity. We need to do that."

"When do you want to get started?"

"How about right now?" he replied as he put his arm around her and gave her a big hug.

"Right now sounds pretty good," Yani responded with a really sensuous kiss to seal the deal. It was settled. They spent the next half hour enjoying the majesty of the Shequaga Falls surrounded by the spirit of Catharine Montour, and then drove directly back to the cottage where they made love for the first time during the day light; something else that was right up near the top of Dan's to-do list.

Chapter 26

They spent the week alternating between rides in the Seneca Song, Dan's little motorboat, or tubing during the day while transitioning to music and bonfires at night. All of this was sandwiched around Dan's semi-compulsory weekly trips home, primarily to appease his mother, but also so he could reload on food, clean clothes, and anything else he needed for the cottage, including firewood or fuel for the boat. When Saturday finally rolled around, Dan turned to Yani as they cruised along in the Seneca Song, "Tomorrow's Sunday. You still on for church, sugar?"

"Yep. Absolutely. What time we leaving?"

"I want to do the high Mass again, so we'll leave around 10:30. You want me to review the rules, or do you remember everything?" he asked laughing.

"I think I remember the important stuff, but if I do something wrong, you'll be sure to let me know, won't you?" she replied sarcastically.

"Hey, I would never do that to you."

"Sure, Dan, sure. We all know how you roll," she replied with her big, sultry smile. "By the way, what's this favor you're asking God for?" she asked, a look of curiosity on her face.

"That has to remain a secret until after Mass. I'll be happy to tell you after that. These will be official prayers."

"Oh, really? Must be important."

"It is, honey."

"Okay, well, I can't wait."

"You'll know soon enough. Just be patient a little while longer."

When Sunday morning arrived, Dan walked down to the Hartmann's place, and, as promised, Yani was ready to go. Just like the last time they went to St. Mary's of the Lake, she was dressed a little bit nicer, wearing a blouse, a matching skirt, earrings, some makeup, and her hair was in a ponytail. She looked really beautiful, but that was expected. Dan had never seen Yani when she didn't look really beautiful. They walked together back to his place, hopped into the Chrysler, and started the short drive to Watkins.

They pulled up in the front of the church, and once they got headed toward the main doors, Dan turned to her, "Okay, I know we were joking around yesterday, but just as a reminder, even though you aren't Catholic, everything except Communion is optional. You can mimic whatever I do or not. It doesn't matter. So, if you want to do the sign of the cross or genuflect, feel free. If you don't want to, that's okay, too. No one is going to say anything or think badly of you. As for Communion, just fold your arms in front of you like you did last time. Okay?"

"Got it," she replied as they walked up the marble steps to the church. "Do you think the priest is going to do that blessing thing again?"

"Hard to say. Again, that was kind of an ad-lib on his part. He can do it if he wants, but there's no hard or fast rule on it. I guess it'll depend on whether the mood strikes him. Be ready either way."

"Okay, will do," and they made their way into the church. Dan immediately went to the holy water font, dipped his finger, and performed the sign of the cross. Though a bit awkwardly and a little heavy on the water part, Yani attempted the same thing with a big drop running down the center of her forehead that she had to wipe away. Dan gave her a nod of approval and led them to seats in the center of the church. The church was already filling up, so they took a seat closer

236

to the rear this time. Dan knelt, said his prayers in silence, and sat back patiently, waiting for the Mass to commence. Not long after, the organ came to life, the small summer choir began the opening hymn with great enthusiasm, and the priest entered with his two altar boys. It was Father Sullivan again as the celebrant. The pomp and circumstance began to unfold, and the Mass proceeded accordingly. It was a high Mass, so just like the last time, it included the burning of incense, the cloud of aromatic smoke filling the sanctuary and carrying their prayers up to heaven.

When the time for the Eucharistic celebration arrived, Dan and Yani took their places in line, waiting to reach the altar and the priest. As they were making their way forward, Dan noticed the priest take a quick glance at Yani and quickly turn to one of his altar boys. He leaned over and whispered something into the boy's ear. The altar boy turned around, disappeared from the sanctuary, and returned a moment later holding something Dan couldn't quite make out. When they reached the priest, Dan took his Eucharist from Father Sullivan, placed it in his mouth, made the sign of the cross, and stepped aside for Yani.

Yani confidently stepped forward in front of the priest with arms folded as instructed. The altar boy held open a small container for the priest, and he carefully dipped his thumb into the liquid. He reached out to Yani and blessed her as he had done before, stating loudly for all the congregation to hear, "In nomine Patris et Filii et Spiritus Sancti. Amen." This time, though, he placed his thumb on her forehead and made the sign of the cross. Dan suddenly recognized a very faint scent in the air and realized that the small container held Chrism. This was incredibly unusual. He knew they did it for the sick and dying, but the only other time Dan had ever seen a priest bless someone with Chrism was during preparation for Baptism. Like a true soldier, though, Yani stood there and didn't even flinch. She allowed the priest to do his thing and, when finished, turned around and walked reverently back to her seat. After they sat back down, she turned to him and gave him this really warm smile, and he nodded back his approval. The smile only increased in size and brilliance.

After Mass concluded and they were walking out, Father Sullivan was standing outside, as usual, greeting parishioners. Out of respect, they paused as they were walking by to see if the priest wanted to speak with them. Dan figured it was a given, considering what had happened during Mass. Sure enough, as they walked up, Father Sullivan eagerly spoke to them. "Well, good morning! Good morning! It is so good to see the two of you here again. How is everything?"

Ever fearless, Yani responded immediately. "Hi, Father Sullivan. It's nice to see you again, too."

"Thank you, young lady. It's wonderful to have you here. How is your summer going?"

"It's going really well. Thanks for asking. There's been some ups and downs, but I've been very happy for the most part. Unfortunately, it's going to end soon, and that's really sad to think about."

"Yes, I'm sure it is. Do you think you'll be able to come back next year?"

"I don't know, but I sure hope so. I've come to really appreciate how special the Finger Lakes are. I think I finally understand why Dan loves it here so much," she stated as she turned to look at Dan standing next to her.

"This area really is a special gift from God. We are so blessed to live here. Well, if I don't see you again this summer, though I really hope I do, I look forward to seeing you next summer. In the meantime, you take care and God bless you both."

"Thank you, Father. That means a lot."

"Yes, thanks, Father," Dan reiterated as the two turned and walked back to the car.

"Okay, Dan. What the heck just happened there?" she asked quietly so the priest wouldn't overhear them.

"Yeah, well, this is a tough one to explain. So, I can tell you what happened there, but I can't tell you why it happened. Anyway, the priest blessed you with a special holy oil. It's called Chrism. They only use this stuff under very special circumstances. Almost no one gets Chrism unless you're dying, which you aren't, or preparing to go through the formal process of becoming a Catholic, which I'm certain he hopes you will do, and maybe that's why he blessed you with that. I'm not sure. This is something that I've never personally witnessed. It's crazy."

"What was that scent I noticed?"

"Right. So, the Chrism oil is different from other oils priests might use to bless things. Chrism has balsam in it. If I remember correctly, the balsam scent is the scent of God or something like that. As I'm not a Catholic priest, I'm not totally clear on that."

"Interesting. Well, what do I do now? I'm not dying."

"No, you aren't. So, you can just leave the Chrism on your forehead for the time being. If you want, you can wash it off before you go to bed or you can leave it on. That's totally up to you. Doesn't matter. Bottom line, though, you think the blessing you got the first time was a big deal? This one is simply over the top. You've received so much grace, it's absolutely oozing out of you," he said laughing. "This is really special."

"You Catholics are really bizarre."

"Yes, we can be. Anyway, you are now the most special person here at the lake so, with that, you ready to go to lunch, young lady?"

"Yes. How about pizza?"

239

"Pizza is a brilliant idea and I know the absolute best place for that!"

"Cool! Okay, let's go," and they started heading that way.

When they got to the pizza parlor, they placed their order, got their drinks, selected a table and waited for their food. While they waited, Yani asked more about the blessing, more about its meaning and if you could see the oil on her forehead. Dan told her you could see the shiny spot, but that it wasn't super obvious. Before long, their pizza arrived and they dug into their lunch. It was hot, cheesy and near perfect. When they were almost finished with their meal, the door opened and in walked two young men that, unfortunately, were all too familiar to them. As they were walking up to the counter to place their order, the two glanced over and noticed Dan and Yani sitting there. The tall one stopped his buddy and they walked over to Dan and Yani's table.

"Well, look what the cat dragged in. If it isn't Ronnie or Lonnie or Tawny or Scrawny or whatever the hell your name is."

"Ha, ha, ha. Such a funny guy. That would be Yani to the likes of you, pal," she replied sarcastically.

"Oh, you're getting mouthy again. I love it!" he replied raising his voice. "And what the hell is that grease spot on your forehead?"

"Something you'll never experience, Jack."

"Oh, is that right?"

"Yeah, that's right. Listen, buddy. I've already told you once to get lost, now get lost."

He laughed at her and they continued firing barbs back and forth at each other, each time the volume of their voices increasing just a little more. It finally reached the point where the owner came out from behind the counter.

"Okay! Okay! I've had enough, you guys. Take it outside! Now please!"

"That's fine," Yani responded to the owner. "We're finished here anyway." The two got up and headed for the back door to the parking lot with the two boys following right behind.

Once they reached the parking lot, Yani and Dan stopped to face the two. "Okay, guys. What do you want?" Dan asked.

"I don't like her mouth," the tall one said aggressively.

"Well, I don't like yours either," Yani fired back.

"Yeah, and what exactly are you going to do about it?" was his taunting retort.

Yani looked at him kind of quizzically. "What's your name?" she asked using a normal and calm tone of voice.

"What?"

"I said, what's your name?"

"Larry. What's it to you?"

"Well, Larry, tell you what. If I show you a little love and affection," and then she paused for what seemed to Dan to be nothing more than dramatic effect, "Then will you leave us alone?" Dan turned and stared at her with this shocked and confused look on his face. He stood there thinking, what the hell is she doing?

Larry turned to his buddy and the two of them started laughing nervously. Larry turned back to her and replied, "Well, hell yes, Yani. Show me some love and I will absolutely leave you two alone. What you got in mind, baby?" he said with this cocky look on his face.

"This," she replied as she calmly walked straight towards to him. As soon as she got within arm's length, she hammered him right in the testicles with this vicious uppercut. Yani really leaned into it and put everything she had behind the blow which, considering her size, wouldn't have been insignificant. Larry made this little gasping sound; his eyes began to bulge and he slumped straight to his knees. It was almost like watching slow motion as he rolled over on his side into a fetal position, his knees pulled up into his belly. She stood over him and spoke in a hushed tone. "Happy now, Larry."

Dan walked up behind her, took her by the arm and told her, "Get in the car," as he nodded in that direction.

Looking back at him, she replied, "If he manages to get up, it's your job to finish things."

"Understood," he replied, raising his eyebrows not exactly sure now what to do next. Yani walked over to the car, got in and sat there waiting. Dan stood there looking at Larry lying in the parking lot moaning as his buddy talked to him trying to figure out what he should do. After several seconds of looking down at Larry, it was obvious he wasn't going to be getting up anytime soon and his buddy wasn't going to do anything about it, so Dan simply walked over to the car and the two drove off. As they started heading back towards the cottage, he turned to her. "Well, that really wasn't the way I wanted things to end on what started out as such a beautiful day, but I have to ask, what possessed you to do that?"

Yani turned to him and just stared with that expressionless face. After a few seconds, she finally spoke pointing right at him. "Dan, I'm a chick. What am I supposed to do? Get in a fist fight with him. Let him kick my ass and beat me to a bloody pulp. He's a bully! You know that I'm already in one abusive relationship and ever since I hit puberty, I've had nothing being a continuous stream of really aggressive guys hitting on me trying to get me in bed. What I've learned so far in life is that if you don't put a stop to it immediately, it only gets worse. Oh, and there's no way in hell they just wanted to go for a ride in our boat."

"Oh, I'm well aware of that, Yani. Those two are trouble and I could sense it as soon as I walked up to them on that dock. There's no way on earth I was going anywhere with those guys."

"And there's no way I'm taking any of Larry's shit. I will fight him to the death before I'll let him abuse me. Trust me. He's not the first, but I certainly hope he's the last."

"You know what, Yani?" he said calmly nodding his head as he looked at her. "I believe you. I really do."

They drove on toward the cottage and she looked over at him again. "Well, you going to tell me what the favor is you asked from God or am I going to have to beat it out of you?"

He only needed to hear that once. "Yeah, well, what with all the excitement, I almost forgot and, no, you don't have to beat it out of me, so please don't do that," he said with a slight grin before continuing. "Okay, here we go. So, the favor I asked of God is this," he said pausing once more to assemble the right words. "I asked God for three things. I asked him that, if possible, to bring you back here to me next summer. I feel especially strong about that. This has been the best summer of my life and I would give almost anything to be able to repeat this. Next, I also asked him to console you and bring you comfort in time of need so that you don't have to suffer alone emotionally. Finally, and most importantly, I asked him to help your mother find it in her heart to be loving and kind to you and that, Yani, is what I asked for."

She looked at him, looked away, and down into her lap. He could see her bite her lip, the tears begin to form, and her voice starting to tremble. "You prayed that for me?" she asked the tears now flowing like a river down her face.

"Yes, Yani. Those were my prayers and you know I believe that prayer works. That's how much I love you. And you know what else I think?"

"Oh, God. I'm not sure I want to know."

"I think that unusually special blessing you received today with the Chrism from the priest is a sign that God heard my prayers. Remember, God knows everything, so he knew in advance what my prayers would be and that's a sign to me that he is going to answer those prayers."

"You're killing me, Dan. Please stop. Don't give me false hope."

"No. Quite the contrary, Yani. I'm not killing you and I'm not bringing you false hope. I'm bringing you a life and a future, whether it be with me or with someone else. I truly believe you're going to be okay and that you'll be loved and that God doesn't care whether you are a Catholic or not to do that for you."

Yani sat there in the car seat staring at him. The tears had now stopped and she wiped her cheeks dry. Nodding at him as she spoke, she said, "You know what, Dan?"

"What's that, honey?"

"In case no one has ever told you, you are a really strange person and you say the most unbelievably bizarre things. You say you aren't, but I swear to God you must be one of those angel things."

"Should I take that as a compliment, sugar?" he asked, laughing softly.

"You can take it any way you want, Dan Wallace."

Chapter 27

Dan could feel the cool water being flicked onto his skin as he sat there floating in his tube and that could only mean one thing. Yani had something on her mind that she felt a compelling urgency to discuss. Turning to look at that stunning face he inquired softly, "Yes, dear? Something I can help you with?"

"How come you haven't taken me fishing yet?" she asked with a serious look on her face. "You said you were going to."

"How come I haven't taken you fishing yet? Well, actually, honey, I did ask you if you wanted to go fishing with me, but you said no."

"That doesn't count. That was like seconds after we first met. I didn't even know you or know if I could even trust you. You told me in Montour that you were going to take me fishing."

"Yeah, you got me there. Okay, I'll be happy to take you fishing, but you know you have to get up early and there's no whining allowed even if you're bored."

"When was the last time you heard me whine about anything?"

"Hmmm. Let me think about that and get back to you," he said laughing.

"Smart aleck," she responded while simultaneously splashing him with more water.

"Oh, no!" he cried out laughing even harder. "She's getting me wet while I'm floating out in the middle of a lake! Oh, the humanity!"

"I'm going to get you!" she responded with this tough girl look on her face as she grabbed at his arm and tried to pull him out of his tube. He put up almost no resistance and just as he started to fall out, he grabbed ahold of her, wrapped his arms around her and pulled her in with him. "Ah!" she hollered right as they were going under. When they popped back to the surface, she started punching him in the chest as he laughed and cried out, "Stop! Please stop! Help! She's hurting me! Help!" he yelled while simultaneously laughing.

"I sure hope I'm hurting you, because you definitely deserve it, you brute!" she responded as she pushed him away, then swimming back to her tube and climbing in. She followed that up by paddling over to his tube and kicking it as hard as she could so that it floated further out into the lake. "There! Now we're even!"

"Even for what?"

"For you pulling me in."

Dan continued laughing as he swam back to his tube, climbed in and paddled back over to her. "Okay, baby. I promise I'll take you fishing tomorrow, but we're going to do this right. First thing in the morning, we'll drive down to the bait store in Watkins and load up."

"Hold on a minute. You mean there's an actual kind of store that sells bait for fishing?"

"Yeah, the bait shop in Watkins only sells bait or any other supplies you might need for fishing, you know, likes poles, reels, hooks, fishing line, stuff like that."

"Huh! Well, why don't we just go down today and get the bait so we already have it?"

"Because I plan to get live bait and live bait doesn't last too long. If we buy it today, by tomorrow morning some or all of it will already be dead. I mean, we could use artificial bait, but I think live bait works much better and there's few things in life worse than going fishing and not catching anything," he stated while nodding his head once for emphasis.

"I see. So what time are we going?"

"You know, I'm thinking the 7:30 to 8:00 o'clock range is plenty good enough. It's not like there's a specific time to go fishing, though it's almost always best done first thing in the morning. Fish typically stop feeding as you get later into the day."

"Okay. That's not too bad. I'll just tell my grandparents to wake me. They're always up by that hour anyway."

"Fine. Then it's settled. Fishing in the morning."

When the next morning arrived, the two of them drove down to Watkins to the bait store where Dan showed her all of the different kinds of things you could buy for fishing. "This is totally crazy," she replied. "All of this stuff in here is just for fishing?"

"Yep. A lot of people around here take their fishing very seriously."

"Dang!" was all she could say in response.

After showing her the wide range of fishing tackle and describing what some of them were for, he bought a supply of both night crawler worms and shiners for their purposes.

"Why aren't you buying any of those?" Yani asked pointing at two other tanks with much larger bait fish.

"Those there are what are called saw bellies and those are what are called smelt," he answered while pointing at the different species. "They're for trout fishing which we aren't going to be doing. We'll be fishing for bass and perch."

"So, are those the same smelt that people eat that you were telling me about?"

"Yep. That's them. Like I told you, they are very tasty, but they also make a really good bait for trout fishing. Trout just love them. Truth be told, I love them. They are without a doubt one of my favorite fish to eat."

"You weren't kidding when you said you'd need a whole lot of them to make a meal."

"Yes. Yes, you sure do. Okay, all set or is there anything else you want to see?"

"Nope. Let's go fishing."

"Fishing it is," he replied and they headed back to the cottage. Dan had loaded the boat with everything they'd need the night before, so when they got back to the cottage, they hopped in the little motorboat and headed right out. There was a large cove not too far from their cottages that he drove to first. Dan had always had pretty good success there over the years so he had decided ahead of time they would start there and just change locations if there wasn't any action. When they got near the center of the cove, he killed the engine, reached under the bow and grabbed the anchor.

"Okay, young lady, here's how it works," he began to explain as he dropped the anchor over the side letting the rope out until it stopped then tying it off on the bow so that the boat would remain pointed into the wind. "We'll anchor here and see what's happening. I've got two poles for each of us so we'll set up two with worms and two with minnows and see which works best. Now, you said you've never been fishing before, right?"

"That's right. This is the first time."

"Okay, so I'll help you get started with baiting your hook, but I expect you to learn how to do it, too, before we finish. Fair enough?"

"Yes. Just as long as you teach me how."

"Don't worry. I'm a good teacher. Before we do that, though, you need to learn how to use the reel," and he proceeded to show her how to open and close the bail, let line out or reel it in. Next, he had her try it a few times until she got the hang of it. "Now, by design, these fishing poles are super sensitive to anything tugging on the line. So, when a fish bites on your bait, the tip of your fishing pole bends down towards the water and it's really obvious a fish is doing what is called 'hitting' your bait," and he demonstrated to her what that looked like. "So, when that happens, you have to do what's called 'setting' the hook. You do that by jerking back on the pole," and, again, he demonstrated how to do that. "The key to it is a nice, good, quick upward jerking motion on the pole, but you can't jerk too hard or you'll pull the hook right of the fish's mouth. You also can't jerk too softly or the hook won't set. Understood?"

"Yep. Watch the end of the fishing pole and when I see it bend, jerk the pole to set the hook and start reeling in the fish."

"Perfect! So, we're going to do what they call catch and release. That is, anything we catch we try not to kill and just release it back into the water. However, we do make exceptions. If we catch something really big, we might keep that and have your grandma make a meal out of it. I'll kind of be the judge on whether the fish is a keeper or not. Okay with you?"

"Okay. You're the judge."

"Awesome. Oh, and one final thing. It's perfectly okay to talk while we're fishing, but don't bang the bottom of the boat with your feet. Scares away the fish."

"Got it. No banging on the bottom of the boat," she replied smiling as he proceeded to bait the hooks and put the lines out.

After he got the baited lines out and everything arranged just the way he wanted, he turned to her, "Okay. Now sit back, relax and keep an eye on your poles."

"Gotcha," and she gave him a thumbs up and a smile. "Hey, how long are we going to fish for?"

"Oh, I'm guessing until we get bored or hungry. Whichever comes first," he replied while nodding at her.

"Okay. Hunger or boredom. That works," she answered back and they settled into the fishing routine.

The first few times a fish hit her bait, she struggled a little bit trying to determine when it was time to set the hook and the right amount of force to use when she jerked the line, but before too long she had the hang of it and was having decent success. Getting her to bait her own hooks, though, ended up being a much greater challenge. Between the slipperiness of the bait itself and sticking a metal hook through a living creature, there was a lot of squirming, cringing and weird faces out of her before she finally became a little more comfortable doing it.

Fortunately, the fishing that day was really good and Dan was silently grateful. Sitting in a boat with little to no activity can get pretty boring pretty fast especially when you're with somebody who is new to the sport. They didn't have to worry about that today, though, catching a steady combination of both perch and rock bass. None were even approaching a size he felt worth keeping but there was ample fight in them making it a ton of fun. Yani would get so excited every time the tip of her pole started bouncing, Dan couldn't help but laugh.

"Hey, Dan?" she asked at one point as they sat in the boat with the waves lapping against the side.

"Yes, my dear."

"What's that black colored bird doing?" she asked pointing out over the water.

Looking where she was pointing, he replied, "Oh, that thing? That's called a loon."

"Yeah, but what's he doing?"

"Loons are fishing birds. They fly over the water looking for fish near the surface, then they dive into the water to catch them. They're really cool. They can actually go under water and swim. As low as he's flying, he must have spotted something," and they both watched as the bird dove and disappeared below the surface before popping back up a few seconds later and starting to fly off.

"Wait. What's happening? Oh. No! Dan! He's got my fishing bait and he's trying to fly away with it!"

"Oh, dang, Yani. You caught yourself a loon," he replied laughing.

"How can you laugh? What am I supposed to do now?" she cried out, anguish all over her face.

"Believe it or not, this is not the first time this has happened to me. So, what I need you to do is start by staying calm. We'll get him loose. Don't worry, sugar."

"What do you mean don't worry? I've hooked a damn bird! How can I not worry?" she shouted. "I don't want to kill a bird!"

"Trust me, Yani. I've got this. What I need you to do is reel him in nice and slow because we don't want the line to snap. Once you get him close to the boat, I'll grab a hold of the line and then cut the hook. Go ahead. Start reeling…slowly," and as she reeled, the bird fought like crazy against the hook with its wings flapping frantically. Eventually, she got the struggling bird close enough for Dan to grab the line and pull the loon close to him while at the same time trying to avoid the beating wings. Reaching out with his side cutting pliers, he cut off the end of the hook and the bird immediately shot up into the sky never to be seen again.

"But the hook is still in his beak. Is he going to die?" she asked with a concerned look.

251

"Nope. According to the Fish and Wildlife folks, I did exactly what I was supposed to. With the tip of the hook cut off, eventually, the rest of the hook will work its way out of its beak and before you know it, Mr. Loon will be good as new. Now, let's get you a new hook and get back to the business of fishing."

"Oh, God," she muttered shaking her head.

After they'd been at it for a couple hours, he finally said to her, "Okay, sugar. I think we've terrorized the local fish population enough for one day. Let's catch a couple more and then we'll head in."

"Okay, that's fine," she replied. "I'm ready."

As they sat there waiting to land a couple more, Dan turned to her, "Hey, we talked about going on an actual date like dinner and a movie. Want to go tonight?"

"Yes. That would be great. What movies are playing?"

"There's only one. The theater in town is really small, so they only show one film at a time. What they're showing right now is called 'Play Misty For Me' and it's a Clint Eastwood movie."

"Huh! That's a strange name for a western."

"Actually, it isn't a western at all. It's supposedly some kind of psycho thriller movie and I think it might be the first one he's ever personally directed."

"Is that right? I thought he only did westerns or killer cop movies."

"Me, too, but apparently not. Anyway, it sounds like fun."

"Okay, count me in," and just as the words left her lips, one of her poles bent over wildly slamming against the inside of the boat and almost bouncing right out into the lake. The line went slack for the briefest of moments before it violently slammed again against the inside of the boat, the pole tip pointing almost straight down.

"Quick, Yani! Grab the pole before it gets yanked in!"

"Help me, Dan. Help!" she yelled.

"No, baby. You've got this. The hook is already set so just start reeling it in."

Yani had this terribly panicked look on her face as she grabbed the pole and began to reel in the fish with the end of the pole bent almost a full ninety degrees. This was one really large fish on the end of her line.

"Steady, girl! Steady! Just a nice, good, consistent pressure on that line. Don't let it get slack. Keep it taught."

Yani stood up in the boat straining to hold the pole and reel in the fish, but the expression on her face had now gone from one of panic to that of determination. As the fish got closer and closer to the boat, Dan reached around her and grabbed the net. He almost didn't pack it the night before thinking there was no way he would need it, but he could tell for sure that whatever was on the end of her line, it would definitely require the net. As he sat there enjoying the show she was putting on while working to reel in the fish, out of the corner of his eye he noticed that the line had started to race back and forth in front of her. "Yani, watch out!" he yelled. "He's getting ready to jump!" and just as he finished warning her, this dark, silver monster broke the surface jumping three feet straight up in the air. It was shaking its head violently back and forth trying to toss the hook, but to no avail falling back into the lake still securely attached.

The line began racing directly away from her and Dan called out again. "Hold on! He's got one more run in him and then I think he's finished!" he yelled. She stood there motionless until he shouted out. "Okay, the line stopped moving. Start reeling!"

Yani began to reel again and continued reeling until she finally yelled to him, "Dan, I can see it!"

"Okay, keep going, honey. When you get it to the side of the boat, hold it for a second while I get it in the net."

"Okay."

When the fish finally broke the surface, Dan slipped the net right underneath it and held it up for Yani to see.

"Oh, my God, Dan. What the heck is that? It's huge!"

"It sure is huge. This, my dear, is a lake trout and it's a whopper. Congratulations, Yani. Well done. I bet this beast must weigh close to four pounds."

"Is that a lot?"

"Is that a lot she says. What a funny girl. That's gigantic, honey! This fish can easily feed four, maybe five people!"

"Oh, my gosh! I can't believe it!"

"Believe it, baby," Dan responded as he went about the business of removing the hook, getting the fish on a stringer and into the bait bucket to keep it alive. "Let's go show your grandparents, Yani. They're going to be shocked."

As they approached the Hartmann dock, Yani began calling out, "Grandpa! Grandpa! Come help!"

Mr. Hartmann hustled out to the end of the dock as she was climbing up the swim ladder. Dan, standing in the boat, handed the bait bucket up to Mr. Hartmann who set it down on the dock, grabbed hold of the stringer and lifted the fish out of the bucket. With a look of astonishment on his face, he turned towards the cottage yelling, "Ma! Ma! Quick! Bring the camera. Yani caught a trout!"

"What? Yani caught a trout! Oh, my heavens!" she exclaimed as she came hurrying up with their camera. "Look at the size of that!" Turning to Yani, "You caught that?"

"Yes, grandma! Isn't it awesome?"

"Awesome? It's a monster. Here, hold it so I can get pictures," Yani's grandmother told her almost breathlessly. Her grandfather had already removed the fish from the stringer and showed her how to hold it by the gill. Yani stood there proudly posing with the fish along with a huge smile while her grandmother got pictures of her and the monster trout that she struggled just to hold up in the air. "Well, I guess I know what we're having for supper this evening."

"Oh, yeah. By the way, grandma, is it a problem if maybe we have the fish tomorrow night?"

"Well, sure, Yani, but what's wrong with tonight, honey?"

"Dan was planning on taking me on a date. We were planning to go out for dinner and a movie," she announced with a big smile on her face.

"I see." Her grandmother replied, then turning to look at her grandfather, he just shrugged his shoulders. "Okay, no problem. I'll cook the fish tomorrow. You two can go out and have some fun."

"Thanks, grandma. I appreciate that."

"It's fine, dear," she replied as Dan came walking out onto the dock.

"What do you think, Mr. Hartmann? Four pounds?"

"Let's weigh it and find out," he responded and he walked to the boathouse to grab the scales. He hung the fish from the scale and staring at the dial he announced, "Just short of four pounds."

"Yani, that is incredible," Dan said to her. "I have never caught one that large. In fact, I know people who have been fishing here for years that have never even caught one. And the first time you ever go fishing, you catch a lunker," he said laughing. "That is so cool. Good for you!" Yani stood there with this big, beaming smile shaking her head in disbelief and laughing out loud. Turning to her grandparents, "By the way, did she mention that we're going to the movies?"

"Yes, she did," replied her grandmother, now smiling back at the two of them.

"You know, I have to be home by dark, so we won't be out late. I was thinking I'd take her to Seneca Lodge to eat. After that, we'll go to the Glen Theater. They're showing a Clint Eastwood movie today called Play Misty For Me. It's supposedly some kind of a psychological thriller."

"Oh, my. That certainly sounds exciting. Okay, well, we'll get the fish cleaned and plan to cook it tomorrow."

"Perfect. Thanks very much, Mrs. Hartmann. By the way, Mr. and Mrs. Hartmann, you know what else Yani caught?"

"What's that, Dan?" her grandfather asked.

"She caught a loon." Yani just stood there on the dock, laughing at the thought of catching a bird while fishing.

"What? She caught a loon? Well, what happened to it?"

"I was able to cut it loose and it flew off pretty much unharmed."

"Well, thank heavens for that. I can honestly say I've never actually caught a loon."

"Almost no one has, Mr. Hartmann," Dan replied, laughing and then turning to Yani, he asked, "Hey, you want to help me unload the boat?"

"Sure." Turning to her grandparents, "We'll be back."

"And we'll be right here," her grandmother replied with a big smile.

Chapter 28

The balance of the day and evening were nowhere near as eventful as their fishing excursion that morning, but still very pleasant, none the less. Because they needed to be back to the cottage by dark, supper had to be held earlier than normal to leave time for the movie. As originally planned, Dan took her to a place on the hillside overlooking Watkins called the Seneca Lodge. It was one of those eclectic businesses in the Finger Lakes region that couldn't decide its real purpose in life. Was it for camping, lodging, or dining? It seemed like the owners couldn't make up their minds, so they decided to provide all three services.

The Seneca Lodge had been in business since long before Dan was born and was actually pretty popular with some of the race teams when they came to town. The restaurant menu was a little more upscale than a diner, and Yani's grandfather had slipped Dan some cash before they left with the instructions to show her a good time so they didn't scrimp on their dinner selections. Once the meal was complete, they drove back to the Glen Theater and their date movie.

The Glen was really small with a single screen which made it almost impossible to generate enough revenue to offer first run movies, so the owners didn't even try. Instead, they focused their efforts on providing a great movie going experience where you could see top movies that were maybe a year or so old. The staff were super friendly and the interior of the theater was amazingly beautiful and comfortable. Play Misty For Me had already finished its run at the major theaters making it a perfect candidate for the Glen. The lights were still up when they entered the theater so Yani got a good look at the really special décor before selecting their seats and settling in for the show.

After the movie ended and they were walking back to the car, Dan looked at Yani, "You know, I was raised with the understanding that under no circumstances is a man to ever hit a woman, but this Evelyn woman did everything possible to get punched like that."

"Oh, mentally insane does not adequately describe her. That chick was just unbelievably nuts and super dangerous."

"What'd you think about the way she died, falling out that window and over the cliff like that after he punched her?"

"Honestly, I was shocked. Caught me completely off guard. I never expected that in a million years."

"Yeah, it was pretty cool. Hey, it's going to be plenty early when we get back to the cottage. You in the mood for a bonfire tonight?"

"Sure. Kind of a celebration bonfire for my first lake trout sounds great."

"Awesome. Let's go."

On their way back to the cottage, Dan looked over at Yani studying her face. Somehow, she sensed it and turned to him, "Something I can help you with, buster, because you know I don't look it when people stare at me."

"Sorry. I didn't mean to stare, and yes, there is something you can help me with. I have a question for you," as he paused momentarily to organize his thoughts. "Have you ever thought about whether you'd like to have children and be a mom?"

"Actually, I have thought about that, and I do hope I can have children of my own someday. You know, I consider myself kind of an expert on how *not* to raise your children, so I think I'd be a pretty good one. Why do you ask?"

"I don't know exactly. It just seems like you hear people talking all the time now about how being a stay-at-home mom isn't cool anymore. For some reason, now women need to have a career outside of the home before their life has any meaning and I'm trying to figure out why that is."

"You know, I heard my mom say something about this subject recently that I thought was really weird. Of course, coming from my mom, that makes it kind of her normal," she stated, her voice trailing off with this quizzical look on her face before continuing. "Where was I? Oh, yeah. So, she said that if a woman just has an interesting hobby or something instead, that's just as rewarding and fulfilling as being a mom. I didn't say anything, but I was sitting there thinking to myself, I'm pretty sure that having a nice rose garden or being really good at jigsaw puzzles isn't nearly as rewarding or fulfilling as having and raising kids, but what do I know? I'm just a stupid teenager."

"Yeah. Those are my thoughts exactly. My mom stayed at home to raise us, and once we got to an age where we didn't need to be looked after constantly, she went back to work part-time, which seemed perfectly reasonable to me. Plus, my parents made sure my older siblings knew they were also responsible for looking after the young ones. Actually, I think all my aunts did the exact same thing. They had my cousins, raised them, and once they were old enough to take care of themselves, they went back to work, too."

"Seems perfectly reasonable to me. My little sisters are a good example. They're home alone all day while my folks are at work and nothing bad ever happens to them."

"Yeah. Good point. Anyway, like I said, I don't know why, but I was thinking about that for some reason."

Yani turned to him with this sly little smile and asked sweetly, "Do you think maybe it's because you might want me to have your babies some day?"

"Stop! You're embarrassing me!" he responded and she just laughed at how uncomfortable that had made him.

"Wait. I'm embarrassing you, Dan Wallace? Oh, I'm so sorry," she said sarcastically. "Well, we certainly can't have that, so I'll stop," she stated, reaching over and pinching his cheek as he flinched and knocked her hand away. They drove onto the cottage smiling and immersed in their own thoughts about having babies while the radio provided entertainment in the absence of conversation.

Back at the cottage, Dan went about his usual routine of building the bonfire while Yani turned on the music and got them drinks from the refrigerator. As the bonfire kicked into high gear, they sat together, holding hands, listening to the music playing, and engaging in small talk while staring at the blaze in the firepit. Once the evening progressed, they went from holding hands to making out, and then things really started to heat up between the two of them. Eventually, Dan whispered in her ear, "Let's make love," and she nodded enthusiastically. They got up and made their way together down to the dock so they could make love under the stars again. Working together as a team, they created their little makeshift bed out of the sleeping bags. Once organized, they lay down together under the moonless night sky.

By this point in the summer, their love making came free, easy, and was a beautiful thing for them. Once they were finished, they held each other while lying on their backs, staring up at the stars and meteors as they waited for the heart rates to return to normal. After a few moments, Yani turned to him, "I have to tell you a secret."

"What's that, sugar?"

"My mom uses sex as a weapon to control my dad," she whispered.

"What? What do you mean she uses sex as a weapon?"

"You've seen my home. It's nice, but it's not large. There are times when I'm in my room, and they think I'm asleep, but I can hear them talking."

"Well, what do they say?"

"My mom makes my dad make an appointment to have sex with her."

"What? Come on! No way!"

"And depending on how she judges his behavior leading up to that evening, that'll determine if she's actually going to have sex with him or not."

"That's crazy. I don't know anything about marriage, but that sounds wrong."

"Oh, it gets worse. Most of the time, she simply refuses him because he did something that made her mad. I'm pretty sure sometimes she refuses him just to remind him who's boss."

"Oh, God. That is just so cruel."

"And on those occasions when she does agree to sleep with him, she'll make him wait like up to an hour sometimes before she'll actually go to bed with him. Think about that for a minute. She makes him wait so that he has to perform on demand like a male prostitute or something."

"So, what you're saying is that you're not the only person in her life that she treats like absolute garbage?"

"I feel really sorry for my dad. I think he's a really good guy. He doesn't deserve this, but for whatever reason, he just doesn't want to leave her."

"Well, I'm told that throwing in the towel on a marriage does have its costs. I've heard my folks talk about other couples they know that have gotten divorced. They said that it's really messy and really expensive. I know hope isn't a strategy, but maybe he's hoping she'll wake up some day and realize what a good guy and a good husband he is. That's the only reason I can think of as to why he'd suffer through that abuse." After pausing for a moment, Dan continued. "So, what do you think about that?"

"Me? Are you kidding? No way do I want a relationship like that with my husband or boyfriend. I mean, I'm just a teenager, but for me, I want making love to be spontaneous. Having a schedule for that? No way. That's never going to happen."

As the two of them lay there thinking about what was just discussed, out of nowhere, Dan suddenly heard footsteps approaching from up top. He quietly turned to Yani, who had frozen at the sound of the same thing. He put his finger to his lips, indicating that she needed to be perfectly still, and she nodded once. Carefully turning his head so he could get a view of the stairs, he could clearly make out the silhouette of a man standing there at the top. Dan knew that where they were laying was completely concealed by darkness and that there was no way the person could see them, so he whispered in her ear. "Don't move until I tell you." She nodded once again in response, indicating her understanding, and they lay there together motionless waiting to see what would happen next.

After a number of seconds had passed, a male called out in a loud voice, "Dan?" It was Gary. Dan wondered to himself, what the hell was he doing here? Again, he put his finger to his lips, and they continued to lay there motionless. "Hello?" After more time had passed, Dan heard him moving and looked up towards the top of the stairs. There, he saw Gary turn and walk away towards the cottage.

Once he was out of sight, he whispered to Yani, "When I give you the signal, you hustle into the boathouse, close and lock the door behind you, and don't open it until I tell you. Okay?" and again, she nodded her understanding. They waited and waited, heard nothing more, so he quietly turned to her, "Okay, go!" he whispered. She grabbed her clothes, got up, and slipped stealthily into the boathouse barely even making a sound. As she was doing that, he slipped on his shorts, pulled his tee shirt over his head, and started walking nonchalantly up the stairs. Once at the top, he walked past the wood pile and proceeded to the firepit.

It didn't take long before Gary reappeared from the shadows around the corner of the cottage, calling out to Dan as he walked towards him, "Hey, man."

Turning to face him, Dan responded, "Oh, hey, Gary. What's going on?"

"I was walking down the road, saw the bonfire, and thought I'd see what you were up to."

"Yeah, at this point, I'm just letting it burn down before I take the hose to it, at which point I'm calling it a night. What's going on down at your place?"

"About the same. Last time I saw my folks, they were inside reading, and I'm sure they'll be going to bed pretty soon. What're you doing tomorrow?"

"Haven't decided yet. I guess we'll see in the morning."

"I know you've been hanging out with that Yani girl a lot cause I've seen you two together. You hanging out with her tomorrow?"

"Maybe. That's kind of up to her."

"Right. Okay, well, if you're getting ready to go in, I guess I better take off. See you tomorrow, maybe."

"Okay, man. See you tomorrow," and Gary turned and walked away towards his cottage. Dan waited a few minutes longer until he was absolutely convinced Gary wouldn't be coming back. He then headed back down to the boathouse, retrieved Yani, and they began walking her home.

Strolling back to her place, she remarked, "That was kind of weird that he would show up here like that."

"Yep. I'm with you. Not sure what that was all about. Sometimes, he does weird things, though. Always has."

"So…that would at least partially explain why you're friends with him here at the lake, but not back in Elmira?" she asked.

"Yes, my dear. That would explain it."

"Do you think maybe he was trying to catch us together in the act? Spying on us?"

"I don't know, baby. He's never stopped by this late before. I'm not sure what was going through his head, but that was definitely uncomfortable there for a minute."

"Boy, that's for sure," and the two left it at that while they continued their short walk back to her cottage and the end of their evening together.

Chapter 29

Dan and Yani were sitting together on his front deck, eating peaches they'd purchased from the farmer up at the top of the hill and engrossed in a highly competitive game of 'First to Identify the Bird Species' when she asked him almost absent-mindedly, "So, anything exciting happening at the lake this weekend?"

"Actually, there is," he mumbled.

She waited a few seconds for him to say more, and when he didn't speak except to point and call out the species of a new bird that had just flown onto his property, she turned and stared at him. "Well, you going to tell me about it or leave me hanging here?"

"Let me think about that for a second. I'm in the middle of something super important right now," he replied, focusing on the trees and the birds flying back and forth.

"Here. Let me help you with that," she offered as she reached over and whacked him on the back of the head. "There. Better?"

"Yes. Thanks so much," he said, laughing and turning to face her. "Okay, seriously, three of the area towns are holding their annual fair this weekend. It's actually a fundraiser for the local volunteer fire department that serves their communities, including right here where we sit, and it's held at the fairgrounds on the firehouse property just a short distance from our private road. You could actually walk to it if you wanted to, though I definitely don't. But it is that close and it runs Friday through Sunday. We go every year if we can. You interested?"

"Do they have rides?"

"Yep."

"Cotton candy?"

"Yes. Not only that, normally, they have an actual parade on Saturday evening before the festivities kick into high gear. It's a really classic kind of country-style parade."

"Perfect. Let's go."

"Okay, it's settled. We'll make a final decision based on the weather, but right now, let's plan on going Saturday. That's the busiest and best night to go."

"Saturday it is," she responded excitedly. "Male blue jay!" she suddenly shouted, pointing at one of the walnut trees.

"Darn you," he muttered dejectedly.

When the weekend rolled around, they stuck with the original plan and went up to the fair on early Saturday evening, parking in the field on the lakeside of the highway. "Why aren't we parking at the firehouse so we don't have to walk so far?" she asked, curious as to why there.

"Well, I'm planning on staying well past dark. If I park here, technically, this way, I can drive home after dark because I won't actually be driving on public roads, just the private road that leads down to our cottages. If I park over at the firehouse, I can't do that legally, and I don't want to take the chance of getting busted. There's going to be a lot of police here at the fair."

"Got it. Okay. Well, I guess we walk."

As they had arrived in plenty of time to see the parade, there were already lots of folks standing along the short parade route on the lake road, now temporarily closed by local law enforcement so the big event could be held safely. Once the parade started, there were plenty of American flags, and it all began with a military color guard from the Seneca Depot leading the way. There were lots of tractors, both antique and new, muscle cars and antique hotrods, people on horseback, school cheerleading squads, and riding lawnmowers the country boys had modified into something that could only be described as racing mowers. Last, but certainly not least, were all the firetrucks, volunteer firefighters, and local law enforcement officers in their squad cars with all the emergency lights and sirens going off. It was true rural Americana at its finest, and the image could have come straight out of a Norman Rockwell painting. After the parade ended and the cheering concluded, Dan and Yani walked across the still-closed highway and down to the fairgrounds.

Saturday brought clouds, a slight breeze, and mid-seventies temperatures. There was a large crowd of both young and old gathered together on the fairgrounds. As it was still early, there were also lots of families with kids running around. The two of them spent the evening trying out all the rides, sampling the food, and, of course, making sure Yani got her cotton candy. There were a lot of people that Dan knew, and he would introduce them to Yani as they randomly bumped into them. It seemed like everyone wanted to meet and talk to this strange and beautiful girl from Ohio, and Yani was extremely patient about it. Being used to this kind of attention, as long as they weren't overly nosy or aggressive, she was friendly to everyone she met.

Once it got dark out, the beer tent quickly filled to overflowing. The dance floor was jammed. Everybody was having a blast and the volunteer firefighters were all smiles thinking about the money they were now raking in. As the evening wore on, they found themselves at a table next to the live band, surrounded by a group of young people from the area that Dan knew. The band was doing a great job, and occasionally, the two of them would get up, dance to a song they especially liked, and then return to their seats afterwards to rejoin the conversation they'd left behind.

As they were sitting there in between songs, out of nowhere a young, male voice yelled out over the crowd noise, "Hello, Yani!" She and Dan turned toward the voice and Larry was standing there glaring down at her. "I thought I might find you here," he shouted with obvious malice as he grinned and then punched her right in the head as hard as he could. The sickening crack of his fist striking her skull temporarily stunned the group, but once they got over the shock, the boys jumped up and immediately started whaling on him while all the girls screamed, "Hit him! Beat his ass!" as the police rushed to the scene. It was total mayhem.

Dan knelt down over Yani, who was now lying unconscious on her back in the field. "Yani," he whispered. "Yani. Look at me. Please." Her eyes fluttered open, and she looked up at him, trying to get into a sitting position. "No. Don't try to sit up yet. Stay there. Talk to me. Okay?"

"Yeah. What the hell happened, Dan?" she asked as a member of the EMS ran up with his emergency medical kit and knelt next to them.

"Can you talk?" he asked.

"Yes," she replied weakly.

"What's your name?"

"Yani."

"What day is it, Yani?"

"Saturday," she whispered.

"How many fingers do you see?"

She hesitated for a moment before answering, "Three."

"Any chance you can sit up for me?"

"I can try," and the two of them helped her into a sitting position. The EMS technician took a miniature flash light out of his kit and checked her eyes. While this was going on, Dan looked back over his shoulder. There was a huge scrum of young people where they'd been sitting seconds earlier. Fists were flying, and somewhere at the bottom of the scrum was a young punk named Larry. There were several sheriffs' deputies and the local police now trying to break up the fight, pulling kids off as fast as they could. There was also another deputy standing right behind him, just staring down at the three of them, taking in the situation.

The technician turned to Dan. "I don't think she has a concussion, but I do think we should take her to the hospital and get her checked out just to be sure. Did she come here with you?"

"Yeah. We're both staying at the cottages down at the bottom of the hill."

"What's your last name?"

"Wallace."

"I know where your place is. What about her?"

"She's the Hartmann's granddaughter."

"Okay." Turning back to Yani, he said in a raised voice to make sure she understood, "Miss Hartmann, I'd like to take you to the hospital. Are you willing to go to the hospital?"

She turned and looked at Dan, "Do I have to? I think I'm okay, Dan. Can't you just take me back to the cottage?"

Dan looked at the EMS technician for guidance. "Well, it's up to you. If she thinks she's okay, take her home. But if that changes later, take her straight to the hospital. Got it?" and Dan nodded his understanding. Turning back to Yani, the technician said, "Okay, we're going to let you go, but you need to go straight home, get some ice on your face and rest. Understood?" and she shook her head acknowledging the instructions. They helped her to her feet, made sure she was steady enough, and the two of them started walking back in the direction of his car. The deputy, now walking along beside them, reached over to help support Yani and then started speaking to Dan.

"Do you know that boy who hit her?"

"We don't know him, but we had a couple of run-ins with him recently. His first name is Larry. We don't know his last name." Unless asked specifically, there was no way Dan was mentioning anything about Yani punching the guy in the nuts.

"When you say run-ins, can you be a little more specific?"

Now, Yani chimed in. "He's a really aggressive guy. I told him to get lost the two times we met him, which was once at that Showboat place and once at the pizza parlor in Watkins. He and his buddy didn't seem to like that very much."

"So, you think he assaulted you because he didn't like the way you spoke to him previously?"

"Yes."

"I see," he said, and he paused for a moment, considering what they'd told him. "Okay, well, will you be at the Hartmann place later if we need to get a statement?" he asked, looking at Dan.

"Actually, I'm a Wallace, and she's a Hartmann, so we're staying in separate cottages, but we'll be down there for sure."

"Okay, understood. Miss Hartmann, do you need help walking to the car?"

"Thanks, officer, but I think I can make it. It's right there," she responded, pointing at the Chrysler.

"Okay, well, you two, please be careful the rest of the evening."

"We will. Thanks, deputy," Dan replied as he and Yani continued walking the rest of the way to his car.

"What the hell is wrong with that Larry guy, Dan?" she asked, now weeping softly. "I mean, what the hell? Am I like that Evelyn girl from that Play Misty movie, and he's Clint Eastwood or something? Damn it, that hurt."

"Easy, honey. Please don't talk. We'll have you home before you know it." He could now clearly see that the swelling of her face had really started to kick in and there was a little bit of blood.

When they got to the cottage, Dan helped her out of the car and walked her inside, shouting as he entered, "Mr. and Mrs. Hartmann!"

They both came rushing into the room, "Dear, Lord! What happened, Dan?" Mr. Hartmann asked.

"She was assaulted."

Mr. Hartmann turned to his wife, "Ma, get some ice and wrap it in a dish towel! Hurry! What do you mean she was assaulted?" he asked. "By what? A pickup truck? Look at her!"

"Some guy we met a couple of times before doesn't like her cause she told him to get lost. He shows up at the fair tonight, sees her sitting there, walks up, and without any warning at all, he punches he in the face and knocks her out."

"Does the sheriff know?"

"Yes, but I don't know what happened with that. After the EMS technician was done with her, he told us we needed to come straight here, so we did. We did speak briefly with a deputy, and he said he might want to get a statement later."

"I don't like this one bit," he said angrily. "Ma, get that ice on her face, then you and Dan get her to the hospital. I'm headed to the sheriff's office," and with that, he charged out the door. Dan got them loaded up into the car, and they drove to the hospital in Watkins. As they walked in, an orderly took one look at Yani, grabbed a wheel chair, loaded her into it, and they disappeared through the doors leading to the examination rooms. Dan took a seat while her grandmother met with the receptionist to get Yani signed in. Once finished with the check in process, she took a seat next to him where they waited together.

Not long after that, four sheriffs' deputies came busting through the door, half holding up, half dragging some guy in handcuffs whose face was a total mess. They didn't even slow down as they passed through the lobby, marching straight through the double doors and disappearing behind them. A half-hour after that, Mr. Hartmann showed up and sat down with them.

"He's been arrested," he announced. "Name's Larry Osbourne, and he's a local kid. The sheriff said it was a good thing it happened at the fair with police presence. Sheriff said your friends were in the process of beating him to death. Apparently, he's not too popular in these parts."

"I can't imagine why," Dan responded sarcastically.

"Once they get him patched up, he's been ordered locked up until there's a hearing."

"What do you mean, 'patched up'?" Dan asked.

"Didn't you see him when they brought him in? They had to have come right through here."

"Are you kidding? That was Larry? Oh, my God! He was beaten to a pulp!"

"Yeah, your friends did that to him because of what he did to Yani."

"Unbelievable!" was all that Dan could say.

Eventually, Yani came back out in a wheel chair with a doctor at her side, except now she had a big bandage over the left side of her head and eye. The doctor explained that she didn't have a concussion but that she should take it easy and continue with the ice packs until the swelling went away. If things changed, they were to bring her back immediately.

Back at the cottage, Mr. Hartmann stopped Dan outside the front door. "I don't know what's going to happen, Dan, but I want you to know that I had a judge take out a restraining order on this Larry guy." Sticking his finger in Dan's chest, he continued, "He comes anywhere near you two, you let me know, and I'll have him thrown right back in jail. In the meantime, I've got to go see how Yani's doing. Good night, Dan," and he went inside leaving Dan standing there alone outside their front door.

"Good night, Mr. Hartmann. I'll see you tomorrow," he sighed and then slowly walked back to his cottage wondering what the hell had happened.

Chapter 30

The next morning, when he went down to see how Yani was doing, rather than knock, he simply followed the narrow sidewalk around the side of the cottage to the porch on the front that overlooked the lake. Their car was in the driveway, so he was pretty certain he'd find them sitting there. Sure enough, the three of them were gathered around the table, sitting there talking quietly. As he rounded the corner, they all looked up simultaneously, and Mrs. Hartmann spoke first. "Good morning, Dan. Come here and sit down."

"Yes, ma'am," and he did as he was told. There was an ice pack on the table in front of Yani, and she had her hair pulled back in the high ponytail. "Can I look?" he asked her gently, and she nodded her permission. Looking at the wound on the side of her head, he could make out the shape of the boy's knuckles in her skin, with plenty of swelling but not nearly as bad as he had feared. "You obviously ducked," he stated, "and that is a very good thing."

"What do you mean?" she asked.

"When he swung at you, I could tell he was aiming for your eye. Your instincts must have taken over and you flinched slightly to avoid the blow. The good news is that he missed his target. Otherwise, he would have probably broken your eye socket, your eye would be completely swollen closed, and you would almost certainly need surgery. I'm pretty sure that's what he was hoping would happen. The bad news is that he hit you right flush in the temple, and that's why you got knocked out. I've got some friends who like to box for fun. They told me they're always looking to land that shot when they're in a match because they know if they can do it, their opponent is taking a nap."

Turning to Mr. and Mrs. Hartmann, Dan stated with great certainty in his voice, "He didn't want to knock her out. He wanted to really hurt her."

"That son of a bitch," Mr. Hartmann responded as Mrs. Hartmann shot him a stern look for using that language.

"Well, I don't know anything about that, but I can tell you for sure that it hurt like hell, and I'm pretty wobbly today," Yani chimed in.

"I'll bet you are. That was a heck of a blow you took, both from his fist and when you slammed the back of your head on the ground. Fortunately, you're going to be just fine in a couple of days. Not sure about that Larry fellow. He wasn't looking too good when they dragged him through the emergency room lobby." Turning to Mr. Hartmann, "Any news on that?"

"No, but I wasn't really expecting any. If the sheriff has any questions, he knows where to find us. Just out of curiosity, where'd you two meet this guy?"

"The other day, when you told me to take Yani for a ride, I stopped at the Showboat so we could get a drink. When we came back out to the slip where I'd moored the boat, he was there with one of his buddies checking out the Seneca Song."

"Okay, so what?"

"Well, he wanted me to take him and his buddy for a ride, and when I said no, he didn't like it and pushed the issue. That led to words being exchanged, and he got mad at the way we spoke to him, but it ended with nothing more than some hard feelings on his part, at least that's what I thought at the time. Then, the other Sunday after church, we decided to stop for pizza. He and his buddy wandered into the shop, saw us, and immediately started another argument. It got heated. The owner kicked us out. The argument moved to the parking lot, and more words were exchanged. This time, it was even more aggressive, and Yani gave him an earful that he didn't appreciate."

"What happened after that?"

"The argument ended, or so we thought. We got in the car and drove back to the cottage."

"And you didn't see him again until he walked up to the table at the fair last night?"

"Yes, sir. That's correct."

Turning to Yani, "Look it, you're certainly going to be laid up for a couple of days and I haven't checked in with my folks in a while. If it's okay with you, I think I'll run down to Elmira for a couple of days. You all right with that?"

"Sure. That's fine. So...what? You're coming back on Tuesday?"

"That's what I'm thinking. Spend the rest of today with them, all day Monday, and I'll drive back up here Tuesday morning. Does that work?"

"Yes, that works."

At that point, Dan turned back to Mr. Hartmann and took a really long pause and a heavy sigh before speaking again. "Mr. Hartmann, Yani, and I are running out of summer and I want to ask you and Mrs. Hartmann for a big favor," he began as he simultaneously looked over at Mrs. Hartmann. "Lord knows you don't owe me anything, but I'm hoping you'll give us permission to make one more road trip."

"Another road trip?" Mr. Hartmann asked with eyebrows raised. "I see. Well, what've you two got in mind this time?"

"Yani and I want to go to Niagara Falls."

"Niagara Falls, huh?"

"Yes, sir, and I promise, this time, no surprises."

Mr. Hartmann turned to his wife, "Ma?"

"Only if they promise not to get too close to the edge. I don't need more worries. I've had more than enough for one summer."

"I promise, ma'am."

"When do you want to go?" Mr. Hartmann asked.

"Thursday morning. I've studied the map, and it looks like it's about two and a half hours each way."

"Okay, just as long as she's better by then," Mrs. Hartmann announced.

"Yes, Ma'am. Understood." Facing Yani, he said, "Okay. I'll see you Tuesday," and got up to leave, placing a hand affectionately on her shoulder as he did. She leaned her head against his hand, turned, and looked up at him, smiling.

"See you Tuesday," and walked out of their cottage.

When he arrived back on mid-morning Tuesday, after unloading and storing away the fresh supplies he'd brought with him, he made the short walk to the Hartmann's. Hearing voices inside as he strolled up, he knocked and waited patiently for someone to greet him. In short order, Mrs. Hartmann came to the door and let him in. "She's sitting at the kitchen table. Make yourself at home, Dan."

"Thanks, Mrs. Hartmann," he replied as he made his way to the kitchen and sat down at the table across from Yani. "Well, young lady, good to see you sitting here looking a lot better than the last time I saw you. How are you feeling?"

"The pain is mostly gone, but now the bruising has set in big time."

"Yeah, I can see that. It's nice and purple with a hint of green setting in. Looks like most of the swelling is gone."

"Yeah, I'm on the mend."

"Feel like going down to the dock to sit for a while?"

"Sure. That sounds great. Let's do that," and she stood from the table. He followed her lead and they made their way down to the dock. Mr. Hartmann was busy organizing the boathouse as they walked up.

"Mind if we grab a couple of beach chairs?" Dan asked.

"Oh, hi, Dan. Of course. Help yourself," he responded, smiling at the two of them. Grabbing chairs, the two walked out to the end of the dock and sat down, staring out at the vast expanse of Seneca Lake.

He didn't know if they approved or not, but at this point, Dan didn't really care anymore what Mr. and Mrs. Hartmann thought about his relationship with Yani. Reaching over, he took her hand and, staring into those eyes, he said, "You can't imagine how relieved I am that you're going to be okay. I didn't tell you at the time, but I was really worried about how bad he might have hurt you. I think your guardian angel might have intervened and turned your head ever so slightly for you."

He paused for a long moment before speaking again. "Sweetheart, I fully understand that men can get super aggressive in their advances towards you and that you need to defend yourself, but you've got to make me a promise. In the future, no more punching guys like that. Next time, you may not be so lucky. If he landed that shot the way he wanted, your face would have been a mess, and there aren't any surgeons at that little hospital in Watkins that could have put you back together. That would have meant leaving immediately for Youngstown, our time together would be over, and, more than likely, your face would

278

be ruined forever. Then, people would always stare at you for an entirely different reason. Okay? You promise?"

"Yes," she replied softly, staring down into her lap. "I promise."

"I haven't told anyone what you did to Larry, and I won't. You don't say anything, either. This needs to be our little secret. Got it?"

"Okay. I understand."

"Excellent! Well, enough of that. You excited to be going to Niagara Falls on Thursday?"

Looking up at him, now smiling, she responded enthusiastically, "Oh, yeah. I'm super excited. This is going to be awesome!"

"So, you heard me tell your grandparents I already studied the map. We're going to head to Geneva, hop on the Interstate, and take that all the way to Niagara Falls. By the way, remember when we went to Geneva the first time?"

"Yes. We saw Hobart College, Willard Insane Asylum, the white deer, and other stuff," she answered back.

"Right. I remarked at the time that you'd probably driven past all of that when your parents brought you here, but you said none of it looked familiar. Well, in fact, it wasn't familiar because you hadn't driven that way. Even though the southern route is a much tougher drive, it is faster, so your parents obviously came that way."

"Huh! Okay, well, I guess they'll probably take that route then when they come back to fetch me on Labor Day."

"That's what I'm thinking. Anyway, the trip to the Falls is very straight forward. We take the New York State Thruway to Buffalo and hop on a different Interstate that takes us the rest of the way to Niagara Falls and to the park. Nothing to it."

"Cool! So, what time do you want to leave on Thursday morning?"

"It's not nearly as far as Youngstown, so I'm thinking we can take our time and leave after breakfast whenever we get around to it. Does that sound okay with you?"

"Sounds great. We taking Henry's Chrysler or my grandparents' car?"

"I don't want to ask if we can use their car. I just don't feel right about that. If they want to offer, then okay, we'll take their car. If not, then we'll drive Henry's Chrysler. Is that all right with you?"

"Yep. That sounds just fine," and they returned to holding hands and staring out at the lake in all its grandeur while thinking about their upcoming road trip to Niagara Falls.

Chapter 31

Come Thursday morning, Dan had been invited by the Hartmann's to join them for breakfast before leaving for Niagara. Afterwards, Dan and Mr. Hartmann sat at the kitchen table, Mrs. Hartmann cleaned up, and Yani got ready for the drive. As they sat watching the girls, Hartmann slid his car keys across the table. Dan stared at the keys and back up at Mr. Hartmann. "Seriously, Mr. Hartmann?"

"I'm not letting you take that girl to Niagara in your brother's car, Dan. Her grandmother can't handle any more stress. This summer has been awful hard on her. You drive our car," he ordered, while nodding at Dan to make his point.

"I can't believe this. Thank you so much, Mr. Hartmann. Of course, if you need them, the keys to the Chrysler are on the counter in the kitchen, and the tank is mostly full."

"Okay," and with a really serious look on his face, he followed that up with, "Dan, just be careful. Please. And no surprises," he emphasized with a finger pointed at Dan.

"Got it, Mr. Hartmann. No surprises and we'll be careful. I promise."

"What time do you suppose you'll be back?"

"Well, we've got about five hours of driving. I'm told that Niagara Falls is really amazing, but I don't know how long you can actually stare at it and remain interested. Just guessing here, but I'm thinking probably around five."

"Okay, we'll start looking for you around the five o'clock hour, but no rushing it if you're running a little late. We'll be right here when you get back. Don't push it."

"Understood."

With that, Yani walked up to the table. "Okay, I'm ready. Let's go." She hugged both her grandparents, and off they went first to Geneva then north from there to the New York State Thruway. Once on the Thruway, they took that all the way to the Buffalo suburbs, getting off at I-290, which led them to I-190 North across Grand Island and, finally, to the little city of Niagara Falls. The traffic moved smoothly the entire time, and it turned out to be a fairly easy drive, but now came the tricky part. In studying the map ahead of time, it looked like the best thing to do was to jump onto the Niagara Scenic Parkway and take that to the Niagara Falls State Park. Dan managed to find the parkway without any difficulty at all, but just as he approached the park, he somehow found himself trapped with a potentially large problem confronting him.

"Oh, crap, Yani. I'm in the wrong lane. This lane is exit only and I want to keep straight towards the park," he stated as he looked into the mirrors as well as glancing over his left shoulder at the traffic next to him.

Looking out the rear window, she offered, "Well, put your signal on and see if someone won't let you in." Following her suggestion, he put his signal on, drifting over towards the center line, hoping someone would take the hint and be kind enough to let him in. That action was immediately greeted with a long, loud blast of a horn and the driver signaling to him with a raised digit as he drove past.

"Huh! They don't seem too friendly around here," he muttered as the 'Exit Only' lane rapidly approached. "Darn it, Yani. I messed up," he announced.

"Don't worry about it, Dan. It'll be fine. We'll just circle back around."

"Well, at this point, we really don't have much choice, so let's give it a go." Taking the exit, he turned right at the next surface street he came to, hoping to backtrack to the parkway. Turning again onto a street he thought would take them back to where they needed to be, he suddenly realized he was now on an access road that actually crossed directly over the top of the parkway. The good news was that he had successfully backtracked to the parkway. The bad news was he was about twenty feet in the air above the road he wanted to be on with no obvious means by which to get to it. "Where the heck is this taking us?" he wondered out loud as they crossed down onto an island with signs stating they were now somewhere called Goat Island and more signs directing them to public parking. Turning to Yani, "Well, what do you think? Do you suppose this is part of the whole Niagara Falls State Park system? I've read there are different sections. You want to just park here and see what this is all about?"

"Sure. I mean, you can see the spray from the falls off in the distance. Obviously, we're really close. I say go ahead and park. Let's take our chances."

"Okay, let's do it,' and he pulled into the very next lot, paid the attendant, who in turn handed him a map. Once parked and out of the car, they followed a broad walkway towards a large building the map identified as the Top of the Falls restaurant and shops. The closer they got, the louder the roar became and the air started filling with a cool mist. Passing around the left side of the building, the whole falls system immediately appeared right there in front of them. They followed the signs to what was identified as Terrapin Point, holding hands as they strolled down the gently sloping walkway to a large, protruding piece of land. When they reached the end and a black metal railing, they immediately realized that they were standing right next to the edge of the Horseshoe Falls. You could almost reach out and touch the water as it rushed by.

"Oh, my, God, Dan! Look at it! This is absolutely incredible!"

"Astonishing!" was all he could say in response as he stood there staring at the immense size of the falls. "This is freaking nuts. The descriptions I've read don't even come close to doing this justice. This is simply awesome!" he proclaimed, wrapping his arm around her waist and pulling her close. They stood there together, silently taking in the view of the falls complex. From their vantage point, they could not only see the Horseshoe Falls, but also a clear view down through the Niagara Gorge along with the park complex on the Canadian side and a rainbow gracing the skyline. Of course, as Niagara Falls is globally famous, just as in the case of Watkins Glen State Park, there were lots of foreign tourists walking around with their obligatory cameras hanging around their necks. When groups walked past, Dan and Yani would look at each other and smile. You always had to keep an eye out for those pesky tourists.

After a while, Dan looked at her and announced, "Okay, let's take a stroll and see what else we can discover. According to the map, there are other viewing areas you can walk to."

"That sounds good. Let's go."

Pointing straight down the river, Dan stated, "If I'm reading the map correctly, I think walking in that direction takes us towards the American Falls, so let's head that way."

"Perfect," she replied, reaching down and taking his hand as they started down river towards where there were supposed to be more falls. "You know, with the cloud cover today and the mist from the falls, it's almost a little cool. I kind of wish I'd brought my jacket."

"You want to walk back to the car and get it?"

"No. I'll tough it out for now," she replied. "Maybe later."

"Okay. Just let me know if you change your mind."

They walked along past the entrance to Cave of the Winds, pausing briefly at the entrance before deciding it might be a little too chilly inside. So, they kept following the trail they were on until it came to the edge of a narrow strip of the Niagara River and a much smaller falls, the sign identified as Bridal Veil. Again, the park provided a nice, sturdy railing you could lean against and look right over the edge down to the bottom of the gorge. It was really quite exhilarating being that close to the edge of the cliff. If you wanted to, you could climb right over and jump to your death, and there was no one around to prevent you from doing it. He was shocked it was that accessible.

For the first time, they could get a good look at the Maid of the Mist down in the gorge and the tourists on board with their raincoats. Putting her arm around his shoulders, Yani said, "I don't know, honey. That just doesn't look like a good time. Those people must be getting soaked, and, as you know, the water around here is pretty cold. No thanks."

After a quick stop for lunch, they took a little bridge across Bridal Veil to Luna Island, and then backtracked to the North Shore Trail. At one point, the trail came within just a few feet of the river with no railings to hold them back. "Come on, Dan. We've got to step in so we can tell everyone we were standing in the Niagara River just upstream from the falls.

"Okay, but for the love of God, please be careful and hold onto me. Please?" She took his arm, and they both stepped into the shallow water.

"Damn! The water is cold," she exclaimed. "What is it about this part of America that the water is always so freaking cold?"

"I don't know, Yani," Dan laughed. "It just is."

"Brrr," she replied, hopping back onto dry land. From there, it was down to the pedestrian bridge to Green Island, over to the Lower Gorge Trail, followed by a short walk to the observation area for the American

Falls. As they stood there, some ladies walked up and stood next to them staring out over the falls. After a few minutes, one of the women turned to them. "Come here often?"

"First time," Yani replied.

"My friends and I come here several times each year. We just love it. What do you think?"

"I'm really glad we came. It is absolutely amazing. I had no idea how beautiful and immense it is. It's definitely worth the effort."

"Yeah, I know. I can never get enough of it," the lady replied. "Hey, uh, honey?" the lady asked gently. "What happened to the side of your face? That looks pretty nasty," she said, staring at Yani's huge, ugly bruise.

"Yeah. I had an accident, but it's getting much better. Thanks for asking," Yani responded to her trying to be nice.

"I see. By the way, have you two seen the falls from the Canadian side yet?"

"No," Dan answered. "Can you do that?"

"Oh, sure. People do it all the time. You just drive over the Rainbow Bridge right there," the lady said pointing. "Soon as you get on the other side, there's signs directing you to parking. You should do it. We go over all the time. You can see everything and the view is exceptional."

Turning to Yani, "I don't know. Do you want to?"

"Well, we've pretty much seen everything here and it's still early. Sure. We can go over to the Canadian side and check it out. After that, we can start heading home."

"Okay. Let's do it." Turning to the ladies, Dan thanked them, and they walked directly back to the car for the short drive to the Canadian side.

Getting off of Goat Island and on the correct road to the Canadian border was a lot easier than they anticipated. Crossing the Niagara Gorge, signs proclaimed Welcome to Canada as they rolled up to the Rainbow Plaza Border Control Station. Upon stopping, the immigration officer walked up to Dan's window, pausing a moment to stare at the two teenagers sitting there. "ID, please." Dan dug into his wallet to get his driver's license while Yani searched for her school identification and Dan presented them to the officer. He stared at the ID's and took a quick glance into the front and back seats of the car. "It says here that you're both seventeen. Is that correct?" Dan and Yani looked at each other wondering what was going on. Dan shrugged and replied, "Yes, sir. That's correct. We're both seventeen."

"And what's your purpose for visiting Canada?"

"Well, we met some ladies over at the American Falls and they told us we really needed to drive over here to see the falls from this side," Dan replied, nodding his head for emphasis.

"Is that right." Looking back into the car at Yani, the officer had this puzzled look on his face. "Miss, what's wrong with the side of your head?"

"I had an accident, officer."

Turning to Dan, "Registration and proof of insurance, please."

Oh, Christ, Dan thought to himself, wondering where the heck Mr. Hartmann might have stored that. "Yani, it's got to be in the glove box. Would you look for it, please?"

"Sure," and she opened the glovebox. Rummaging around, she finally found the documents, handed them to Dan who passed them to the officer. Now he was starting to get nervous. What had he gotten the two of them into?

"Says here, the car belongs to someone named Hans Hartmann who lives in Wellsboro, PA, but your ID says your name is Daniel Wallace and that you live in Elmira, NY." Looking at Yani, "And your ID says you live in Youngstown, OH, so this isn't your car."

"No, sir."

"Well, whose is it?"

Yani leaned over to face the officer. "It's my grandfather's."

Shaking his head, the officer exclaimed, "Okay, let's review here folks: The car's registered in Pennsylvania and you don't own it." Pointing at them, he continued, "You're from New York. You're from Ohio, you're both minors and you've got a big, huge bruise on the side of your head. So, now I'm going to need you to park right over there, turn your vehicle off and wait. Understood?" he ordered them. Removing the radio from his belt, he began speaking into it. "Base?"

"Yeah, Davis."

"Possible 207-A."

"We're sending a team right now." Before they knew what was happening, the two of them were being marched into the immigration offices and as soon as they got inside, they were separated. As Yani was being led away, she turned back to Dan raising her hands and asking with her eyes what was going on. Led into an interrogation office, she was told to sit where a female officer started questioning her as another officer stood in the corner watching.

"You told the border officer that the big bruise on your face is from an accident. We're a little skeptical about that statement. So, again, how'd you get that bruise?"

288

Hands folded in her lap, Yani looked down and right back up at the officer. "I was assaulted," at which point she suddenly realized they must be thinking Dan was responsible. This was a problem.

"Why'd you lie to the officer?"

"I don't know, but I'm sorry."

"Who assaulted you?"

"His name is Larry Osbourne."

"And how do you know this Mr. Osbourne?"

"I don't. He's a stranger."

"What happened to Mr. Osbourne?"

"He was arrested."

"When and where did this happen?"

"Last Saturday night near Watkins Glen, NY."

"If we place a call down there, are they going to corroborate your story?"

"Yes, ma'am."

Turning to her partner, "Make the call," and he left the room.

Down the hall, Dan was getting grilled by a different team. It was obvious they felt he might be responsible for Yani's injury, that she was potentially in danger and they weren't taking this lightly. Back in Yani's room, she looked up at the officer. "Officer, that guy I'm traveling with is my boyfriend. He loves me and would never do anything to hurt me." The officer didn't respond. She just sat there staring at Yani and waiting for her colleague to return.

Forty-five minutes later, the two were being ushered back out of the offices and led to their vehicle with instructions to take the U-turn at the end of the parking lot, get their butt back to America and never darken Canada's doorway again until they were at least eighteen. In the car and under way, Yani spoke first. "That scared the living crap out of me. They thought you were responsible for assaulting me and that I was probably in some kind of danger; maybe kidnapping and fleeing America to avoid arrest."

"I know. They grilled me pretty hard. I was awful nervous there for a while," and they continued on their way driving along thinking about what had happened. "Well, that certainly took some of the guild off the lily," he finally said. "Go to Canada. Everyone does. It'll be fine. Yeah, right," he remarked sarcastically.

"Yeah, it definitely wasn't the way I expected it to end. On the bright side, we both got to do something new. We got to see Niagara Falls, we got interrogated by the police and we got kicked out of a country," she replied laughing. "Now, just get us home with no more surprises. Okay, Dan?"

"You got it."

Once back at her cottage, Dan dropped Yani and the car, next heading down to his cottage to drop off his gear. As he was walking, he heard something he'd never heard before. "NO!" Yani was shrieking at the top of her lungs. Next thing he knew, she was charging out the cottage heading straight for him with this really angry look on her face. As she got to him, she reached down and took his hand. "You're taking me for a boat ride right now!" she ordered.

Once underway, he called to her, "Where we going?"

"Take me out into the middle and just shut off the engine."

Once out in the center of Seneca, he killed the Evinrude, they started drifting when she turned to face him. "You were right."

"About what?"

"When we were sitting at the falls down in Montour, you told me to be mentally prepared because my mom might change the dates."

"How bad is it?"

"They're coming a whole week earlier than originally planned."

"Damn it!" and the two of them just sat there despondently in total silence. After half an hour or so had passed, he looked at her. "What happened?"

"My grandfather got a message from a neighbor that he needed to call my folks. When he called, my dad he told him my mom has some music festival she wants to go to Labor Day weekend, so they have to come a week early to get me."

Dan just shook his head in frustration and sadness. There was absolutely nothing they could do about it and they both knew it. It was over. They knew when they started down this path it was going to happen. But to have it end like this was awfully painful and a really bitter pill to swallow.

Chapter 32

"The way I see it," Dan stated as Yani slowly rowed along in front of the point. "Today is Friday, August 11th. If I'm correct and your parents don't change plans again, that means we've got about sixteen days left before you'll be leaving."

"Dan?" she said softly, as she paused in between strokes.

"Yeah, sugar?" he answered staring off at the horizon.

"I know this is childish, but have you ever wished you were a bird and you could simply fly away?"

"Many times, honey. I'd love to be able to fly away from my problems. Just never figured out a way of doing that. Not only that, seems like if I ignore them hoping they'll go away, they just end up getting worse." Pausing, he looked at her, "Okay, so if you were a bird and you could fly away, what kind would you be?"

Looking up into the sky and hesitating for a moment, she declared, "I think possibly a song bird, like maybe a cardinal or something. Yes, a cardinal would be perfect."

"When cardinals appear, angels are near."

"What'd you just say?"

"When cardinals appear, angels are near. It's an old expression that's been passed down over the generations."

"Seriously? All these cardinals here at the lake and everytime I see one, there's an angel flying around nearby?"

"What can I tell you. Anyway, you say you'd like to be a song bird, but I've never heard you sing. Do you sing?"

"I used to, but I don't any more."

"Why not?"

"My mom told me to stop because she found it irritating."

"Sing for me."

"What?" she asked, as she stopped rowing.

"I don't believe for one second that your singing is irritating. Sing for me."

She stared at him expressionless and then sighed. "Okay," she said. Clearing her throat, she began singing softly and then abruptly stopped. "Wait. I want to start over." She shifted in her seat, sat up straight and quietly began singing the Carol King song, 'Will You Love Me Tomorrow'. She sang in this lilting, almost spiritual, a cappella voice, gradually increasing in intensity as she continued singing the lyrics. When the song reached its conclusion, she looked him in the eyes. "Will you still love me, Dan?" she asked, staring at him with that same expressionless face.

"Well? Will you, Dan?" she asked again, having gotten no immediate response.

"Yes. Yes, Yani. I will still love you both tomorrow and forever."

"Thank you," she whispered.

"My God, sweetheart. I'm absolutely touched by how beautiful your voice is. That was just so incredible."

"Thank you, Dan," and with her solo performance now complete, she went right back to rowing without speaking another word. She acted as if nothing at all just took place. Dan sat in the back of the boat studying the girl in total silence for the longest time. The only sounds were the oars cutting through the water, the song birds in the trees along the shore, and the occasional call of a seagull as it flew overhead. She made no eye contact with him until he finally challenged her with a question.

"Yani?"

"Yes," she replied, now looking back at him.

"If you no longer sing any more, how is it that you know that song by heart?"

"If a tree falls in a forest and no one is there to hear it, does it make a sound?" was her response, answering his question with a question of her own.

"Ah, yes. My English teacher dropped that quote on us the other day. I could be wrong about this, but I think she credited that to some philosopher by the name of George Berkeley, although there seems to be some question as to whether he ever actually said it," he stated. "Of course, the answer to the question depends upon your perspective, now, doesn't it?" She said nothing in reply and just continued rowing while staring at him.

"Here. Let me translate this," he offered. "Except for me, there were no witnesses when you sang. If you ask me not to tell anyone, I won't. Therefore, there are no witnesses and therefore, you have not sung." That remark created just the slightest hint of a smile forming at the corners of her mouth revealing that Dan had uncovered yet another one of her secret defense mechanisms. If no one hears her sing, she can't be attacked or scolded for singing. Therefore, she doesn't 'officially' sing. You can't prove it, so it never actually happened. He sat there thinking about that until she broke the silence with another question of her own.

"Dan?"

"Yes."

"Can you take me somewhere I haven't yet been to?"

"Some place you haven't been to, huh?" and he paused for a moment considering her request before coming up with an idea. "Okay, I think I've got it!" he announced excitedly. "I know just the place. We'll go bird watching. Yani, take us in."

Now in the car and heading south out of Watkins, she turned to him. "It looks like we're going to Elmira."

"We are headed towards Elmira, but we aren't going that far."

"Well, where are we going?"

"I told you. We're going bird watching."

"So…this is like another one of your surprise mystery things?"

"Yep."

"Interesting," was her sole response and she sat back to relax while they drove along with the windows down and the radio on. Reaching the very northern outskirts of the Elmira area, Dan turned off onto a different highway that the signs said led towards the regional airport. After going a short distance, he turned again onto a two-lane country road that immediately started up a steep hill taking them into what looked like a really remote area of dense forest.

"Where the heck are we going?"

"Be patient, Yani. We're almost there and you won't be disappointed." They continued on the narrow road until they cleared the crest of the hill, immediately bursting out of the forest and into a wide-open green area where a large sign declared 'Welcome to Harris Hill-The Soaring Capital of America'. At almost the exact same moment the sign came into view, a tow motor, engine blaring, with a glider tethered behind flew right over their heads seriously startling Yani.

"Ah!" she shrieked. "What the heck is that? It almost hit us!" she shouted.

"Easy, girl. It wasn't that close. I said we were going bird watching. Those are the birds; sailplane birds, if you will. You watch now. That little plane in front towing the glider is going to cut him loose. When that happens, the glider is going to start flying around with no engine, just like a bird." Sure enough, as they watched from the car, the tow motor pulled the glider higher up into the sky and once the pilot had reached his desired elevation, he released the line. Released from the tow plane, the glider gracefully soared out over the valley below and then back along the mountain ridge lines where the lift was greatest.

Dan pulled into the viewing area provided for visitors and they parked near some other cars whose passengers were already watching the gliders flying and started watching the sailplanes take off, fly out over the valley, return from their flight and land, if you could call it that. To Dan, it always looked more like the gliders were making a sort of crash landing than a controlled one. Of course, with no motor, wheels or brakes, you were basically relying on the friction of the sailplane scraping across the landing strip to stop, with no way to actually steer.

"This is both really beautiful and truly amazing," Yani said as she took Dan's hand. "Do they do this all the time?"

"Nope. It's seasonal. I took a chance they'd be flying today and we got lucky. They call it soaring and, weather permitting, they only do it between like April and November and they don't fly at night."

"Why's that?"

"Well, they don't fly at night because it's simply too darned dangerous. I mean, it's not like they have headlights, nor is the field lit. If they tried, they'd be crashing left and right and people would be dying all over the place."

"And that would not be good."

"No, it sure wouldn't," he replied laughing at the thought of sailplanes crashing all over Harris Hill. "As for the seasonal part, I'm not entirely sure about that. It might be something as simple as it being too cold. I don't think these things have heaters and it's cold up in the atmosphere. Heck, I'm sure it's a few degrees cooler up here than down in the valley. Without a heater, if you did go up in winter, you wouldn't be able soar long anyway without getting hypothermia."

"Well, I know it's really cold up there. Otherwise, really tall mountains wouldn't be snow covered year-round. So why don't they just put in heaters?"

"It's all about weight and aerodynamics, Yani. I'm guessing if they put a heater in, they'd need a battery. Batteries are heavy and they take up a lot of space. It starts to get complicated from an engineering standpoint, but the bottom line is that the cost benefit simply doesn't add up, so there's probably no heaters. At the same time, it could just be the normal wind conditions during winter. These things really like wind and lift and if there isn't any, they don't fly. Simple as that."

"Fascinating. How high can they fly?"

"The ones we're watching don't go much over ten thousand feet."

"Why's that?"

"Once you go over ten thousand, you need a pressurized cabin and oxygen like a true airplane. Where we are right now is about 1,750 feet elevation so it's not like they're getting way up over the hill top here. Again, it's the old cost benefit analysis. A pressurized cabin and an oxygen system add weight and cost. Besides, the people that fly these things aren't interested in how high they can go. They're interested in how fast they can go. I'm told that some of these can do as much as about 175 mph and that's with no engine. These people are seriously into speed."

"That is absolutely crazy. Is it dangerous? It has to be dangerous, right?"

"The people that fly them don't think so," Dan replied laughing. "Let's put it this way. It's more dangerous than driving a car, but I've never heard of anyone dying here."

"This is so cool."

"Yep. It really is. So, if you want to fly like a bird, here's your solution, sugar."

"Someday I'm going to do this. I'm going to go soaring, Dan."

He put his arm around her, pulled her close and kissed her on the forehead. "And someday I'm going to take you. Just not today, baby. Sailplane rides are a little expensive for a humble guy like me."

She looked at him with a really warm smile and kissed him right back on the lips. "It's okay. I can wait until we can afford it," and he gave her a big squeeze in appreciation. They spent the next two hours together watching the 'birds' until the wind died down and so did the corresponding number of flights. With the frequency of flights rapidly dwindling, they decided it was time to leave.

Sailplane watching over, they got back in the car and headed straight for the lake. Dan dropped Yani off at her place and as he was turning the car around to go home, she came popping back out of the cottage all excited and hollering, "Wait! Wait!"

He stopped the car and called back, "What's wrong?"

"I need to show you something. Quick! Park and come inside! Hurry!"

"Okay. Okay," he answered back. Dan put the car in park, got out, and hustled into the Hartmann cottage along with Yani. Her grandparents were already standing there together in the living room waiting for the two of them to arrive.

"Look!" Yani said pointing at the wall. Professionally mounted and hanging on the wall in vivid living color was a full-sized portrait of Yani standing there holding her lake trout. "How about that, huh?" she blurted out with that big radiant smile adorning her face.

"Oh, my, God! That is so awesome! Look at that," Dan responded excitedly. He was just so happy and proud of her. He started laughing like crazy, unable to control himself at the thought of Yani catching this trout when grown men had been fishing here their entire adult lives and had never caught anything even close to the size of this.

"Okay, you two," her grandmother announced. "Let's get a picture of you standing right here together on either side of Yani's trout picture. Come on over here," and the two of them dutifully took their positions posing for Mrs. Hartmann in front of the picture. "Okay, hold still."

Her grandmother followed that up with, "You two can hold hands if you want to," she stated coyly. "We've already seen you doing it." They both blushed a little, then Yani reached over and Dan took her hand. "Okay, ready? Now smile," and they both did exactly as they were told while Mrs. Hartmann started clicking away to capture the image for posterity's sake. "Thank you, very much!" she said after she was satisfied that she'd captured the perfect picture.

Chapter 33

Even though Yani's last weekend at the lake was rapidly approaching, her grandmother had patiently told them that they could stay out late that evening, just don't push the boundaries. Those were the rules and out of respect for the Hartmann's, the rules would be followed. They had walked down to the point, skipped stones and sat for a while at the end of the dock holding hands engaged in small talk.

"I can't believe this is actually coming to end."

"Me either, Yani. This was probably the best summer of my life. No, it was definitely the best summer of my life." He kissed her while staring into those amazing eyes as they sat silently together watching the sun set. Once it had dropped below the mountain on the opposite side of the lake and the darkness began to gather, they dutifully got up and made the walk back to the Hartmann cottage. They stopped briefly to make out once more before they got there, then Dan walked her up to the door. "I'll see you in the morning," turned and walked away heading back to his place. As he was leaving, he noticed a light burning down on the dock and figured that Mr. Hartmann must be doing some repairs or something to the Seneca Song, then never gave it another thought.

Back at the cottage, he went down to sit on the end of the dock staring at the lights on the opposite side of the lake and watching the vehicles driving up and down the highway. Although it was more than two miles away, when the wind was blowing in a certain direction, you could actually hear the sound of the individual vehicles. All of a sudden, he heard a really loud thud and felt a huge concussion in the air. What the hell was that he, thought? He glanced down in the direction of the Hartmann property and noticed a bright light that was definitely out of the ordinary. "Oh, no!" he yelled, jumping up from his chair and bounding through the boathouse then up the steps two at a time. When he got to the road, he sprinted in the direction of the Hartmann property and stopped at the top of their stairs. Gasping in horror, he saw that the source of the loud thud was a fire now building in the Seneca Song. Racing down the stairs as fast as he could he found Mr. Hartmann with a fire extinguisher trying to put the flames out.

"Dan, grab Yani and take my car up to the firehouse. Hurry!" he shouted.

"No, Mr. Hartmann. We've got to get the boat out or it'll take the boathouse with it."

"Okay, hit the brake!" he yelled.

Normally, Dan would release the brake so that there was a nice, gentle descent of the boat. This time he just cut the brake loose completely. The flywheel started spinning like crazy with cables unwinding like ropes of spaghetti. The lift cradle and boat immediately dropped like a rock creating a massive splash as it slammed into the lake. At the same time, the fire extinguisher was sputtering and running out of chemicals. Mr. Hartmann threw it onto the dock behind him and went to the boat.

While the fire was greatly subdued, he hadn't been able to put it out completely. With the engine cowling closed, it was only a matter of time before the fire reignited. Hartmann bent down grabbing the gunwale with both hands and gave the Seneca Song a mighty shove. With the boat floating past, he grabbed the bow line, walked parallel to it as it slipped by and tied it off as it slid past the end of the dock. It was now safely away from the dock and boathouse, but the flames were flickering back to life again.

While all of this was going on, Dan had run back up the stairs to find Yani standing there with the car keys. It was well past eight o'clock and most definitely dark. Dan wasn't supposed to be driving, but he

301

decided he'd deal with that later, if necessary. They jumped into the Hartmann's car and took off down the road throwing stones and dirt everywhere. Starting up the hill, the first thing Dan had to do was navigate the corner leading out of their little community.

Even at low speed, there was barely enough room for two vehicles. He switched on the high beams and the emergency flashers, hugged the corner as tightly as he dared and cleared it. Thank God, there were no cars coming from the other direction. Now it was a straight line to the top of the hill. He quickly glanced over at Yani and she looked scared to death. All the color was completely gone from her face. Dan floored it and kept it floored until he was almost at the top, braking hard as he approached the highway. He'd have to make a left and he'd also have to make sure there were no cars coming.

Approaching the intersection, he looked left, right and then both directions once again just to be sure. There were no vehicles coming so he didn't bother stopping. He turned north on the highway and floored the engine. Fortunately, the firehouse was only about 500 yards down the road. When he reached the entrance, he pulled in and laid on the horn. He raced up to the firehouse, skidded to a stop, jumped out and started yelling at the volunteer fireman he saw standing outside the open bay door about the fire now burning at the Hartmann's cottage.

"Yeah, son. We got the call. We're on our way right now," was their response. Obviously, one of the neighbors who actually had a phone line realized there was a fire and had made the call to the firehouse.

"Please hurry."

"We are, son. Now get back in your vehicle and get out of the way."

Dan got back in the car, wheeled it around and headed back to the Hartmann's place. As he got back out on the highway, he saw flashing blue lights coming in both directions. These were the volunteer firefighters. Right before he turned onto the lake road, he saw one of the cars with the blue flashing lights already making the turn. Going down the steep hill was a lot more dangerous than going up so he made sure he didn't carry too much speed into the corner and end up in the forest. That would be disastrous. They made it safely and once he and Yani got back to the Hartmann's place, rather than park the car in the driveway, he drove just past the cottage so it wouldn't be in the way of the firetruck.

Now out of the car, they ran to the area adjacent to the top of the stairs so they wouldn't interfere with the firefighters. Mr. Hartmann was down below standing at the end of the dock staring at the Seneca Song floating out in the lake. The fire was now engulfing the entire stern and making its way towards the seats. It never occurred to him at the time, but the fire was also slowly, but methodically, making its way toward the fuel tank. When it blew, it went off with a thunderous explosion shooting pieces of the transom and the gas tank straight into the air. There was little Hartmann could do except cover his face and head with his arms as the shrapnel rained down around him. All hope of saving the Seneca Song was now lost.

Right after the explosion subsided, Dan heard the sounds of the sirens and when he turned around, he could see the red emergency lights bouncing off the tree tops. The firetruck pulled up right in front and the volunteers went straight to work. Two of them grabbed the firehose from the side of the truck and raced down the stairs to the dock where Hartmann stood in total shock staring out at what was left of his burning Century Resorter.

Once they had the hose stretched out and in place, they signaled up to the driver. He opened the main valve, the firehose swelled from the pressure and a huge volume of water erupted from the nozzle. They directed the stream onto the fire and in no time at all, it was out, but it was way too late. The damage was done. Once the firemen were convinced the fire wouldn't reignite, they gave the signal back to the truck to turn off the water. The volunteers stood there taking in the scene of destruction while talking to Mr. Hartmann the whole time.

As all of this was going on, Dan and Yani stood there speechless and never even noticing the sheriff deputy walking up behind them. As he approached, he put his hand on Dan's shoulder. Dan turned around and found himself staring right into the face of the deputy. "Son, I received a report about someone speeding, throwing up stones everywhere and driving like a crazed maniac. By any chance, would that have been you?" Dan was busted and he knew it.

He hesitated before speaking. "Yes, deputy. It was me and I'm really sorry. I didn't know what else to do. Mr. Hartmann told me I needed to get up to the firehouse as fast as possible, so that's what I did."

"You look awfully familiar. Where do I know you from?"

"Maybe the fair this summer? We had a little problem there."

"I knew you looked familiar." Turning to Yani, he studied her face carefully for a moment. "Glad to see you're all healed up, Miss."

"Yes, officer. Thank you."

Now facing Dan, he started speaking, "Well, son, let's see here. We've got speeding, we've got reckless driving and, let me guess, you don't have a senior operator's license, do you?"

"No, deputy. No, I don't." Dan replied staring down at his feet. He figured he was definitely in a ton of trouble. It wasn't like he'd be going to jail or anything, but he might be getting a handful of tickets. That would be expensive and, more than likely, he'd lose his insurance and maybe his license.

"Well, son, seems to me like this was a kind of emergency and when there's an emergency, sometimes you just gotta do what you gotta do." He stood there for several seconds staring at Dan. "I'll tell you what.

304

There's no harm done. Let's just keep this between the two of us for now. Fair enough?"

"Yes, deputy. Thank you, sir. I really do appreciate that," Dan replied letting out a big sigh.

"You're welcome. Have a good evening and I'm real sorry about your grandfather's boat, Miss."

"Thank you, officer," she quietly replied. The officer said nothing more, simply walked back to his cruiser and drove off. Dan had gotten very lucky and he knew it.

"Holy cow, Dan."

"Yeah, for sure. He could have given me a bunch of tickets. I could've definitely lost driving privileges until I turned eighteen, if not longer. Plus, it would have cost a fortune."

They returned their attention back to the fire scene and saw that the firefighters were now in the process of loading everything up. They had done their duty and it was time to go home. Mr. Hartmann was still standing at the end of the dock with this terribly forlorn look on his face as he stared at what was left of his once beautiful and iconic boat. The waves on the lake were rocking it slowly back and forth and you could still see some steam rising from it. "I'll be right back," he said quietly and walked toward the stairs leading down to the lift. When he reached the bottom, he walked up to Mr. Hartmann, "I am so sorry, Mr. Hartmann. Anything I can do right now to help you?"

"No, Dan. Thanks, but it's late. We'll deal with this in the morning."

"Okay," and he walked back up the stairs to Yani and told her, "I think I better be leaving, Yani. Goodnight, honey."

"Okay. Goodnight, Dan. See you in the morning," she said sadly while giving him a big hug.

The next morning, Dan walked down to the Hartmann's place. There was already a group of men from the neighborhood, several of whom Dan knew, standing down on the dock talking as a group. Dan went down, joined them and learned they had devised a plan to get the boat out of the lake. Mr. Hartmann was going to back a trailer down the steep access road to the point. The other men and Dan would walk the burnt shell down through the shallows, load it onto the trailer at which point Mr. Hartmann would drive it down to Watkins and figure out how to dispose of it.

As they were transporting the boat, Dan listened to the men discussing the fire and learned what had caused it. Mr. Hartmann had been working on the fuel lines and decided afterwards that he would start the engine and let it run briefly. However, he had violated his own rules. He had not turned on the blower to exhaust any gas fumes that might have accumulated inside the engine cowling. When he turned on the ignition, it had obviously generated a spark causing the explosion that Dan had heard as the loud thud when he was sitting on the dock. With the fire enclosed inside the engine cowling, there was no stopping it with the single fire extinguisher Hartmann had. It was doomed from the moment it ignited.

The charred hull stunk terribly from the burnt upholstery and the oil-based varnish. Most of the music notes and the words "Seneca Song" were also gone. The only thing left of the American flag was the little pole it was attached to. Who knew how badly the engine was damaged. Dan realized there would be no fixing this. The Seneca Song would never see water again. It was history.

After the Seneca Song was hauled away and the men were gone, Dan found Yani. It was now Saturday and she'd be leaving tomorrow so he wanted to spend as much time with her as possible. In spite of how sad things were, they spent the day doing the things that she enjoyed the most hoping to make the best of the situation. They skipped stones from the water's edge on the community beach. They went for a ride in Dan's boat. After lunch, they went for a swim and, after that, they took a walk up through their private gorge to see some of the little water falls she liked so much. Finally, they walked up to the vineyards to see the grapes now very plump and having turned a deep purple color. The growing season and summer were coming to an end. The sweet corn, stone fruit, alfalfa and produce crops had all been harvested. The only thing left was the field corn that would be turned into sileage to feed the dairy cow herds over the winter and the wine grapes. Their time together had come to an end, just like the season.

Yani's grandmother invited him to join them for dinner, but Dan didn't think he could bare to sit there with a very sad Mr. Hartmann, so he politely declined. He had spoken to him earlier in the day, though. Mr. Hartmann had thanked him profusely for his help and for keeping a cool head the night before. He went out of his way to tell Dan he had almost certainly saved the boathouse with his quick thinking. Dan didn't know what to say, so he simply told him that he was glad he could help and how terribly sorry he was about the Seneca Song.

After he'd eaten and was sure the Hartmann's were done with their meal, Dan walked back down and found Yani sitting on the little bench just outside the front door waiting for him. She stood, walked over, put her hand on the back of his head, pulled him towards her and kissed him. This was it; their last night together and she intended to make the most of it. They walked back to his cottage and went down to the dock to watch the sunset. They sat together quietly holding hands and watching the sun as it slowly dropped over the horizon on the opposite side of the lake. Neither really felt like talking. They just wanted to be close and in the company of each other on their final evening together.

It was also her last Saturday night, so Yani could stay out much later than usual. Soon the darkness started to descend. It would be another cloudless night. There would be no moon and the Milky Way would be in its full glory. With any luck, there'd be lots of shooting stars to provide a light show. It would also be pitch black out so no one would be able to see them.

Once Dan saw all the dock lights turn off one by one and was convinced everyone had gone inside for the evening, he got the sleeping bags from the boathouse and spread them out on the dock. He and Yani laid down together and made love for what they hoped would not be the final time. After they had exhausted themselves, they lay together holding hands staring up at the star filled canopy overhead while searching the universe for the next meteor to streak across the sky.

It turned out to be a very active night and they were thrilled over and over with a near continuous stream of meteors. It was simply glorious to watch. Eventually they decided, very reluctantly, that it was time for Yani to leave. Dan packed up their makeshift bed and they walked together back up to the road and down to the Hartmann's cottage. It was so dark they walked very slowly and very carefully. One wrong step on the rocks that littered the road surface and you could easily turn an ankle. Once they were close, all of a sudden, Yani froze.

"What's wrong now?" Dan asked quietly.

"Oh, my God. That's my parent's car. I thought they weren't coming until tomorrow. Damn it! You better leave me here, Dan. I don't want them to see you. Who knows what my mom might do. You know how crazy she is."

They kissed one last time and Dan gave her hand a reassuring squeeze then a big hug. They quietly said goodnight and he headed back to his cottage in the pitch black. God, it was dark. You couldn't even see your hand in front of your face. He made it safely to the cottage and went to sleep immediately while dreaming about Yani and their summer together.

Chapter 34

The next morning, Dan was sitting on the deck staring out at the lake. It was now August 27th, 86 days since they'd first laid eyes on each other while she was sitting in the Seneca Song. Yani was leaving. He hadn't seen her yet today and he didn't even know if he would, though he sure hoped so. But now her mom had turned her life upside down again, just like she always did. All they wanted was one more half day to properly say their goodbyes and maybe talk about the future, but she took that from them. It was almost expected.

Next weekend was the Labor Day holiday and the Wednesday after that he'd be back in school to start his senior year. Summer was over. He'd already decided that once Yani left, there was no point hanging around any longer, so he'd head home, too. His gear was already packed and loaded in the car. He had emptied the boats of the life jackets, cushions, oars and gas tank, stored them away in the boathouse and locked the door behind him as he exited.

Down at the Hartmann cottage, things were quickly erupting. Yani and her parents were sitting at the kitchen table and her mom was screaming at her.

"We have to go! It's a long drive. We both have to work tomorrow and we aren't sitting here waiting for you while you go down to say goodbye to that stupid boy."

"Of course, mom. It's all about you. It's always all about you. You can't even wait fifteen freaking minutes for me to go say goodbye."

"Don't you speak to me like that!"

"Are you serious? Grandma and grandpa have been great, but he's the only friend I've had here all summer long and now you're not even going to let me say goodbye? Thanks for nothing."

"Yani, I am telling you. You are not going down to say goodbye to that low class, white trash boy you've been sleeping with all summer."

"Low class and white trash, huh. And what if I did sleep with him, Mom? You've been telling me since I was fifteen that I'm nothing but a slut. Isn't that what you expected?" she yelled back leaning right into her words. "And who left the birth control pills in my dresser drawer here? Huh, mom?"

"That was only to save your ass from an unwanted pregnancy so you wouldn't ruin your life," her mother hissed.

"You mean kind of like how getting pregnant with me ruined your life?"

"That's exactly right," she shouted back and immediately there was a collective gasp from everyone in the room. Her mom followed up that remark with, "You know, you disgust me you little tramp."

"I disgust you? How do you think you make me feel talking to me like that?"

At this point, Yani's grandmother simply couldn't take it any longer and jumped into the fray. "Cathy, I am not going to tolerate talk like that about Yani and Dan," she exclaimed indignantly. "He's a fine boy from a good family. She's been an absolute joy this summer and I don't appreciate you saying that one bit." The entire time, Yani's father sat there just staring at his hands like some kind of a Buddha statue.

"Oh, is that right? Well, did you know your little angel here drove your car to Youngstown a few weeks back? That's right, Missy," she spat, turning to Yani. "Our neighbor told me they saw you pull into our driveway with some strange boy behind the wheel of your grandparents' car."

Shocked and completely caught off guard, Yani thought of what Dan had told her when they were making their plans for the trip; you

310

don't know what you don't know and there's always things you can't anticipate. They had been busted and didn't even know they had.

"Hold on there a second, Cathy." Mr. Hartmann now interrupted. "We know all about their trip to Youngstown. They told us they were going and they told us why. Yani wanted to see her sisters and we gave them permission to make the drive," he stated in a bald-faced lie.

Yani turned and stared at her grandfather. How did he know? Then it dawned on her. Dan had obviously told them without sharing that with her. He was covering for her. He'd had her back the whole time. Turning to face her mother she stated, "That's right, mom. We drove home so I could see Lisa and Robin."

Turning to Yani's mom, her grandmother responded in her defense. "Well, do you blame her, Cathy? She hasn't seen or spoken to her sisters all summer long."

"Bullshit," was her mom's response. "You just drive home and don't even tell me you're coming. Well, I'm not buying that for a second. Yani, I've had enough. We're leaving. Get in the car! Now!"

Yani slowly stood up. Her eyes had suddenly changed from their normal luminescent blue to a hard cobalt and her expression was one of both determination and total contempt for her mother. "Really, mom?" she replied. After a short pause and staring at her mother the whole time, Yani quietly said, "Here. Watch me." With that, she spun around, charged out of the cottage slamming the screen door behind her and took off in a sprint running as fast as she could.

She didn't even bother to turn around when she heard her mother yelling, "Yani! Get your ass back here!" She simply didn't care, but she had literally nothing to lose anyway so it didn't even matter. The trip home with her parents was already going to be four and a half hours of hell. So what if at this point she disobeyed her mom? It couldn't possibly get any worse.

311

Once she hit the fork in the road, she started yelling, "Dan! Dan!" When he heard her call out, he instantly jumped out of his chair and ran up to the road catching her in his arms in an embrace as she fell into him crying uncontrollably. He wrapped his arms around her so tightly it almost crushed the air from her lungs. "Dan, she wasn't even going to let me say goodbye," she sobbed.

"I know, Yani. We expected that to happen. That's just who she is," he said softly. She was still crying when he took her face in his hands and said, "Yani, I want you to know something. I really love you and I am going to miss you like you cannot possibly imagine." She stopped crying for a moment and smiled up at him gently caressing his cheek.

"Oh, God, Dan, and I love you, too." She kissed him with all the passion she had in her soul and then gently pushed him away as she looked into his eyes. "Dan, I'm promising you. I will be back here again next summer. Please tell me you'll be here, too."

"Yani, honey, you know I've been coming here every summer since I was born, and unless, God forbid, I get drafted, I'll be here next summer, too. I promise you that."

"I know you will, Dan. I know you will and we'll see each other again right here next year. There. It's settled. I'll see you back here next summer," she sobbed. She momentarily stared down at her sandals, "In the meantime, I have to go," she said in a hushed tone. Looking back up at him, "I love you, Dan."

"I love you, too, Yani, and yes, it's settled. I'll see you right here at Seneca Lake." They gave each other one last hug and she slowly turned away heading back to her grandparents'.

"Yani!" he shouted and she looked back at him, a puzzled expression on her face. "Your angel's got this, Yani! You have faith, honey!" She nodded at him with a look of determination and continued onto her cottage. Dan stood there watching and waiting. It wasn't long

312

before he saw her parents' car back out of the driveway and head towards him. When they reached the fork, they turned right and headed up the hill to the highway. Yani was sitting in the back behind her dad. It was as far away from her mother as she could possibly get. Her face was buried in her hands and Dan could tell she was crying.

He stood there until he could no longer hear the sound of their car and the gravel dust cloud trailing behind had drifted away. With Yani now officially gone, he silently went back to the cottage and locked up. Walking back to the Chrysler, he looked down the road and saw Mr. Hartmann standing there just staring at him. He didn't call out or even wave. He just stood there staring at Dan for several seconds before slowly turning and disappearing into his cottage.

Other than Led Zeppelin singing the 'Thank You' song on the radio, he remembered little about the drive. As he was passing through Watkins, he glanced at his watch while at the same time whipping the car onto the side street leading to St. Mary's. It was time to throw up a proverbial Hail Mary of his own. He parked, went inside, stopping at the font and performed the sign of the cross. Dan knelt in the last row and began praying. "Dear Lord, here I am once again asking for a favor. I am so pathetic. I only pray for help when I don't stand a prayer of dealing with my own problems. Lord, the favor I'm asking for this time is to please help me stop the pain. I am just so sad." Suddenly realizing he wasn't alone Dan looked and saw Father Sullivan standing there next to him. Was God already answering his prayers? Maybe.

"She's gone, isn't she?" he asked quietly.

"Yes," he replied, biting his lip to keep from crying.

Father Sullivan put his hand on his shoulder. "It's always the same. The more you love them, the more it hurts when you lose them. Let us pray, son." With that, Father Sullivan began whispering prayers in Latin. When he finished, he made the sign of the cross on Dan's forehead. "Good luck, young man," he said softly as he removed his hand and silently walked away.

When he finally arrived home, Dan walked inside with his gear. As usual, his mom was in the kitchen preparing food. "Oh, hi, Dan. I wasn't expecting you so soon. Everything okay?"

"Yeah, everything's fine, ma." He walked on past her through the kitchen into the living room where his dad sat reading the newspaper while some of his siblings watched TV.

"Hi, Dan. I thought that was you pulling into the driveway. How are you?"

"Good, Dad. I'm good," he replied making a U-turn and immediately heading upstairs to his bedroom. He was in no mood for conversation. When he got into his room, he tossed his bag on the floor and laid down on his bed, his hands clasped behind his head staring up at the ceiling. A few minutes later, his dad walked into his room and stood there looking at him.

"You seem awfully quiet, son. Everything okay?"

"The Seneca Song is gone."

"What do you mean gone?"

"It caught fire Friday night and burnt to the water line, Dad. It's history."

"Oh, my God. That's awful."

"Yeah, and Yani left today, too," he said quietly.

"I see," his dad replied. He stood there for a moment, not speaking. "I think I'll go back downstairs. You want me to close the door, son?" he asked.

"No. That's fine." After his dad had left, he lay there on the bed for a few minutes thinking. Yani's gone. The Seneca Song is gone. Young men are going off to war in some God-forsaken place called Vietnam. They're getting shot or maimed or killed. I'll be turning eighteen next year and might end up the exact same way. He got up off the bed and walked back downstairs. As he passed through the kitchen, he told his mom he was going for a drive. She responded with, "Okay, we'll see you later," and out the door he went.

He slipped in behind the steering wheel of the Chrysler, headed down the driveway and turned on the radio. 'She's A Rainbow' by the Rolling Stones was playing, so he cranked up the volume. When he reached the bottom of the driveway, he thought to himself, okay, Dan, which way you heading, right or left? Responding to his own question, he thought to himself, well, I guess it don't really matter. He turned onto the highway and simply drove off to nowhere.

THE END

Epilogue

Summer in the Finger Lakes was normally a time of great pleasure, but this year felt very different. After riots, a pandemic, inflation and years of political turmoil, citizens on both sides were at each other's throats. Major cities in America were overwhelmed with crime and the economy was shaky, at best. Now retired, Dan sat there looking out on Seneca Lake wondering when, or if, life in America would ever return to some semblance of the pre-Covid normal. Down at the stone beach he could see his adult children, their spouses and grandkids playing in the water along the shore line. Old age now approaching, he worried what their futures might hold, certainly nothing like that summer he spent here when he was seventeen worrying about his own.

After graduating from high school, rather than wait for the draft, Dan had simply enlisted in the Army hoping he might get assigned to something that didn't include the possibility of combat. As hope is never a strategy, after Basic and Advanced Infantry Training, he was assigned to the Ranger Indoctrination Program at Fort Benning, GA. Completion of this advanced combat training resulted in his worst fears being realized when he received orders to report for a tour of duty as a Ranger Advisor in support of a South Vietnamese Ranger Battalion.

While in country, the battalion he was assigned to was attacked by the NVA. Over the course of the three-day battle, Dan was shot twice: once in the left hand resulting in the partial loss of two digits along with a flesh wound to the lower body. Unable to medevac out, he continued supporting the Vietnamese Rangers tending to casualties, calling in air strikes, directing fire and assisting the troops on the perimeter. By the time they were able to safely retreat, he was one of only two Ranger Advisors still in the fight. For his valor, Dan was awarded the Army's Distinguished Service Cross along with a Purple Heart.

On the wall inside the cottage where he now sat was a display case. Inside the case was a tri-folded American flag and two medals. On top of the case was a little, golden angel. Hanging on the wall next to it was a mounted and framed portrait of two teenagers holding hands in front of another picture of that same girl holding up her lake trout.

In the fifty-plus years since that life altering summer, one of the few things that remained steadfast all that time sat directly across from him. When Dan looked over at Yani, to him, she was as stunningly beautiful now as the first time he'd laid eyes on her sitting in the Seneca Song. She returned the gaze, looking over at her hero with that big, radiant smile and those luminescent eyes. Around her neck hung a small, gold crucifix. He had given it to her the day they were married at St. Mary's of the Lake. The only time she ever took it off was when she bathed. She'd even worn it during the birth of their three children.

"Hey, there, sweetheart. What do you think? Time for a ride?"

"Yes!" she replied with a laugh and a small fist pump.

They walked hand in hand to the dock, her high ponytail bouncing in perfect rhythm, to where their old boat sat in its lift. It was a 1948 Century Resorter, fully restored and in mint condition. Painted across the stern was 'Seneca Song II' with little music notes as quotation marks around the name. Their kids had the radio on and, at that moment, 'She's A Rainbow' was playing. As they walked past, Dan called out to his boy, "Hey, son!"

"Yeah, Dad?" he replied, smiling up at his parents.

"Crank it up, buddy!"

"You got it!"

Made in United States
Orlando, FL
21 March 2024

45007248R00176